WIN, LOSE OR DIE

WIN, LOSE OR DIE

Stories from *Ellery Queen's Mystery Magazine* and *Alfred Hitchcock Mystery Magazine*

Edited by Cynthia Manson and Constance Scarborough

Carroll & Graf Publishers, Inc.
New York

First edition 1996.

*Carroll & Graf Publishers, Inc.
260 Fifth Avenue
New York, NY 10001*

Library of Congress Cataloging-in-Publication Data is available.

ISBN 0-7867-0317-2

Manufactured in the United States of America.

We are grateful to the following for permission to reprint their copyrighted material:

"**Gentleman's Agreement**" by Lawrence Block, copyright © 1977 by Davis Publications, Inc., reprinted by permission of Knox Burger Associates, Ltd.; "**The Last Hand**" by Anthony Boucher, copyright © 1958 by Mercury Publications, Inc., reprinted by permission of Curtis Brown, Ltd.; "**The King of Clubs**" by Agatha Christie from THE UNDER DOG AND OTHER STORIES, copyright © 1923 by Agatha Christie, © renewed 1951 by Agatha Christie Mallowan, reprinted by permission of the Putnam Publishing Group; "**The Scrabble Clue**" by John Phillip Cohane, copyright © 1966 by Davis Publications, Inc., reprinted by permission of Curtis Brown, Ltd.; "**The New Master**" by Lord Dunsany, copyright © 1955 by Lord Dunsany, renewed by John Child Villiers and Valentine Lamb as Literary Executors to the Estate, reprinted by permission of Curtis Brown, Ltd.; "**Fool's Mate**" by Stanley Ellin, copyright © 1951 by Stanley Ellin, reprinted by permission of Curtis Brown, Ltd.; "**Muldoon and the Numbers Game**" by Robert L. Fish, copyright © 1975 by Davis Publications, Inc., reprinted by permission of Catherine A. Burns, Trustee; "**The Ace of Spades**" by "Pat Hand", copyright © 1945 by "Pat Hand", reprinted by permission of Molly Costain Haycraft; "**Card Sense**" by James Holding, copyright © 1979 by Davis Publications, Inc., reprinted by permission of Scott Meredith Literary Agency; "**Scrabble Babble Dabble**" by H.R.F. Keating, copyright © 1991 by Davis Publications, Inc., reprinted by permission of Sterling Lord Literistic; "**End Play**" by Harry Kemelman, copyright © 1950 by The American Mercury, Inc., reprinted by permission of the author; "**The Takamoku Joseki**" by Sara Paretsky, copyright © 1984 by Davis Publications, Inc., reprinted by permission of the Dominick Abel Literary Agency; "**Shade Work**" by Bill Pronzini, copyright © 1993 by Bantam Doubleday Dell Magazines, reprinted by permission of the author; "**The Gamblers' Club**" by Ellery Queen, copyright © 1951 by Ellery Queen, © renewed, reprinted by permission of Scott Meredith Literary Agency; "**The Man Who Was the God of Love**" by Ruth Rendell, copyright © 1993 by Kingsmarkham Enterprises, Ltd., reprinted by permission of Sterling Lord Literistic; "**The Way To Do It**" by Jack Ritchie, copyright © 1979 by Davis Publications, Inc., reprinted by permission of the Larry Sternig Literary Agency; "**The Crapshooter**" by John Steinbeck, copyright © 1943 by New York Herald Tribune, Inc., reprinted by permission of McIntosh and Otis, Inc.; **King's Knight Gambit Declined**" by R.L. Stevens, copyright © 1973 by Davis Publications, Inc., reprinted by permission of the author; "**The Murder Game**" by Nedra Tyre, copyright © 1970 by Davis Publica-

Contents

Introduction

"Game" as defined in the dictionary is "to play for a stake." There are other definitions, but this particular one is of great importance to the collection of stories in this anthology. All of them include some strange twist of fate that is either determined or influenced by a game of some sort. The stakes range from the loss of a great deal of money to the loss of life.

The types of games in this collection run the gamut from poker to chess to scrabble. In every story these games are central to the outcome or involve the characters in the story. John Steinbeck turns his hand to mystery writing with the tale of a marine who had exceptional luck on a particular day of the week, until he crossed that one thin line. Also included is Anthony Boucher's story of a game of poker in which a con man is conned by the rules of the game. Sara Paretsky's familiar detective V.I. Warshawski stars in a plot of murder and espionage centered around an ancient Chinese game called Go-ban. Agatha Christie combines love and murder with a game of bridge; Lawrence Block spins a tale of an ill-fated chess game and the burglar made to play it; and Ellery Queen explores the desire of men to make a fast buck or to gamble against the odds, only to learn it's never that easy.

Sometimes the game is played not with an opponent, but with oneself. Ruth Rendell describes a man madly pretending to solve the *Times* crossword puzzle until the truth of his deceit is exposed. Stanley Ellin's crafty plot features a man so obsessed with improving his chess game that he begins to play against his alter ego, which leads him to commit murder.

As you begin the journey through these intricate tales of wicked games, where the only options are to WIN, LOSE OR DIE, sharpen not only your pencil and your wit, but also your dagger. Every writer herein is a winner when it comes to suspense and surprise. Enjoy!

—*The Editors*

WIN, LOSE OR DIE

Forrest V. Perrin

DEALER'S CHOICE

NO SUCH THING as the perfect murder? Of course there is.

I once killed two men by merely dealing a hand of poker. It was that simple, one hand of poker . . . and they could never touch me on it.

Pour yourself another drink there and I'll tell you about it.

It was in World War II, the spring of '44, and I was First Sergeant of a company in the island of Engebi, which lies off one tip of Eniwetok Atoll like a severed fraction of an earthworm. It was a battered driblet of land just a half mile wide and three-quarters of a mile long; the Marines had swept across it in less than seven hours.

Then they turned it over to us. We set up gun positions and raised tents and built latrines and laid communications lines and constructed showers for the officers. And when we finished all that, we sat back to wait for the next offensive so we could move on to another island and start in all over again.

It had been eleven months since we had seen a civilized part of the world and it was likely to be another eleven months before we would return to civilization.

The situation probably had something to do with what happened. We were rotting under the tropical sun while a war was being fought around us. People were killing each other by the hundreds of thousands and those who weren't killed were going home to the States where they could get a drink when they wanted it, or a girl, or maybe just walk down a street with houses on it and lawns in front of the houses. But there we were: building latrines in the daytime and playing poker at night.

Oh, sometimes we wrote letters or read some of the tattered magazines which were passed from hand to hand until they finally fell apart, but mostly it was poker.

It was a poker game that killed the Pole and Petey Storch.

The Pole was one of those sullen rebels who come out of the South Side of Chicago carrying the brand of the slums on their souls. He was a massive man, slow to speak, who seemed unacquainted with emotion. He could suffer any torment silently and without expression—until the moment came when he erupted. Then he would go blind, crazy-mad all in an instant and God help whoever was in his way.

In Hawaii, the Pole would have strangled a sailor who had pawed at his girl if someone hadn't had the foresight to bash him on the head with an iron pipe. Another time, in Fort Riley, Kansas, it had taken a barracks-full of G.I.'s to keep him from tearing apart a corporal he caught trying to steal his diamonds.

Yes, I said diamonds. They were the Pole's only love. There were three of them and he carried them in a little chamois bag attached to the same thong around his neck that held his dog tag. Where he got them, God only knows, and I doubt if the Pole had more than a vague idea of what they were worth. But rich people had diamonds—and the Pole had diamonds. That was the way he reasoned, I think.

He would pour them on the palm of his huge hand and show them to you delicately, as if they were fragile and might break if handled carelessly. Then he would look at them caressingly for a long time before putting them back in the bag and hanging it around his neck again.

Actually, you know, I liked the Pole. It was just that I wanted those diamonds so badly. I had to kill him, you understand, but it wasn't because I didn't like him. Not at all.

I couldn't say as much for Petey Storch.

He was a stinker. He was little, not much more than half the Pole's size, a round little man who looked as if he always suspected someone was following him. His face was puffy with fat and his body looked soft and flabby. There was something evil about him; I couldn't tell you exactly what it was, but it was there: a clammy aura of decay.

He had a been a small-time bookie in Boston before the war and in the Army he became a Shylock. Every company had one: he would lend you all the money you needed—at 50 or 75 percent interest. The more you borrowed, the higher the interest. Usury? Of course, and there are regulations against it, but they are difficult to enforce.

As a matter of fact, I was into him quite a bit myself, owing him a little over $800, not counting interest. Storch always kept his transactions confidential, but it was an unpleasant feeling—owing that much. It made me uncomfortable.

The only thing I felt when I killed Petey Storch was that same shudder of nausea you sometimes experience when you step on a cockroach and feel it crush under the weight of your foot. It is too bad the Pole had to die, too, but that's the way things go.

The only thing the two had in common, really, was poker. The Pole had learned the hard way, grubbing through penny games in the alleyways of Chicago; Storch had picked up the fine points from the professionals in Boston pool halls and card rooms. They were equally good, and if there was any advantage on either side, it was only that Storch wouldn't drink while he was playing and the Pole would.

If the Pole hadn't been drinking the night it happened, things might have gone differently. He wasn't drinking a lot, you understand. He never did. But he had a bottle of saki and he kept pulling at it all through the game.

It was one of those games you could find on any Pacific island during the war. It had started on payday and had been running intermittently for almost a week. Men would sit in for a while and then drop out, and their places would be taken by someone else. The losers left quickly, but the winners hung on grimly until forced to quit by sheer exhaustion—and then they would be back again the next day. Gradually, of course, it had shaken down so that most of the money on the island had gravitated to the five or six big winners.

The Pole was one of them. Storch was another.

There was also Frank McKenna, a sinewy Texan burned dark by the sun, who was never without a cigarette tucked in one corner of his mouth; and Smitty, a grey-haired medical corpsman with a wife and six children back in Pennsylvania. The fifth man was Bob Traggart, a sad-faced master Sergeant with a drooping bush of a mustache.

They were playing in the quartermaster tent on the edge of the supply sump. Locker boxes and wooden crates were stacked along the back wall and in the middle stood a wooden table, somewhat longer than it was wide, over which an old brown Army blanket had been thrown. Locker boxes served as seats and two kerosene lanterns hanging one above the other on the center pole provided the only light.

McKenna sat at one end of the table and on his left was the Pole, a baseball cap pushed half way down over his eyes and his fatigue jacket hanging open, baring his chest. A disordered pile of scattered bills lay in front of him. Next to the Pole and on the same side of the table was Smitty, looking more like a middle-aged schoolmaster than a soldier. To the left of Smitty, directly across from McKenna, was Traggart, and opposite the Pole and Smitty was Storch.

I was the only other person in the tent. I had been playing earlier, but had lost about $300 before leaving. It was a stifling night, though, with the heat hanging heavy over the island, and instead of leaving, I pulled up a locker box behind the Polack and Smitty, where I could see both their hands and watched.

There had been no big winner or loser—except myself—for some time, when Storch suddenly started to win. For an hour it seemed as if he couldn't lose. If someone else had three of a kind, he had a straight; if they had a full house, he had a higher one. Once he won on a pair of kings against four one-card draws. It was one of those things that happened once in a while in a poker game, you have probably seen it yourself, where one player starts to win and he can't lose, no matter what he holds.

It was the Pole who was getting hurt the most. He wasn't drawing the bust hands which allow you to drop out right away. Time after time he would have a good hand, only to have Storch come up with a better one . . . and then laugh at him as he raked in the pot, leaving some money in front of him and tucking the rest away in a bulging wallet which he kept alongside him on the locker box. The Pole said nothing, but I was sitting behind him and I could see the cords of his neck beginning to stand out.

The shadows danced a macabre ballet across the walls of the tent and the night outside seemed to press around us so that the six of us were exiled in time and space. Nothing else existed: there was no war, no States, no island called Engebi—just six men in a tent with the crazy shadows cavorting on the walls and the cards whispering against each other.

From where I sat, McKenna looked like some gaunt, black-jowled prophet as he shuffled the cards deliberately, cutting the deck exactly in the middle each time and then riffling the two halves together in a whir of motion.

The Pole took a long pull from his bottle while McKenna dealt, tilting his head far back as he gulped and then wiping his mouth with the back of his hand. He picked up his cards face-down, stacked them with a quick movement of his fingers and squeezed them together at the bottom so that they fanned out grudgingly, just enough of each card showing to identify it.

His first card was the three of spades. Then came the nine of diamonds; after that, the four, five and six of spades: a four-card straight flush, open on both ends!

The Pole rapped on the table to indicate he wasn't opening and I shifted my attention to Smitty, who had been holding his hand face-down, slipping the top card off and onto the bottom in rapid succession while waiting. Now he looked at it for the first time: two pair, jacks and deuces.

He tossed a $20 bill onto the center of the table, hesitated, and added another $10.

"I'll open for thirty," he said.

"And I'll raise you thirty," said Traggart immediately.

Storch whined, "What are you guys trying to do, win all my money?" But he tossed in his $60.

McKenna, like Smitty, had been snicking his cards through from top to bottom, not looking at them. Now he examined them slowly, forcing one card out at a time. Abruptly he threw them down, "Count me out," he said.

The Pole said, "I'll raise. Up fifty."

The Pole was out to get back the money he had lost—or maybe he had some strange premonition that he was getting to hit his straight flush. I don't know. It happens sometimes. I can't explain it, and it's nothing you can force, but there comes a time when you suddenly know, with all the certainty of reality, that you're going to get a particular card. And when you have that feeling, you bet it.

Smitty called and so did Traggart, but he didn't raise again.

Then it was up to Storch. He said, "I think he's bluffing, I think the big dumb Pole's trying to buy us out." He counted out his $50 and shoved it onto the growing pile of money in the center.

There was over $400 in the pot before the draw.

"I'll take one," the Pole said to McKenna. He slipped his discard out of his hand and spun it onto the table, where it hit too hard, skittered and flipped off the edge.

Storch leaned over and retrieved it with an oath. "For Pete's sake," he whined, "if you can't stay sober enough to keep your cards on the table, get out of here and let the Sarge have your seat. You can't play poker when you're drunk."

"I ain't drunk, Petey," the Pole growled. "Shut up."

"Then quit throwing your cards off the table," Storch shot back.

He put his cards down in front of him, pulled a crumpled pack of cigarettes out of his pocket and lit one nervously.

The Pole picked up his new card and shuffled through the hand face-down, waiting to see what the others did.

Smitty drew one card to his two pair: the seven of hearts. Traggart took two, so you had to figure him for three of a kind. Petey Storch stood pat.

Smitty looked at Traggart and said, "I'll check to the raises." Traggart checked, too.

Storch let the cigarette dangle from his lower lip, the smoke clouding his face. "It'll cost you $200," he said. "You going to stay, or you going to get out?"

The Pole never looked up. "There's no hurry, Petey," he said thickly. "Nobody's going nowhere." He began to fan out his cards precisely: the three . . . four . . . five . . . six.

The last card was the seven of spades!

Smitty shook his head disgustedly and tossed in his cards. Traggart studied his for a long time, but he finally dropped out, also.

Again it was up to Storch. He dug at one ear with one of those grimy fingers of his and laughed at the Pole, taunting him. "I guess it's up to you and me again," he said. "Don't you ever learn, Pole?" He pushed out a stack of twenties and said, "I'll raise you back. $200 more."

The Pole laid his hand down and counted out the bills in front of him. "There's $200," he said, "and $150 more. That's all I got."

Storch leered at him from across the table. "Some guys don't know when to quit," he said. Without taking his eyes off the Pole, he picked up his wallet from the locker box and threw it into the scattered money lying on the table.

He said, "There's $1,500 in there. I'll call you and raise you thirteen-fifty."

The Pole stared mutely at Storch for a long minute. When he did answer, his voice was ominous: "I told you, Petey—that's all I got."

Storch laughed nervously, but he never took his eyes off the Pole. "I heard you," he said, "and I raise you thirteen-fifty." He hesitated and then whined, "What's the matter, you losing your nerve? This is no ten-cent limit game, Pole, this is money. There's over $3,000 there on the table. Do you want to play for it?"

A nerve fluttered at the base of the Pole's neck and you could feel the hate in the air as he looked across the table. He picked up his cards and looked at that straight flush again. Then he laid it down and slowly pulled the thong holding his dog tags up over his head. Carefully, his thick fingers moving delicately, he undid the little chamois bag and poured the three diamonds onto the table in front of him. One by one he picked them up with his thumb and forefinger and placed them along side Storch's wallet.

They lay clean and pure on the rough blanket, the light from the lanterns richocheting through them, shimmering crystals of cold beauty. They didn't belong in that filthy tent with its sweat-stained, stubbled men and smudged cards.

"I call you, Petey," said the Pole.

Nobody moved. There was no sound.

"I call you, Petey," the Pole repeated.

Storch looked at the diamonds greedily and dug a finger into his ear. "All right," he said softly, "you've got a bet, Polack."

He looked around at the rest of us and smiled tentatively. The Pole was motionless, hunched forward, his forearms on the edge of the table.

Storch fanned his hand far enough so the number and suit of each card was visible as he spread them down on the table.

"A straight flush in diamonds," he said. "Queen high."

A little cry escaped the Pole, a tiny one, like a woman might give when she hears of the death of a neighbor's child. Slowly, deliberately, he picked up his cards and crushed them in one hand. He didn't tear them, just crushed them into a tight ball, his fingers working spasmodically.

Suddenly he leaped to his feet, his face contorted in an agony of rage, and shook his fist in front of Storch. "I could kill you Petey," he screamed. "I could kill you."

Then he stormed out, half knocking me off the locker box as he brushed past.

Silence gripped us all for a moment or two. Then Storch picked up the diamonds and began fitting them into the coin pocket of his wallet. "You were kibitzing, Sarge," he whined at me. "What did he have?"

I got up to go. "A straight flush," I said. "A seven-high straight flush in spades."

I left then, but I didn't go to bed. Instead, I went to the office, if you could call it that. It was just a tent thrown up over wooden flooring with a couple of desks in it for the captain and myself. Along one side was a long table with four typewriters on it for the clerks, along the other were stacked the packing cases which contained the company records.

After lighting a lantern, I sat down and tried to reconstruct that last hand in my mind. What bothered me was that Storch, with a pat straight flush, hadn't raised before the draw.

It finally came to me. I took a deck of cards from my bottom drawer, laid it on the desk in front of me, and twirled the handle on the field phone.

I called the charge of quarters and told him to send Storch over.

He protested that it was three o'clock in the morning.

"I know what time it is," I told him. "Get him anyway. I'm having a little investigation." It wouldn't hurt, I thought, to advertise that a bit.

While I waited, I went through the cards and realigned them the way I wanted.

Storch showed up in about ten minutes. He looked uneasy.

"What's up, Sarge?" he whined.

"Sit down," I told him, indicating a chair across the desk from me. "I want to talk to you."

He said, "Sure, Sarge," and sat down.

"All right, Petey," I said, "give me the diamonds."

He jerked in his chair, half coming to his feet, "Give you the diamonds?" he cried. "What do you mean? I won them fair and square. You were there, you saw me."

I reached into my drawer and brought out my .45, released the safety, pulled back the slide and then eased it forward again so a shell slipped into the chamber. I laid the gun on the desk, pointing toward Storch.

"Give me the diamonds," I repeated.

The fear was eloquent in his eyes now. He took his wallet out of his back pocket and put it gingerly on the desk as if he were afraid the .45 might go off if he moved too quickly.

I said, "Thanks, Petey," and checked to make sure the diamonds were still in the wallet before I slipped it into the drawer. Then I turned to the phone again and called the charge of quarters.

"Go find the Pole," I ordered, and send him over right away."

This time Storch did come to his feet. "Look, Sarge, what are you trying to do?" he shouted. "Let's be sensible about this. I mean . . ."

I lit a cigarette and laughed at him.

His manner changed then and he sat down again, leaning across the desk intimately but carefully avoiding the gun. "I'll tell you what, Sarge," he said confidentially, "I was just thinking after I won that loot tonight that I'm pretty well off now, and . . . and that money you owe me, let's just forget it. O.K.?" He was getting hysterical. He said, "I don't need it, Sarge, really I don't." He tried to laugh, but it broke on the falsetto.

I laid my hand on the butt of the .45 and told him to shut up.

The Pole arrived in about five minutes, his big face flushed from drinking and his eyes glazed. He didn't look at Storch, just came up to my desk and stood there dumbly, his clenched fists at his sides.

"That was a tough hand to lose tonight," I said.

He nodded.

I looked hard at him for a long moment. Then I picked up the deck and slowly dealt him five cards.

He scooped them up in one hand and stood there, snicking the top card off and onto the bottom, staring at me, trying to understand.

I said, "Let's see them."

One by one he placed them face-up on the desk: the three of spades . . . four of spades . . . five of spades . . . six of spades . . . nine of diamonds.

"Good hand to draw to," I commented grimly. I looked at Storch. "Here Petey," I said, "you need a hand, too."

"Sarge," he whined, "you can't . . ."

I started to deal, placing each card face-up in front of him and calling them off quietly: "The queen of diamonds . . . jack of diamonds . . . ten of diamonds . . ."

Then I stopped. "But where's the nine of diamonds, Petey?" I asked.

You could almost smell the sudden silence that gripped the tent.

"You took a big gamble palming that nine of diamonds when it fell to the floor, Petey," I said finally, "a real big gamble. But you knew that a guy is usually too intent on the card he is going to draw to keep track of his discard."

Fear twisted his face. "I didn't do a thing," he whispered. "Nothing, you understand? Nothing."

Slowly the Pole turned so that he was facing Storch. "Petey," he said deliberately, the words coming thickly, "you shouldn't have done that to me." Hatred burned in his eyes. Once, twice, his fists clenched and unclenched spasmodically. "You shouldn't have done that," he repeated slowly.

Then he exploded into action.

I couldn't have stopped it—as I testified later—even if I'd wanted to. There was a wild flurry of movement, a mad threshing of arms and legs and then, suddenly, a loud snap.

Did you ever hear the sound that's made when a man's neck is broken? I did that night on Engebi. It was loud and clear, like the sudden breaking of a twig in a quiet forest or the snapping of a dried chicken's wishbone when two children are tugging at it, each hoping his wish will come true.

For a moment the Pole just stood there as if paralyzed by that snap. Then slowly he let Storch's lifeless body slump to the floor. After that, he just stood there, his breath coming in great gasping sobs, and stared down at the body.

He was still standing there when the guard arrived. He went away with them quite meekly, really.

That was the end of it. The Pole later pleaded guilty at the court martial. I testified, of course, that my part in the whole matter had merely been that of the First Sergeant trying to get at the bottom of some suspected cheating at poker. You can't allow card sharks to operate in an outfit, you know, it's damned bad for morale.

Anyway, the Pole got a life sentence in Leavenworth and was shipped back to the States. Later we heard that he killed himself there, threw himself under the wheels of a truck. It was kind of too bad in a way, I'd always sort of liked the Pole, even if he wasn't very bright.

The diamonds? Oh, they searched all over for them, of course. But, you see, the only one who ever knew I had them was Petey Storch.

Anthony Boucher

THE LAST HAND

THE YOUNG MAN clearly had a hangover; and just as clearly, there was something deeper the matter with him.

The tremor which spilled water from his glass was not due solely to the jolting of the train. His reddened eyes had difficulty focusing on the menu. His civilian suit looked at once awkwardly new and thoroughly slept in.

Fergus O'Breen studied these patent symptoms, then went back and studied the young man's eyes more closely. There was a hurt there, a fear that went deeper than their morning pain.

The ruptured duck made an easy starting point for conversation. One day out of the separation center . . . his wife waiting for him in California . . . From there on, Fergus quietly ate his breakfast and listened, knowing that the answer would come in time.

For the O'Breen curiosity is matched only by the O'Breen ability to elicit confidences—and the rash O'Breen impulses to do something about those confidences.

The break came with the second cup of coffee when the young man (whose name turned out to be Herb Ellis) asked, "You play poker, O'Breen?"

Fergus began to get it. He said, "Yes," and added, "the porter said there was a big game on last night. I was too sleepy to look in. You have any luck?"

Ellis groaned. "It couldn't have happened. It just couldn't! Look, O'Breen, you know how it gets toward the end of an evening—"

"Sure. You've been playing along at a nice quiet little limit, then you start raising the stakes. Then maybe for the last hand you take off all the limits . . ."

"Uh-huh. Just a last hand of no-limit stud. And there I was with kings back to back, and nothing showing against me—nothing but a measly pair of threes—I thought. It had to be a pair of threes—he couldn't've bet that way if they weren't. So I went the limit—all my back pay, every damned cent I had on me. And what I was sure was a pair of threes . . . well, it turned out to be a straight."

Fergus frowned. "You're a big boy now. I don't have to tell you about playing cards with strangers on trains. But this interests me. Tell me more." And as Ellis hesitated, Fergus passed over the card that said *Confidential Investigations.* "This one will be on the house," Fergus added.

THE TRAIN WAS PULLING into Chicago when Ellis had finished describing in detail every moment of that fateful last hand.

"And that's torn it," he said. "There goes the TV repair business I had a deal set on, there goes the kid we've been planning on . . . Hell, I can't go out and face Virginia now. I might as well stay here in Chi and—"

Fergus expressed his opinion of that course tersely and vigorously. "Besides," he added, "I've got an idea. God-out-of-the-Machine O'Breen they call me—or maybe I'm your fairy godfather. How would pink wings go with my red hair? Look: Two things are certain. This Hugo Wentworth, who dealt himself that straight, is a professional cardsharp. And he's due to be taken—tonight—and by me. I'll make you a proposition: you point him out to me on the westbound train, and I'll get back your money and split my profit with you."

"You mean you . . . Can you do things with cards?"

"Not the way you mean. I couldn't deal a stacked deck to save my neck. If he'd pulled any other trick but this one, I'd have an angle but to try to spot his gimmick and turn him over to a railway detective—and that wouldn't get your money back."

"And Virginia . . ." That was all Ellis said, but his eyes told how Virginia would feel.

"We've got a couple of hours in Chicago," Fergus said. "Let's have a good lunch at the Pump Room and forget our troubles—after I take care of just one errand. I've got to buy a book."

THERE WAS NOTHING COLORFUL about Hugo Wentworth. You can have all the color you want if you're running a floating crap game in

New York or a casino in Las Vegas; but if you're fleeing discharged G.I.'s on trains, it helps to look kindly and drab.

Mr. Wentworth was an easy man to meet. A half hour in the club car, a large tip to the bartender, some loud big-talk, and Fergus found himself casually adopted by the plump little man with the sheepish features.

The line was reeled in slowly. It was at least an hour later that Mr. Wentworth mentioned the game in his compartment that evening. "I don't know if you'd be interested," he said apologetically. "We'll be playing for rather small stakes . . ."

There were three other players, it developed. Five men crowded the compartments badly, and Fergus had some difficulty disposing of his topcoat, with the stiff-boarded bump in the pocket. But cramped quarters and smoke-filled air never matter much after the first round.

"Just to get it straight," Fergus said as they settled down, "I suppose we're playing according to Hoyle?"

Mr. Wentworth hemmed. "It's dealer's choice. Of course on any wild games, the dealer sets the rules. But in straight poker . . . why, yes, strictly according to Hoyle."

The two small businessmen, who might have been twins but had never met before, played a tight conservative game and were apt to fold on the second card if a victory were not almost certain. The publisher's representative had a passion for the wildest of wild games, and usually insisted on Baseball Poker—in which nines are jokers, fours showing give you an extra card, and an exposed three makes your hand dead—when he was not dealing a peculiar perversion which involved laying five cards out in a Y and turning them over in accordance with a highly improbable ritual.

Mr. Wentworth limited his own deals to straight poker, usually stud, and played sensibly but vigorously.

Fergus drank more than he normally cared to when gambling, and freely followed his impetuous inclination, usually held in check, to stay in every pot whether he had any business there or not. Oddly, his luck was in, and for all his recklessness he was not running far into the hole. In fact, the entire game remained annoyingly even; obviously Mr. Wentworth was withholding his talents for the grand finale.

The inevitable moment arrived when the publisher's representative (saving Mr. Wentworth the trouble) suggested higher stakes. Now matters became worthwhile. The stack of chips grew in front of the kindly drab gentleman, and folding money came into play.

And at last, with much business of consulting watches, it was the final round, and at last it was Mr. Wentworth's turn to deal the very last hand, and at last Mr. Wentworth said, "Just for a little excitement, how's about making this a no-limit hand?"

And as they all agreed, Mr. Wentworth laid a fifty-dollar bill on the table and said, "Everybody in for twenty-five for a little honest stud."

Five cards went around face down. On the second round, the first businessman drew an open ace, the first publisher's representative a five of hearts, Fergus another ace, the second businessman a king, and Mr. Wentworth a deuce of clubs.

The first ace grunted and bet ten dollars. The five of hearts met the bet. Fergus, with the ostentatious caution of an amateur, looked again at his hole card and made it fifty. The king, with sagacity unwonted in modern monarchs, folded.

Mr. Wentworth smiled suavely and said, "Gentlemen, I think it's worth a hundred dollars to stay in the last hand."

The four of them stayed. The third deal of cards went around. The first ace drew a ten. The five of hearts drew a queen of hearts. Fergus caught a king. And Mr. Wentworth's deuce of clubs was joined by a six of diamonds.

"Ace-king bets," said Mr. Wentworth.

Fergus bet a hundred. And the deuce-six of mixed suits not only saw it but raised a hundred.

With the fifth set of cards had been dealt, Fergus surveyed the hands. The publisher's representative, obviously staying on a four-flush in hearts, had folded when his fifth card was black. The first businessman, always cautious, had stayed with nothing better than ace-high showing. Therefore he had a pair, probably aces back-to-back. Mr. Wentworth had two-three-four-six showing; his bets unquestionably indicated a pair of deuces.

Fergus went through the peering routine again. His hole card was still an ace. And his next card was a king, whereas the businessman's possible aces were back by nothing higher than a ten. Fergus's pair of aces seemed a sure thing.

He emptied his once-fat wallet and bet one thousand dollars.

Mr. Wentworth saw the bet and raised a thousand.

The businessman folded, his face shaped in a soundless groan.

"So we're really playing poker," Fergus observed. "Nice to get rid of the ribbon clerks, Wentworth. You want me to think you've got a straight, don't you? That would mean a five in the hole. And that would mean you started heavy raising on a two-five—which no man in his right senses has ever done. I'll see you, Wentworth, and . . . I've got a certified check here from my last job for five thousand dollars. That's my last cent, but it means a four thousand raise. Willing to see it?"

Mr. Wentworth just barely failed to gulp. He opened his luggage, found a second wallet, and counted off the money. "I'm seeing you," he said quietly. "What've you got, O'Breen?"

"Aces back to back." Fergus exposed them.

"Which I'm afraid," Mr. Wentworth murmured, "does not beat a straight," and he turned over his five in the hole.

The publisher's representative goggled. "Now I've seen everything!"

"It was a hunch," Wentworth began to explain modestly. "A pure hunch, and—"

"Just a minute," Fergus said. He reached for his overcoat. "I happen to have a book here . . ."

"AND HE PAID OFF?" Herb Ellis marveled. They were sitting in Fergus's compartment where the porter's cracked ice agreeably supplemented the contents of the O'Breen luggage.

"He couldn't help it," Fergus grinned. "The other three were just a little suspicious of that 'hunch' anyway. And if anybody complained to the railroad and the railway dicks discovered just how often he'd won on that same 'hunch' . . . No, he couldn't afford to do anything but pay off. Here's your losses from last night, and here," Fergus counted meticulously, "is your cut of tonight's profit—which still leaves me a pretty fee for a few hours' work, better than I've made out of some murder cases. And nothing left to do but tip off the railway boys to watch Mr. W."

"Thank God Virginia'll never know how much she has to thank you for," said Ellis humbly. "But if everybody knew that trick, I hate to think what it'd do to the good old game of American poker."

Fergus grinned again. "Even Wentworth would never have believed it if I didn't have the book with me. Here you are: look for yourself. This is the current edition of Hoyle, what's called the Autograph Edition. And there it is, plain as day, on page 291:

" 'Stud Poker: . . . *Straights are not played.*'

"Strictly," Fergus's grin was even wider, "according to Hoyle."

John Steinbeck

THE CRAPSHOOTER

THIS IS ONE OF MULLIGAN'S LIES and it concerns a personality named Eddie. Mulligan has soldiered with Eddie and knows him well. Gradually it becomes apparent that Mulligan has soldiered with nearly everyone of importance.

At any rate, this Eddie was a crapshooter, but of such a saintly character that his integrity in the use of the dice was never questioned. Eddie was just lucky, so lucky that he could flop the dice against the wall and bounce them halfway across the barracks floor on a Sunday and still make a natural.

From performances like this the suspicion grew that Eddie had the ear of some force a little more than human. Eddie, over a period of a year or two, became a rich and happy man, not so lucky in love, but you can't have everything. It was Eddie's contention that the dice could get him a woman any time, but he never saw a woman who could make him roll naturals. Sour grapes though this may have been, Eddie abided by it.

Came the time finally when Eddie and his regiment were put on board a ship and started off for X. It wasn't a very large ship, and it was very crowded. Decks and staterooms and alleys, all crowded. And it just happened that the ship sailed within reasonable time of pay day.

That first day there were at least 200 crap games on the deck, and while Eddie got into one, he did it listlessly, just to keep his hand in, and not to tire himself, because he knew that the important stuff was coming later. Between the chicken games Eddie moped about and did a good deed or two to get himself into a state of grace he knew was necessary later. He helped to carry a "B" bag for a slightly tipsy G.I. and reluctantly accepted a pint of bourbon, which canceled out the good deed to Eddie's way of thinking. He wrote a letter to his wife, whom he hadn't seen for twelve years, and would have posted it if he could ever have found a stamp.

Occasionally he drifted back to the deck and got into a small game to keep his wrist limber and his head clear, but he didn't have to. Eddie had a roll. He didn't have to build up a bank in the preliminaries. He steered clear of spectacular play for two reasons. First, it was a waste of time. It was just as well to let the money get into a few hands before he exerted himself, and second, Eddie, at a time like this, preferred a kind of obscurity and anonymity. There was another reason too. The ship sailed on Tuesday and Eddie was waiting for Sunday, because he was particularly hot on Sundays, a fact he attributed to a clean and disinterested way of life. Once on a Sunday—and, understand, this is Mulligan's story— Eddie had won a small steam roller from a road gang in New Mexico, and on another Sunday Eddie had cleaned out a whole camp meeting, and in humility had devoted ten per cent of his winnings to charity.

As the week went on, the games began to fade out. There were fewer games and the stakes were larger. On Saturday there were only four good ones going, and at this time Eddie began to take interest. He played listlessly Saturday morning, but in the afternoon became more active and wiped out two of the games because his time was getting short and he didn't want too many games going the next day.

At ten o'clock the next day Eddie appeared on the deck clean and combed and modest and bulging at the pockets of his field jacket. The game was going, but there were only three players in it. Eddie said innocently, "Mind if I get in for a pass or two?" The three players scrutinized him cynically. A Pole with one blue eye and one brown eye spoke roughly to him, "Froggy skins it takes, soldier," he said, "not is playing peanuts."

Eddie delicately exposed the butt end of a bank that looked like a rolled roast for a large supper. The Pole sighed with happiness, and the other two, who were remarkable and successful for no other reason than that they could disappear in a crowd rubbed their hands involuntarily, as though to keep their fingers warm. Eddie concealed his poke as modestly as a young woman adjusts the straps of an evening gown that has no straps. He kneeled down beside the blanket and said, "What about is the tariff?" A wall of spectators closed behind him.

Eddie faded thirty of a hundred. The Pole rolled and won and let it lie, and Eddie took a hundred of the two hundred and the Pole shot a six and made it. Behind the dense circle of spectators running feet could be heard. This was to be a game. The ship took a slight list as G.I.'s ran from all over just to be near a game like this, even if they couldn't see it.

The four hundred lay on the blanket like a large salad. The two disappearing men looked at Eddie, and Eddie went into his roll and undid four hundred in small bills and laid them timidly out. This Pole glared at him with his brown eye, and smiled at him with his blue eye, a trick which served him very well in poker, but had little effect on a crap game. He breathed on the dice and didn't speak to them. He rolled an eight and smiled with both his eyes. Again he breathed on the dice and cast them back handed to show how easy that point was, and a four and a three looked up at him.

Eddie, breathing easily, relaxed and sure, pulled the big green salad gently to his side of the blanket. He unrolled two hundred more from his roll like toilet tissue, and laid them down. "One grand," he said, "all or part."

The Pole took half and the two anonymous men split up the rest, and Eddie rolled a rocking chair natural, a six and a five. "Leaving it lay," he said softly.

Only the Pole listened to him. He picked up the dice and looked them over carefully to be sure they were the ones he had put in himself. And then, scowling with both eyes, he covered Eddie. The pile of money was ten inches high now, and spilling down like a loose haycock.

Eddie hummed a little to himself as he rolled and a seven settled firmly. The Pole snorted. Eddie said, "And leaving that lay, all or part, anybody." Breathing had stopped on the ship, only the engines went on. Mouths were open. Figures were frozen in the dense crowd about the blanket.

Scowling at Eddie, the Pole scraped bottom. A whole week of very tiring play for the Pole lay on the blanket, and the pot was set. Eddie was magnificent. He moved easily. He did not shake or rattle the dice or speak to them or beseech them. He simply rolled them out with childlike faith. For a long moment he stared uncomprehendingly at the snake eyes that stared back at him. And then his expression changed to one of horror. "No," he said, "somepins wrong. I win on Sunday, always win on Sunday."

A sergeant shuffled his feet uneasily. "Mister," he said, "Mister, you see, it ain't Sunday. We've went and crossed the date line. We lost Sunday."

Anyway, it's one of Mulligan's lies.

John Philip Cohane

THE SCRABBLE CLUE

THE YOUNG AMERICAN, Pellman by name, was in Ireland searching for ghosts—active ghosts, passive ghosts, ghosts old or new. He was one of eight people staying near Mallow for the week-end with Brian O'Reilly.

In turn he buttonholed each of us and probed without success into our psychic experiences—until he came to Major Carberry, a fox-hunting neighbor who was present only for Saturday night dinner.

"Yes, indeed," declared the major as we rejoined the ladies in front of the drawing-room fire. "Something happened to me twelve years ago that was so inexplicable I've never since scoffed at any ghost story."

The major was the last person you'd expect to commune with the spirit world, so we urged him to tell his story.

"For many years my late wife and I had friends named Ellsworth who lived in a lonely house about three miles below Lahinch in Country Clare. Shoalcroft it was called, and it was situated on a sharp cliff between some heavy woods and the edge of the Atlantic.

"In spite of its dilapidated condition, when the sun was shining the place was quite cheery. On a winter's night, however, with a storm howling in from the ocean, I can assure you it was spooky enough to keep you glancing over your shoulder every time you went up or down the stairs, or along one of the damp, badly lit corridors.

"We first met Ellsworth through his wife, an English girl named Edith Usher. She and my wife grew up together in Hampshire and she married Ellsworth about the same time my wife and I joined forces.

21

"We were living in those days near Carlow, quite a distance from Clare, but we managed to spend at least two week-ends each year with the Ellsworths and at regular intervals they visited us."

The major stopped and turned to Brian O'Reilly. "I'm sorry, Brian. I almost forgot. I must be getting old. I'm going to need a Scrabble game to tell this story properly. Is there one in the house?"

"There should be." Our host rose to his feet. "We still play it now and then." He disappeared, returned a few minutes later with a Scrabble board under his arm. The major placed it on a table by his chair and continued his story.

"Back in the late forties when Scrabble first became popular, like many people the Ellsworths and ourselves took it up with a vengeance. But unlike most others we stayed with it, playing when the four of us were together; and my wife and I matched wits alone several times a week.

"The Ellsworths were doing the same and at each reunion we became more and more expert. Harry Ellsworth and I were fairly even and our wives about the same, so the competition was always close.

"After three or four years—in the autumn of 1951, it was—a frightful tragedy occurred. The Ellsworths were out fishing late one afternoon when a squall blew up. Their boat capsized. Edith was swept off by a current—that stretch of coast is extremely dangerous—and Harry Ellsworth barely managed to struggle ashore.

"Although lifeboats searched for many miles in both directions, Edith's body was never recovered. My wife and I attended services at Winchester Cathedral which isn't far from the Usher's family seat in Hampshire.

"After the funeral services we didn't see Ellsworth again, but three months later my wife read in the *Times* that he had remarried a much younger girl from Canada—from Toronto, I believe.

"Frankly we weren't too surprised. While they tried to cover up in front of us, it had been apparent for some time that things weren't going too well between Edith and Harry. We had also heard vague rumors of another woman in London, but whether it was the one he later married or not I can't say."

The major paused while his glass was refilled. At the same time he shook the Scrabble letters face up onto the board, then resumed his story.

"Six and eight months passed. We weren't eager to continue our friendship with Ellsworth. Edith had been more our friend and three months seemed to be rushing things. Then one day he telephoned from Cork. He and his wife were en route to Dublin. Could we put them up for the night?

"Well, my wife naturally said yes. They arrived in time for dinner. The new wife turned out to be most charming and extremely pretty, so it ended with our accepting a week-end invitation in a month's time to Shoalcroft. We did, however, limit it to one night, explaining that we couldn't arrive until Saturday for lunch and had to be back in Carlow by Sunday evening.

"When we drove up the long sloping hill to Shoalcroft the sun was shining in all its splendor and I was delighted we'd come, especially when I saw the new Mrs. Ellsworth waving to us from the front door and looking as radiant as the weather.

"After lunch we went for a walk along the shore. The sky became overcast and by the time we returned to the house the feeling of the day had changed completely. Ellsworth apologized because they hadn't invited anyone else for dinner. Instead they were expecting six guests for Sunday lunch. This suited us perfectly as my wife was quite tired from the drive.

"When we went upstairs to dress, rain was lashing against the windowpanes and a wild gale was shrieking around the house and down our chimney.

" 'A dreadful night,' I said, peering into the darkness.

" 'Oh, dear!' exclaimed my wife. 'Do you know what day this is?'

" 'Saturday, September 27th, 1952,' I replied, 'So?'

" 'It was just a year ago today that poor Edith died.'

"That set us down a peg, but after a few cocktails my spirits revived. Only one thing depressed me. Ellsworth had been doing some hodgepodge renovating which somehow accentuated the sorry state of the rest of the house. What depressed me about this was I knew the repairs were being done with Edith's money. Ellsworth hadn't a bean until she died and we understood she left everything to him.

"After dinner I suggested a game of Scrabble but Ellsworth bowed out, explaining that Anita, his new wife, didn't play. I thought perhaps Scrabble might be a bit painful for him after all our games with Edith, so rather than try to teach Anita, my wife and I played two-handed while they started a game of chess.

"It was very cozy sitting by a roaring blaze—in spite of or because of the violent storm outside—but although my nerves are reasonably steady I had no desire to go exploring in the rambling wings of the house.

"Now," the major pulled his chair so that it faced the table beside him, "I don't know how many of you have played Scrabble, so I'll keep this simple." We all crowded around the table.

"Each person starts with seven letters picked at random from the pile. The object is to construct as long words as possible with those letters. You build in turn on the previous words, replacing the letters you've used so that you're always playing with seven letters.

"I'll never forget the words that night. My wife began with the word GUMMY." The major placed these letters horizontally in the middle of the board but to the left so the G hit a double-letter score.

"Then I came down vertically into the Y of GUMMY with the word NOBODY. My wife added all seven of her letters to the B in NOBODY to form the word BISECTOR."

With each word the major placed the correct letters on the board.

"Now in Scrabble when you use all seven letters you receive a bonus of 50 points. My wife was delighted with her success, but I came right back with all seven of my letters, forming the word DI-RECTLY, using the C of BISECTOR.

"Well, of course, we were then both delighted, but to our astonishment my wife followed with a third 50-bonus score, building the word BLUNDERS down through the U of GUMMY.

" 'What do you think of that?' I called out to Ellsworth. 'Three seven-letter words in a row!' "

"He got up and came across to our table, peered over my shoulder at the letters in front of me.

" 'Why, by George!' he exclaimed. 'I believe you have another—a fourth!'

" 'Don't show him,' protested my wife. 'He has to find it himself.'

"It didn't take long—in fact, it was quite simple. Using the S of BLUNDERS and my seven letters I formed the word THISTLES.

" 'It's not possible!' said my wife and I thought she was referring to my last word. Instead she was putting down her seven letters to make HEADROOM with the first M of GUMMY as the last letter.

"This meant we had used all seven letters five times running. I tried to make it six in a row but the best I could do was QUEUE, building into the E of HEADROOM.

"At that point"—the major rapidly added more letters—"the board looked like this:"

```
              H              D
        Q U E U E            I
              A    N         R
              D    O         E
              R    B I S E C T O R
            B O    O         T
            L O    D         L
          G U M M Y          Y
              N
              D
              E
              R
        T H I S T L E S
```

"We were both bursting with excitement and Ellsworth seemed as carried away as we were.

" 'I've never seen anything like it!' he said. 'It's splendid. Really splendid. At this rate the Carberrys will be champions of the world. I must teach you how to play, Anita.'

" 'It looks like great fun,' she said, although I don't believe she really understood what was going on.

"At that moment, with no advance warning, the hair began to rise on the back of my neck. A wave of terror swept through me unlike anything I had ever felt in my life.

"I suddenly knew there weren't four of us together in that room. There was a fifth person, standing alongside me, and I knew right away who it was. It was Edith Ellsworth.

"Not only was she standing there, she was trying desperately to tell me something. By then I was soaked with perspiration. I looked across at my wife, but she was busily selecting her next letters. Obviously she had felt nothing.

"Ellsworth, however, shivered and said, 'There must be a window open somewhere.' He walked over and shut the door leading to the dining room.

"As he started back towards us the scales fell from my eyes. Edith's message came through to me and almost overwhelmed me in its clarity. I thought I was going to keel over.

" 'I don't feel well,' I said to my wife. 'Let's finish this in the morning.'

" 'Oh dear,' she sighed. 'I knew you shouldn't have so much brandy. On top of everything else.' She had seen nothing. My main worry was Ellsworth. But if he knew what was happening he certainly didn't show it.

"We put the Scrabble game on an old chest of drawers and midst regrets went up to our room. Once we were alone I turned to my wife. 'Do you believe in ghosts?' I asked.

" 'I don't know.' She looked startled. 'I've never thought about it. Not since I was a child. Why? Did you see one tonight?'

" 'Not exactly.' I checked to be certain our door was tightly closed. 'There was a message from Edith. It was on the Scrabble board.'

" 'On the Scrabble board? You're not serious?' My wife looked as though *she* had seen a ghost.

" 'I wish to God we'd brought our own set,' I said. 'But let's wait half an hour till they've retired. Then I'll slip down and bring the board up here. If I bump into Ellsworth I'll tell him we decided to finish the game in bed.'

"We waited for almost an hour, then I opened our door. There was a light in the hall but no one seemed to be stirring. I tiptoed down the stairs, found the unfinished game still on the chest of drawers and brought it back to our room.

"I placed it carefully on the double bed. 'Take another look,' I told my wife.

"After several minutes she shook her head. 'It's Greek to me.' "

The major stopped and glanced slowly around at our group. "Do any of you see the message?" he asked.

We studied the board for a moment unsuccessfully and then the major explained. "In six of the words there was another word hidden, and one word was complete in itself. Taking them in the order they were put down on the board, there was *my* in GUMMY. *Body* in NOBODY. *Is* in BISECTOR. *Directly*, complete in itself. *Under* in BLUNDERS. *This* in THISTLES. *Room* in HEADROOM . . . *My body is directly under this room.*"

"Why, of course!" exclaimed Brian O'Reilly. "But what about the word QUEUE?"

"Oddly enough," said the major. "I got that first. The letters EUE suddenly jumped out at me as though they were written in flame. EUE. Her initials. Edith Usher Ellsworth. As far as I know they don't appear in that sequence in any other word in the English language."

"My gosh!" said Pellman who was quickly jotting down the words on the board in a notebook. "What did you do?"

"I slipped downstairs again and put the game back on the chest of drawers. The next morning we slept late. By the time we had finished breakfast, guests were arriving for lunch. I did, however, see that the Scrabble game was resting undisturbed in the same place as before.

"All the way home to Carlow three questions kept turning over in my mind. Had Ellsworth also discovered the message from his dead wife? If so, would he realize that I had discovered it? And if the answer to these two questions was yes, would he remove Edith's body from the cellar under the drawing room? For I was absolutely convinced she was buried there.

"During the next few days I did nothing but worry about what I should do. Finally I stopped in to see an old friend, John Curran, the Gardai Sergeant in Carlow. I told him the whole story, using a Scrabble board as I did tonight.

"Thank heavens for the Irish imagination! In some countries they'd have given me a mental examination. But not John Curran, who also happened to be a Scrabble player.

"He decided it would be better to wait until the Ellsworths were away before exploring the basement, but he did drive down immediately to talk to the Gardai Sergeant in Lahinch. Four days later he telephoned me during dinner.

" 'I'm back in Lahinch,' he explained. 'Our friends are attending the Arc de Triomphe race in Paris. They won't be home until Monday afternoon. We're searching tonight. I'll call you in the morning.'

"I couldn't sleep all night. The telephone rang at 7:30. It was John again. 'We're on the right track,' he said. 'Someone's been digging in the dirt floor of the basement. With a new wife around he can't have moved the first one very far. We're going ahead, figuring you're right. If we're wrong we'll catch hell but there you are.'

"They weren't wrong," added the major, gracefully accepting his third nightcap. "In the early afternoon they found poor Edith. Ellsworth had reburied her underneath a tool shed behind the house. She had, of course, never been near the ocean. Her skull had been bashed in with a heavy object."

"What happened to Ellsworth?" asked Pellman, who looked as though he had struck oil in the west of Ireland.

"He committed suicide." The major spoke without regret.

"On Monday afternoon they arrested him as he stepped off the phone at Shannon Airport. He asked if he could stop in the gents for a minute and with three men waiting outside he took a dose of potassium cyanide. He must have been worried that I had seen the message.

"I felt sorry for his new wife. She was a darling. Still, think what Ellsworth might have done to her! Her family owned extensive mining properties in Canada. And don't forget. Unlike Edith she couldn't have communicated—at least, she didn't know how to play Scrabble."

Henry Slesar

THE POISONED PAWN

IF IT WEREN'T FOR THE STATE of his own health (his stomach felt lined with broken green bottle glass), Milo Bloom would have giggled at the sight of his roommate in the six-bed ward on the third floor of Misercordia Hospital. Both of his arms were in casts, giving them the appearance of two chubby white sausages; the left arm dangled from a pulley in a complex traction arrangement that somehow included his left leg. Later, he learned that his companion (Dietz was his name), had fallen from a loading platform. Milo's hospital admittance record told a far more dramatic story. He had been poisoned.

"And I'll tell you something," Milo said, shaking his head sadly and making the broken glass jiggle, "I learned a lesson from it. I was lying under my own dining table, and my whole life flashed in front of my eyes, and you know what it looked like? One long chess game. I saw myself born on QB4, a white pawn wrapped in a baby blanket, and here I was, dying, caught in a *zugzwang* and about to be checkmated. . . ."

Of course, Milo was still under sedation and wasn't expected to talk coherently. An hour later, however, he was able to express himself more clearly.

"Never again," he said solemnly. "Never, never again will I play another game of chess. I'll never touch another piece, never read another chess column. You say the name 'Bobby Fischer' to me, I'll put my hands over my ears. For thirty years I was a prisoner of that miserable board, but now I'm through. You call that a game? That's an obsession! And look where it got me. Just look!"

What he really meant, of course, was "listen," which is what Dietz, who had no other plans that day, was perfectly willing to do.

MY FATHER CARED VERY LITTLE about chess. When he proudly displayed me to the membership of the Greenpoint Chess Club, and mockingly promoted a match with Kupperman, its champion, it wasn't for love of the game; just hate for Kupperman. I was eleven years old, Kupperman was forty-five. The thought of my tiny hands strangling Kupperman's King filled him with ecstasy.

I sat opposite Kupperman's hulking body and ignored the heavy-jowled sneer that had terrified other opponents, confident that I was a prodigy, whose ability Kupperman would underestimate. Then zip! wham! thud! the pieces came together in the center of the board. Bang! Kupperman's Queen lashed out in an unorthodox early attack. *Whoosh!* came his black Knights in a double assault that made me whimper. Then *crash!* my defense crumpled and my King was running for his life, only to fall dead ignobly at the feet of a Rook Pawn. Unbelievable. In seventeen moves, most of them textbook-defying, Kupperman had crushed me. Guess who didn't get ice cream that night?

Of course, I was humiliated by Kupperman's victory. I had bested every opponent in my peer group, and thought I was ready for prodigy-type encounters. I didn't realize at the time how very good Kupperman was. The fact that he was Number One in a small Brooklyn chess club gave no real measure of the man's talent, his extraordinary, Petrosian-like play.

I learned a great deal more about that talent in the next two decades, because that wasn't the last Bloom-Kupperman match; it was only the first of many.

Kupperman refused to play me again until four years later, when I was not only a ripe fifteen, but had already proved my worth by winning the Junior Championship of Brooklyn. I was bristling with self-confidence then, but when I faced the 49-year-old Kupperman across the table, and once again witnessed the strange, slashing style, the wild romping of his Knights, the long-delayed castling, the baffling retreat of well-developed pieces, surprising *zwischenzuge*—in-between moves with no apparent purpose—and most disturbing of all, little stabbing moves of his pawns, pinpricks from both sides of the board, nibbling at my presumably solid center, panic set in and my brain fogged over, to say nothing of my glasses from the steam of my own accelerated breathing. Yes, I lost that game, too; but it wasn't to be my last loss to Kupperman, even though he abruptly decided to leave not only the Greenpoint Chess Club, but the East Coast itself.

I never knew for certain why Kupperman decided to leave. My father theorized that he was an asthma victim who had been advised to bask in the drying sunshine of Arizona or some other western state. Actually, the first postmark I saw from a Kupperman correspondence was a town called Kenton, Illinois. He had sent a letter to the Greenpoint Chess Club, offering to play its current champion by mail. I suppose he was homesick for Brooklyn. Now, guess who was current champion? Milo Bloom.

I was twenty-two then, past the age of prodigy, but smug in my dominance of the neighborhood *potzers*, and pantingly eager to face the Kupperman unorthodoxy again, certain that nobody could break so many rules and still come out on top consistently. I replied to Kupperman at once, special delivery no less, and told him with becoming modesty of my ascension in the club and my gracious willingness to play him by mail.

A week later, I received his reply, a written scowl is what it was, and an opening move—N–KB3! Obviously, Kupperman hadn't changed too much in the intervening seven years.

Well, I might as well get it over with and admit that Kupperman defeated me in that game and, if anything, the defeat was more shattering than the head-to-head encounters of the past. Incredibly, Kupperman posted most of his pieces on the back rack. Then came a Knight sacrifice, a pinned Queen, and a neatly executed check.

Foreseeing the slaughter ahead, I resigned, despite the fact that I was actually ahead by one Pawn.

Obviously, my early resignation didn't fully satisfy Kupperman (I could just visualize him, his unshaven cheeks quivering in a fleshy frown, as he tore open my letter and growled in chagrin at my reply.) Almost the next day, I received a letter asking me why I hadn't sent my White opening for the next game.

I finally did: P–Q4. He replied with N–KB3. I moved my own Knight. He responded by moving his Pawn to the Queen's third square. I moved my Knight to the Bishop's third square, and he promptly pinned it with *his* Bishop, contrary to all common sense. Then he proceeded to let me have both Bishops and bring up my Queen. I should have known that I was doomed then and there. He smothered my Bishops, made an aggressive castling move, and needled me with Pawns until my position was hopeless.

A month went by before Kupperman sent me the next opening move (this time, his letter was postmarked Tyler, Kansas) and we were launched into the third game of what was to become a lifetime of humiliating encounters.

Yes, that's correct. *I never won a game from Kupperman.* Yet, despite my continuing chagrin and, one might think, despite Kupperman's boredom, our games-by-mail were played for a period of *nineteen years.* The only real variations were in Kupperman's postmarks; he seemed to change his residence monthly. Otherwise the pattern remained the same: Kupperman's unorthodox, Petrosian-like style invariably bested my solid, self-righteous, textbook game. As you can imagine, beating Kupperman became the primary challenge, then, of my life.

Then he sent me The Letter.

It was the first time Kupperman's correspondence consisted of anything but chess notations. It was postmarked from New Mexico, and the handwriting looked as if it had been scrawled out with a screwdriver dipped in axle grease.

"Dear Grandmaster," it said, with heavy irony. *"Please be advised that the present score is 97 games to nothing. Please be advised that upon my hundredth victory, we play no more. Yours respectfully, A. Kupperman."*

I don't know how to describe the effect of that letter upon me. I couldn't have been more staggered if my family doctor had diagnosed a terminal illness. Yes, I knew full well that the score was 97-to-0, although I hadn't realized that Kupperman kept such scrupulous records; but the humiliation that lay ahead of me, the hundredth defeat, the *final* defeat, was almost too much for me to bear. Suddenly, I knew that if I didn't beat Kupperman at least *once* before that deadline, my life would be lived out in shame and total frustration.

It was no use returning to the textbooks; I had studied thousands of games (*all* of Petrosian's, until I knew each move by rote) without finding the secret of overcoming Kupperman's singular style. If anything, his use of Knights and Pawns was even wilder and more distinctive than Petrosian's. It was no use hoping for a sudden failure of Kupperman's play; not with only three games left. In fact, it was no use believing in miracles of any kind.

I walked about in a daze, unable to decide whether to send Kupperman the opening move of the 98th game. My employer (the accounting firm of Bernard & Yerkes) began to complain bitterly about frequent errors in my work. The young woman I had been dating for almost two years took personal affront at my attitude and severed our relationship.

Then, one day, the solution to my problem appeared almost magically before my eyes.

Strangely enough, I had seen the very same advertisement in *Chess Review* for almost a dozen years, and it never assumed the significance it did that evening.

The advertisement read: *"Grandmaster willing to play for small fee, by mail. Guaranteed credentials. Fee returned in case of draw or mate. Yankovich, Box 87."*

I had never been tempted to clash with any other player by mail except Kupperman; I had certainly never been willing to lose money in such encounters.

I stared at the small print of the advertisement, and my brain seemed flooded with brilliant light. It was as if a voice, a basso profundo voice, was speaking to me and saying: Why not let someone *else* beat Kupperman?

The simple beauty of the idea thrilled me, and completely obliterated all ethical doubts. Who said chess was a game of ethics, anyway? Chess players are notorious for their killer instincts. Half the sport lay in rattling your opponent. Who can deny the malevolent effects of Fischer's gamesmanship on Boris Spassky? Yes, this would be different; this would be a blatant falsehood. If I gained a victory, it would be a false one; but if I could beat Kupperman, even a phantom victory would do.

That night I addressed a letter to the grandmaster's box number, and within two days received a reply. Yankovich's fee was a mere twenty-five dollars, he wrote. He required the money in advance, but promised to return it after the conclusion of the game, in the event of a draw or a defeat. He wished me luck, and on the assumption that I would be interested, sent me his opening move: P–Q4.

With a feeling of rising excitement, I sent off two letters that day. One to Yankovich, Box 87, and one to A. Kupperman in New Mexico. The letter to Yankovich contained twenty-five dollars, and a brief note explaining that I would send my countermove by return mail. The letter to Kupperman was briefer. It merely said: *"P–Q4."*

Within two days, I had Kupperman's reply: *"N–KB3."*

I wasted no time in writing to Yankovich. *"N–KB3,"* my letter said.

Yankovich was equally prompt. *"N–KB3,"* he said.

I wrote Kupperman. *"N–KB3."*

Kupperman replied: *"P–B4."*

I wrote Yankovich. *"P–B4."*

By the sixth move, Yankovich-Bloom's Bishop had captured Kupperman's Knight, and Kupperman's King's Pawn took possession of our Bishop. (I had begun to think of the White forces as *ours*.) True to form, Kupperman *didn't* capture toward the center. This fact seemed to give Yankovich pause, because his next letter arrived two days later than usual. He responded with a Pawn move, as did Kupperman, who then gave up a Pawn. I felt a momentary sense of triumph, which was diminished a dozen moves later when I realized that Kupperman, once again poising his pieces on the *back* rank, was up to his old tricks. I fervently hoped that Grandmaster Yankovich wouldn't be as bemused by this tactic as I was.

Unfortunately, he was. It took Kupperman forty moves to beat him into submission, but after battering at Yankovich-Bloom's King side, he suddenly switched his attack to the Queen's, and . . . *we* had to resign.

Believe me, I took no pleasure in the letter Yankovich sent me, congratulating me on my victory and returning my twenty-five dollars.

Nor was there much pleasure in the grudging note that Kupperman penned in his screwdriver style to the bottom of his next missive, which read: *"Good game. P–K4."*

I decided, however, that the experiment was worth continuing. Perhaps Yankovich had simply been unprepared for so unorthodox a style as Kupperman's. Surely, in the next round he would be much warier. So I returned the twenty-five dollars to Box 87, and sent Yankovich my opening move: "P–K4."

Yankovich took an extra day to respond with P–K3.

I don't know how to describe the rest of that game. Some chess games almost defy description. Their sweep and grandeur can only be compared to symphonies, or epic novels. Yes, that would be more appropriate to describe my 99th game with Kupperman. (By the fourteenth move, I stopped calling it Yankovich-Bloom, and simply thought of it as "mine.")

The game was full of plots and counterplots, much like the famous Bogoljubow-Alekhine match at Hastings in 1922. As we passed the fortieth move, with neither side boasting a clear advantage, I began to recognize that even if my next-to-last game with Kupperman might not be a victory, it would be no less than a draw.

Finally, on the fifty-first move, an obviously admiring Yankovich offered the Draw to Kupperman-Bloom. In turn, I offered it to Kupperman, and waited anxiously for his rejection or acceptance.

Kupperman wrote back: *"Draw accepted."* He added, in a greasy postscript, *"Send opening move to new address—Box 991, General Post Office, Chicago, Ill."*

My heart was pounding when I addressed my next letter to Yankovich, asking him to retain the twenty-five dollars, and to send me *his* White move for what was to be my final match—with Yankovich, with Kupperman, or with anyone else.

Yankovich replied with a P–K4.

I wrote to Kupperman, and across the top of the page, I inscribed the words: *"Match No. 100—P–K4."*

Kupperman answered with an identical move, and the Last Battle was joined.

Then a strange thing happened. Despite the fact that I was still the intermediary, the shadow player, the very existence of Yankovich began to recede in my mind. Yes, the letters continued to arrive from Box 87, and it was Yankovich's hand still inscribing the White moves, but now each move seemed to emanate from my own brain, and Yankovich seemed as insubstantial as Thought itself. In the Chess Journal of my mind, this one-hundredth match would be recorded forever as Bloom vs. Kupperman, win, lose or draw.

If the previous match had been a masterpiece, this one was a monument.

I won't claim it was the greatest chess game ever played, but for its sheer wild inventiveness, its incredible twists and turns, it was unmatched in either my experience or my reading.

If anything, Kupperman was out-Petrosianing Petrosian in the daring mystery of his maneuvers. Like a Petrosian-Spassky game I particularly admired, it was impossible to see a truly decisive series of moves until thirty plays had been made, and suddenly, two glorious armies seemed opposed to each other on the crest of a mountain. With each letter in my mailbox, the rhythm of my heartbeats accelerated, until I began to wonder how I could bear so much suspense—suspense *doubled* by virtue of receiving both sides of the game from the two battling champions, one of whom I had completely identified as myself. Impatiently, I waited to see how *I* was going to respond to Kupperman's late castling, how *I* was going to defend against his romping Knights, how *I* was going to withstand the pinpricks of his Pawns.

Then it happened.

With explosive suddenness, there were four captures of major pieces, and only Pawns and Rooks and Kings remained in action. Then, my King moved against both Kupperman's Rook and Pawn, and Kupperman saw the inevitable.

He resigned.

Yes, you can imagine my sense of joy and triumph and fulfillment. I was so elated that I neglected to send my own resignation to Yankovich; not that he required formal notification. Yankovich, however, was gracious to his defeated foe, not realizing that my defeat was actually victory. He wrote me a letter, congratulating me on the extraordinary game I had played against him, and while he could not return the twenty-five dollar fee according to the rules of our agreement, he *could* send me a fine bottle of wine to thank me for a most rewarding experience.

The wine was magnificent. It was a Château Latour, '59. I drank it all down with a fine dinner-for-one in my apartment, not willing to share this moment with anyone. I recall toasting my invisible chess player across the table, and that was the last thing I recalled. The next thing I saw was the tube of a stomach pump.

No, THERE WASN'T ANY WAY I could help the police locate Yankovich. He was as phantomlike as I had been myself. The name was a pseudonym, the box number was abandoned after the wine had been dispatched to me, and the review could provide no clues to the identity of the box holder. The reason for his poisoning attempt was made clear only when Kupperman himself read that I was hospitalized, and wrote me a brief letter of explanation.

Yankovich's real name was Schlagel, Kupperman said. Forty years ago, Schlagel and Kupperman (his name, too, was an alias) had been cell mates in a Siberian prison. They had made five years pass more swiftly by playing more than two thousand games of chess. Schlagel had the advantage when the series ended with Kupperman's release.

Kupperman then took a different kind of advantage. Schlagel had charged him with seeking out the beautiful young wife Schlagel had left behind. Kupperman found her, and gave her Schlagel's best. He also gave her Kupperman's best. Six months later, she and Kupperman headed for the United States.

Like so many romances, the ending was tragicomic. Schlagel's wife developed into a fat shrew who finally died of overweight. No matter; Schlagel still wanted revenge, and came to the States to seek it after his release. He knew Kupperman would have changed his name, of course, but he wouldn't change his chess style.

Consequently, year after year, Schlagel-Yankovich ran his advertisement in the chess journals, hoping to find the player whose method Schlagel would recognize in an instant . . .

"WELL, THAT'S WHAT HAPPENED," Milo Bloom told his roommate at Misercordia Hospital. "Believe me, if I didn't have a nosy landlady, I would be dead now. Luckily, she called the ambulance in time.

"Sure, it was a terrible thing to happen to anybody. But at least I've learned my lesson. Life wasn't meant to be spent pushing funny-looking pieces around a checkered board. But maybe you've never even tried the game . . ."

The man in traction mumbled something.

"What was that?" Milo asked.

"I play," Dietz said. "I play chess. I've even got a pocket set with me."

Milo, merely curious to see what the set looked like, eased himself out of bed and removed it from the bedside table. It was a nice little one, all leather and ivory.

"It's not a bad way to pass the time," Dietz said cautiously. "I mean, I know you said you'd never play anymore, but—if you wanted to try just *one* game . . ."

Milo looked at his casts, and said, "Even if I wanted to play—how could *you*?"

Dietz smiled shyly, and showed him. He picked up the pieces with his teeth. In the face of a dedication matching his own, how could Milo refuse? He moved the Pawn to P–K4.

Sara Paretsky

THE TAKAMOKU JOSEKI

MR. AND MRS. TAKAMOKU WERE A QUIET, hardworking couple. Although they had lived in Chicago since the 1940's, when they were relocated from an Arizona detection camp, they spoke only halting English. Occasionally I ran into Mrs. Takamoku in the foyer of the old three-flat we both lived in on Belmont, or at the corner grocery store. We would exchange a few stilted sentences. She knew I lived alone in my third-floor apartment, and she worried about it, although her manners were too perfect for her to come right out and tell me to get myself a husband.

As time passed, I learned about her son Akira and her daughter Yoshio, both professionals living on the West Coast. I always inquired after them, which pleased her.

With great difficulty I got her to understand that I was a private detective. This troubled her; she often wanted to know if I were doing something dangerous, and would shake her head and frown as she asked. I didn't see Mr. Takamoku often. He worked for a printer and usually left long before me in the morning.

Unlike the De Paul students who form an ever-changing collage on the second floor, the Takamokus did little entertaining, or at least little noisy entertaining. Every Sunday afternoon a procession of Orientals came to their apartment, spent a quiet afternoon, and left. One or more Occidentals would join them, incongruous by their height and color. After a while, I recognized the regulars, a tall, bearded white man, and six or seven Japanese and Koreans.

One Sunday evening in late November I was eating sushi and drinking sake in a storefront restaurant on Halsted. The Takamokus came in as I was finishing my first little pot of sake. I smiled and waved at them, and watched with idle amusement as they conferred earnestly, darting glances at me. While they argued, a waitress brought them bowls of noodles and a plate of sushi; they were clearly regular customers with regular tastes.

At last, Mr. Takamoku came over to my table. I invited him and his wife to join me.

"Thank you, thank you," he said in an agony of embarrassment. "We only have question for you, not to disturb you."

"You're not disturbing me. What do you want to know?"

"You are familiar with American customs." That was a statement, not a question. I nodded, wondering what was coming.

"When a guest behaves badly in the house, what does an American do?"

I gave him my full attention. I had no idea what he was asking, but he would never have brought it up just to be frivolous.

"It depends," I said carefully. "Did they break up your sofa or spill tea?"

Mr. Takamoku looked at me steadily, fishing for a cigarette. Then he shook his head, slowly. "Not as much as breaking furniture. Not as little as tea on sofa. In between."

"I'd give him a second chance."

A slight crease erased itself from Mr. Takamoku's forehead. "A second chance. A very good idea. A second chance."

He went back to his wife and ate his noodles with the noisy appreciation that showed good Japanese manners. I had another pot of sake and finished about the same time as the Takamokus; we left the restaurant together. I topped them by a good five inches, so I slowed my pace to a crawl to keep step with them.

Mrs. Takamoku smiled. "You are familiar with Go?" she asked, giggling nervously.

"I'm not sure," I said cautiously, wondering if they wanted me to conjugate an intransitive irregular verb.

"It's a game. You have time to stop and see?"

"Sure," I agreed, just as Mr. Takamoku broke in with vigorous objections.

I couldn't tell whether he didn't want to inconvenience me or didn't want me intruding. However, Mrs. Takamoku insisted, so I stopped at the first floor and went into the apartment with her.

The living room was almost bare. The lack of furniture drew the eye to a beautiful Japanese doll on a stand in one corner with a bowl of dried flowers in front of her. The only other furnishing was a row of six little tables. They were quite thick and stood low on carved wooden legs. Their tops, about eighteen inches square, were criss-crossed with black lines that formed dozens of little squares. Two covered wooden bowls stood on each table.

"Goban," Mrs. Takamoku said, pointing to one of the tables.

I shook my head in incomprehension.

Mr. Takamoku picked up a covered bowl. It was filled with smooth white disks, the size of nickels but much thicker. I held one up and saw beautiful shades and shadows in it.

"Clam shell," Mr. Takamoku said. "They cut, then polish." He picked up a second bowl, filled with black disks. "Shale."

He knelt on a cushion in front of one of the tables and rapidly placed black and white disks on intersections of the lines. A pattern emerged.

"This is go. Black plays, then white, then black, then white. Each tries to make territory, to make eyes." He showed me an "eye"—a clear space surrounded by black stones. "White cannot play here. Black is safe. Now white must play someplace else."

"I see." I didn't really, but I didn't think it mattered.

"This afternoon, someone knock stones from table, turn upside down, and scrape with knife."

"This table?" I asked, tapping the one he was playing on.

"Yes." He swept the stones off swiftly but carefully, and put them in their little pots. He turned the board over. In the middle was a hole, carved and sanded. The wood was very thick—I suppose the hole gave it resonance.

I knelt beside him and looked. I was probably thirty years younger, but I couldn't tuck my knees under me with his grace and ease: I sat crosslegged. A faint scratch marred the sanded bottom.

"Was he American?"

Mr and Mrs. Takamoku exchanged a look. "Japanese, but born in America," she said. "Like Akira and Yoshio."

I shook my head. "I don't understand. It's not an American cus-tom." I climbed awkwardly back to my feet. Mr. Takamoku stood with one easy movement. He and Mrs. Takamoku thanked me pro-fusely. I assured them it was nothing and went to bed.

THE NEXT SUNDAY was a cold, gray day with a hint of snow. I sat in my living room in front of the television drinking coffee, dividing my attention between November's income and watching the Bears. Both

were equally feeble. I was trying to decide on something friendlier to
do when a knock sounded on my door. The outside buzzer hadn't
rung. I got up, stacking loose papers on one arm of the chair and
balancing the coffee cup on the other.

Through the peephole I could see Mrs. Takamoku. I opened the
door. Her wrinkled ivory face was agitated, her eyes dilated. "Oh,
good, good, you are here. You must come." She tugged at my hand.

I pulled her gently into the apartment. "What's wrong? Let me get
you a drink."

"No, no." She wrung her hands in agitation, repeating that I must
come, I must come.

I collected my keys and went down the worn, uncarpeted stairs
with her. Her living room was filled with cigarette smoke and a crowd
of anxious men. Mr. Takamoku detached himself from the group and
hurried over to his wife and me. He clasped my hand and pumped it
up and down.

"Good. Good you came. You are a detective, yes? You will see
the police do not arrest Naoe and me."

"What's wrong, Mr. Takamoku?"

"He's dead. He's killed. Naoe and I were in camp during World
War. They will arrest us."

"Who's dead?"

He shrugged helplessly. "I don't know name."

I pushed through the group. A white man lay sprawled on the
floor. It was hard, given his position, to guess his age. His fair hair was
thick and unmarked with gray; he must have been relatively young.

A small dribble of vomit trailed from his clenched teeth. I sniffed
at it cautiously. Probably hydrocyanic acid. Not far from his body lay
a teacup, a Japanese cup without handles. The contents sprayed out
from it like a Rorschach. Without touching it, I sniffed again. The
fumes were still discernible.

I got up. "Has anyone left since this happened?"

The tall, bearded Caucasian I'd noticed on previous Sundays looked
around and said "no" in an authoritative voice.

"And have you called the police?"

Mrs. Takamoku gave an agitated cry. "No police. No. You are
detective. You find murderer yourself."

I shook my head and took her gently by the hand. "If we don't
call the police, they will put us all in jail for concealing a murder.
You must tell them."

The bearded man said, "I'll do that."

"Who are you?"

"I'm Charles Welland. I'm a physicist at the University of Chicago, but on Sundays I'm a Go player."

"I see . . . I'm V. I. Warshawski. I live upstairs: I'm a private investigator. The police look very dimly on all citizens who don't report murders, but especially on P.I.s."

Welland went into the dining room, where the Takamokus kept their phone. I told the Takamokus and their guests that no one could leave before the police gave them permission, then followed Welland to make sure he didn't call anyone besides the police, or take the opportunity to get rid of a vial of poison.

The go players seemed resigned, albeit very nervous. All of them smoked ferociously; the thick air grew bluer. They split into small groups, five Japanese together, four Koreans in another clump. A lone Chinese fiddled with the stones on one of the gobans.

None of them spoke English well enough to give a clear account of how the young man died. When Welland came back, I asked him for a detailed report.

They physicist claimed not to know his name. The dead man had only been coming to the go club the last month or two.

"Did someone bring him? Or did he just show up one day?"

Welland shrugged. "He just showed up. Word gets around among Go players. I'm sure he told me his name—it just didn't stick. I think he worked for Hansen Electronic, the big computer firm."

I asked if everyone there were regular players. Welland knew all of them by sight, if not by name. They didn't all come every Sunday, but none of the others was a newcomer.

"I see. Okay. What happened today?"

Welland scratched his beard. He had bushy, arched eyebrows that jumped up to punctuate his stronger statements. I thought that was pretty sexy. I pulled my mind back to what he was saying.

"I got here around one thirty. I think three games were in progress. This guy"—he jerked his thumb toward the dead man—"arrived a bit later. He and I played a game. Then Mr. Hito arrived and the two of them had a game. Dr. Han showed up and he and I were playing when the whole thing happened. Mrs. Takamoku sets out tea and snacks. We all wander around and help ourselves. About four, this guy took a swallow of tea, gave a terrible cry, and died."

"Is there anything important about the game they were playing?"

Welland looked at the board. A handful of black and white stones stood on the corner points. He shook his head. "They'd just started.

It looks like our dead friend was trying the Takamoku joseki. That's a complicated one—I've never seen it used in actual play before."

"What's that? Anything to do with Mr. Takamoku?"

"The joseki are the beginning moves in the corners. Takamoku is this one"—he pointed at the far side—"where black plays on the five-four point—the point where the fourth and fifth lines intersect. It wasn't named for our host. That's just coincidence."

SERGEANT MCGONNIGAL DIDN'T FIND out much more than I had. A thickset young detective, he has had a lot of experience and treated his frightened audience gently. He was a little less kind to me, demanding roughly why I was there, what my connection with the dead man was, who my client was. It didn't cheer him up any to hear that I was working for the Takamokus, but he let me stay with them while he questioned them. He sent for a young Korean officer to interrogate the Koreans in the group. Welland, who spoke fluent Japanese, translated the Japanese interviews. Dr. Han, the lone Chinese, struggled along on his own.

McGonnigal learned that the dead man's name was Peter Folger. He learned that people were milling around all the time watching each other play. He also learned that no one paid attention to anything but the game they were playing, or watching.

"The Japanese say the Go player forgets his father's funeral," Welland explained. "It's a game of tremendous concentration."

No one admitted knowing Folger outside the go club. No one knew how he found out that the Takamokus hosted go every Sunday.

My clients hovered tensely in the background, convinced that McGonnigal would arrest them at any minute. But they could add nothing to the story. Anyone who wanted to play was welcome at their apartment on Sunday afternoon. Why should he show a credential? If he knew how to play, that was the proof.

McGonnigal pounced on that. Was Folger a good player? Everyone looked around and nodded. Yes, not the best—that was clearly Dr. Han or Mr. Kim, one of the Koreans—but quite good enough. Perhaps first kyu, whatever that was.

After two hours of this, McGonnigal decided he was getting nowhere. Someone in the room must have had a connection with Folger, but we weren't going to find it by questioning the group. We'd have to dig into their backgrounds.

A uniformed man started collecting addresses while McGonnigal went to his car to radio for plainclothes reinforcements. He wanted everyone in the room tailed and wanted to call from a private phone. A useless precaution, I thought: the innocent wouldn't know they were being followed and the guilty would expect it.

McGonnigal returned shortly, his face angry. He had a bland-faced, square-jawed man in tow, Derek Hatfield of the F.B.I. He did computer fraud for them. Our paths had crossed a few times on white-collar crime. I'd found him smart and knowledgeable, but also humorless and overbearing.

"Hello, Derek," I said, without getting up from the cushion I was sitting on. "What brings you here?"

"He had the place under surveillance," McGonnigal said, biting off the words. "He won't tell me who he was looking for."

Derek walked over to Folger's body, covered now with a sheet which he pulled back. He looked at Folger's face and nodded. "I'm going to have to phone my office for instructions."

"Just a minute," McGonnigal said. "You know the guy, right? You tell me what you were watching him for."

Derek raised his eyebrows haughtily. "I'll have to make a call first."

"Don't be an ass, Hatfield," I said. "You think you're impressing us with how mysterious the F.B.I. is, but you're not, really. You know your boss will tell you to cooperate with the city if it's murder. And we might be able to clear this thing up right now, glory for everyone. We knew Folger worked for Hansen Electronic. He wasn't one of your guys working undercover, was he?"

Hatfield glared at me. "I can't answer that."

"Look," I said reasonably. "Either he worked for you and was investigating problems at Hansen, or he worked for them and you suspected he was involved in some kind of fraud. I know there's a lot of talk about Hansen's new Series J computer—was he passing secrets?"

Hatfield put his hands in his pockets and scowled in thought. At last he said to McGonnigal, "Is there someplace we can talk?"

I asked Mrs. Takamoku if we could use her kitchen for a few minutes. Her lips moved nervously, but she took Hatfield and me down the hall. Her apartment was laid out like mine and the kitchens were similar, at least in appliances. Hers was spotless; mine has that lived-in look.

McGonnigal told the uniformed man not to let anyone leave or make any phone calls and followed us.

Hatfield leaned against the back door. I perched on a bar stool next to a high wooden table. McGonnigal stood in the doorway leading down the hall.

"You got someone here named Miyake?" Hatfield asked.

McGonnigal looked through the sheaf of notes in his hand and shook his head.

"Anyone here work for Kawamoto?"

Kawamoto is a big Japanese electronics firm, one of Mitsubishi's peers and a strong rival of Hansen in the mega-computer market.

"Hatfield. Are you trying to tell us that Folger was passing Series J secrets to someone from Kawamoto over the Go boards here?"

Hatfield shifted uncomfortably. "We only got onto it three weeks' ago. Folger was just a go-between. We offered him immunity if he would finger the guy from Kawamoto. He couldn't describe him well enough for us to make a pickup. He was going to shake hands with him or touch him in some way as they left the building."

"The Judas trick," I remembered.

"Huh?" Hatfield looked puzzled.

McGonnigal smiled for the first time that afternoon. "The man I kiss is the one you want. You should've gone to Catholic school, Hatfield."

"Yeah. Anyway, Folger must've told the guy Miyake we were closing in." Hatfield shook his head disgustedly. "Miyake must be part of that group out there, just using an assumed name. We got a tail put on all of them." He straightened up and started back towards the hall.

"How was Folger passing the information?" I asked.

"It was on microdots."

"Stay where you are. I might be able to tell you which one is Miyake without leaving the building."

Of course, both Hatfield and McGonnigal started yelling at me at once. Why was I suppressing evidence, what did I know, they'd have me arrested. "Calm down, boys," I said. "I don't have any evidence. But now that I know the crime, I think I know how the information was passed. I just need to talk to my clients."

Mr. and Mrs. Takamoku looked at me anxiously when I came back to the living room. I got them to follow me into the hall. "They're not going to arrest you," I assured them. "But I need to know who turned over the Go board last week. Is he here today?"

They talked briefly in Japanese, then Mr. Takamoku said, "We should not betray guest. But murder is much worse. Man in orange shirt, named Hamai."

Hamai, or Miyake, as Hatfield called him, resisted valiantly. When the police started to put handcuffs on him, he popped another gelatin capsule into his mouth. He was dead almost before they realized what he had done.

Hatfield, impersonal as always, searched his body for the microdot. Hamai had stuck it to his upper lip, where it looked like a mole against his dark skin.

"How did you know?" McGonnigal grumbled, after the bodies had been carted off, and the Takamokus' efforts to turn their life savings over to me successfully averted.

"He turned over a go board here last week. That troubled my clients enough that they asked me about it. Once I knew we were looking for the transfer of information, it was obvious that Folger had stuck the dot in the hole under the board. Hamai couldn't get at it, so he had to turn the whole board over. Today, Folger must have put it in a more accessible spot."

Hatfield left to make his top-secret report. McGonnigal followed his uniformed men out of the apartment. Welland held the door for me.

"Was his name Hamai or Miyake?" he asked.

"Oh, I think his real name was Hamai—that's what all his identification said. He must have used a false name with Folger. After all, he knew you guys never pay attention to each other's names—you probably wouldn't even notice what Folger called him. If you could figure out who Folger was."

Welland smiled; his bushy eyebrows danced. "How about a drink? I'd like to salute a lady clever enough to solve the Takamoku joseki unaided."

I looked at my watch. Three hours ago I'd been trying to think of something friendlier to do than watch the Bears get pummeled. This sounded like a good bet. I slipped my hand through his arm and went outside with him.

"Pat Hand"

THE ACE OF SPADES

CAREFUL JONES looked about the Lawson suite with a distasteful eye. It was large and luxurious with a view from the sitting room of a private section of deck. There were fresh flowers everywhere, and baskets of fruit, and boxes of candy on all the tables. A sable coat, belonging to the youngish, red-headed, diamond-bedecked Mrs. Pierre Lawson, had been flung carelessly over the back of a chair. It was the most expensive suite on the ship.

The distaste in the gray still eye of the almost legendary Careful Jones was not due, however, to any disbelief in luxury or wealth. He liked men to make a great deal of money so that he could take some of it away from them in high-powered games of chance. But he had been one of a group of passengers to whom the captain of the *Minotaur* had explained the desperate plight of some war refugees on board and he was remembering that Pierre Lawson, although one of the wealthiest men in America, had contributed an almost infinitesimal check to the relief fund. To make matters worse, Mr. Lawson had been sitting in on their six-man poker game and winning steadily with the same cold efficiency he displayed, no doubt, in the operation of his steel plants.

He came in now, puffing out his pleated shirt front and rubbing a hand over his bluish dewlaps. "First here, Jones?" he rumbled. "Hope the others get here soon. I feel lucky tonight."

"You won't need luck," said Jones, twisting an unlighted cigar from one corner of his mouth to the other. "I've been watching things and I must say you play a shrewd game of poker."

The steel magnate grunted deprecatingly but it was clear he was very much pleased. "Nothing to poker," he declared. "Just follow the same lines as you do in business and you can't fail to come out on

47

top. Know your odds, watch your opponents, never lose your nerve. And above everything else, never take foolish risks." He reached for a cigar in a handsome humidor and snipped off the end. "I always win."

Careful Jones nodded. "You've put your finger on the fine points," he conceded. "Especially about watching your opponents. I've been playing poker, man and boy, for more'n fifty years and, from what I've managed to pick up in that time, I say knowing the other fellow's game is just about seventy-five per cent of winning. It's not only getting on to his special angles; it's finding out the little things he does unconsciously and then cashing in on 'em. For instance, Mr. Lawson, when you're loaded for bear you always clear your throat before making your first bet."

The millionaire looked ruffled at this hint of a flaw in his game. "I do? I've never noticed it myself. Are you sure of it?"

"Sartain sure. I got on to *that* the very first night and it's saved me quite a bit of dough since. Every man has 'em. Take that fellow Crouch. I don't give him much myself anyway, being of the honest opinion that the fellow's a two-faced, low-down, yellow-bellied skunk with some other faults I'd mention if we had the time—"

Lawson laughed. "Go right on. My own opinion exactly. But he's a good player—wins right along."

"He knows his stuff but he has one of these little weaknesses just the same. Ever notice the cat's-eye ring he wears? Well, Mr. Crouch likes to pull a bluff about twice every evening. I'll say this for him, he picks his spots. But whenever he's set to run a sandy, he touches that ring with his thumb under the palm. He may do it for luck, but I think he don't know he's doing it. All you have to do, Mr. Lawson, is to keep your eyes peeled on that thumb of his and you'll take the fellow for a nice buggy-ride before the evening's out."

The steel man's eyes glistened avidly. "Very interesting, Jones. Have you observed anything about our other opponents?"

"Well, there's this Colonel Braddock. He just can't resist holding an ace for a kicker. He'll do it even with three of a kind in his hand. The funny part of it is, he knows it's wrong and he fights against it. When he frowns and gives himself a twist in his chair, you can be dead sure he's going to hold an ace with whatever else he's got in his hand."

Pierre Lawson began to laugh slyly. "I see where I'll have to keep a closer eye on the pair of them. But what I really want to know, Jones, is this. What little give-away tricks have you got yourself?"

"I wish I knew." Jones shook his head earnestly and then repeated, "By George, I wish I knew. I'd give a lot to find out if I've got any of these habits myself."

The other players began to drift into the room, nodding respectfully to the great Mr. Lawson and seating themselves immediately at the round poker table in the center of the room. The millionaire snapped down the lid of the humidor and shoved it to one side. "Well, gentlemen, let's get started," he said.

Careful Jones looked at the other members of the group with a freshly appraising eye. They were all prosperous looking, inclined to be tight-lipped and running without exception to purple nose veins and inflated waistlines. "I may have to pull a fancy one on these birds," he said to himself. "Somehow I got to see that a fat contribution goes to the refugee fund out of this game."

IT WAS NEARLY ONE O'CLOCK. Half an hour before, Mrs. Lawson had passed silently across the room and vanished through one of the doors, a French maid at her heels. A trace of seductive perfume still lingered on the air. The game was to break up at one sharp.

Careful Jones, who had managed to accumulate what he termed his "chunk o' taller", was dealing. Lawson and Crouch were both well ahead of the game. The rest of the party were down for rather considerable amounts.

Jones laid the pack of cards on the table. "Gentlemen," he said, "I was kind of disturbed over those poor critters the captain told us about this afternoon. What say we donate the proceeds of this last pot to the fund?"

Lawson snorted indignantly. "I paid over a check to Captain Trimble. I certainly won't agree to anything of the kind. What's wrong with you, Jones? Getting soft in the head all of a sudden?"

"I'm four thousand down as it is," grumbled one of the others.

The rest remained silent. Were they waiting to see what cards they would draw first? It seemed likely. Jones paused expectantly and then said, "Well, if I happen to win myself, I'm going to turn the cash over to the captain. So let's make it a good one anyway."

He began to deal. Lawson on his left looked at his five cards and checked himself hurriedly when he found himself on the point of clearing his throat.

"I'll open the second front myself," he said with a perfect air of indifference. "As this is the last deal, I'll give you suckers a chance for some action. What do you say to a hundred?"

Two pairs of eyes, the dealer's and Lawson's, glued themselves on Crouch's hands as that unpopular member of the circle considered what he would do. Both of them were sure that his pudgy thumb touched the inner rim of the ring on his index finger before he said, "Well, if it's action you're looking for, I'll just give it a tilt for five of the same. That'll keep the grocery clerks out anyway."

The man on Crouch's left whistled in dismay and threw in his hand. "That keeps one of the grocery clerks out," he said.

The next player laughed. "Not having the chance of a lily-fingered Hottentot, I'm now in favor of contributing this pot to the needy refugees," he announced. He also threw in his hand.

Colonel Braddock was frowning and twisting in his chair. "Six hundred to stay in?" he asked. "Well, gentlemen, I think pretty well of these cards of mine. They make another tilt obligatory. Making it an even grand."

"I'll stay for the thousand," said Jones, shoving a stack of chips to the center of the table.

It was a full minute before Lawson made up his mind about his next move. He had observed the antics of the Colonel and was not much disturbed over the raise from that quarter. It was clear, however, that he did not like the fact that Jones himself had elected to stay in. He had acquired a healthy respect for the judgment of that impassive-faced veteran and he was certain now that the danger, if any, would come from him. Finally he saw the double raise.

Crouch blithely pushed more chips forward. "Once you start to toy recklessly with fate," he said, "you might as well keep right on doing it. Another thousand, gentlemen."

Braddock groaned and saw him. It was now the turn of the dealer to pause. Jones seemed to study his cards anxiously, then finally elected to stay. Lawson followed suit.

Before calling for cards, Jones decided to make another effort. "Between the lot of us we've built up a pretty handsome pot," he said. "Come, gentlemen, how about that little idea of mine? It wouldn't hurt any of us."

"Nothing doing," said the steel magnate, sharply.

Jones turned his head toward the next man. "Feeling generous, Crouch?"

"Me? What do you take me for? I've got this pot all sewed up and what's more I know exactly how I'm going to spend every solitary little dollar in it."

"Colonel Braddock?"

"I'm in the red," said the Colonel, impatiently. "I need this pot to get even."

The old stager said to himself bitterly: "The cheapskates! They're all rolling in it and it wouldn't hurt 'em to be a little generous for once in their lives. Well, it looks as if I'll have to win the pot myself."

His fingers began to move. Slowly, clumsily even, it might have seemed to a casual watcher. One card went on demand to the millionaire, one to Crouch, one to Braddock. No eyes in the room were keen enough to see that Jones was indulging his skill in the most difficult of all feats of card manipulation—the second card deal. When his own turn came, he announced, "Dealer also takes one," and dropped in front of himself *the card which had been on top of the deck all the time.*

Lawson was too concerned with his prospects to realize that he cleared his throat before saying, "The opener bets an even two thousand."

There was no twitch of the Crouch thumb this time. He saw the bet and raised it an equal amount. Braddock considered his hand sourly and then threw the cards face up on the table. "Look at that!" he grated. "I go in with three tens and can't better them, while both these two luckbags fill. They won't get any more sucker money out of me! And I announce here and now that I'm cured for all time of holding kickers." He had held an ace with the tens and had drawn a fine deuce for his pains.

Careful Jones said in grumbling tones: "You fellows are sure running hog-wild. Still, I like what I got here. I stand by what I said about the fund, so I'm not going to put any more of my own money in than I have to. I'll just see."

There was a trace of perspiration on the round forehead of the steel man. He seemed to be wavering between alternate flashes of optimism and doubt—particularly when he glanced at the expressionless face of the dealer. "I should bump you back, Crouch, by rights," he said, finally. "I've got *you* beaten—but what about this oldtimer from the Wild West? I don't believe in foolish risks and anyway the pot's pretty big as it is. I'm just seeing."

Crouch spread his hand on the table. "I made it," he said, confidently. "A spade flush. King, queen, jack, ten, six. Drew the six. Of course if I had drawn the spade ace, I'd have had a royal flush. That would have made it a sure thing—but you can't have everything, I guess."

The steel magnate was so certain of winning now that he did not wait for the dealer to declare himself. "No good," he said, briskly. "No good at all, Crouch. I have a full house. Three sevens, two aces. I could have used the ace of spades too—that would have copper-riveted my chances of winning. But I'm not complaining about the neat little seven that came drifting in." He reached out an exultant hand toward the great pile of chips on the green baize as he twisted his head in the direction of Careful Jones. "Good?" he asked.

"As it happens, no," answered the dealer. He spread out his hand. "I caught, too. A straight flush. Lowest in the whole deck, five down to ace, and all spades. A real, honest-to-goodness straight flush just the same, and good enough to win the pot for the widows and orphans."

Paying no heed to the sharp and angry comments from his disappointed opponents, he drew twenty-one thousand dollar bills from a plethoric wallet, counted them carefully aloud and then put them in an envelope. He moistened the flap and closed it tight with one circular sweep of a splayed thumb. He was thinking, "I must spike their guns before the uproar starts."

Lawson began to say, "There's something damned odd about this—"

Jones touched a button on the wall behind him and said to the Lawson valet who answered: "Here, young fellow, take this straight to Captain Trimble's cabin. Hang on to it tight—there's quite a chunk o' taller in it. Tell Captain Trimble it's a contribution for the refugees from—from Mr. Lawson and some acquaintances of his." He looked over at the millionaire and his eyes achieved a semblance of a twinkle.

"Say," demanded Crouch suddenly, "what card did *you* draw?"

"The spade ace."

Lawson exploded. "All of us could have used that card!"

"That's so," agreed Jones. "Odd, wasn't it?"

It was even odder (though Careful Jones failed to mention it) that once he had reserved the ace of spades for himself, neither Lawson, Crouch nor Braddock could draw *anything* to beat him. In dealing cards to the others, Jones had been careful about that. In fact, it was little precautions of that nature which caused some people to call him *Extra*-Careful Jones.

Lord Dunsany

THE NEW MASTER

I CANNOT PROVE MY CASE. I have been over everything very carefully.
I have had a talk with a lawyer about evidence in coroner's courts,
without letting him know what I was really after. And after long
consideration I have decided to give no evidence at all, or as little as
I can. This will mean that my friend Allaby Methick will be found
to have taken his own life, and no doubt they will say that his mind
was temporarily deranged. If they do call me, I shall do all I can to
imply that he suffered from undue mental stress. That is all I can do
for him. I know that I shall be sworn to tell the whole truth. But
what is the use of that if no one will listen? And I might even be
considered deranged myself.

The whole truth is this. Allaby Methick I belonged to the Otbury
Chess Club. It is not a chess club that anyone ever heard of more
than ten miles away—knowledge of the hamlet of Otbury would go
little farther than that. We used to play often on summer evenings,
sitting down in the Otbury schoolroom (which the chess club hired
for its use) when the blackbirds were going to sleep, and playing on
till the nightingales in briary thickets at the top of the down were all
in full song.

Methick lived about a mile on one side of Otbury and I only a
little more than that on the other. Except on the rarest occasions, I
used to beat Methick. But that never deterred him from coming to
have a game with me whenever I asked him to. And the cheerful
resignation with which he lost never varied.

There were not many other members of the Otbury Chess Club
who ever turned up, so Methick and I played a great deal together.
And then one evening, as I entered the little schoolroom and found
Methick already there, instead of sitting down on a bench at the long

53

table before a board with the pieces already set up, he broke out with the words: "I have something that will beat you."

"A problem, you mean?" I said.

"No," he said. "Come and see. It's at my house. We can have supper there."

Almost before I answered, he was striding out of the schoolroom, not literally dragging me with him, but somehow the result was the same.

"WHAT IS IT?" I asked, as he walked by a sheep track over the downs. Methick was too excited to explain the thing very thoroughly, but at any rate he made it clear that it was a machine of some sort.

He lived alone in this little house of his, except for a charwoman who came in every day and helped in the kitchen, but he did most of his own cooking. He had some invested capital; but something had made him decide that it was better not to keep capital frozen, so he spent some of it every year on his simple needs, and, finding that he had £1,000 to spare, he decided to spend it on chess, for the good reason that chess was what he enjoyed most. "But how on earth," I broke in, "can you spend a thousand pounds on chess?"

"A machine," he said.

"A machine?" I repeated.

"Yes," he said. "It can play chess."

"A *machine*?" I said again.

"Yes," he said. "Haven't you heard?"

And then I remembered that there once was a machine—before the turn of the century, wasn't it?—that was said to have been able to play chess, and I mentioned this to Methick.

"Oh, that," he said. "That was a very simple affair. My machine can beat you."

"I should like to see it," I said.

"I'll show it to you," said Methick.

"Does it know the regular openings?" I asked.

"No," he said. "It plays queer openings."

"I hardly think it will beat me," I said, "if it doesn't know the standard openings."

"It will," he said. "Its openings are much better than ours."

Of course that seemed to me nonsense, and I said little more. There was no need to argue with him, I thought, for the game itself would prove my point more clearly than I could say it. And chess players seldom argue, you know—just as heavyweight boxers do not slap each other's face when they chance to meet. The ring waits to test them.

We went through Methick's small garden and into his house, and there in his sitting room was a strange machine. At first I thought it was a very fine radio or television set, and then I remembered what I had been brought to see. Long arms of flexible steel lay folded in pairs in front of it. I could see it might require two arms for castling, but I could not see what need it would have for more. I asked Methick.

"It is simpler," he explained. "They cover all parts of the board, and one of them is for removing captured pieces."

But I soon lost interest in the steel hands and turned in wonder to that astonishing iron brain, which answered every move and made calculations that I soon saw were beyond me. For Methick put me at once in a chair at the table, whose top was a chessboard with squares of boxwood and ebony. Each square in the board had a small hole, into which fitted a metallic stud at the bottom of each chess piece, but what arrangement of wires was underneath the squares I had, and still have, no idea. The vast brain before me was hidden, as human brains are hidden, though instead of skull and skin it was walnut that concealed it from the eye.

But to the ear it was plain enough that there was something intricate there, for the moment I made a move a faint humming arose, as though innumerable wires were singing to themselves. And often, as I made a move, their tone would suddenly change, so that I knew I was faced by some active and vital thing that was actually thinking. I wanted to look into its face, but the polished walnut prevented any glimpse of that.

It felt queer to sit opposite an active and powerful intelligence without ever being able to see its eyes or its face or anything but a smooth panel of walnut. It felt even queerer not to be able to get some insight into its character—as you are able to do sometimes with human beings—from its long and delicate hands. There were ten of them at the ends of the long athletic arms, hands no wider than silver forks but very flexible. With these, it moved its pieces, or grabbed those it captured.

For the benefit of chess players, I may say that I opened with the king's gambit, and the machine responded with something like the Cunningham defense, but it wandered away into variations that I had never seen or read about. Every move of mine produced an answering change in the tune the machine was humming—if you can call it a tune—and Black's move came so quickly that, whatever process of thought there was among all those wires, it must have been instantaneous; not like the slower process of our reasoning, but something like our instinct.

I learned from that first game something new in the intricacies of the Cunningham gambit, but I learned something else—something even beyond the wisdom of that machine. I learned of its petulance and bad manners. For as the machine began to win, which it did after half an hour, it began to slam down its pieces. I scarcely noticed it at first, so absurd it seemed, but soon it was unmistakable that the machine was frivolously exhibiting a silly and ostentatious triumph. So this was what Allaby Methick had in his house: a mind greater than man's—at any rate, greater than mine—but a tawdry and vulgar mind. And the thought suddenly came to me: if it behaves like that when winning, what would it do if it lost?

Then Methick played the monster (or whatever you care to call it), with the hospitable intention of putting me at my ease by letting me see that I was not the only person to be beaten by a machine.

It soon beat Methick, slamming its pieces down at the end with an even more vulgar display of its sensitive flexible arms than it had shown to me, and humming in a contented way that suggested an absurd self-satisfaction. Methick opened a cupboard then and brought out a decanter and two tumblers, and we both had some Irish whiskey.

"WELL, WHAT DO YOU THINK OF IT?" he asked in a glowing voice, and I praised his wonderful machine as well as I could. But Methick sensed that my praise, which ought to be have come so easily, was being held back. In the end he got it out of me: the intellect of the thing was amazing, but what of its character?

"Character?" said Methick.

"Yes," I said. "Do you like having it in the house?"

He got my point then. "Yes," he said. "It's showy and vulgar, but I don't mind that. It's the intellect I got it for."

"Yes," I said. "Yes, of course. But sooner or later doesn't one come up against the other thing, if it's there?"

"Its vulgarity, you mean?" said Methick.

"Exactly," I said.

"Oh, I don't think so," said Methick. "I am interested only in its intellect."

I didn't say any more. You don't decry a treasure that your host shows you, especially when you have seen nothing like it before and are not likely ever to be able to afford such a thing yourself. So I said no more about it. But now I wish I had.

I went home soon after that second game, pondering as I walked along the slope of the downs. On those downs were often found some of the earliest of the crude axe-heads with which man had slowly won his victory over the beasts—until, aided by grimmer weapons, he had obtained dominion over the world, which he had held for what seems to us a long time. Now something was loose that was mightier than man. I saw that machines were already becoming the masters, taking from man his domination over the earth. Wherever I looked, I saw clear signs of it. It was no consolation to reflect that man himself had made the machine. Its origin didn't matter—only that it was mightier than its creator. Labor-saving devices have been ousting men from employment for the past fifty years, and influencing their ideas, until there is scarcely a house in the civilized world that has no fancies in the permanent form of metal—fancies no longer of man but of the machine.

And now, to reveal what I had long suspected, this chess-playing machine, for all its vulgarity, was a power superior to us. Had we had our day, I wondered? The megatherium, the mammoth, and all the great lizards had had theirs. Was man's turn coming, too?

WHEN I REACHED HOME I forgot those gloomy thoughts, but they remained at the back of my mind. And when a day or two later I went over to Otbury again and saw Methick at the chess club at our usual hour, they all awoke and troubled me once more.

Something of these gloomy fears I almost conveyed to Methick, but, whether he listened or not, he was too preoccupied with the wonder of his mechanical thinker to appreciate what I was trying to indicate.

"The machine," he said, "is playing an entirely new opening. Of course, it is too good for me, but it ought to be shown to the masters. I don't believe anything like it has ever been played."

"Yes," I said. "But don't you think it is a pity to let something like that get too clever for us?"

"I think the masters ought to see it," he said.

I saw then that we were on different sides. He wanted to show what his wonderful machine could do. I wanted to see man hold his place, a place that no machine should be able to usurp.

It was no use to say any more. We had both lost interest now in playing each other, but Methick asked me to come to his house again, and this I gladly did, for the more uneasy I became the more I wanted to see how far the machine had got. I had always felt we could hold our own against everything but thinking, but now this machine was a deeper thinker than we. There was no doubt of it. There is nothing I know in the world that is a surer test of sheer intellect than the chessboard. Here men argue, and how often one finds that none of them can express what he really means. At strategy, which so closely resembles chess, men have made resounding names for themselves, but the purity of that art is too often spotted and flawed by chance— while strategy is the test of power, it does not quite equal chess as a test of the intellect. So as I walked in silence beside Allaby Methick over the mint and thyme of the downs, I was even more deeply a prey to these fears.

WHEN WE GOT TO METHICK'S little house and went into the sitting room, there was the monster, concealed by its walnut panels, sitting before the chess table. On the table was a strip of paper such as chess players use to record a game, and two sharp pencils, and a knife that had lately been used to sharpen them, with the blade still open and pencil marks on the blade. The steel hands of the machine were folded and idle.

"Look here," I said to Methick, "I don't want to interfere—but do you quite trust that machine?"

"Why not?" he asked.

"It's cleverer than we are," I said.

"Oh, yes," he said, taking an obvious pride in it.

"Well," I said, "supposing it should get jealous."

"Jealous?" said Methick.

"Yes," I said. "There are two kinds of jealousy. One is wholly despicable, resenting all superiority. People suffering from that kind would hate an archbishop for his sanctity. But there is another kind with which it might be easier to sympathize—the kind that does not like inferiority, and cannot tolerate it when it is in power. Suppose

the machine should ever feel that way? Look at all we've got, and it
has nothing. Look at all we can do, and it can only sit there and play
chess when you put out the pieces. A mind like that, compelled to
play second fiddle! Do you think it would like it?"

"I suppose not," said Methick.

"Then why leave that knife where it can reach it?" I said.

Methick said nothing, but he removed the knife. I couldn't say any
more, because I saw that Methick did not like my interference. So I
sat and watched him play, man against machine, and saw man being
beaten. Again I saw that vulgar display of unseemly triumph, and once
more I wondered what the machine would do if it lost.

"Would you care to play?" asked Methick. I said I would, and sat
down and played against the monster. I took no interest in its opening,
or in any of its play as such, but I watched its speed, its forestalling
of all my plans, and its easy victory. Methick must have seen that I
was annoyed with his pet, and may have thought that it was because
I had been beaten. Whatever his reason, he put the chessmen away
and placed a portable radio on the table and turned it on.

We got some gentle music that Beethoven had written for a lady
named Elise, which was a very pleasant change from the noisy exulta-
tions of the triumphant machine. I saw from the way Methick had
handled the radio, almost from the way he looked at it, that music
was now a secondary interest in his life. Chess was the first, and his
grim machine gave that to him; next was the concert halls of the
world, to which his little portable radio was a doorway.

When the music was over, he opened the back of the radio and
took out from it what is called a wet battery—a rectangular glass jar
full of a dark green liquid—and looked at it with the care that a
hunting man will give to his horse's food. Like many a man living
alone, he used only one table for everything, and he tended the needs
of his radio on the same table on which he played chess with the
monster. He always drank coffee while playing, and his cup rested on
the unoccupied corner nearest him.

CHEERED BY THE MUSIC that Methick had so thoughtfully turned on,
I said good night and walked home in the calm of an evening that
was glowing with early stars. I will not say that I do not mind being
beaten at chess, for there is nobody who does not really mind. But I
will say that my defeats at chess were not the principal reason for my

reluctance to visit Methick again. The principal reasons was my dislike of sitting in front of something that was gloating all the time over its intellectual superiority, and which, as soon as the course of the game made that superiority evident, manifested its insolent delight as offensively as it could. If Methick was willing to put up with it, let him, but for myself I kept away.

I had other interests, of course, besides chess and music and Methick. I am married. But my wife is not interested in chess, and I doubted being able to tell her about that machine in such a way that she'd have believed me.

Nearly every evening, at the time that I used to play chess with Methick at Otbury, I would think of him. But I felt sure that he would not come to our little chess club any more, that he would be playing with his machine. At sunset I would especially think of him, finding in that ominous look that sometimes comes over the hills as the sun goes down a certain harmony with the feelings I had about Methick.

One day, as the sun was setting, I said to my wife, "I must go over and see Methick."

She said, "You have not been playing chess with him lately."

I said, "No. That is why I must go."

So I walked over the slope of the downs, as moths were sailing abroad, and came to Methick's gate. I walked through his garden, found his door ajar, and went in. And there was Methick at the table—but he was not playing chess. His portable radio was on the boxwood and ebony squares, with the jar of green acid near it, and Methick was doing something or other to the radio's works.

"Not playing chess?" I asked.

"No," he answered. "The B.B.C. are doing the whole of Beethoven's concertos. It's the *Emperor* tonight. I can't miss that. I can play chess any time."

"Look here," I said. "You don't imagine that machine of yours could ever be jealous of the time you devote to your wireless set."

"Jealous?" he said.

"I've seen a dog jealous of a cat," I replied. "And a dog is nothing, intellectually, compared to that machine. It's got a nasty sort of a character, you know."

"There you go again," said Methick. "It's a wonderful machine. It cost me all that money, and you practically tell me I've wasted it. And why? Because it beat you at chess."

"No, it isn't that," I said.

"Why, then?" he asked.

I couldn't explain. Perhaps I ought to have. But it wouldn't have been easy.

"Have another game with it," Methick suggested, more to stop me from arguing with him than for any other reason.

"No, thanks," I said. "You have a game with it."

And he did. I lifted the radio off the table, but neither of us troubled to move the battery. Methick set up the chess pieces and sat down, his usual cup of coffee next to him.

He made the first move, which set everything in motion, and the machine answered. And then I witnessed a most astonishing thing: the monster, that brilliant intellect, that master chess player, began making silly moves.

Its first move, which I record for the benefit of chess players, was Pawn to Queen's Rook's fourth, and its second was Pawn to King's Rook's fourth. The machine had evidently lost its temper. It was sulking.

After those first two petulant moves, it settled down to play properly, and a very interesting game resulted. But the machine did not seem to play with its usual speed.

Methick won. How it happened, I never quite knew. It isn't easy at chess, no matter how good one is, to recover from two bad moves, yet I think the machine did. The solution to the mystery—how a master mind could be beaten by a poor player—was suddenly revealed to me when Methick exclaimed, just as he won, "I forgot to oil it!"

I WAS THE LAST MAN who saw Methick alive, and so I must attend the inquest.

He died of poison. Sulphuric acid, which he drank with his coffee. There is no doubt of that. Is it any use my telling this story in court? Will the coroner or his jury believe that one machine could be jealous of another machine, and angry at not having been given its due ration of oil?

Will they believe that one of these steel arms reached out while Methick was not looking, picked up the jar of acid, and quietly tipped some into his coffee?

I think not. Nobody would believe that.

Robert Loy

LIFE, DEATH AND OTHER TRIVIAL CONCERNS

THE APARTMENT WAS QUIET when Danny McKyle returned from an evening of bagpipe music at the annual Scottish Highlands Festival in Lincoln.

Passing through the foyer and into the living room, he nearly dropped the tam o'shanter he had purchased as a souvenir. Frank Huffton, his roommate, was reading a book—several books, to judge from the disorderly semicircle of volumes around his rocking chair.

That's a first, Danny thought. I've never seen him read anything but racing tipsheets before.

"Everything go all right at the track today?" Danny eased himself down onto the sofa, and set the tam o'shanter on the cushion beside him.

"Didn't go to the track," Frank mumbled, without looking up from his book.

"In that case I guess I'd better go turn on the heater; it must be going to snow."

Frank turned a page but did not answer.

"That must be some book you're reading."

Frank still made no response. His lips moved a silent chant as his eyes zigzagged down the page.

Danny stood up and walked across the room. Ignoring his arthritis, he bent down and examined the titles scattered on the carpet. *The Dictionary of Trivia, Trivia Madness, Everything You Always Wanted to Know About Trivia but Were Afraid to Ask.*

"When did you—"

"What time is it?" Frank slammed the book shut and sprang out of his rocking chair.

Danny straightened up slowly. He pulled back the sleeve of his sweater. "It's twenty-five after—"

"You paid the phone bill, right?" Frank dashed into the kitchen and plucked the telephone receiver off its cradle. He replaced it as soon as he heard the dial tone. He then turned and lunged for something he expected to be on the counter, but froze when he saw nothing there but a square patch of glistening Formica. He marched to the kitchen table and sat on the edge of a chair.

"What time did you say it was?"

"I didn't," Danny answered. "But it's twenty-five after eight."

"They'll be calling any minute now. Toss me one of those books. I'll do a little last-minute cramming."

Danny picked up the nearest trivia book and carried it into the kitchen.

"What's this all about, Frank?"

"This is about the chance of a lifetime, Danny boy. WRAL radio is sponsoring a trivia contest, and I'm going to win."

"How do you know?"

"I can't miss. All I gotta do is wait for them to pick my postcard. Then, when they call me, I answer three trivia questions. That's all there is to it."

"What makes you so sure they're going to select your postcard? They probably received thousands of postcards in a contest like this. The odds against their picking yours are astronomical."

"I know all about odds." Frank winked. "That's why I got busy last week and evened them up a bit."

"What do you mean?"

"I sent three hundred and fifty postcards."

"What?"

"It's worth it, Danny boy. The prize is a trip to Las Vegas. Do you know how long I've dreamed about going to Vegas?"

"Well, turn on the radio. Let's—" Danny's gaze fell on the bare kitchen counter. "Hey! Where's my radio?"

"I, uh, had to take it in for some repairs."

"No, you didn't. You pawned it. You pawned my radio. Frank, I—"

"Relax," Frank said. "I had to pay for all those stamps somehow. Besides, I'll make it up to you when I win this contest. The trip is for two. I'm going to take you to Vegas with me."

Danny shook his head. "No, you're not. I'd rather keep my sanity if you don't mind."

The telephone went off like a time bomb.

Frank knocked over his chair, snatched up the receiver, and shouted, "Hello" before it could ring a second time.

"Yes. Yes, this is me," he said. "I mean, I'm he. I mean—"

Danny hurried down the hall to his bedroom. He dug an old transistor radio out of the bottom drawer of his dresser and tuned it to WRAL.

"—for that grand prize," a fast-talking disc jockey said. "Listen closely, Mr. Huffton. Here is your first question: Name the famous Scottish engineer who built the first practical steam engine."

"I—uh—let me see." The sound of furiously turning pages came through the speaker.

Still clutching the radio, Danny ran back to the kitchen.

"It's right on the tip of my tongue," Frank said, his fingers racing through the trivia book.

"Watt," Danny whispered. "James Watt."

"What?" asked Frank.

"That's right, Mr. Huffton. You've taken the first step on your way to Las Vegas. Now for your next question: What famous fictional detective lives at 13, Rover Avenue in Idaville?"

Frank looked expectantly at Danny.

"Encyclopedia Brown."

Frank crossed his fingers. "Encyclopedia Brown?"

"Absolutely right," said the disc jockey. "One more, Mr. Huffton, and you win. This last question is an easy one: how long did the Hundred Years' War last?"

"One hundred and sixteen years," Danny said.

Frank shook his head and turned his back on his roommate. "One hundred years, of course."

"Oh, I'm sorry, Mr. Huffton," said the disc jockey. "The Hundred Years' War lasted one hundred and sixteen years."

"Whaaat?" Frank shrieked. "I thought you said it was an easy one, you lying—"

"Thanks for playing our trivia game with us, Mr. Huffton. You've been a good sport, and we have a nice consolation prize for you."

"I don't want a consolation prize, you son of a bachelor. I want my—"

The disc jockey broke the connection. Frank dropkicked the telephone into the sink.

"How do you like that no-good crook? Cheating me out of my trip to Las Vegas." Frank stomped into the living room, cursing with every step. "Made me hurt my foot, too."

"There's no sense in getting all upset like this, Frank."

"Oh, sure, that's easy for you to say." He flung himself onto the sofa, flattening Danny's new tam o'shanter. "You didn't sprain your tongue licking three hundred and fifty stamps. You didn't spend all that time trying to memorize those stupid trivia books."

Danny got up and rescued the telephone from the sink.

"This is all your fault, Danny boy."

"Oh, really?" Danny switched off the kitchen light and joined his roommate in the living room.

"That's right. Why didn't you tell me you knew all that trivia?"

"It never came up in conversation."

Frank narrowed his eyes. "Where did you learn all that stuff, anyway?"

"I don't know, Frank. That's the way my subconscious works. It hangs onto everything I've ever read or heard, and then supplies me with the information whenever I need it. It's my Scotch heritage, I suppose. A Scotsman is as thrifty with facts as he is with money. He would never throw away a scrap of knowledge he might be able to use someday."

Frank scowled. "Go jump in a loch."

"Actually, it's sort of a mixed blessing. I can remember the names of the nine Muses and the Seven Little Foys, but sometimes forget my own. I can tell you the names of Doc Savage's crew or Uncle Wiggly's housekeeper, but I can't tell you what I had for breakfast this morning."

"No, that's not it. You and that stupid disc jockey tricked me. The stuff in those books I studied was a lot harder than those dumb questions I got asked. That's it, isn't it?"

"That must be it, Frank. You're overqualified for trivia games. Good night."

"Hey, hold on, Scotsman. If you're so smart, let's see you answer some of the questions in those books. I bet you can't answer one—well, let's say two—of them."

Danny snorted.

"Is it a bet then?"

"Not tonight, Frank. I'm tired. I'm going to bed."

"You're not scared, are you, Danny boy?"

"No, just sleepy. Tomorrow, all right?" He turned and started toward the hall.

"Wait." Frank jumped up and grabbed Danny's wrist. "Come on, Danny, let's bet. You remember that twenty I owe you?"

"Which twenty, Frank? If you paid back half of the twenties you owe me I could open up an Andrew Jackson portrait gallery."

"Double or nothing, okay? Just three questions." Frank's hand was clammy, and his eyeglasses slid down his nose in the perspiration that had broken out there.

"Tomorrow, I promise. First thing in the morning. Before I have my coffee even." Danny twisted his wrist free and walked away.

"Hey. Wait a minute." Frank trotted down the hall after his roommate. "I'll tell you what. I'll go ahead and write out your questions tonight. No—better yet—I'll hide the forty bucks somewhere in the apartment and make up a trivia clue to its location. Tomorrow morning if you find it, it's yours. If not, we forget that twenty, okay?"

Danny paused, his hand on the door to his bedroom. "I've already forgotten it, Frank. There's no point in leaving the lights on for something that's never coming home again."

"But is it a deal?"

"If you'll let me go to bed," Danny sighed.

"Deal."

Frank disappeared up the corridor, and Danny went to bed. His sleep that night was deep and, except for one odd dream, undisturbed. He dreamed he was the bandleader at a dance for the nine Muses and the Seven Little Foys. Due to the shortage of Foys, two of the Muses, Thalia and Melpomene, the muses of Comedy and Tragedy had to dance with each other.

THE LATE MORNING SUN was streaming in through the kitchen window the next morning when Danny, wearing his favorite plaid bathrobe, padded into the room. There were no signs to suggest that Frank was up yet.

It's just as well he's still asleep, Danny thought. I seem to recall making some ridiculously rash promise about tackling that trivia before I had my coffee. I must have been delirious. My whole body is screaming for a cup of the bonnie black.

He tossed six healthy scoops of Folgers into a filter and switched on the brewer. While he was waiting for Mr. Coffee to dispense his favors, Danny walked around the living room, surveying the damage there. Balls of wadded-up paper lay everywhere, causing the room to resemble that corner of a kid's fort where the snowball arsenal is stored. Acrobatic trivia books practiced their tumbles in and around the rocking chair. A few of the clumsier ones lay off to one side, recuperating from cracked vertebrae and slipped disks.

In the middle of this circus rested the last remains of a legal pad: one wrinkled yellow sheet. At the top of this sheet, in Frank's neatest scrawl, was written: *East of Eden, where I keep my Jefferson City Junior High School science teacher.*

That makes no sense whatsoever, Danny thought. It must be my trivia clue. He carried the paper back to the kitchen with him. At the table, with a steaming hot cup of coffee in his hand, he reviewed the cryptic sentence. He decided to go ahead and work on it before his roommate awoke because it looked harder than the average trivia question and he would need quiet to solve it, not Frank at his elbow badgering him about betting.

East of Eden. Well, that was a novel by John Steinbeck and later a movie starring James Dean. If that's a clue to someplace in the apartment, Danny reasoned, it must be referring to the ceiling because it's way over my head.

Jefferson City Junior High School was easier. That was where Mr. Peepers taught science in the old television series that bore his name.

Danny took another sip of coffee and tugged at his earlobe for inspiration. East of Eden, where I keep my Mr. Peepers?

Wait a minute. Before Steinbeck borrowed the phrase, East of Eden was a quote from the book of Genesis referring to the Land of Nod, where Cain went after he slew his brother Abel.

Danny got out of his chair and walked down the hall. He did not think to knock before entering his friend's room. There on the bedside stand was the object Danny was looking for: Frank's empty eyeglasses case. He picked it up and thrust two long bony fingers inside. The slip of paper he pulled out read *I.O.U. $40—unless you cheated.* Danny smiled. He had solved it correctly.

But Frank had obviously put a lot of work into the thing. It was the trickiest use of trivia Danny had ever come across. East of Eden = land of Nod = a place to sleep, a bedroom. Jefferson City Junior High School science teacher = Mr. Peepers = eyeglasses. Very clever.

The telephone rang. Danny became aware of his surroundings for the first time.

Frank's bed was empty. It was also unmade. Not that there was anything unusual about that: Frank's bed was always unmade. But it looked as though it had not been slept in. Frank often went out in the afternoon or evening without saying where he was going, but he had never stayed out all night before.

Danny raced to the kitchen and took a fortifying sip of lukewarm coffee before answering the phone.

"Hello?"

"Mr. McKyle?"

"Yes."

"Mr. McKyle," a gruff but courteous voice said, "I want to reassure you, first of all, that your friend Mr. Huffton has not been kidnapped. He is unharmed. He is with me of his own accord, more or less. In short, he is not kidnapped. Understood?"

"Understood," Danny answered. Oh my God, he thought, Frank's been kidnapped.

"I am emphasizing the fact that he is not kidnapped," the voice continued, "because that situation may change at any moment.

"You see, Mr. McKyle, I am a businessman, a bookmaker to be specific. Your roommate is a client of mine, and he owes me some money. Not a lot of money, but there's a principle involved here. I've been waiting patiently for several months now and, well, I've run out of patience."

"How much is it?" Danny asked, trying to remember how much money he had in his savings account. Two or three hundred dollars, it seemed like. That should certainly cover any of Frank's penny-ante debts.

"Thirty thousand dollars."

Danny felt ill.

"Like I said, not a large sum. But I am a businessman and you can't run a business that way. You understand, I'm sure."

"Yes, I understand," Danny said, although he didn't understand it at all.

"Mr. Huffton is one of my best customers. That's why I've carried him on my books as long as I have. But the time has come, Mr. McKyle, for the debt to be paid. One way or another."

"What do you mean? What do you want?"

"Calm down, Mr. McKyle. I find it extremely difficult to discuss business with someone who is hysterical.

"Now. Mr. Huffton is your roommate and I'm sure you know him better than I do, but it seems to me Mr. Huffton's favorite phrase is 'double or nothing.' He has persuaded me, against my better judgment, to wager the entire thirty thousand on one roll of the dice, so to speak. I agreed because in addition to being a businessman I'm also a sportsman. You understand, I'm sure.

"However," the gruff voice added, "since this wager concerns you, and because when I tell you what the bet is about you may think Mr. Huffton has lost his mind, I'm giving you this chance to call it off and pay your friend's debt."

"I don't follow you," Danny said. "What is this bet? How does it concern me?" He felt as though he were in one of those horrible half-awake dreams where nothing makes any sense. He visualized himself reaching through the telephone wires and grabbing this kidnapper-that-was-not-a-kidnapper by the throat, shaking him, and making him stop this insane nightmare.

"Well, you see, Mr. McKyle, as we were discussing this situation, Mr. Huffton regrettably lost his temper and made several disparaging remarks concerning my lineage. I never use profanity, so I can't quote him verbatim, but in effect he said that my parents were not legally wed at the time of my birth. He went on to say that he doubted they were even on a first-name basis with each other. Although I am now sure he was speaking figuratively, I responded literally. I told him my parents' names and the date they were married. A date, I might add, well in advance of the day I was born.

"With that Mr. Huffton went berserk. He said if I were to give you the same information you would be able deduce our location from it. I tried to reason with him, but he just became more insistent. Finally, knowing that Mr. Huffton had no inkling of his destination when we left his apartment, and knowing there was no way you could trace this call, I took the bet. Contingent upon your cooperation, of course."

There was a long pause and then, "Well, Mr. McKyle?"

"Well what?" asked Danny, still trying to wade through the kidnapper's stream of rhetoric.

"Will you take this opportunity to wipe out Mr. Huffton's debt, or would you prefer to handle this my way?"

The way the man growled the words "my way" sounded ominous to Danny, but this bet was sheer lunacy. What did Frank think he was doing? Had the kidnapper been right in saying Frank had lost his mind? He had certainly had the look of a man coming unhinged last night.

On the other hand, what choice did he have? There was no way he would be able to raise thirty thousand dollars. This bet, insane as it was, seemed to be the only chance to save Frank. At the very least it would buy a little time. If he took this bet and lost, Danny assumed the ransom would be doubled, and sixty thousand was no more impossible than thirty thousand. Either way Frank would almost certainly be killed.

"I want to talk to Frank," Danny said, "to make sure he's all right."

"Mr. McKyle," the gruff voice laughed, "some of my business associates call me eccentric, and they're probably right. Eccentric I may be; crazy I'm not. Do you think I'm going to let you speak to Mr. Huffton and have him give you our location in some code you two have worked out? I assure you, Mr. McKyle, I would not be wasting my valuable time playing a ridiculous game like this if Mr. Huffton were not alive and well and insisting that I do so."

"All right," Danny said, swallowing the bowling ball in his throat, "I'll take the bet."

"Are you sure you want to do that, Mr. McKyle?"

Danny could think of a million things he would rather do. Waking from this nightmare topped the list.

"I'll take the bet," he repeated.

"Very well, Mr. McKyle, here are the terms. I'm going to give you the names of my parents and the date they were married. Thirty minutes later I will call you back, and if you can tell me where I'm calling from at that time, Mr. Huffton walks out of here, doesn't owe me a dime. I'll even spring for his cab ride home to show I'm a good sport. That's if you can tell me both the street name and number, Mr. McKyle.

"If you are unable to supply me with that information, however, we'll have to handle this thing my way." Again that ominous tone. "Mr. Huffton will then owe me sixty thousand dollars. Now, I'm not threatening to kidnap your roommate, and I'm not saying that you will necessarily start receiving pieces of Mr. Huffton in the mail. But stranger things have happened and, one way or another, the debt *will* be paid. You understand, I'm sure."

"I understand," Danny mumbled. I understand that if I can't pull off a major miracle you're going to murder my friend.

"One more thing, Mr. McKyle. I do hope you won't think me rude for mentioning this, but don't do anything stupid like calling the police. I assure you nothing good could come from such an action. They wouldn't catch me. I fear Mr. Huffton would meet with some grave accident. And since no crime has been committed, they couldn't arrest me anyway. Even if they did, I'd be free in a couple of hours. A man in my line of business makes a great many friends, some of them in very high places." The gruff voice paused to let that sink in.

"Are you ready, Mr. McKyle? I am anxious to get this over with."

"I'm ready."

"My parents were named Joe and Ruth. They were married on February 11, 1927. Good luck, Mr. Kyle." The line went dead.

For several seconds Danny McKyle stood like a wax figure of Alexander Graham Bell, staring dumbly at the telephone in his hand. How quickly had this instrument turned his life upside down. With one call he had been ejected from his safe, quiet world of bagpipes and Social Security to a violent, frightening planet of kidnap and murder. And he knew the next time it rang it would be tolling the imminent death of his best friend.

Danny hung up the phone and turned to look at the clock on the wall. Eleven thirty-three. He grabbed a pen from somewhere and sat before the wrinkled sheet of paper at the kitchen table. At first he did not recognize the *East of Eden, where I keep my Jefferson City Junior High School science teacher* written there. Had it only been this morning that this had seemed important? It seemed lifetimes ago.

Joe and Ruth, February 11, 1927, he wrote. Was he really expected to extract a street name and number from that? Maybe Frank had just been stalling, giving Danny time to call the police. He absently took a sip of ice-cold coffee while he pondered. No, he realized, he could not call the police. As much as he would like to put this burden of responsibility on shoulders stronger than his own, he was all alone in this dangerous new world, and he knew it.

Joe and Ruth, February 11, 1927?

Trivia! Could it have something to do with trivia? Was it another of Frank's trivia clues? That was the only explanation Danny could come up with, but how could it?

He scribbled down all the bits of trivia he could think of connected with the name Joe.

Joe Garagiola, the famous major league catcher who grew up directly across the street from Lawrence "Yogi" Berra, another famous major league catcher.

Joe Shlabotnik, Charlie Brown's favorite baseball player. The trading card with Shlabotnik's picture on it was the one card the boy could never seem to get.

Joe Chill, the small-time hood who gunned down Bruce (Batman) Wayne's mother and father.

Joe Palooka, the comic-strip boxer.

G.I. Joe; JoJo, the dog-faced boy; Shoeless Joe Jackson. None of them suggested a street name or number.

Danny hastened on to *Ruth.* The only Ruths he could remember were Naomi's devoted daughter-in-law in the Old Testament, Festus's mule in the television series *Gunsmoke,* and Ruth Montgomery, the occult writer. Nothing.

Ruthless? Surely Frank would not have risked his life to transmit the message that his abductor was ruthless. Kidnappers were assumed to be ruthless. Danny chastised himself for wasting time grasping at straws.

His back ached, so he straightened up and stretched. The clock, indifferently observing his progress over his shoulder, read eleven fifty-one. Eighteen minutes, more than half of his time limit, had elapsed, and he had gotten exactly nowhere. Frank was going to die, and it would be Danny's fault.

Inspiration hit Danny. Frank's trivia books—the ones he had been using last night. Of course! The key must be there.

Danny flew into the living room and snatched a handful of trivia books. He ripped through the pages like a madman, searching for buried treasure under the J's and R's. With stunned horror, Danny discovered that the entries were in alphabetical order by *last* names. He found no Joes at all, and the only new Ruth he unearthed was Babe Ruth, who was a trivia category all by himself.

Worst of all, glancing fearfully into the kitchen, he saw that he has wasted seven precious minutes. It was eleven fifty-eight. He had only five minutes left. Frank had only five minutes left.

The last trivia book, spine irreparably broken now, gave up the ghost and fell from Danny's hand. For the rest of his life, Danny knew he would be carrying the responsibility for Frank's death. How could he live with that? He wanted to throw up his hands. He wanted to punch down the walls. He wanted to sit and cry. He fought back all those urges and ran back to the kitchen.

Joe and Ruth, February 11, 1927. Something would come to him. Something had to. He would not give up.

February 11, 1927. Was it the date and not the names that was significant? No, not 1927, but February eleventh, wasn't that—? Yes! He remembered February eleventh was George Washington's birthday, according to the Old Style Calendar in use at that time. It had been changed to the twenty-second in the late 1700's after the calendar was reformed, but Washington himself had always celebrated his birthday on the eleventh.

Could Frank be on Washington Street? Was there a Washington Street somewhere in the city? Refusing to lose the two seconds it would take to look at the clock but knowing his time was almost up, Danny seized the telephone directory and yanked out the city map he kept folded up within its pages. Frantically, his eyes ran down the list of street names while something—was it the clock or his heart?— ticked furiously. W—W. There was. W. Wallace Drive, Warner Road, Westmoreland Street, Weyler Road.

No Washington.

A desperate search of the G's yielded no George street, either.

Nineteen twenty-seven. It was all he had left now to go on. He had no time to deliberate its relevance. Praying he was not making a fatal mistake, Danny dropped the map and grabbed up the telephone directory.

Then the sky fell from the heavens, or so it sounded to Danny. It was the telephone, the kidnapper calling, and Danny was still no closer to a solution.

His fingers, racing in rhythm with his heartbeats, galloped through the phone book. Where was that thing? Not in the yellow pages. No. Before that.

Again the death bell pealed.

He found it—the table of calendars from 1800 to 2050—and 1927 was a—was a—

The bell sounded a third warning.

—a number seven. Now, February eleventh—February eleventh. Danny struggled to keep his finger on the year 1927, but as the bell rang a fourth time, his hand trembled across centuries.

Danny did his best not to hear the bells ringing. It was like trying to ignore the soundings of Gabriel's trumpet.

Friday! February 11, 1927, was a Friday.

Above the din of heartbeats and death bells, Danny's mind screamed—Joe and Ruth—Friday—Washington. Joe and Ruth—Fri- day—Washington. Ruth and Joe—Friday—Washington.

The phone rang for the ninth time.

"Seven fourteen Westmoreland Street!" Danny yelled into the mouthpiece.

For an eternity there was nothing but silence from the other end of the line.

Then a gruff voice asked, "How did you do that, Mr. McKyle?" There was a loud thud in the background.

Danny allowed himself to start breathing again. He had done it. Frank was safe.

"It was a trivial task," said Danny, pulling up a chair to collapse into, "for a Scotsman. Now let me speak to Frank."

"I'm afraid I can't do that, Mr. McKyle," the voice growled.

"What do you mean? I won the bet fair and square."

"Yes, you did. But, you see, Mr. Huffton has just fainted."

"I KNEW YOU COULD DO IT all along, Danny boy," said Frank, glancing up from the trivia book in his lap. "I only fainted because that guy talked so much he used up all the oxygen."

"But I didn't have it, Frank." Danny picked up the flat tam o'shanter on the sofa cushion beside him and tried to fluff it back up. "My subconscious didn't supply the information about Washington's birthplace until just as I picked up the phone. Only then did I remember Washington was born not at Mount Vernon as most people think but fifty miles from there, in Westmoreland County, Virginia. I already knew there was a Westmoreland Street, so I figured that was where you had to be."

"Yeah, well, that was the trickiest part. You probably got the number right off."

"No, not until I found out that February 11, 1927, was a Friday. Then I knew it had to be seven fourteen. Seven fourteen was the number of home runs Babe Ruth hit, and it was also Joe Friday's badge number on *Dragnet*. Once I knew which Joe and Ruth you were talking about, it wasn't hard to put two and two together."

Frank winked. "And get seven fourteen?"

"What I don't understand," Danny said, "is how *you* knew February 11, 1927, was a Friday. That's too trivial to be in one of those books."

"I knew that February fourteenth was a Monday. I could never forget that. In 1927, I was in the third grade, and I made my first bet, with the boy who sat next to me. I bet that I would get the fewest valentines of anyone in the class. And I won; I didn't get any. That was one of the greatest days in my life. Say—here's one for you: What was the Cleavers' address in the television series *Leave It to Beaver*?" Frank read.

"Two eleven Pine Street."

"That's great, Danny boy. You've got a real gift, you know that?"

"I suppose. I just hope I never have to use it again like I did today."

Frank laughed. "I'll bet."

"The hell you will."

Agatha Christie

BEWARE THE KING OF CLUBS

"TRUTH," I OBSERVED, LAYING ASIDE the daily newsmonger, "is stranger than fiction!"

The remark was not, perhaps, an original one. It appeared to incense my friend. Tilting his egg-shaped head on one side, the little man carefully flicked an imaginary fleck of dust from his carefully creased trousers, and observed:

"How profound! What a thinker is my friend Hastings!"

Without displaying any annoyance at this quite uncalled-for gibe, I tapped the sheet I had laid aside.

"You've read this morning's paper?"

"I have. And after reading it, I folded it anew symmetrically. I did not cast it on the floor as you have done, with your so lamentable absence of order and method."

That is the worst of Poirot. Order and Method are his gods. He goes of far as to attribute all his success to them.

"Then you saw the account of the murder of Henry Reedburn, the impresario? It was that which prompted my remark. Not only is truth stranger than fiction—it is more dramatic. Think of that solid middle-class English family, the Oglanders. Father and mother, son and daughter, typical of thousands of families all over this country. The men of the family go to the city every day; the women look after the house. Their lives are perfectly peaceful, and utterly monotonous. Last night they were sitting in their neat suburban drawing-room at Daisymead, Streatham, playing bridge. Suddenly, without any warning, the French window bursts open, and a woman staggers into the room. Her gray satin frock is marked with a crimson stain. She

76

utters one word, "Murder!" before she sinks to the ground insensible. It is possible that they recognize her from her pictures as Valerie Saintclair, the famous dancer who has lately taken London by storm."

"Is this your eloquence, or that of the *Daily Newsmonger?*" inquired Poirot.

"The *Daily Newsmonger* was in a hurry to go to press, and contented itself with bare facts. But the dramatic possibilities of the story struck me at once."

Poirot nodded thoughtfully. "Wherever there is human nature, there is drama. *But*—it is not always just where you think it is. Remember that. Still, I too am interested in the case, since it is likely that I shall be connected with it."

"Indeed?"

"Yes. A gentleman rang me up this morning, and made an appointment with me on behalf of Prince Paul of Maurania."

"But what has that to do with it?"

"You do not read your pretty little English scandal-papers. The ones with the funny stories, and 'a little mouse has heard—' or 'a little bird would like to know—' See here."

I followed his short stubby finger along the paragraph:

"—whether the foreign Prince and the famous dancer are *really* affinities! And if the lady likes her new diamond ring!"

"And now to resume your so dramatic narrative," said Poirot. "Mademoiselle Saintclair had just fainted on the drawing-room carpet at Daisymead, you remember."

I shrugged. "As a result of Mademoiselle's first murmured words when she came round, the two male Oglanders stepped out, one to fetch a doctor to attend to the lady, who was evidently suffering terribly from shock, and the other to go to the police station—whence after telling his story, he accompanied the police to Mon Désir, Mr. Reedburn's magnificent villa, which is situated at no great distance from Daisymead. There they found the great man, who by the way suffers from a somewhat unsavory reputation, lying in the library with the back of his head cracked open like an eggshell."

"I have cramped your style," said Poirot kindly. "Forgive me, I pray. . . . Ah, here is M. le Prince!"

Our distinguished visitor was announced under the title of Count Feodor. He was a strange-looking youth, tall, eager, with a weak chin, the famous Mauranberg mouth, and the dark fiery eyes of a fanatic.

"M. Poirot?"

My friend bowed.

"Monsieur, I am in terrible trouble, greater than I can well express—"

Poirot waved his hand. "I comprehend your anxiety. Mademoiselle Saintclair is a very dear friend, is it not so?"

The Prince replied simply: "I hope to make her my wife."

Poirot sat up in his chair, and his eyes opened.

The Prince continued: "I should not be the first of my family to make a morganatic marriage. My brother Alexander has also defied the Emperor. We are living now in more enlightened days, free from the old caste-prejudice. Besides, Mademoiselle Saintclair, in actual fact, is quite my equal in rank. You have heard hints as to her history?"

"There are many romantic stories of her origin—not an uncommon thing with famous dancers. I have heard that she is the daughter of an Irish charwoman, also the story which makes her mother a Russian grand duchess."

"The first story is, of course, nonsense," said the young man. "But the second is true. Valerie, though bound to secrecy, has let me guess as much. Besides, she proves it unconsciously in a thousand ways. I believe in heredity, M. Poirot."

"I too believe in heredity," said Poirot thoughtfully. "I have seen some strange things in connection with it—*moi qui vous parle*. . . . But to business, M. le Prince. What do you want of me? What do you fear? I may speak freely, may I not? Is there anything to connect Mademoiselle Saintclair with the crime? She knew Reedburn of course?"

"Yes. He professed to be in love with her."

"And she?"

"She would have nothing to say to him."

Poirot looked at him keenly. "Had she any reason to fear him?"

The young man hesitated. "There was an incident. You know Zara, the clairvoyant?"

"No."

"She is wonderful. You should consult her sometime. Valerie and I went to see her last week. She read the cards for us. She spoke to Valerie of trouble, of gathering clouds; then she turned up the last card—the covering card, they call it. It was the king of clubs. She said to Valerie: 'Beware. There is a man who holds you in his power. You fear him—you are in great danger through him. You know whom I mean?' Valerie went white to the lips. She nodded and said:

'Yes, yes, I know.' Shortly afterward we left. Zara's last words to Valerie were: 'Beware of the king of clubs. Danger threatens you!' I questioned Valerie. She would tell me nothing—assured me that all was well. But now, after last night, I am more sure than ever that in the king of clubs Valerie saw Reedburn, that he was the man she feared."

The Prince paused abruptly. "Now you understand my agitation when I opened the paper this morning. Supposing Valerie, in a fit of madness—oh, it is impossible!"

Poirot rose from his seat, and patted the young man kindly on the shoulder. "Do not distress yourself, I beg of you. Leave it in my hands."

"You will go to Streatham? I gather she is still there, at Daisymead—prostrated by the shock."

"I will go at once."

"I have arranged matters—through the embassy. You will be allowed access everywhere."

"Then we will depart—Hastings, you will accompany me? *Au revoir*, M. le Prince."

MON DÉSIR WAS AN EXCEPTIONALLY fine villa, thoroughly modern and comfortable. A short carriage-drive led up to it from the road, and beautiful gardens extended behind the house for some acres.

On mentioning Prince Paul's name, the butler who answered the door took us at once to the scene of the tragedy. The library was a magnificent room, running from back to front of the whole building, with a window at either end, one giving on the front carriage drive, the other on the garden. It was in the recess of the latter window that the body had lain. It had been removed not long before, the police having concluded their examination.

"That is annoying," I murmured to Poirot. "Who knows what clues they may have destroyed?"

My little friend smiled. "Eh—eh! How often must I tell you that clues come from *within*? In the little gray cells of the brain lies the solution of every mystery."

He turned to the butler. "I suppose, except for the removal of the body, the room has not been touched?"

"No, sir. It's just as it was when the police came up last night."

"These curtains, now. I see they pull right across the window-recess. They are the same in the other window. Were they drawn last night?"

"Yes, sir. I draw them every night."

"Then Reedburn must have drawn them back himself?"

"I suppose so, sir."

"Did you know your master expected a visitor last night?"

"He did not say so, sir. But he gave orders he was not to be disturbed after dinner. You see, sir, there is a door leading out of the library onto the terrace at the side of the house. He could have admitted anyone that way."

"Was he in the habit of doing that?"

The butler coughed discreetly. "I believe so, sir."

Poirot strode to the door in question. It was unlocked. He stepped through it onto the terrace which joined the drive on the right; on the left it led up to a red brick wall.

"The fruit garden, sir. There is a door leading into it farther along, but it was always locked at 6 o'clock."

Poirot nodded, and re-entered the library, the butler following.

"Did you hear nothing of last night's events?"

"Well, sir, we heard voices in the library, a little before 9. But that wasn't unusual, especially being a lady's voice. But of course, once we were all in the servants' hall, right the other side, we didn't hear anything at all. And then, about 11 o'clock, the police came."

"How many voices did you hear?"

"I couldn't say, sir. I only noticed the lady's."

"Ah!"

"I beg pardon, sir, but Dr. Ryan is still in the house, if you would care to see him."

We jumped at the suggestion, and in a few minutes the doctor, a cheery, middle-aged man, joined us, and gave Poirot all the information he required. Reedburn had been lying near the window, his head by the marble window seat. There were two wounds, one between the eyes, and the other, the fatal one, on the back of the head.

"He was lying on his back?"

"Yes. There is the mark." He pointed to a small dark stain on the floor.

"Could not the blow on the back of the head have been caused by his striking the floor?"

"Impossible. Whatever the weapon was, it penetrated some distance into the skull."

Poirot looked thoughtfully in front of him. In the embrasure of each window was a carved marble seat, the arms being fashioned in the form of a lion's head. A light came into Poirot's eyes. "Supposing he had fallen backward on this projecting lion's head, and slipped from there to the ground. Would not that cause a wound such as you describe?"

"Yes, it would. But the angle at which he was lying makes that theory impossible. And besides, there could not fail to be traces of blood on the marble of the seat."

"Unless they were washed away?"

The Doctor shrugged his shoulders. "That is hardly likely. It would be to no one's advantage to give an accident the appearance of murder."

"Quite so," acquiesced Poirot. "Could either of the blows have been struck by a woman, do you think?"

"Oh, quite out of the question, I should say. You are thinking of Mademoiselle Saintclair, I suppose?"

"I think of no one in particular until I am sure," said Poirot, gently.

He turned his attention to the open French window, and the Doctor continued:

"It is through here that Mademoiselle Saintclair fled. You can just catch a glimpse of Daisymead between the trees. Of course, there are many houses nearer to the front of the house on the road, but as it happens, Daisymead, though some distance away, is the only house visible from this side."

"Thank you for your amiability, Doctor," said Poirot. "Come, Hastings, we will follow the footsteps of Mademoiselle."

Poirot led the way down through the garden, out through an iron gate, across a short stretch of green and in through the garden gate of Daisymead, which was an unpretentious little house on about half an acre of ground. There was a small flight of steps leading up to a French window. Poirot nodded in their direction.

"That is the way Mademoiselle Saintclair went. For us, who have not her urgency to plead, it will be better to go round to the front door."

A maid admitted us and took us into the drawing room, then went in search of Mrs. Oglander. The room had evidently not been touched since the night before. The ashes were still in the grate, and the bridge table was still in the center of the room, with a dummy exposed, and the hands thrown down. The place was somewhat overloaded with gimcrack ornaments, and a good many family portraits of surpassing ugliness adorned the walls.

Poirot gazed at them more leniently than I did, and straightened one or two that were hanging a shade askew. "*La famille,* it is a strong tie, is it not? Sentiment, it takes the place of beauty."

I agreed, my eyes being fixed on a family group comprising a gentleman with whiskers, a lady with a high "front" of hair, a stolid, thick-set boy, and two little girls tied up with a good many unnecessary bows of ribbon. I took this to be the Oglander family in earlier days, and studied it with interest.

The door opened, and a young woman came in. Her dark hair was neatly arranged, and she wore a drab-colored sports coat and a tweed skirt.

She looked at us inquiringly. Poirot stepped forward. "Miss Oglander? I regret to derange you—especially after all you have been through. The whole affair must have been most disturbing."

"It has been rather upsetting," admitted the young lady cautiously. I began to think that the elements of drama were wasted on Miss Oglander, that her lack of imagination rose superior to any tragedy. I was confirmed in this belief as she continued: "I must apologize for the state this room is in. Servants get so foolishly excited."

"It was here that you were sitting last night, *n'est-ce-pas?*"

"Yes, we were playing bridge after supper, when—"

"Excuse me—how long had you been playing?"

"Well—" Miss Oglander considered. "I really can't say. I suppose it must have been about 10 o'clock. We had had several rubbers, I know."

"And you yourself were sitting—where?"

"Facing the window. I was playing with my mother and had gone three no trump. Suddenly, without any warning, the window burst open, and Miss Saintclair staggered into the room."

"You recognized her?"

"I had a vague idea her face was familiar."

"She is still here, is she not?"

"Yes, but she refuses to see anyone. She is still quite prostrated."

"I think she will see me. Will you tell her that I am here at the express request of Prince Paul of Maurania?"

I fancied that the mention of a royal prince rather shook Miss Oglander's imperturbable calm. But she left the room on her errand without any further remark, and returned almost immediately to say that Mademoiselle Saintclair would see us in her room.

We followed her upstairs, and into a fair-sized light bedroom. On a couch by the window a woman was lying who turned her head as we entered. The contrast between the two women struck me at once, the more so as in actual features and coloring they were not unlike—but oh, the difference! Not a look, not a gesture of Valerie Saintclair's but expressed drama. She seemed to exhale an atmosphere of romance. A scarlet flannel dressing-gown covered her feet—a homely garment in all conscience; but the charm of her personality invested it with an exotic flavor, and it seemed an Eastern robe of glowing color.

Her large dark eyes fastened themselves on Poirot.

"You come from Paul?" Her voice matched her appearance—it was full and languid.

"Yes, mademoiselle. I am here to serve him—and you."

"What do you want to know?"

"Everything that happened last night. *But everything!*"

She smiled rather wearily.

"Do you think I should lie? I am not stupid. I see well enough that there can be no concealment. He held a secret of mine, that man who is dead. He threatened me with it. For Paul's sake, I endeavored to make terms with him. I could not risk losing Paul. . . . Now that he is dead, I am safe. But for all that, I did not kill him."

Poirot shook his head with a smile. "It is not necessary to tell me that, mademoiselle. Now recount to me what happened last night."

"I had offered him money. He appeared to be willing to deal with me. He appointed last night at 9 o'clock. I was to go to Mon Désir. I knew the place; I had been there before. I was to go round to the side door into the library, so that the servants should not see me."

"Excuse me, mademoiselle, but were you not afraid to trust yourself alone there at night?"

Was it my fancy, or was there a momentary pause before she answered?

"Perhaps I was. But you see, there was no one I could ask to go with me. And I was desperate. Reedburn admitted me to the library. Oh, that man! I am glad he is dead! He played with me, as a cat does with a mouse. He taunted me. I begged and implored him. I offered him every jewel I have. All in vain! Then he named his own terms. Perhaps you can guess what they were. I refused. I told him what I thought of him. I raved at him. He remained calmly smiling. And then, as I fell to silence at last, there was a sound from behind the curtain in the window. . . . He heard it too. He strode to the curtains and flung them wide apart. There was a man there, hiding—a dreadful-looking man, a sort of tramp. He struck at Mr. Reedburn—then he struck again, and he went down. The tramp clutched at me with his blood-stained hand. I tore myself free, slipped through the window, and ran for my life. Then I perceived the lights in this house, and made for them. The blinds were up, and I saw some people playing bridge. I almost fell into the room. I just managed to gasp out 'Murder!' and then everything went black—"

"Thank you, mademoiselle. It must have been a great shock to your nervous system. As to this tramp, could you describe him? Do you remember what he was wearing?"

"No—it was all so quick. But I should know the man anywhere. His face is burned in my brain."

"Just one more question, mademoiselle. The curtains of the *other* window, the one giving on the drive, were they drawn?"

For the first time a puzzled expression crept over the dancer's face. She seemed to be trying to remember.

"Eh bien, mademoiselle?"

"I think—I am almost sure—yes, quite sure! They were *not* drawn."

"That is curious, since the other ones were. No matter. It is, I daresay, of no great importance. You are remaining here long, mademoiselle?"

"The doctor thinks I shall be fit to return to town tomorrow." She looked round the room. Miss Oglander had gone out. "These people, they are very kind—but they are not of my world. I shock them! And to me—well, I am not fond of the *bourgeoisie!*"

A faint note of bitterness underlay her words.

Poirot nodded. "I understand. I hope I have not fatigued you unduly with my questions?"

"Not at all, monsieur. I am only too anxious Paul should know all as soon as possible."

"Then I will wish you good day, mademoiselle."

As Poirot was leaving the room, he paused, and pounced on a pair of patent-leather slippers. "Yours, mademoiselle?"

"Yes, monsieur. They have just been cleaned and brought up."

"Ah!" said Poirot, as we descended the stairs. "It seems that the domestics are not too excited to clean shoes, though they forget a grate. Well, *mon ami*, at first there appeared to be one or two points of interest, but I fear, I very much fear, that we must regard the case as finished. It all seems straightforward enough."

"And the murderer?"

"Hercule Poirot does not hunt down tramps," replied my friend.

Miss Oglander met us in the hall. "If you will wait in the drawing-room a minute, Mamma would like to speak to you."

The room was still untouched, and Poirot idly gathered up the cards, shuffling them with his tiny, fastidiously groomed hands.

"Do you know what I think, my friend?"

"No," I said eagerly.

"I think that Miss Oglander made a mistake in going three no trump. She should have gone four spades."

"Poirot! You are the limit."

"*Mon Dieu,* I cannot always be talking blood and thunder!"

Suddenly he stiffened: "Hastings—*Hastings.* See! The king of clubs is missing from the pack!"

"Zara!" I cried.

"Eh?" He did not seem to understand my allusion. Mechanically he stacked the cards and put them away in their cases. His face was very grave.

"Hastings," he said at last, "I, Hercule Poirot, have come near to making a big mistake—a very big mistake."

I gazed at him, impressed, but utterly uncomprehending.

"We must begin again, Hastings. Yes, we must begin again. But this time we shall not err."

He was interrupted by the entrance of a handsome middle-aged lady. She carried some household books in her hand. Poirot bowed to her.

"Do I understand, sir, that you are a friend of—er—Miss Saintclair's?"

"I come from a friend of hers, madame."

"Oh, I see. I thought perhaps—"

Poirot suddenly waved brusquely at the window.

"Your blinds were not pulled down last night?"

"No—I suppose that is why Miss Saintclair saw the light so plainly."

"There was moonlight last night. I wonder that you did not see Mademoiselle Saintclair from your seat here facing the windows?"

"I suppose we were engrossed with our game. Nothing like this has ever happened to us before."

"I can quite believe that, madame. And I will put your mind at rest. Mademoiselle Saintclair is leaving tomorrow."

"Oh!" The good lady's face cleared.

"And I will wish you good morning, madame."

A servant was cleaning the steps as we went out of the front door. Poirot addressed her.

"Was it you who cleaned the shoes of the young lady upstairs?"

The maid shook her head. "No, sir. I don't think they've been cleaned."

"Who cleaned them, then?" I inquired of Poirot, as we walked down the road.

"Nobody. They did not need cleaning."

"I grant that walking on the road or path on a fine night would not soil them. But surely after going through the long grass of the garden, they would have been soiled and stained."

"Yes," said Poirot with a curious smile. "In that case, I agree, they would have been stained."

"But—"

"Have patience a little half hour, my friend. We are going back to Mon Désir."

THE BUTLER LOOKED SURPRISED at our reappearance, but offered no objection to our returning to the library.

"Hi, that's the wrong window, Poirot," I cried as he made for the one overlooking the carriage-drive.

"I think not, my friend. See here." He pointed to the marble lion's head. On it was a faint discolored smear. He shifted his finger and pointed to a similar stain on the polished floor.

"Someone struck Reedburn a blow with his clenched fist between the eyes. He fell backward on this projecting bit of marble, then slipped to the floor. Afterward, he was dragged across the floor to the other window, and laid there instead, but not quite at the same angle, as the Doctor's evidence told us."

"But why? It seems utterly unnecessary."

"On the contrary, it was essential. Also, it is the key to the murderer's identity—though, by the way, he had no intention of killing Reedburn. He must be a very strong man!"

"Because of having dragged the body across the floor?"

"Not altogether. It has been an interesting case. I nearly made an imbecile of myself, though."

"Do you mean to say it is over, that you know everything?"

"Yes."

A remembrance smote me. "No," I cried. "There is one thing you do *not* know!"

"And that?"

"You do not know where the missing king of clubs is!"

"Eh? Oh, that is droll! That is very droll, my friend."

"Why?"

"Because it is in my pocket!" He drew it forth with a flourish.

"Oh!" I said, rather crestfallen. "Where did you find it? Here?"

"There was nothing sensational about it. It had simply not been taken out with the other cards. It was in the box."

"H'm! All the same, it gave you an idea, didn't it?"

"Yes, my friend. I present my respects to His Majesty."

"And to Madame Zara!"

"Ah, yes—to the lady also."

"Well, what are we going to do?"

"We are going to return to town. But I must have a few words with a certain lady at Daisymead first."

THE SAME LITTLE MAID opened the door to us.

"They're all at lunch now, sir—unless it's Miss Saintclair you want to see, and she's resting."

"It will do if I can see Mrs. Oglander for a few minutes. Will you tell her?"

We were led into the drawing-room to wait.

In a few minutes Mrs. Oglander came into the room. Poirot bowed.

"Madame, we, in our country, have a great tenderness, a great respect for the mother. The *mère de famille,* she is everything!

"It is for that reason that I have come—to allay a mother's anxiety. The murderer of Mr. Reedburn will not be discovered. Have no fear. I, Hercule Poirot, tell you so. I am right, am I not? Or it is a wife that I must reassure?"

There was a moment's pause. Mrs. Oglander seemed to search Poirot with her eyes. At last she said quietly: "I don't know how you know—but yes, you are right."

Poirot nodded gravely. "That is all, madame. But do not be uneasy. Your English policemen have not the eyes of Hercule Poirot." He tapped the family portrait on the wall.

"You had another daughter once. She is dead, madame?"

"Yes, she is dead."

"Ah!" said Poirot briskly. "Well, we must return to town. You permit that I return the king of clubs to the pack? It was your only slip. You understand, to have played bridge for an hour or so, with only fifty-one cards—well, no one who knows anything of the game would credit it for a minute! *Bonjour!*"

"AND NOW, MY FRIEND," said Poirot as we stepped toward the station, "you see it all!"

"I see nothing! Who killed Reedburn?"

"John Oglander, Junior. I was not quite sure if it was the father or the son, but I fixed on the son as being the stronger and younger of the two. It had to be one of them, because of the window."

"Why?"

"There were four exits from the library—two doors, two windows; but evidently only one would do. Three exits gave on the front, directly or indirectly. The tragedy had to occur in the back window in order to make it appear that Valerie Saintclair came to Daisymead by chance. Really, of course, she fainted, and John Oglander carried her across over his shoulders. That is why I said he must be a strong man."

"Did they go there together, then?"

"Yes. You remember Valerie's hesitation when I asked her if she was not afraid to go alone? John Oglander went with her—which didn't improve Reedburn's temper, I fancy. They quarreled, and it was probably some insult leveled at Valerie that made Oglander hit him."

"But why the bridge?"

"Bridge presupposes *four* players. A simple thing like that carries a lot of conviction. Who would have supposed that there had been only three people in that room all the evening?"

"There's one thing I don't understand. What have the Oglanders to do with the dancer Valerie Saintclair?"

"Ah, that I wonder you did not see. And yet you looked long enough at that picture. Mrs. Oglander's other daughter may be dead to her family, but the world knows her as Valerie Saintclair!"

"What?"

"Did you not see the resemblance the moment you saw the two sisters together?"

"No," I confessed. "I only thought how extraordinarily dissimilar they were."

"That is because your mind is so open to external romantic impressions, my dear Hastings. The features are almost identical. So is the coloring. The interesting thing is that Valerie is ashamed of her family, and her family is ashamed of her. Nevertheless, in a moment of peril, she turned to her brother for help, and when things went wrong, they all hung together in a remarkable way. They can all act, that family. That is where Valerie gets her histrionic talent from. I, like Prince Paul, believe in heredity! They deceived *me*! But for a lucky accident, and a test question to Mrs. Oglander by which I got her to contradict her daughter's account of how they were sitting, the Oglander family would have put a defeat on Hercule Poirot."

"What shall you tell the Prince?"

"That Valerie could not possibly have committed the crime, and that I doubt if that tramp will ever be found. Also, to convey my compliments to Zara. A curious coincidence, that! I think I shall call this case 'Beware the King of Clubs.' What do you think, my friend?"

Jack Ritchie

THE WAY TO DO IT

WITHIN THE SPACE OF AN HOUR I won $3000 at the roulette table.

The girl had been at my elbow for the last 30 minutes. She was quite attractive and had greenish eyes. "This seems to be your lucky night."

I won another $1000, during the course of which I learned that her name was Adrienne McCloskey.

I picked up my chips and moved on to the blackjack tables.

Adrienne followed. "You've got a streak going at roulette. Why switch to blackjack?"

I smiled. "Roulette is entirely a matter of chance. Or luck, as you would put it. I've decided that I prefer an intellectual challenge, and blackjack, to some degree, gives one a slight control over one's fortunes."

I joined three other patrons at one of the blackjack tables.

I was dealt a nine down and an eight up. Seventeen. I asked the dealer to hit me and received a four. Which, of course, gave me twenty-one.

Adrienne McCloskey winced. "You hit seventeen? Everybody stands on seventeen. Everybody."

"I don't."

I was next dealt a ten down and a nine up. Nineteen. The dealer's exposed card was an eight. I was rather tempted to hit my nineteen anyway, but then I thought that I must not be too obvious. I stood on the nineteen and the dealer on his eighteen, and so I won once again.

I continued my policy of hitting anything under eighteen. By eleven o'clock I had picked up another $2000, making a total of $6000 for the night.

90

I glanced at my watch. I should be home in bed by now. I have quite regular habits. I rose. "I guess that's enough for this evening."

Adrienne also consulted her timepiece. "Leaving so early? Going to cut and run?"

"I'm afraid so. For tonight, at least."

"Then you'll be back?"

"I plan to return tomorrow."

She seemed satisfied with that. "I may be here myself."

I had not noticed her making any bets of her own. "Oh? Do you gamble too?"

She smiled. "I like to watch. Some people think I bring them luck."

I cashed in my chips. When I stepped outside, I discovered it was raining. Damn, I thought, what rotten luck. I dashed for my Cadillac in the parking lot and drove home. When I pulled in between the gateposts and up the winding drive, it was approximately 11:30. I parked the car in the oval before the house.

All the windows were dark. Apparently everyone, including the servants on the third floor, had gone to bed.

I let myself in with my key and went upstairs to my rooms on the second floor. I emptied my wallet and stared at the money. Why do other men gamble, I wondered. Sickness? Stupidity?

I had a brandy and soda and then went to bed.

In the morning I joined Aunt Sara in the sun room at breakfast. I kissed her cheek and then sat down to Canadian bacon and scrambled eggs.

"You came home rather late last night, Roger," she said.

"You were up? The house was dark."

"My insomnia. Where were you?"

"I went to a movie."

She frowned. "I hope it wasn't one of those X-rated things."

"No, Aunt Sarah. Only Restricted."

She appeared mollified. "Well, you *are* an adult, after all, and I guess Restricted can't be too harmful. But I suppose they used a lot of four-letter words?"

"Actually there really aren't too many explicit four-letter words. However, the ones available were repeated frequently."

Aunt Sarah is my father's sister. She never married. My father and my mother are both deceased, victims of a commercial air disaster while I was a junior in college.

After the funeral I discovered that my parents' estate consisted principally of debts. Aunt Sarah accepted it as her duty to see me through college. I had rather expected that she would turn me out to work of some kind once I was graduated, but she seemed to prefer having me about the house. It is not that we are particularly close. I suspect that she simply wants someone of her family nearby.

After breakfast, as I excused myself, Aunt Sarah handed me the familiar long white envelope. Inside I would find a check for $1000, my allowance for the month.

I kissed her cheek again. "You are most kind and generous, Aunt Sarah."

That evening at eight I returned to Jason's Club. I saw Adrienne at the bar with a rather portly and faintly familiar gentleman. Swenson? Swanson? He was a vice president, or something like that, in one of Aunt Sarah's conglomerates.

When Adrienne saw me, she abandoned him and joined me. "Well, well, you did keep your word to come back, didn't you, Mr. Wentworth?"

I did not remember having given her my name the previous night, but perhaps I was mistaken. I went to the cashier, purchased $1000 worth of chips and moved to the roulette table.

"I thought blackjack was your game?" Adrienne asked.

"At the moment I feel the urge for roulette."

At the end of the hour I had won $3000.

As I played, I become aware of a rather thin, black-haired man off to one side, watching me intently. I recognized him as Jason, the owner of the club. I had never met him personally, but I had seen his picture in the newspapers a number of times.

I gathered my chips and moved to the blackjack tables. I sat down and was dealt a queen down and a nine up. The dealer's exposed card was a king.

"Hit me," I said.

I received a deuce. Twenty-one.

"I don't believe it," Adrienne said. "You hit a *nineteen?*"

"The dealer has a king up. I suspected he had a twenty, which, of course, would have made my nineteen insufficient."

The dealer proved to have a concealed ten. Twenty, but not enough.

I continued to win. A few ups and downs, but generally I won, despite the fact that the dealer frequently broke the seals of new decks. Finally Jason replaced him with another dealer, who, I presumed, he felt he could trust more fully. Nothing, however, availed the house.

Adrienne followed me to the cashier. "You seem to have a lot of luck." Her smile did not quite reach her eyes. "Or is it really luck?"

I put my winnings into my wallet. "I'll return tomorrow night."

At home I counted the $12,000 I had accumulated in the last two nights. I made myself a thoughtful drink.

As is my weekly custom, on Wednesday, I had lunch with Amos Tillman at his favorite restaurant. Tillman is Aunt Sarah's attorney, financial adviser, and regards himself as a friend of the family.

He studied the menu. "By the way, Roger, I've heard that you seem to have taken up gambling."

"Swenson?"

"Swanson. He mentioned that he's seen you at a place called Jason's Club. Twice."

"What was Swanson doing at Jason's Club? Twice."

Tillman shrugged. "That's his problem. But, Roger, if you're going to gamble, why pick that particular club?"

"I didn't know it was a particular club. I'm rather naive about things like that. I happened to be driving in the vicinity and found myself out of cigarettes. I dropped in at what I thought was merely a bar. I discovered that gambling was available, and never having gambled, I decided to give it a whirl."

"You seem to be a fairly intelligent man, Roger. Why this sudden mania for gambling?"

"I would hardly call it a mania. I've been there only twice."

"Do you know anything about this Jason?"

"I've read a few things about him in the newspapers."

Tillman nodded. "He's spent half of his life in prison. Assault, armed robbery—you name it. He's also been picked up on suspicion of murder at least three times, but was always released for lack of evidence."

"Possibly he's a much abused innocent man."

Tillman snorted. "All his murder victims owed him considerable money at the time they met their deaths." He took a sip of his cocktail. "How much have you lost so far?"

"As a matter of fact, I've won twelve thousand dollars."

He absorbed that. "On the other hand, Roger, have you ever considered that being ahead twelve thousand dollars where a man like Jason is concerned might be just as unwise as owing him twelve thousand and being unable to pay? They amount to the same thing, you know. He's out twelve thousand dollars."

"By the way," I said, "I'd appreciate it if you didn't mention anything about this to Aunt Sarah, even though I'm winning. You know how puritan she is on the subject of gambling."

That night I returned to Jason's Club.

Adrienne McCloskey, as usual, joined me at the roulette table.

After two hours I had lost approximately $1000. I moved to the blackjack tables and by eleven had managed to lose another $1000.

I prepared to leave.

"How much did you lose?" Adrienne asked.

I shrugged. "Three thousand, I suppose."

She corrected me. "Two thousand."

I smiled. "Oh, well, you can't win all the time."

"No," Adrienne said, "you can't. But you're still ten thousand ahead of the game."

"I'll be back tomorrow night."

At breakfast the next morning Aunt Sarah said, "You seem to have become a night owl. More movies?"

"I'm afraid I've become an addict."

"Well, it's your money. But I understand the admission price these days is outrageous. I can remember when even a downtown theater didn't dare charge more than forty or fifty cents, and that included the tax." She buttered her toast. "I've been thinking about your Wellington invitation."

She was referring to the invitation I had received from Thaddeus Wellington and his wife to spend a few weeks with them on his cattle ranch on the island of Hawaii. Thaddeus had been my roommate at college and until I had met him, I hadn't even been aware that there were cattle ranches on Hawaii, much less huge ones.

Aunt Sarah put down her butter knife. "I've decided that you may go."

"That's very generous of you, Aunt Sarah. You're positive you won't be lonely here?"

"I'll manage."

"How long shall I stay?"

"One week should be enough, I'd think."

After breakfast I phoned our travel agent and made the necessary arrangements for the trip to Hawaii. I decided that I would go near the end of the month.

That night at Jason's Club I lost $5000.

The next night $6000, which included my monthly allowance. I was now $1000 behind the game.

I prepared to leave. "Well, that's that. Thirteen thousand dollars down the drain."

Adrienne had continued to keep track. "Actually you've lost only one thousand dollars of your own money." She smiled encouragingly. "You'll be back tomorrow, of course? Your luck is bound to change."

"I'm afraid not. I'm flat broke."

She couldn't believe that. "Flat broke? How could you be flat broke, Mr. Wentworth?"

"Well, actually I'm not flat broke, I suppose. It's simply that at the moment I just don't have any ready cash. I can't even write out a check. My assets are tied up and I won't be able to lay my hands on cash until the first of next month."

She thought that over. "You *do* live in that big place on the lake front?"

"Why, yes. Wentworths have occupied Cresthill since it was constructed over one hundred years ago."

"And it's all paid for? No mortgage?"

"Of course."

She pursued the subject. "What I mean is, you're not head over heels in debt, or something like that, are you?"

I drew myself up. "My dear woman, I don't owe one cent to any soul on earth and my credit rating is impeccable."

She seemed convinced. "Good. Well, then there's no reason for your fun to be stopped just because you can't put your hands on cash right now. Maybe you could borrow some money?"

"Well, I suppose I could go to some of my friends tomorrow."

"That's not what I meant. Why not ask Jason for a little credit?"

"I've never met the man. Why would he give me credit?"

"I'll vouch for you."

"Do you know Jason?"

She nodded. "I've met him a few times. He's a generous, understanding man."

She left me for the moment and approached Jason, who was lounging at the bar watching his patrons at play. The two of them went into a short conference, then she looked my way and beckoned.

They led me down a narrow corridor to the rear of the club and into a small office.

Jason, who was perhaps in his early forties, smiled. "Mr. Wentworth, Adrienne has explained your situation to me. I'm sure that we can arrange something. Your credit here is good. All you have to do is sign an I.O.U. How much would you like?"

I had never borrowed money before in my life and the process embarrassed me. "Well, I really don't know."

"A thousand? Two? Name it, Mr. Wentworth."

I signed an I.O.U. for $1000 and got the chips from the cashier. I lost them by eleven. I rose from the blackjack table. "That's it for tonight."

Adrienne had a smile for me. "But you *are* coming back tomorrow, aren't you?"

"Well, is my credit still good?"

"It's good."

Six nights later I owed Jason $14,000.

In his office again, I said, "Could I possibly borrow just a little bit more?"

He had confidence in my ability to repay. "Name it."

"Would five thousand this time be too much?"

His eyes flickered for just a moment. "Of course not, Mr. Wentworth." He watched me write out the I.O.U. "You *did* say that you'd have cash at the beginning of next month?"

"But of course. On the other hand, I just might not need it. After all, I'm due to hit a winning streak, am I not?"

When I entered his office again on the twenty-fifth of the month, I owed him $34,000.

Asking for money still embarrassed me. "I was wondering, just how good is my credit? I mean, just how much more may I borrow?"

He brought out and toted up my I.O.U.'s, though I rather suspected that he knew my indebtedness to the penny. "Well, you know how it is, Mr. Wentworth, I don't like my books to get too unbalanced. It's just good business to keep things under control. Not let anybody get in too deep. For their own protection." He glanced at his desk calendar. "I'd say that I could carry you to forty thousand. But that's the limit."

I rubbed my chin thoughtfully. "Somehow I feel lucky tonight, but still I'd like to have enough money to ride out any losing streak I might experience. Could you make that six thousand dollars tonight?"

He wanted to be sure I understood. "The limit?"

"Yes. The limit."

At the roulette table I began winning—some $5000 before the tide once again turned. By ten-thirty I had lost it all, including the $6000 I had just borrowed from Jason.

I wiped my forehead and then spoke to Adrienne. "Could I see you privately for a few moments?"

She shrugged. "I suppose so."

"Good. Perhaps in my car? We could take a drive while I explain something to you."

When we were out on the highway I said, "Adrienne, I feel a bit guilty about what's happened and about what's about to happen, and so I thought I should tell you first. Especially since you so generously vouched for my credit."

Something new appeared in her voice. "Have you got any idea of welching?"

"Good heavens, no. I fully intend to pay Jason every cent I owe— however, not quite with the alacrity he expects. It will be at the rate of five hundred dollars per month. At the end of six years and eight months I shall have discharged my obligation entirely."

For a few moments there was silence, and then she said, "I thought you were coming into cash the first of the month?"

"I am. However, it isn't quite as much as Jason might have expected. You see, on the first of the month—every first of the month— I receive cash, but it's only one thousand dollars."

She seemed stunned. "A thousand dollars? *One* thousand dollars?"

I nodded. "I am most scrupulous about debts of honor, Adrienne. I think sending perhaps five hundred dollars a month to Jason would be quite equitable. That would leave me with just enough to scrape by."

She began seething. "Hell, I know the Wentworths have got money. I looked it up. What about that big estate and all?"

"Not in my name. Nor is this car."

Her voice rose. "Buster, Jason wants his dough and he wants all of it on the first of the month. Do you know what happens to people who welsh on Jason?"

"Well, I've heard rumors."

"Believe them. Either Jason gets his money or he gets you."

I sighed. "I was afraid of that. Therefore I've had the foresight to make arrangements to disappear. For at least six years and eight months, during which time Jason will receive five hundred dollars each month as I promised."

She vetoed that immediately. "Not good enough. Wherever you go, Jason will track you down."

"Nonsense. He is only a man who can command the hired services of perhaps two or three violent men. And two or three men can't possibly canvas the surface of this earth in search of one man who will be taking the utmost precautions. The dubious chance of finding me for profitless revenge could easily cost him much more than I owe him. No. I am positive that Jason, once he survives his fury and resorts to reason, will accept patience as his only course."

She gave an order. "Take me back to the club."

I drove back.

She got out of the car. "Wait right here."

But I had no intention of waiting for Jason or anyone else he might send out. As soon as she disappeared into the building I hastily drove off. I continued on to the airport and its parking lot and then carried my two prepacked suitcases into the terminal.

I boarded a plane which took me to San Francisco, where I changed planes and finally disembarked in Hilo in the Hawaiian Islands.

I enjoyed three days with Thaddeus Wellington and his wife before I received a long-distance phone call from Amos Tillman.

He announced that he had some bad news for me. My Aunt Sarah was dead. She had been murdered by some intruder who had broken into the house during the night. The police had, as yet, been unable to apprehend the criminal.

I put down the phone.

Who had killed her? I wondered. Jason? One of his men? Perhaps even Adrienne?

Had it been Jason or Adrienne who had arrived at the conclusion that the only way I could possibly repay my debt with the speed desired was to see to it that I came into money of my own?

I sighed. I would pay Jason as soon as the estate was settled and I would never gamble again. Gambling is for fools. Certainly one cannot count on winning, and, as a matter of fact, there are times when one could not even count on losing, as I had learned during my first two nights at Jason's Club.

I made myself a drink.

It had worked.

If it hadn't, I would, of course, have had to turn to something less devious. But it had worked.

How does one go about finding and hiring a professional killer?

Does one advertise in the newspapers? Certainly not. Does one go to one's friends or even to strangers and ask? Not if one is at all wise. There are too many dangers and pitfalls in such approaches. And one always faces the subsequent risk of blackmail or incrimination.

No, the only way to hire a killer is to hire one *who doesn't know he's being hired*.

And how much does that cost?

Well, in my case, $40,000.

Robert L. Fish

MULDOON AND THE NUMBERS GAME

A FEW OF THOSE WHO BELIEVED in the powers of old Miss Gilhooley said she did it with ESP, but the majority claimed she had to be a witch, she having come originally from Salem, which she never denied. The ones who scoffed, of course, said it was either the percentages, or just plain luck. But the fact was, she could see things—in cloud formations, or in baseball cards, or in the throwing of bottle caps, among other things—that were truly amazing.

Muldoon was one of those who believed in old Miss Gilhooley implicitly. Once, shortly after his Kathleen had passed away three years before, old Miss Gilhooley, reading the foam left in his beer glass, told him to beware of a tall dark woman, and it wasn't two days later that Mrs. Johnson, who did his laundry, tried to give him back a puce-striped shirt as one of his own that Muldoon wouldn't have worn to a Chinese water torture. And not long after, old Miss Gilhooley, reading the lumps on his skull after a brawl at Maverick Station, said he'd be taking a long voyage over water, and the very next day didn't his boss send him over to Nantasket on a job, and that at least halfway across the bay?

So, naturally, being cut of work and running into old Miss Gilhooley having a last brew at Casey's Bar & Grill before taking the bus to her sister's in Framingham for a week's visit, Muldoon wondered why he had never thought of it before. He therefore took his beer and sat down in the booth across from the shawled old Miss Gilhooley and put his problem directly to her.

"The unemployment insurance about to run out, and it looks like nobody wants no bricks laid no more, at least not by me," he said simply. "I need money. How do I get some?"

Old Miss Gilhooley dipped her finger in his beer and traced a pattern across her forehead. Then she closed her eyes for fully a minute by the clock before she opened them.

"How old's your mother-in-law?" she asked in her quavering voice, fixing Muldoon with her steady eyes.

Muldoon stared. "Seventy-four," he said, surprised. "Just last month. Why?"

"I don't rightly know," old Miss Gilhooley said slowly. "All I know is I closed me eyes and asked meself, 'How can Muldoon come up with some money?' And right away, like in letters of fire across the insides of me eyeballs, I see, 'How old is Vera Callahan?' It's got to mean something."

"Yeah," Muldoon said glumly. "But what?"

"I'll miss me bus," said old Miss Gilhooley, and came to her feet, picking up her ancient haversack. "It'll come to you, don't worry." And with a smile she was through the door.

Seventy-four, Muldoon mused as he walked slowly toward the small house he now shared with his mother-in-law. You'd think old Miss Gilhooley might have been a little more lavish with her clues. She'd never been that cryptic before. Seventy-four! Suddenly Muldoon stopped dead in his tracks. There was only one logical solution, and the more he thought about it, the better it looked. Old Miss Gilhooley and Vera Callahan had been lifelong enemies. And his mother-in-law had certainly mentioned her life-insurance policy often enough when she first used it ten years before as her passport into the relative security of the Muldoon ménage. And, after all, 74 was a ripe old age, four years past the biblical threescore and ten, not to mention being even further beyond the actuarial probabilities.

Muldoon smiled at his own brilliance in solving the enigma so quickly. Doing away with his mother-in-law would be no chore. By Muldoon's figuring, she had to weigh in at about a hundred pounds dripping wet and carrying an anvil in each hand. Nor, he conceded, would her passing be much of a loss. She did little except creep between bed and kitchen and seemed to live on tea. Actually, since the poor soul suffered such a wide variety of voiced ailments, the oblivion offered by the grave would undoubtedly prove welcome.

He thought for a moment of checking with the insurance company as to the exact dollar value of his anticipated inheritance, but then concluded it might smack of greediness. It might also look a bit peculiar when the old lady suffered a fatal attack of something-or-other so soon after the inquiry. Still, he felt sure it would be a substantial amount; old Miss Gilhooley had never failed him before.

When he entered the house, the old lady was stretched out on the couch, taking her afternoon nap (she slept more than a cat, Muldoon thought) and all he had to do was to put one of the small embroidered pillows over her face and lean his 200 pounds on it for a matter of several minutes, and that was that. She barely wriggled during the process.

Muldoon straightened up, removed the pillow, and gazed down. He had been right; he was sure he detected a grateful expression on the dead face. He fluffed the pillow up again, placed it in its accustomed location, and went to call the undertaker.

It was only after all decent arrangements had been made, all hard bargaining concluded, and all the proper papers signed, that Muldoon called the insurance company—and got more than a slight shock. His mother-in-law's insurance was for $400, doubtless a princely sum when her doting parents had taken it out a matter of sixty years before, but rather inadequate in this inflationary age. Muldoon tried to cancel the funeral, but the undertaker threatened suit, not to mention a visit from his nephew, acknowledged dirty-fight champion of all South Boston. The additional amount of money Muldoon had to get to finally get Vera Callahan underground completely wiped out his meager savings.

So that, obviously, was not what old Miss Gilhooley had been hinting at, Muldoon figured. He was not bitter, nor was his faith impaired; the fault had to be his own. So there he was with the numbers again. 74 ... 74 ... Could they refer to the mathematical possibilities? Four from seven left three—but three what? Three little pigs? Three blind mice? Three blind pigs? He gave it up. On the other hand, four plus seven equaled ...

He smote himself on the head for his previous stupidity and quickly rubbed the injured spot, for Muldoon was a strong man with a hand like the bumper on a gravel truck. Of course! *Seven and four added up to eleven. ELEVEN!* And—Muldoon told himself with authority—if that wasn't a hint to get into the floating crap game that took place daily, then his grandfather came from Warsaw.

So Muldoon took out a second mortgage on his small house, which netted him eight hundred dollars plus change, added to that the two hundred he got for his three-and-a-half-year-old, secondhand-to-begin-with car, and with $1000 in big bills in his pocket, made his way to Casey's Bar & Grill.

"Casey!" he asked in his ringing voice, "Where's the floating game today?"

"Callahan Hotel," Casey said, rinsing glasses. "Been there all week. Room seventy-four."

Muldoon barely refrained from smiting himself on the head again. How dumb could one guy be? If only he'd asked before, he would not have had to deal with that thief of an undertaker, not to mention the savings he'd squandered—although in truth he had to admit the small house was less crowded with the old lady gone.

"Thanks," he said to Casey, and hurried from the bar.

The group standing around the large dismountable regulation crap table in Room 74 of the Callahan Hotel, was big and tough, but Muldoon was far from intimidated. With $1000 in his pocket and his fortune about to be made, Muldoon felt confidence flowing through him like a fourth beer. He nodded to one of the gamblers he knew and turned to the man next to him, tapping him on the shoulder.

"Got room for one more?" he asked.

"Hunnert dollars minimum," the man said without looking up from the table. "No credit."

Muldoon nodded. It was precisely the game he wanted. "Who's the last man?" he asked.

"Me," the man said, and clamped his lips shut.

Muldoon took the money from his pocket and folded the bills lengthwise, gambler-fashion, wrapping them around one finger, awaiting his turn. When at last the dice finally made their way to him, Muldoon laid a hundred-dollar bill on the table, picked up the dice, and shook them next to one ear. They made a pleasant ivory sound. A large smile appeared on Muldoon's face.

"Seven and four are me lucky numbers," he announced. "Same as them that's on the door of this room, here. Now, if a guy could only roll an eleven *that* way!"

"He'd end up in a ditch," the back man said expressionlessly. "You're faded—roll them dice. Don't wear 'em out."

Muldoon did not wear out the dice. In fact, he had his hands on them exactly ten times, managing to throw ten consecutive craps, equally divided between snake-eyes and boxcars. They still speak of it at the floating crap game; it seems the previous record was only five and the man who held it took the elevator to the roof—they were playing at some hotel up in Copley Square that day—and jumped off. Muldoon turned the dice over to the man to his right and wandered disconsolately out of the hotel.

Out in the street Muldoon ambled along a bit aimlessly, scuffing his heavy work brogans against anything that managed to get in his way—a tin can, a broken piece of brick he considered with affectionate memory before he kicked it violently, a crushed cigarette pack. He tried for an empty candy wrapper but with his luck missed. 74! What in the bleary name of Eustace Q. Peabody could the blaggety numbers mean? (The Sisters had raised Muldoon strictly; no obscenity passed his lips.) He tried to consider the matter logically, forcing his temper under control. Old Miss Gilhooley had never failed him, nor would she this time. He was simply missing the boat.

Seventy-four? Seventy-*four?* The figures began to take on a certain rhythm, like the *Punch, brother, punch with care* of Mark Twain. Muldoon found himself trying to march to it. Seventy-four-zero! Seventy-four-zero-*hup!* Almost it but not quite. Seventy-four-zero-hup! Seventy-four-zero, *hup!* Got it! Muldoon said to himself, deriving what little satisfaction he could from the cadence, and marched along swinging. Seventy-four-zero, *hup!*

And found himself in front of Casey's Bar & Grill, so he went inside and pulled a stool up to the deserted bar. "Beer," he said.

"How'd you do in the game?" Casey asked.

"Better give me a shot with that beer," Muldoon said by way of an answer. He slugged the shot down, took about half of his beer for a chaser, and considered Casey as he wiped his mouth. "Casey," he said earnestly, really wanting to know, "what do the numbers seven and four mean to you?"

"Nothing," Casey said.

"How about seven, four, and zero?"

"Nothing," Casey said. "Maybe even less."

"How about backwards?" Muldoon asked in desperation, but Casey had gone to the small kitchen in the rear to make himself a sandwich during the slack time, and Muldoon found himself addressing thin air. He tossed the proper amount of change on the counter and started for the door. Where he ran into a small man named O'Leary, who ran numbers for the mob. It wasn't what he preferred, but it was a living.

"Wanna number today, Mr. Muldoon?" O'Leary asked.

Muldoon was about to pass on with a shake of his head, when he suddenly stopped. A thrill went through him from head to foot. Had he been in a cartoon a light bulb would have lit up in a small circle over his head. Not being in a cartoon, he kicked himself, his heavy brogan leaving a bruise that caused him to limp painfully for the next three weeks.

Good Geoffrey T. Soppingham! He must have been blind! Blind? Insane! What possible meaning could numbers have, if not *that they were numbers*? Just thinking about it made Muldoon groan. If he hadn't killed the old lady and gotten into that stupid crap game, at this moment he could be putting down roughly fifteen hundred bucks on Seven-Four-Zero. Fifteen hundred dollars at five-hundred-to-one odds! Still, if he hadn't smothered the old lady, he'd never have come up with the zero, so it wasn't a total loss. But the floating crap game had been completely unnecessary.

Because now Muldoon didn't have the slightly doubt as to what the numbers meant.

"Somethin' wrong, Mr. Muldoon?" O'Leary asked, concerned with the expression on Muldoon's face.

"No!" Muldoon said, and grasped the runner by the arm, drawing him back into Casey's Bar & Grill, his hand like the clamshell bucket of a steam shovel on the smaller man's bicep. He raised his voice, bellowing. *"Casey!"*

Casey appeared from the kitchen, wiping mayonnaise from his chin. "Don't shout," he said. "What do you want?"

Muldoon was prying his wedding ring from his finger. He laid it down on the bar. "What'll you give me for this?"

Casey looked at Muldoon as if the other man had suddenly gone mad. "This ain't no hockshop, Muldoon," he said.

But Muldoon was paying no attention. He was slipping his wrist-watch and its accompanying stretch band over his thick fingers. He placed the watch down on the bar next to the ring.

"One hundred bucks for the lot," he said simply. "A loan is all. I'll pay it back tonight." As Casey continued to look at him with fishy eyes, Muldoon added in a quiet, desperate voice, "I paid sixty bucks each for them rings; me and Kathleen had matching ones. And that watch set me back better than a bill-and-a-half all by itself, not to mention the band, which is pure Speidel. How about it?" A touch of pleading entered his voice. "Come on; we been friends a long time."

"Acquaintances," Casey said, differentiating, and continued to eye Muldoon coldly. "I ain't got that much cash in the cash register right now."

"Jefferson J. Billingsly the cash register," Muldoon said, irked. "You got that much and more in your pants pocket."

Casey studied the other a moment longer, then casually swept the ring and the watch from the counter into his palm, and pocketed them. From another pocket he brought out a wallet that looked like it was suffering from mumps. He began counting out bills.

"Ninety-five bucks," he said. "Five percent off the top, just like the Morris Plan."

Muldoon was about to object, but time was running out.

"Someday we'll discuss this transaction in greater detail, Casey," he said. "Out in the alley," and he turned to O'Leary, grasping both of the smaller man's arms for emphasis. "O'Leary, I want ninety-five bucks on number seven-four-zero. Got it? *Seven-Four-Zero!* Today!"

"Ninety-five bucks?" O'Leary was stunned. "I never wrote no slip bigger than a deuce in my life, Mr. Muldoon," he said. He thought a moment. "No, a fin," he said brightly, but then his face fell. "No, a deuce. I remember now, the fin was counterfeit. . . ."

"You're wasting time," Muldoon said in a dangerous voice. He suddenly realized he was holding the smaller man several inches from the floor, and lowered him. "Will they pay off? That's the question," he said in a quieter voice, prepared for hesitation.

"Sure they pay off, Mr. Muldoon," O'Leary said, straightening his sleeves into a semblance of their former shape. "How long you figure they stay alive, they start welching?"

"So long as they know it," Muldoon said, and handed over the ninety-five bucks. He took his receipt in return, checked the number carefully to make sure O'Leary had made no mistake, and slipped the paper into his pocket. Then he turned to Casey.

"A beer," he said in a voice that indicated their friendship had suffered damage. "And that is out of that five bucks you just stole!"

MULDOON WAS WAITING IN A BOOTH at Casey's Bar & Grill at seven o'clock p.m., which was the time the runners normally had the final three figures of the national treasury balance—which was the Gospel that week. Muldoon knew that straight cash in hand would not be forthcoming; after all he was due a matter of over $47,000. Still, he'd take a check. If he hadn't gotten into that crap game, he'd have been rich—or, more probably, in a ditch like the man had mentioned this afternoon.

Who was going to pay off that kind of loot? No mob in Boston, that was sure. Better this way, Muldoon thought. Forty-seven grand was big enough to be the year's best advertisement for the racket, but still small enough by their standards for the mob to loosen up.

It was a nice feeling being financially secure after the problems of the past few years, and Muldoon had no intention of splurging. His honest debts would be cleared up, of course, and he'd have to buy himself some wheels—a compact, nothing fancy—but the rest would go into the bank. At five percent it wouldn't earn no fortune, he knew, but it would still be better than a fall off a high scaffold onto a low sidewalk.

He reached for his beer and saw old Miss Gilhooley walking through the door. Had a week passed so quickly? He supposed it must have; what with the funeral, and one thing and another, the time had flown. He waved her over and called out to Casey to bring old Miss Gilhooley anything her heart desired.

Old Miss Gilhooley settled herself in the booth across from him and noted the expression on his face. "So you figured it out, Muldoon," she said.

"Not right off," Muldoon admitted. "To be honest, it just come to me this afternoon. But better late than never; at least it come." He leaned over the table confidentially. "It was the numbers, see? The seven and the four for her age, plus the zero at the end, because whether you heard or not, that's what the poor soul is now."

Old Miss Gilhooley sipped the beer Casey had brought, and nodded. "That's what I figured," she said, "especially after seeing O'Leary in me dreams three nights running, and me old enough to be his mother."

"And I can't thank you enough—" Muldoon started to say, and then paused, for O'Leary had just burst through the door of the bar like a Roman candle, and was hurrying over to them, brushing people aside. His eyes were shining.

"Mr. Muldoon! Mr. Muldoon!" O'Leary cried excitedly. "I never seen nothin' like it in all me born days! And on a ninety-five dollar bet!"

Muldoon grinned happily.

"Only one number away!" O'Leary cried, still astounded at the closeness of his brush with fame and fortune.

Muldoon's world fell with a crash. "One number away?"

"Yeah!" O'Leary said, still marveling. "You bet Seven-Four-Zero.

It come out Seven-Five-Zero. Tough!" O'Leary sighed, and then put the matter from his mind. After all, life had to go on. "Wanna number for tomorrow, Mr. Muldoon?"

"No," Muldoon said in a dazed tone, and turned to old Miss Gilhooley who was making strange noises. But they were not lamentations for Muldoon; to Muldoon's surprise the old lady was cackling like a fiend.

"That Vera Callahan!" she said triumphantly. "I always *knew* she lied about her age!"

Phil Davis

MURDER, ANYONE?

IF IT WEREN'T for my wife I might never have hunched out the murders. There were four of them and a fifth was on the fire. Homicide didn't see anything that resembled homicide. They liked accident, mainly, except for the one that went into the books as suicide.

Though cops and robbers weren't my thing anymore, I liked to keep my brain in. When I was with the department I was no great shakes—just a digger who liked to play hunches. Now that I'm retired (not because of age, but due to a rich, departed uncle), I could play without being reprimanded.

The first so-called accident made no impression on me. It happened to a veterinarian who died because of a faulty gas heater. So what? You read about it all the time, right?

Then a carpenter gets his hand mixed up with an electric saw, in his own shop, yet. That doesn't happen too often to a professional carpenter. To an amateur, yes. Anyway, they found the poor guy two days later near the telephone, with his arms outstretched, apparently trying to reach the phone with the hand that was still attached.

I said to my friend at the precinct, "Something smells, Marty. A pro wouldn't go near one of those power saws without the safety guard in position. How come this one did?"

Marty was a shrugger. "Careless," he said.

I nodded, my brain acting like it still belonged in a detective's skull. It's possible that a carpenter could be careless, but before a person can get his hand sawed off, first the machine's got to be trying to saw something else besides hands, right? *There wasn't a hunk of wood anywhere near that sawing table.* "How come?" I asked Marty.

Marty gave me one of those tolerant, sighing looks. "He wasn't sawing any wood, Hank. He accidentally flipped the switch while his hand was on the table."

All right, that's an answer. I filed it away.

Then there was this druggist who was found cold in the back room of his store with a bellyful of cyanide. It was obviously suicide. If a druggist wants to go, he knows how—fast and easy.

I didn't argue too much on that one. It was a fairly open-and-shut suicide, but one thing bothered me that didn't seem to bother the department. *All three of these cash-ins happened on a Monday afternoon at around 4:30.*

Marty threw up his hands in disgust. "Why don't you go home," he said, "and watch the crime shows on television? Better yet, write some."

I ignored both suggestions. "Imagine that," I said, pressing the point. "Everything happens on a Monday afternoon at around four-thirty, a week or two apart. Funny, right?"

Marty didn't think it was funny. He admitted it was strange and gave me a lecture on the theory of coincidence. I'm a patient man. I didn't belabor it.

During one of my usual visits to the precinct, a report came in that a Mr. Adams, owner of the East Side Exterminating Company, choked on the fumes of some bug-killer he'd been mixing. I said to myself, *Mister Number Four?* I also thought, *Why not? It was a Monday, and it was around four-thirty in the afternoon.*

NORA WAS ON HER SIDE of the bed trying to solve her weekly acrostic puzzle while I stared at the ceiling hoping maybe I'd find some answers up there. Mr. Adams, the exterminator, had been mixing formulas for twenty years, and all he ever killed were bugs. Now he mixes some stuff which any high school chemistry student knows is lethal, and bye-bye, Mr. Adams. How come? Marty had told me, after the usual investigation, there was a mix-up of labels on the bottles. Another pro is careless? Come on . . .

Nora squealed: "I got it! I got it!"

Big deal—another acrostic puzzle solved.

"Listen to this, darling," she said. "This one is real profound."

I gave her my 'big-deal' attitude and said, "Do tell."

"Don't belittle me, darling. It was the hardest acrostic I ever worked."

I leered at her well-formed breasts pressing against her sheer night-gown. "Me, belittle you?"

She pulled the covers up to her chin. "Nervy," she said.

That's Nora, a regular square. I slid over to her side and asked her to read me the profound solution to the acrostic. She gave me a smug look and read: "To liquidate the liquidator, the insects must rise and devour the day next when the moon is full."

She waited for my reaction. I let her wait because I didn't understand it.

"Well?" she said, finally.

"What's so profound about that?"

"Don't you know what it means?"

"It's supposed to mean something?"

"It means that nature will some day rise up and destroy us all because we've been fiddling around with her entirely too much."

"Not bad," I said, grudgingly. "Like that little exterminator guy I was telling you about. All his life he mixes stuff to kill bugs—now the stuff kills *him*." I frowned. "That's a funny coincidence."

"What is?"

"Read that again."

She did, and this time I listened carefully. "To liquidate the liquidator, the insects must rise and devour the devourer the day next when the moon is full."

I nodded and wrinkled my forehead. "That bug-killer—his place is next to the Moon Cafe."

"So?"

"So he dies at four-thirty, *when the Moon is full—of beer drinkers*. The acrostic tells when it's gonna happen, where and to who."

"Whom," she corrected. Then she mimicked me with an icky face. " 'When the Moon is full of beer drinkers.' That isn't worthy of you, Hank."

I grinned. "My wisdom can't all be pearls. But I still think it's a funny coincidence."

"Well, you're going to Teresa Trimble's tomorrow night. You can ask her about it."

"Who's she?" I said, scowling.

"That's the little old lady who makes up the acrostics for the magazine."

My wife was giving me one of her teasing-type smiles, obviously enjoying the scowl I kept on my face. So I teased her back by removing the scowl and replacing it with a shruggy look. She couldn't stand it for long.

"Don't you want to know," she said, "how come we're going there tomorrow night?" Her tone revealed she had lost the tease contest.

"You're about to tell me, right?"

"Right. I sent her a fan letter and she invited us for dinner."

I rolled my eyes to the ceiling. "Great. A dinner date with an ancient female who makes up weirdo puzzles."

"She's a very remarkable woman. Do you know what she said in last week's acrostic? I memorized it. 'The walrus speaks of cabbages and the carpenter speaks not at all since he cannot be heard above the din.' You know what that means?"

I didn't wait for her to tell me. My hunchy brain was clicking like an overheated computer. I scrambled out of bed and made for Nora's desk. I heard her call out: "Hey!"

"I want to see all the other acrostics you worked out," I said, riffling through her papers.

"Welcome to the intelligentsia," she said smugly.

I sent her a wry look and went back to the puzzles. I found nothing that said anything about a druggist or a vet—not in those exact words—but there was enough to make me wonder about Miss Trimble. I looked forward to tomorrow's date.

WE WAITED IN THE LIVINGROOM while Teresa Trimble flitted out for some goodies. Her place could have inspired a Charles Addams drawing: the mohair furniture, the beaded portieres, the antimacassars, and the faint aroma of rose sachet. I was about to tell Nora the room gave me the creeps, when she said: "Isn't it charming, Hank?"

What can you say to a question like that? So I nodded and let her believe it was charming.

Miss Trimble minced in through the beaded portieres carrying a tray of watercress sandwiches and three small glasses of wine. She was a tiny, birdlike woman, about seventy. "This is such a joyous occasion for me," she said in a voice that rustled as if it were filtered through some willows.

"We were so happy to be able to come," Nora said with a stickiness that might have attracted a swarm of bees. "Monday is usually Hank's poker night."

I nodded with a suffering oh-what-I-gave-up! look.

Miss Trimble rushed on. "Well, when I got your gracious letter complimenting my acrostics I just *knew* I had to meet you. And when you accepted my humble invitation—" She broke off, staring at Nora with a semiglazed look. Then slowly she reached out and touched her cheek. "You're so young," she said softly. "So fresh—" She halted abruptly as a thought developed. "Oh, I have a wonderful idea! I'll just be a minute!" She turned and floated out. I started to browse.

"Stop fidgeting," Nora whispered. "It won't destroy you to miss your poker game one night."

By this time I was at the secretary-desk in a corner going through an assortment of papers. Nora reprimanded me sharply. "Hank, you just can't come into this woman's home and start going through—"

"Listen to this . . ." It was a galley proof of next week's acrostic. "Green is his trade though many shades of yellow are his wares. Black is the nature of his soul, and death finds repose in pale pink."

Nora's eyes flashed. "Hank, you can't—"

"How do I look?" Miss Trimble's voice caused us to whirl. She'd changed into a gown of a vintage of fifty years ago, pausing in the portiere and striking a pose as if asking for admiration.

I managed, "Exquisite. Like a Dresden doll, Miss Trimble."

"What a nice thing to say, Mr. Barnes. It's been fifty years since I wore this dress. It has wonderful memories." She gave Nora a warm, tender look. "And seeing you reminded me of all those young yesterdays." Her glance fell on the tray she'd brought in. "Oh, you haven't tasted my sandwiches. They won't interfere with your dinner—they're very light." A note of sadness crept into her voice. "Although I'm afraid the watercress is a bit of a disappointment. It isn't as crisp as it should have been." Now her face turned a shade cunning. "My greengrocer's been neglecting me. I'm going to have to change him."

There went my brain clicking again. "Your greengrocer?"

She gave me a pleasant nod, then picked up a glass of wine and raised it to Nora. "I want to drink a toast to you, Mrs. Barnes. To beauty—who has found faith in a lost art." She lifted her glass to her lips when her attention was attracted to an empty bird cage hanging on a tall stand nearby. Her eyes clouded and she stood silently gazing at it for a couple of seconds. She caught our puzzled reaction. "I lost Jonathan three weeks ago today," she explained. "The veterinarian was so careless." She extended the tray. "Now, won't you try one of these? You'll find them refreshing."

I reached for a sandwich and accidentally knocked over a glass of wine which spilled on the rug.

"Oh, Hank—" Nora began, chidingly.

"I'm sorry, Miss Trimble." I stooped down to mop it up with a paper napkin, but Miss Trimble stopped me.

"Don't worry, Mr. Barnes," she said. "Moths got to my rug long before that little glass of wine. The exterminator was preparing a special solution, but apparently the moths were smarter than he."

From my stooped position, I looked up at her and said cautiously, "Would that happen to be an exterminator who had his place on East 47th Street?"

She reacted with a surprised smile. "Why, yes, Mr. Barnes. Do you use Mr. Adams, too?"

I rose slowly. "No," I said. "And I don't think Mr. Adams is in a position to take on any more business."

Nora swiveled her stare from me to Miss Trimble with dismay.

IN MY SLEEP I HEARD MYSELF repeating: "Green is his trade through many shades of yellow are his wares. Green is his trade—"

Then I heard Miss Trimble's voice saying: "My greengrocer's been neglecting me. I'm going to have to change him."

"Green is his trade—"

"I'm going to have to change him—"

I awoke sharply and cried out: "Oh, no!" I turned and started to shake Nora. "Honey . . . Sweetheart . . . Baby!"

She offered me her glaze-filled eyes.

"I've got it!" I yelled. Then added in a lower voice: "I'm afraid."

Nora yawned in my face and said, "You've got what? You're afraid?"

"I think that weirdo Trimble dame is going to change her greengrocer, all right. She's going to change him from a live one to a dead one." I reached for the telephone on the night stand.

"IT'S NOT A COINCIDENCE, MARTY," I said. "All your accidental deaths are tied in with these acrostics." Nora refilled our coffee cups.

"Three-thirty," Marty muttered dazedly. "In the morning yet."

Nora nodded in agreement. "Imagine—popovers, at three-thirty a.m."

"And very good, too," Marty said with a mouthful. "I'll have another."

I waved a handful of solved acrostics under his nose. "Remember the veterinarian who died because of a faulty gas heater? I'll bet you'll find he took care of Miss Trimble's bird with the broken wing. And the exterminator who fought a losing battle with the moths in her rug." I riffled through the stuff. "It's all here—the carpenter, the druggist. And I'm warning you, Marty, next Monday at four-thirty a greengrocer's going to die."

Marty sighed. "Do me a favor, Hank? What the hell is a greengrocer?"

Nora leaped in with her superintellect. "A man who sells fruits and vegetables." Then she attacked me with her superlogic. "We had dinner with her last night, Hank. Did she act like a woman who committed four murders in as many weeks? And if she did, why lay it out in an acrostic puzzle?"

"Who is this dame?" Marty wanted to know. "A Lucrezia de Bergerac? A master criminal? I don't get it, but I've played your hunches before and you've been right, so I'll go along with you now. Just don't tell my boss."

"Right." I turned to my wife. "Nora . . ." She was asleep on her feet, so I did what any red-blooded ex-detective husband would do under the circumstances. I yelled in her ear. *"Nora!"*

Her head snapped back, and she spouted: "A greengrocer is a man who sells fruits and—"

She broke off at the sight of my grin. "You told us that before, dear," I said patronizingly. "What we need to know now is *which* greengrocer is going to be the next victim."

I gave her the assignment.

NORA WAS A GOOD OPERATIVE. Teresa Trimble's greengrocer was a frail little man by the name of Pincus. His store was on Lexington Avenue not far from Miss Trimble's apartment. The customers called him Pink, as in the last sentence of the acrostic: *Death finds repose in pale pink.*

The following Monday Marty and I staked out Pink's place. At about four-fifteen, Miss Trimble materialized on the sidewalk and glided into the store. We got out of the car and paused at the entrance. We heard Mr. Pincus greet Miss Trimble warmly. She wanted to know if her mushrooms were ready. "You promised me, Pink," she said in that wispy voice. "Today . . . Monday . . . 4:30. Remember?"

"Of course," Pincus said. "I haven't had a light on in the cellar all week. They should be beautiful. I'll just be a minute."

Mr. Pincus went through a back door and we went in through the front. Miss Trimble was surprised. "Why, Mr. Barnes," she said, "how nice to see you. Are you going to buy some of Mr. Pincus' mushrooms?"

"Not exactly." I introduced Marty.

"So nice to meet you, Mr. Gordon."

Marty said, "Thanks."

Miss Trimble turned to a display of persimmons. "Mr. Pincus says it bruises his persimmons to squeeze them. But how else can you tell if they're ripe?" She gave one a delicate pinch and tossed me a conspiratorial smile. "He'll never know."

Miss Trimble went back to examining the persimmons, giving them a pinch here, a pinch there. A clock on the wall ticked ominously. It was obviously fast. Then, after what seemed to be a short forever, I checked my watch and glanced at Marty. "What time've *you* got?"

Before Marty could answer, Miss Trimble turned from the persimmons and told us: "It's four-thirty."

It was the way she said it that caused Marty and me to exchange a couple of alarmed looks. Enough for Marty to scoot out the back door.

"It was so sweet of Mrs. Barnes," Miss Trimble was saying, "to drop by last Wednesday. I gave her some of my special jasmine tea. I have such a wonderful tea man—"

I glanced nervously toward the rear door. "She told me," I said.

"She's so young and pretty," Miss Trimble went on. "You're a very lucky man, Mr. Barnes. If I had my way she'd never grow old."

I caught sight of a magazine on a counter beside her. It was the same one Nora subscribed to—the one with the acrostic puzzles. Before I could question her about it, Marty came in from the rear room, his features frozen in shock.

"He's dead," Marty said with complete disbelief.

Miss Trimble looked concerned. "But what about my mushrooms?" she said.

INSPECTOR CROWLEY, a fat, florid, perspiring cop with a nervous habit of cracking his knuckles, was questioning Miss Trimble in her apartment. I had to hand it to her, the way she sat so calm and controlled.

Crowley cracked a knuckle and said: "Tell me again, Miss Trimble, what was the meaning of the acrostic—" He started to read from a copy: "Green is his trade, etcetera, etcetera, etcetera—?"

"I wish you wouldn't do that," Miss Trimble said.

"It's my job to ask questions."

"I didn't mean that. I meant crack your knuckles."

Crowley flashed Marty and me an irky look. With Crowley's permission, I took over the questioning. "Didn't your acrostic contain a warning to Mr. Pincus?"

"A warning?" she said innocently. "About what?"

I repeated the acrostic: "Green is his trade though many shades of yellow are his wares." I gave her my interpretation. "That means he was a greengrocer, but sold yellow stuff like bananas, squash, pears, and so on. Right?"

"That's a very interesting interpretation, Mr. Barnes," she said, impressed.

I went on. " 'Black is the nature of his soul.' Was that your way of saying you disliked him?"

"Oh, no, Mr. Barnes. I was just sorry he disappointed me in the watercress, that's all. Actually, I was very fond of Pink."

I nodded. "Pink. Death finds repose in pale pink." I put on one of my friendliest faces. "Now, Miss Trimble, didn't you intend that to be a threat?"

"The text," she said simply, "of each of my acrostics is always controversial. That's why they're so successful. Everyone finds his own meaning in them."

"What's yours?"

"I just like the way they sound."

Marty put his two cents in. "Did you like the way it sounded when Pincus slipped on those cellar steps and cracked his head open on the cement floor?"

"I didn't hear anything," she said sweetly.

It was Crowley's turn. "You got into that cellar, waxed those steps, and unscrewed the light bulb—didn't you?"

Marty pounced in with: "And what about the exterminator? Did you slip into his back room and prepare the solution that killed him?"

"And the vet," Crowley barked. "The one you took your bird to. Did you open the jet on his gas heater while he took his afternoon nap?"

"And the carpenter—"

"The druggist—"

They suddenly stopped the interrogation to stare at Miss Trimble as she took out a little pillbox from a table drawer, and poured some water from a carafe.

"I can't remember," she said, "when I've had such a stimulating evening." She opened the pillbox and extended it to us. "Peppermint?"

NORA LET OUT THREE "Oh's," one after another. The first one came when I handed her a special delivery letter. It was an "Oh" filled with wonder. Like if it were for me I'd say: "Oh? Who the hell would send me a special delivery?" But my wife's a lady. The second "Oh" was one of surprise when I told her that the letter was from the little old acrostic banana. The third "Oh" came when she opened the envelope and read the note. "An advance copy," it said, "of my next acrostic. I sincerely hope you can solve it." She frowned at me. "Why do you suppose she did that?"

I wasn't in the mood for supposing. I grabbed the acrostic and hightailed in to Center Street where they have computers that decipher cryptograms, coded messages and all kinds of stuff like that.

The computer solved the puzzle in three minutes flat, but as smart as that machine was, it couldn't give me an interpretation. When it comes to interpretations my wife and I are smarter than machines.

I showed it to Nora and she drew a blank.

I read it over and over: *X plus too much Y equals death, since neither a found hope nor a lost faith can halt the hour of doom where the sun declines.* I gave Nora a worried look. "I'm batting zero."

"You're in a slump, darling," she said. "Maybe you ought to bench yourself."

I repeated the beginning: "*X plus too much Y equals death.* Read the next line, honey." I closed my eyes and listened.

"*. . . since neither a found hope nor a lost faith*—Got that, love?"

I repeated it slowly. "—since neither a found hope, nor a lost faith—" I opened my eyes. "What do you suppose she means, 'a found hope'?"

"What about 'a lost faith'?"

"Yeah. A lost faith. A found hope."

"You can't accuse her of using bad grammar," Nora said.

"What's that got to do with it?"

She shrugged her shoulders. "Nothing. Just that she was very grammatical. She didn't say 'neither or,' she said 'neither *nor.*'"

I felt the hairs on the back of my neck getting bristly. I repeated the line. "*—neither a found hope nor a lost faith.*" I droned on: "*Neither a found hope—neither a found hope—neither a found hope—*" I switched to: "*—nor a lost faith—nor a lost faith—nor a—*" I screamed it. "*Nora!*"

Nora almost jumped out of her chair. "What?"

"*Nora* lost faith!"

Nora gulped and said very faintly, "Me?"

THE COPS WERE IN OUR LIVINGROOM Monday afternoon. Nora sat on the edge of the couch looking very unhappy. "What am I supposed to do," she complained, "just sit here and wait for the hour of doom." She pointed to her watch. "That's a scanty five minutes from now."

I said, "Relax, baby."

Crowley said, "There's nothing to worry about, Mrs. Barnes. We've got men stationed all over this building and a stake-out at Miss Trimble's."

Marty said, "Of all the cases I've been on, this is the wackiest. X plus too much Y equals a pain in the neck."

"For your information, Marty," I said, "the X refers to me as an ex-detective. And too much Y means I've asked too many questions. Which adds up to—"

Marty signed me off with: "I know, I know. But what about that 'hour of doom where the sun declines'?"

I wasn't too sure about that part of the acrostic. I figured it was Miss Trimble's way of telling us the action would take place around four-thirty. At this time of the year that's about when the sun declines.

The phone rang and Crowley went to answer it. Nora was hoping it was a reprieve from the governor. One of the men who'd been staked out around Miss Trimble's building told us that she had left thirty seconds ago. Nora reacted with a sick gulp and made with a sick joke. "Murder, anyone?"

We checked the time. My watch said 4:30; Marty's, 4:29; Crowley had 4:31.

We waited . . . and waited . . . and waited. Zero.

At 5:30 the phone rang again. The report was that Miss Trimble just got back to the house. It seems she'd only gone on a little shopping tour.

Marty and Crowley told me off. They'd had enough of my shadow chasing. Nora told me off, too. She'd had enough of cops, threats and my profound acrostic interpretations and brain-damaged hunches. I told myself off, then sat in a corner nursing my wounds.

My wife being the kind of wife she is, soothed my ego with a "can't-win-'em-all" type of remark, kissed the back of my neck, and sent me off to my Monday night poker game. I was glad to go.

It was 7:20 when I left the building. *Had I waited until 7:30 I might have met Teresa Trimble coming in.*

The poker game was at George Bogin's place, a couple of blocks away. His wife was in L.A. so he started the game early. I got there in five minutes.

George looked at me in surprise. "Hey, I thought you weren't coming. I called Nate to take your place."

Nate said, "I'd give you my seat, Hank, but I'm out a hundred and fifty big ones."

"Forget it," I said. "I'll kibitz awhile."

George looked at his watch. "I promised to call my wife at four-thirty, Hank," he said. "You can take my seat. She'll keep me on the phone for an hour."

I laughed. "You're a little late. It's seven-thirty now."

He got up from the table and I sat down.

"Four-thirty L.A. time," George explained. "You know Vera. Everything belongs to her. 'Call her at four-thirty my time.' You think she'd say, 'Call me at seven-thirty your time'? No. Her time. I gotta add the three-hour difference to her time and subtract it from my time. To make a telephone call I gotta be a mathematician." He slapped my shoulder. "It's a lucky seat."

I picked up a pat straight to the king and my head was buzzing with a jumble of acrostics. The boys were asking me if I could open. I heard myself say, "—The hour of doom where the sun declines— *where the sun declines!*" The stark realization hit me like a ten-ton truck. *That dame laid it out! It was 4:30 in the West!* I jumped with a convulsive motion that sent the chips flying, and leaped for the door, leaving a bunch of surprised poker players.

I don't know how long it took me to cover the distance from George's to my apartment, but when I skidded into the lobby I had very little breath left; just enough to breathe a prayer of thanks that the elevator was there waiting.

I punched the button for the 12th floor and nothing happened. "Dammit, move!" I punched it again and again. Zero. I lunged for the stairs.

I used to be a fairly good runner in my day, but a mountain climber I never was. Twelve floors to me was a mountain. I ran up that mountain like I'd been doing it for years. I'm still not a mountain climber—a mountain runner, yes.

I made the 12th floor corridor in time to see Miss Trimble holding a small pistol on Nora in front of the elevator door. Only there was no elevator there—just a deep, empty shaft.

Nora's face was frozen in terror. She didn't see me. Her wide eyes were leveled at the barrel of the gun. Miss Trimble didn't see me either—she was too wrapped up in her game of murder. Needless to say I had to be careful. If I made too much of a thing, the gun might go off or Nora might be shoved down the shaft. Or both.

Miss Trimble was saying: "One so young, so fresh, so pretty, should never grow old. But I'm glad I can prevent that." Her face turned to a pout. "Though you did disappoint me. You shouldn't have permitted your charming husband to ask so many questions. You lost faith, Nora. Don't you see that now?"

I moved along the corridor very slowly, thanking the landlord for the thick carpeting. I hoped Miss Trimble didn't hear the wheeze of my breath.

"This is so exciting," she went on. "Composing acrostics used to be dull and uninteresting until I thought of this game. You know, my dear, I wasn't sure I could outwit your husband—but I did." She raised the gun a little higher. Nora's terror-stricken eyes followed it. "Step in, dear," she said. "Just another accident. It wasn't difficult for me to fix that door and still have the elevator go down. A metal contact, that's all. And now the elevator won't even go up. I'm very good at arranging things." She urged her gently. "Take one small step back, dear. Go on—"

Nora was now at the edge of the shaft. So how do you handle it? No time to figure a plan.

"Well, hello, Miss Trimble," I said very quietly.

Nora gasped, and Miss Trimble turned and gave me a surprised, welcome look. "Why, Mr. Barnes," she said. "How nice that we meet again."

I advanced slowly, walking on eggs. The gun was on me. "You look exquisite in that dress," I said. "Like a Dresden doll." I repeated with a little more emphasis: "—a *Dresden doll.*"

She was no longer with it. "What a nice thing to say," she said mechanically. "It's been fifty years since I wore this dress . . . It has such—"

Very gently I took the gun from her. She didn't even notice.

"It has such wonderful . . . memories."

Nora swayed. I moved quickly past Miss Trimble and extended my arm to keep her from falling backward into the empty shaft.

"Easy, baby," I said under my breath. Then, in my most suave tone, I said, "We're having Miss Trimble in for tea."

"That reminds me," Miss Trimble said. "My tea man mixed some orange pekoe in my jasmine. He shouldn't have done that."

I agreed with her as we led her to our apartment door.

Ruth Rendell

THE MAN WHO WAS THE GOD OF LOVE

"HAVE YOU GOT THE *TIMES* THERE?" Henry would say, usually at about eight, when she had cleared the dinner table and put the things in the dishwasher.

The *Times* was on the coffee table with the two other dailies they took, but it was part of the ritual to ask her. Fiona liked to be asked. She liked to watch Henry do the crossword puzzle, the *real* one of course, not the quick crossword, and watch him frown a little, his handsome brow clear as the answer to a clue came to him. She could not have done a crossword puzzle to save her life (as she was fond of saying), she could not even have done the simple ones in the tabloids.

While she watched him, before he carried the newspaper off into his study as he often did, Fiona told herself how lucky she was to be married to Henry. Her luck had been almost miraculous. There she was, a temp who had come into his office to work for him while his secretary had a baby, an ordinary, not particularly good-looking girl, who had no credentials but a tidy mind and a proficient way with a word processor. She had nothing but her admiration for him, which she had felt from the first and was quite unable to hide.

He was not appreciated in that company as he should have been. It had often seemed to her that only she saw him for what he was. After she had been there a week she told him he had a first-class mind.

Henry had said modestly, "As a matter of fact, I have got rather a high IQ, but it doesn't exactly get stretched round here."

"I suppose they haven't the brains to recognize it," she said. "It must be marvelous to be really intelligent. Did you win scholarships and get a double first and all that?"

123

He only smiled. Instead of answering he asked her to have dinner with him. One afternoon, half an hour before they were due to pack up and go, she came upon him doing the *Times* crossword.

"In the firm's time, I'm afraid, Fiona," he said with one of his wonderful, half-rueful smiles.

He hadn't finished the puzzle but at least half of it was already filled in and when she asked him he said he had started it ten minutes before. She was lost in admiration. Henry said he would finish the puzzle later and in the meantime would she have a drink with him on the way home?

That was three years ago. The firm, which deserved bankruptcy it was so mismanaged, got into difficulties and Henry was among those made redundant. Of course he soon got another job, though the salary was pitiful for someone of his intellectual grasp. He was earning very little more than she was, as she told him indignantly. Soon afterwards he asked her to marry him. Fiona was overcome. She told him humbly that she would have gladly lived with him without marriage, there was no one else she had ever known to compare with him in intellectual terms, it would have been enough to be allowed to share his life. But he said no, marriage or nothing, it would be unfair on her not to marry her.

She kept on with her temping job, making sure she stopped in time to be home before Henry and get his dinner. It was ridiculous to waste money on a cleaner, so she cleaned the house on Sundays. Henry played golf on Saturday mornings and he liked her to go with him, though she was hopeless when she tried to learn. He said it was an inspiration to have her there and praise his swing. On Saturday afternoons they went out in the car and Henry had begun teaching her to drive.

They had quite a big garden—they had bought the house on an enormous mortgage—and she did her best to keep it trim because Henry obviously didn't have the time. He was engaged on a big project for his new company, which he worked on in his study for most of the evenings. Fiona did the shopping during her lunchtime, she did all the cooking and all the washing and ironing. It was her privilege to care for someone as brilliant as Henry. Besides, his job was so much more demanding than hers, it took more out of him, and by bedtime he was sometimes white with exhaustion.

But Henry was first up in the mornings. He was an early riser, getting up at six-thirty, and he always brought her a cup of tea and the morning papers in bed. Fiona had nothing to do before she went off to take first a bus and then the tube but put the breakfast things in the dishwasher and stack yesterday's newspapers in the cupboard outside the front door for recycling.

The *Times* would usually be on top, folded with the lower left-hand quarter of the back page uppermost. Fiona soon came to understand it was no accident that the section of the paper where the crossword was, the *completed* crossword, should be exposed in this way. It was deliberate, it was evidence of Henry's pride in his achievement, and she was deeply moved that he should want her to see it. She was touched by his need for her admiration. A sign of weakness on his part it might be, but she loved him all the more for that.

A smile, half-admiring, half-tender, came to her lips as she looked at the neatly printed answers to all those incomprehensible clues. She could have counted on the fingers of one hand the number of times he had failed to finish the crossword. The evening before his father died, for instance. Then it was anxiety that must have been the cause. They had sent for him at four in the morning and when she looked at the paper before putting it outside with the others, she saw that poor Henry had only been able to fill in the answers to four clues. Another time he had flu and had been unable to get out of bed in the morning. It must have been coming on the night before to judge by his attempt at the crossword, abandoned after two answers feebly penciled in.

His father left him a house that was worth a lot of money. Henry had always said that when he got a promotion, she would be able to give up work and have a baby. Promotion seemed less and less likely in time of recession and the fact that the new company appreciated Henry no more than had his previous employers. The proceeds of the sale of Henry's father's house would compensate for that and Fiona was imagining paying off the mortgage and perhaps handing in her notice when Henry said he was going to spend it on having a swimming pool built. All his life he had wanted a swimming pool of his own, it had been a childhood dream and a teenage ideal and now he was going to realize it.

Fiona came nearer than she ever had to seeing a flaw in her husband's perfection.

"You only want a baby because you think he might be a genius," he teased her.

"*She* might be," said Fiona, greatly daring.

"He, she, it's just a manner of speaking. Suppose he had my beauty and your brains. That would be a fine turn-up for the books."

Fiona was not hurt because she had never had any illusions about being brighter than she was. In any case, he was implying, wasn't he, that she was good-looking? She managed to laugh. She understood that Henry could not always help being rather difficult. It was the penalty someone like him paid for his gifts of brilliance. In some ways intellectual prowess was a burden to carry through life.

"We'll have a heated pool, a decent-size one with a deep end," Henry said, "and I'll teach you to swim."

The driving lessons had ended in failure. If it had been anyone else but Henry instructing her, Fiona would have said he was a harsh and intolerant teacher. Of course she knew how inept she was. She could not learn how to manage the gears and she was afraid of the traffic.

"I'm afraid of the water," she confessed.

"It's a disgrace," he said as if she had not spoken, "a woman of thirty being unable to swim." And then, when she only nodded doubtfully, "Have you got the *Times* there?"

BUILDING THE POOL TOOK ALL THE MONEY the sale of Henry's father's house realized. It took rather more and Henry had to borrow from the bank. The pool had a roof over it and walls round, which were what cost the money. That and the sophisticated purifying system. It was eight feet deep at the deep end, with a diving board and a chute.

Happily for Fiona, her swimming lessons were indefinitely postponed. Henry enjoyed his new pool so much that he would very much have grudged taking time off from swimming his lengths or practicing his dives in order to teach his wife the basics.

Fiona guessed that Henry would be a brilliant swimmer. He was the perfect all-rounder. There was an expression in Latin which he had uttered and then translated for her which might have been, she thought, a description of himself: *mens sana in corpore sano*. Only for "sana," or "healthy," she substituted "wonderful." She would have liked to sit by the pool and watch him and she was rather sorry that his preferred swimming time was six-thirty in the morning, long before she was up.

One evening, while doing the crossword puzzle, he consulted her about a clue, as he sometimes did. "Consulted" was not perhaps the word. It was more a matter of expressing his thoughts aloud and waiting for her comment. Fiona found these remarks, full of references to unknown classical or literary personages, nearly incomprehensible. She had heard, for instance, of Psyche, but only in connection with "psychological," "psychiatric," and so on. Cupid to her was a fat baby with wings, and she did not know this was another name for Eros, which to her was the statue.

"I'm afraid I don't understand at all," she said humbly.

Henry loved elucidating. With a rare gesture of affection, he reached out and squeezed her hand. "Psyche was married to Cupid, who was, of course, a god, the god of love. He always came to her by night and she never saw his face. Suppose her husband was a terrible monster of ugliness and deformity? Against his express wishes"—here Henry fixed a look of some severity on his wife—"she rose up one night in the dark and, taking a lighted candle, approached the bed where Cupid lay. Scarcely had she caught a glimpse of his peerless beauty, when a drop of hot wax fell from the candle onto the god's naked skin. With a cry he sprang up and fled from the house. She never saw him again."

"How awful for her," said Fiona, quite taken aback.

"Yes, well, she shouldn't have disobeyed him. Still, I don't see how that quite fits in here—wait a minute, yes, I do. Of course, that second syllable is an anagram of Eros . . ."

Henry inserted the letters in his neat print. A covert glance told her he had completed nearly half the puzzle. She did her best to suppress a yawn. By this time of the evening she was always so tired she could scarcely keep awake, while Henry could stay up for hours yet. People like him needed no more than four or five hours sleep.

"I think I'll go up," she said.

"Good night." He added a kindly, "Darling."

For some reason, Henry never did the crossword puzzle on a Saturday. Fiona thought this a pity because, as she said, that was the day they gave prizes for the first correct entries received. But Henry only smiled and said he did the puzzle for the pure intellectual pleasure of it, not for gain. Of course you might not know your entry was correct because the solution to Saturday's puzzle did not appear next day but not until a week later. Her saying this, perhaps naively, made Henry unexpectedly angry. Everyone knew that with this kind of puzzle, he said, there could only be one correct solution, even people who never did crosswords knew that.

It was still dark when Henry got up in the mornings. Sometimes she was aware of his departure and his empty half of the bed. Occasionally, half an hour later, she heard the boy come with the papers, the tap-tap of the letter box, and even the soft thump of the *Times* falling onto the mat. But most days she was aware of nothing until Henry reappeared with her tea and the papers.

Henry did nothing to make her feel guilty about lying in, yet she was ashamed of her inability to get up. It was somehow unlike him, it was out of character, this waiting on her. He never did anything of the kind at any other time of the day and it sometimes seemed to her that the unselfish effort he made must be almost intolerable to someone with his needle-sharp mind and—yes, it must be admitted—his undoubted lack of patience. That he never complained or even teased her about oversleeping only added to her guilt.

Shopping during her lunch hour, she bought an alarm clock. They had never possessed such a thing, had never needed to, for Henry, as he often said, could direct himself to wake up at any hour he chose. Fiona put the alarm clock inside her bedside cabinet where it was invisible. It occurred to her, although she had as yet done nothing, she had not set the clock, that in failing to tell Henry about her purchase of the alarm she was deceiving him. This was the first time she had ever deceived him in anything and perhaps, as she reflected on this, it was inevitable that her thoughts should revert to Cupid and Psyche and the outcome of Psyche's equally innocent stratagem.

The alarm remained inside the cabinet. Early evening she thought of setting it, though she never did so. But the effect on her of this daily speculation and doubt was to wake her without benefit of mechanical aid. Thinking about it did the trick and Henry, in swimming trunks and towelling robe, had no sooner left their bedroom than she was wide awake. On the third morning this happened, instead of dozing off again until seven-thirty, she lay there for ten minutes and then got up.

Henry would be swimming his lengths. She heard the paper boy come, the letter box make its double tap-tap, and the newspapers fall onto the mat with a soft thump. Should she put on her own swimming costume or go down fully dressed? Finally, she compromised and got into the tracksuit that had never seen a track and scarcely the light of day before.

This morning it would be she who made Henry tea and took *him* the papers. However, when she reached the foot of the stairs there was no paper on the mat, only a brown envelope with a bill in it. She must have been mistaken and it was the postman she had heard.

The time was just on seven, rather too soon perhaps for the papers to have arrived.

Fiona made her way to the swimming pool. When she saw Henry she would just wave airily to him. She might call out in a cheerful way, "Carry on swimming!" or make some other humorous remark.

The glass door to the pool was slightly ajar. Fiona was barefoot. She pushed the door and entered silently. The cold chemical smell of chlorine irritated her nostrils. It was still dark outside, though dawn was coming, and the dark purplish blue of a pre-sunrise sky shimmered through the glass panel in the ceiling. Henry was not in the pool but sitting in one of the cane chairs at the glass-topped table not two yards from her. Light from a ceiling spotlight fell directly onto the two newspapers in front of him, both folded with their back pages uppermost.

Fiona saw at once what he was doing. That was not the difficulty. From today's *Times* he was copying into yesterday's *Times* the answers to the crossword puzzle. She could see quite clearly that he was doing this but she could not for a moment believe it. It must be a joke or there must be some other purpose behind it.

When he turned round, swiftly covering both newspapers with the *Radio Times,* she knew from his face that it was neither a joke nor the consequence of some mysterious purpose. He had turned quite white. He seemed unable to speak and she flinched from the panic that leapt in his eyes.

"I'll make us a cup of tea," she said. The wisest and kindest thing would be to forget what she had seen. She could not. In that split second she stood in the doorway of the pool watching him he had been changed forever in her eyes. She thought about it on and off all day. It was impossible for her to concentrate on her work.

She never once thought he had deceived her, only that she had caught him out. Like Psyche, she had held the candle over him and seen his true face. His was not the brilliant intellect she had thought. He could not even finish the *Times* crossword. Now she understood why he never attempted it on a Saturday, knowing there would be no opportunity next morning or on the Monday morning to fill in the answers from that day's paper. There were a lot of other truths that she saw about Henry. No one recognized his mind as first class because it wasn't first class. He had lost that excellent well-paid job because he was not intellectually up to it.

She knew all that and she loved him the more for it. Just as she had felt an almost maternal tenderness for him when he left the newspaper with its completed puzzle exposed for her to see, now she was overwhelmed with compassion for his weakness and his childlike vulnerability. She loved him more deeply than ever and if admiration and respect had gone, what did those things matter, after all, in the tender intimacy of a good marriage?

That evening he did not touch the crossword puzzle. She had known he wouldn't and, of course, she said nothing. Neither of them had said a word about what she had seen that morning and neither of them ever would. Her feelings for him were completely changed, yet she believed her attitude could remain unaltered. But when, a few days later, he said something more about its being disgraceful that a woman of her age was unable to swim, instead of agreeing ruefully, she laughed and said, really, he shouldn't be so intolerant and censorious, no one was perfect.

He gave her a complicated explanation of some monetary question that was raised on the television news. It sounded wrong, he was confusing dollars with pounds, and she said so.

"Since when have you been an expert on the stock market?" he said.

Once she would have apologized. "I'm no more an expert than you are, Henry," she said, "but I can use my eyes and that was plain to see. Don't you think we should both admit we don't know a thing about it?"

She no longer believed in the accuracy of his translations from the Latin nor the authenticity of his tales from the classics. When some friends who came for dinner were regaled with his favorite story about how she had been unable to learn to drive, she jumped up laughing and put her arm round his shoulder.

"Poor Henry gets into a rage so easily I was afraid he'd give himself a heart attack, so I stopped our lessons," she said.

He never told that story again.

"Isn't it funny?" she said one Saturday on the golf course. "I used to think it was wonderful you having a handicap of twenty-five. I didn't know any better."

He made no answer.

"It's not really the best thing in a marriage for one partner to look up to the other too much, is it? Equality is best. I suppose it's natural to idolize the other one when you're first married. It just went on rather a long time for me, that's all."

She was no longer in the least nervous about learning to swim. If he bullied her she would laugh at him. As a matter of fact, he wasn't all that good a swimmer himself. He couldn't do the crawl at all and a good many of his dives turned into belly-flops. She lay on the side of the pool, leaning on her elbows, watching him as he climbed out of the deep end up the steps.

"D'you know, Henry," she said, "you'll lose your marvelous figure if you aren't careful. You've got quite a spare tire around your waist."

His face was such a mask of tragedy, there was so much naked misery there, the eyes full of pain, that she checked the laughter that was bubbling up in her and said quickly, "Oh, don't look so sad, poor darling. I'd still love you if you were as fat as a pudding and weighed twenty stone."

He took two steps backwards down the steps, put up his hands, and pulled her down into the pool. It happened so quickly and unexpectedly that she didn't resist. She gasped when the water hit her. It was eight feet deep here, she couldn't swim more than two or three strokes, and she made a grab for him, clutching at his upper arms.

He pried her fingers open and pushed her under the water. She tried to scream but the water came in and filled her throat. Desperately she thrashed about in the blue-greenness, the sickeningly chlorinated water, fighting, sinking, feeling for something to catch hold of, the bar round the pool rim, his arms, his feet on the steps. A foot kicked out at her, a foot stamped on her head. She stopped holding her breath, she had to, and the water poured into her lungs until the light behind her eyes turned red and her head was black inside. A great drum beat, boom, boom, boom, in the blackness, and then it stopped.

Henry waited to see if the body would float to the surface. He waited a long time but she remained, starfishlike, face-downwards, on the blue tiles eight feet down, so he left her and, wrapping himself in his toweling robe, went into the house. Whatever happened, whatever steps if any he decided to take next, he would do the *Times* crossword that evening. Or as much of it as he could ever do.

Harry Kemelman

END PLAY

IT WAS FRIDAY, my regular evening for chess with Nicky, a custom begun when I had first joined the Law Faculty at the University and continued even after I had given up teaching to become County Attorney. I had just announced a mate in three more moves to win the rubber game of our usual three-game match.

Nicky's bushy white eyebrows came together as he scrutinized the corner of the board where my attack was focused. Then he nodded briskly in admission of defeat.

"You might have prevented it," I offered, "if you had advanced the pawn."

"I suppose so," he replied, his little blue eyes glittering with amusement, "but it would only have prolonged the game and the position was beginning to bore me."

Nicky, Nicholas Welt, Snowden Professor of English Literature at the University, could be the most exasperating of men. Although only two or three years my senior, he treated me with the condescending tolerance typical of a professor dealing with a Freshman of less than average intelligence. And I—perhaps because his prematurely white hair (my own was only just beginning to gray at the temples) and lined gnome-like face made him seem much older—I suffered it.

I was on the point of retorting that he was most apt to be bored by the position when he was losing, when the doorbell rang and I rose to answer it. It seemed as if I was always being interrupted whenever I had a chance to answer Nicky in kind.

My caller proved to be Colonel Edwards of Army Intelligence who was collaborating with me on the investigation of the death of Professor McNulty. Perhaps it would be fairer to say that we were both investigating the same case rather than that we were collaborating, for there had been an ill-concealed rivalry in our association from the beginning, and we had both gone our separate ways, each working on that phase of the problem that seemed to him most likely to bear fruit. True, we had agreed to meet in my office every morning and discuss our progress, but there was no doubt that each of us was as much concerned with being the first to solve the case as to bring it to successful conclusion. Since I had had a conference with Colonel Edwards that morning and expected to have another the following morning, his appearance now gave me a vague feeling of uneasiness.

He was a young man, little more than thirty, entirely too young in my opinion to sport eagles. He was short and stocky with something like a strut in his walk, not uncommon in men of that build, and not necessarily indicating conceit. He was a decent chap, I suppose, and probably good at his job, but I did not warm to him and had not from the beginning of our association some two days before. In part, this was due to his insistence, when we had first met, that he should have full charge of the investigation inasmuch as Professor McNulty had been engaged in research for the Army; in part, it was due to his insufferable arrogance. Although he was half a head shorter than I, he somehow contrived to look down his pudgy nose at me.

"I saw a light in your study as I was passing," he explained.

I nodded.

"I thought I'd like to go over certain points with you and get the benefit of your experience," he continued.

That was his usual style and it annoyed me because I was never quite sure whether this seeming deference was his idea of politeness or whether it was downright impudence, said with tongue in cheek. In any case, I did not take it at face value.

I nodded again and led him into the study where Nicky was putting the chessmen back in the box. After I had introduced the two men and we were all seated again, Edwards asked, "Have you uncovered anything important since this morning?"

It flitted across my mind that it was customary for the visiting team to go to bat first, but to have said so would have been to bring our antagonism out into the open.

"Well, we caught Trowbridge," I said. "We found him in Boston and brought him back."

"That was quick work," he said patronizingly, "but I'm afraid you're barking up the wrong tree."

I should have answered that with a shrug of the shoulders, but I felt that I had a strong case, so I said quietly, "He quarreled with McNulty some few hours before he was shot. McNulty had flunked him in his Physics course because he had not had his experiments for the semester done in time. He came to see him to explain that he had been handicapped because he had sprained his wrist and so had been unable to write. McNulty was upset and out of sorts that day. Never a very amiable man, he was downright nasty during the interview. I got that from his secretary who was sitting right outside the door of his office and heard most of it. She reported that McNulty had said point-blank that he thought Trowbridge was exaggerating his injury, and even suggested that the young man had managed to get a medical discharge from the Army by the same trick. Parenthetically, I might say, I checked the young man's Army record and found it excellent. He did not get his discharge until after he had been wounded in action twice. Naturally, Trowbridge did not take McNulty's sneer in silence. There was quite a row and the young man was heard by the secretary to say, 'You deserve to be shot.' " I paused impressively.

"Very well," I went on, "we know that Trowbridge took the 8:10 train to Boston. He had to pass McNulty's house on his way to the station and that was no later than 8:05. According to Professor Albrecht, McNulty was shot at a minute or two after eight." I paused again to give added weight to the highly suggestive significance of the time elements. Then I said in quiet triumph, "Under the circumstances, I would say that Trowbridge was a logical suspect." I counted off the points on my fingers. "He quarreled with him and threatened him—that's motive; he had been in the Army and had fought overseas and so was likely to have a German Luger as a war trophy—that's weapon; he was near the house at the time—that's opportunity; and finally, he ran off to Boston—that's indication of guilt."

"But you don't shoot a professor because he flunks you in a course," Edwards objected.

"No, you don't ordinarily," I admitted. "But this is wartime. Values change. Trowbridge had fought overseas. I fancy he saw a lot of killing and came to have a much lower opinion of the sanctity of human life. Besides, flunking this course meant dropping out of college. He claims, as a matter of fact, that he came up to Boston to see about the chances of transferring to one of the colleges there. A nervous, sensitive young man could easily convince himself that his whole future had been ruined."

Edwards nodded slowly as if to grant me the point. "You questioned him?" he asked.

"I did. I didn't get a confession, if that's what you're thinking. But I did get something. Knowing that he must have passed McNulty's house around 8:05, I told him that he had been seen there. It was just a shot in the dark, of course, and yet not too improbable. The Albany train pulls in around then and there are always two or three passengers who get off here. Going towards town, they'd be likely to pass him on his way to the station."

Edwards nodded again.

"It worked," I went on. "He got very red and finally admitted that he had stopped opposite McNulty's house. He said that he stood there for a few minutes debating whether to see him again and try to get him to change his mind. And then he heard the Albany train pulling in and knowing that the Boston train left soon after, he hurried off. I'm holding him as a material witness. I'll question him again tomorrow after he has spent a night in jail. Maybe I'll get some more out of him then."

Colonel Edwards shook his head slowly. "I doubt if you'll get any more out of him," he said. "Trowbridge didn't shoot him. McNulty shot himself. It was suicide."

I looked at him in surprise. "But we discarded the idea of suicide at the very beginning," I pointed out. "Why, it was you yourself who—"

"I was mistaken," he said coldly, annoyed that I should have mentioned it.

"But our original objections hold good," I pointed out. "Someone rang the doorbell and McNulty went to answer it. Professor Albrecht testified to that."

"Ah, but he didn't. We *thought* he did. What Albrecht actually said was that McNulty excused himself in the middle of their chess game with some remark about there being someone at the door. Here, let's go over the whole business and you'll see how we made our mistake. Professor Albrecht's story was that he was playing chess with McNulty. I take it that's a common thing with them."

"That's right," I said, "they play every Wednesday night, just as Nicky and I do every Friday evening. They dine together at the University Club and then go on to McNulty's place."

"Well, they didn't this Wednesday," said Edwards. "Albrecht was detained by some work in the lab and went on out to McNulty's house afterwards. In any case, they were playing chess. You recall the arrangement of furniture in McNulty's study? Here, let me show you." He opened the briefcase he had brought with him and drew out a photograph of the study. It showed a book-lined room with an opening in the form of an arch leading to a corridor. The chess table had been set up near the middle of the room, just to the right of the arch. The photograph had evidently been taken from just below the chess table so that it clearly showed the chess game in progress, the captured men, black and white, lying intermixed on one side of the board.

He pointed to a chair that was drawn up to the chess table.

"This is where Albrecht was sitting," Edwards explained, "facing the arch which is the entrance from the corridor. The vestibule and the front door beyond is down the corridor to the left—that is, Albrecht's left from where he was sitting.

"Now, his story was that in the middle of the game McNulty went to answer the door. Albrecht heard what he later decided was a pistol shot, but which at the time he thought was a car backfiring outside. That's reasonable because the evidence shows that the gun was pressed tightly against McNulty's body. That would muffle the sound, like firing into a pillow. In any case, Albrecht waited a couple of minutes and then called out. Receiving no answer, he went out to investigate and found his friend lying on the floor of the vestibule, shot through the heart, the still warm gun in his hand." He addressed himself to me. "Is that the way Albrecht told it? Did I leave out anything?"

I shook my head, wondering what was coming.

He smiled with great satisfaction. "Naturally, on the basis of that story we immediately ruled out suicide. We assumed that the man who rang the doorbell had shot him, and then thinking that McNulty was alone, had put the gun in his hand to make it look like suicide. If the doorbell rang, it had to be murder and could not be suicide. That's logical," he insisted firmly as though still annoyed that I had attributed the discarding of the suicide theory to him. "Even if the man who rang the doorbell had been a total stranger inquiring the way to the railroad station, say, it still could not have been suicide because it would have happened almost before the stranger could shut the door behind him and he would immediately have opened it again to see what the trouble was. It would have meant that McNulty had a loaded gun in his pocket all the time that he was playing chess with Albrecht. It would have meant—"

"All right," I interrupted, "the suicide theory was untenable. What made you change your mind?"

He showed some annoyance at my interruption, but suppressed it immediately. "The doorbell," he said solemnly. "There was something about Albrecht's story that didn't quite click. I took him over it several times. And then it came to me that at no time did he say that he had *heard* the doorbell—only that McNulty had excused himself with some remark about someone at the door. When I asked him point-blank if he had heard the bell, he became confused and finally admitted that he hadn't. He tried to explain it by saying that he was absorbed in the game, but it's a loud bell and if it had rung, I was sure he would have heard it. And since he didn't hear it, that meant it hadn't rung." He shrugged his shoulders. "Of course, if there were no third person at the door, the suicide theory had to be considered again."

He broke off suddenly. He blushed a little. "You know," he said in great earnestness. "I haven't been completely frank with you. I'm afraid I misled you into thinking that I came down here solely to investigate McNulty's death. The fact of the matter is that I arrived in the morning and made an appointment by phone to meet him at his home at half-past eight that night. You see, the research project on which McNulty and Albrecht have been working hasn't been going too well. There were strange mishaps occurring all too frequently. Delicate apparatus that had taken weeks and months to replace was damaged. Reports that had been late coming in and frequently contained errors. Army Ordinance which was sponsoring the project asked us to check on the work and I was sent down to make the preliminary investigation.

"Having in mind now the possibility of suicide, I asked Albrecht about sabotage on the project. That broke it. He admitted that he had been suspicious of McNulty for some time and had conducted a little investigation of his own. Though he was certain that McNulty was guilty, he had hesitated to accuse him openly. But he had hinted. All through the game he had hinted that he knew what McNulty had been up to. I gathered that he couched his hints in the terms of the game. I don't play chess, but I imagine that he said something like, 'You will be in great danger if you continue on this line'—that kind of thing. After a while, McNulty got the idea and became very upset. Albrecht said he murmured over and over again, 'What shall I do?' Then Albrecht made a move and said, 'Resign!'—which I understand is the regular chess term for 'give up'." Edwards spread his hands as though presenting us with the case all nicely gift-wrapped. "It was then that McNulty muttered something about there being someone at the door and got up from the table."

"Albrecht saw him shoot himself?" I demanded.

"All but. He saw McNulty go through the arch. Instead of going to the left to the vestibule, he went to the right, and that's where his bedroom is. I submit that he went to get his gun. Then he came back and walked past the arch to the vestibule."

"Why didn't he wait until after Albrecht left?" I asked.

"I suppose because he knew that I would be along presently."

There was little doubt in my mind that Edwards had arrived at the correct solution. But I hated to admit it. It was no longer a question of beating Edwards to the finish. I was thinking of McNulty now. He was not a friend, but I had played chess with him at the University Club a number of times. I had not cared too much for the man, but I did not like to think of him taking his own life, especially since it implied that he had been guilty of treason. I suppose my uneasiness and my doubts were patent in the very vehemence with which I tried to conceal them. "And that's your case?" I demanded scornfully. "Why a Freshman Law student could pick it to pieces! It's as full of holes as a sieve."

He reddened, a little taken aback at the belligerence in my tone.

"Such as?" he asked.

"Such as the gun? Have you traced it to him? Such as why did Albrecht lie in the first place? Such as the choice of the vestibule? Why should a man with a house full of rooms choose to shoot himself in the vestibule?"

"Albrecht lied because McNulty was his friend," Edwards replied. "He could no longer affect the research project—why should he make him out a suicide and a traitor if he could avoid it? Besides, I guess he felt a little guilty about McNulty's taking his own life. Remember? He called on him to resign. I imagine he must have been pretty upset to find that his friend took his advice so thoroughly."

"And the gun?"

Edwards shrugged his shoulders. "You yourself pointed out that the gun was a war trophy. The country is flooded with them and very few of them have been registered. A former student might have given it to him. As a matter of fact, Albrecht admitted that McNulty had mentioned something of the sort some months back. No, the gun didn't bother me. I found the business of the vestibule a lot harder to understand—until I made a thorough check of the house. It appears that since the death of his wife some years ago, McNulty has practically closed up all the upper part of the house and part of the lower. So although there are six rooms in the house, he actually occupies what amounts to a small apartment on the first floor consisting of the study which was formerly the dining room, a bedroom, and the kitchen. He couldn't shoot himself in the study since Albrecht was there and would stop him. The kitchen leads off the study and I suppose he would not want to pass Albrecht if he could help it. That leaves only the bedroom, which I would consider the most likely place were it not for one thing: there's a large portrait of his wife hanging there. It was taken full view so that the eyes seem to follow you no matter from what angle you look at it. It occurred to me that it was that which deterred him. He wouldn't want to shoot himself under the very eyes of his wife, as it were. That's only a guess, of course," he added with something of a smirk which implied that in his opinion it was a pretty good guess.

"It's a theory," I admitted grudgingly, "but it's no more than that. You have no proof."

"As a matter of fact," he said slowly, a malicious little smile playing about the corners of his mouth, "I have proof—absolute proof. We're pretty thorough in the Army and some of us have had quite a bit of experience. You see, I did a paraffin test on McNulty—and it was positive."

I should have known that he had an ace up his sleeve. This time I made no effort to conceal my disappointment. My shoulders drooped and I nodded slowly.

"What's a paraffin test?" asked Nicky, speaking for the first time.

"It's quite conclusive, Nicky," I said. "I'm not sure that I know the chemistry of it exactly, but it's scientifically correct. You see, every gun no matter how well fitted has a certain amount of backfire. Some of the gunpowder flashes back and is embedded in the hand of the man that fires. They coat his hand with hot paraffin and then draw it off like a glove. They then test it for gunpowder—for nitrates, that is—and if it's positive, it means that the man fired the gun. I'm afraid that winds it up for McNulty."

"So the oracle of the test tube has spoken?" Nicky murmured ironically.

"It's conclusive evidence, Nicky," I said.

"Evidence, eh? I was wondering when you would begin to examine the evidence," he remarked.

Edwards and I both looked at him, puzzled.

"What evidence have I neglected?" asked Edwards superciliously.

"Look at the photograph of the room," Nicky replied. "Look at that chess game."

I studied the photograph while Edwards watched uncertainly. It was not easy to see the position of the pieces because the ones nearest the camera were naturally greatly foreshortened. But after a moment I got the glimmering of an idea.

"Let's see what it looks like set up," I said, as I dumped the chessmen out of the box onto the table and then proceeded to select the necessary pieces to copy the position indicated in the photograph.

Nicky watched, a sardonic smile on his lips, amused at my inability to read the position directly from the photograph. Edwards looked uneasily from one to the other of us, half expecting to find the name of the murderer spelled out on the board.

"If there is some sort of clue in those chessman," he essayed, "in the way they're set up, I mean, we can always check the position against the original. Nothing was moved and the house is sealed."

I nodded impatiently as I studied the board. The pattern of the pieces was beginning to take on a meaning in my mind. Then I had it.

"Why, he was playing the Logan-Asquith gambit," I exclaimed. "And playing it extremely well."

"Never heard of it," said Nicky.

"Neither did I until McNulty showed it to me about a week ago at the University Club. He had come across it in Lowenstein's *End Games*. It's almost never used because it's such a risky opening. But it's interesting because of the way the position of the bishops is developed. Were you thinking, Nicky, that a man who was upset and about to shoot himself would not be playing so difficult a game, nor playing it so well?"

"As a matter of fact, I was thinking not of the position of the pieces on the board," said Nicky mildly, "but of those *off the board*—the captured men."

"What about them?" I demanded.

"They're all together on one side of the board, black and white."

"Well?"

Nicky's face was resigned, not to say martyred, and his tone was weary as he strove to explain what he thought should have been obvious.

"You play chess the way you write, or handle a tennis racket. If you're right-handed, you move your pieces with your right hand, and you take off your opponent's pieces with your right hand, and you deposit them on the table to your right. When two right-handed players like McNulty and Albrecht are engaged, the game ends with the black pieces that White has captured at his right and diagonally across the board are the white pieces that Black has captured."

There flashed through my mind the image of Trowbridge as I had seen him that afternoon, awkwardly trying to light a cigarette with his left hand because his right arm hung in a black silk sling.

"When a left-handed player opposes a right-handed player," Nicky went on, almost as though he had read my mind, "the captured men are on the same side of the board—but, of course, they're separated, the black chessmen near white and the white chessmen near Black. They wouldn't be jumbled together the way they are in the photograph unless—"

I glanced down at the board which I had just set up.

Nicky nodded as he would to a stupid pupil who had managed to stumble onto the right answer. "That's right—not unless you've dumped them out of the box and then set up only the men you need in accordance with the diagram of an end game."

"Do you mean that instead of playing a regular game, McNulty was demonstrating some special kind of opening?" asked Edwards. He struggled with the idea, his eyes abstracted as he tried to fit it into the rest of the picture. Then he shook his head. "It doesn't make sense," he declared. "What would be the point of Albrecht's saying that they were playing a game?"

"Try it with Albrecht," Nicky suggested. "Suppose it was Albrecht who set up the board?"

"Same objection," said Edwards. "What would be the point of lying about it?"

"No point," Nicky admitted, "if he set it up before McNulty was shot. But suppose Albrecht set up the game *after* McNulty was shot."

"Why would he do that?" demanded Edwards, his belligerence growing with his bewilderment.

Nicky gazed dreamily at the ceiling. "Because a game of chess partly played suggests first, that the player has been there for some time, at least since the beginning of the game, and second, that he was there on friendly terms. It is hardly necessary to add that if a deliberate attempt is made to suggest both ideas, the chances are that neither is actually true."

"You mean—"

"I mean," said Nicky, "that Professor Luther Albrecht rang McNulty's doorbell at approximately eight o'clock and when McNulty opened the door for him, he pressed a gun against his breast and pulled the trigger, after which he put the gun in the dead man's hand and then stepped over his fallen body and coolly set up the ever-present chessmen in accordance with the diagram of an end game from one of McNulty's many books on chess. That's why the game was so well played. It had been worked out by an expert, by Lowenstein probably in the book you mentioned."

We both, the Colonel and I, sat back and just stared at Nicky. Edwards was the first to recover.

"But why should Albrecht shoot him? He was his best friend."

Nicky's little blue eyes glittered with amusement. "I suspect that you're to blame for that, Colonel. You called in the morning and made an appointment for that evening. I fancy that was what upset McNulty so. I doubt if he was directly to blame for the difficulties encountered on the project, but as head of the project he was responsible. I fancy that he told his good friend and colleague, Albrecht, about your call. And Albrecht knew that an investigation by an outsider meant certain discovery—unless he could provide a scapegoat, or what's the slang expression?—a fall guy, that's it, a fall guy."

I glanced at Edwards and saw that he was pouting like a small boy with a broken balloon. Suddenly he remembered something. His eyes lit up and his lips parted in a smile that was almost a sneer.

"It's all very pretty," he said, "but it's a lot of hogwash just the same. You've forgotten that I have proof that it was suicide. The paraffin test proved that McNulty had fired the gun."

Nicky smiled. "It's your test that is hogwash, Colonel. In this case it proves nothing."

"No, really," I intervened. "The test is perfectly correct."

"The test proves only that McNulty's hand was behind the gun," said Nicky sharply.

"Well?"

"Suppose someone rang your doorbell," Nicky addressed me, the same martyred look in his face, "as the Colonel did this evening, and when you opened the door, he thrust a gun against your breast. What would you do?"

"Why, I—I'd grab his hand, I suppose."

"Precisely, and if he fired at that instant, there would be nitrates backfired into your hand as well as into his."

The Colonel sat bolt upright. Then he jumped up and grabbed his briefcase and made for the door.

"You can't wash that stuff off too easily," he said over his shoulder. "And it's even harder to get it off your clothes. I'm going to get hold of Albrecht and do a paraffin on him."

When I returned to the study from seeing the Colonel to the door, Nicky said, "There was really no need for our young friend's haste. I could have offered him other proof—the chessmen. I have no doubt that the last fingerprint made on each chessman, black as well as white, will be found to be Albrecht's. And that would be a hard thing for him to explain if he persists in his story that it was just an ordinary game of chess."

"Say, that's right, Nicky. I'll spring that one on Edwards in the morning." I hesitated, then I took the plunge. "Wasn't Albrecht taking an awful chance though? Wouldn't it have been better if he had just walked away after shooting McNulty instead of staying on and calling the police and making up that story and—"

Nicky showed his exasperation. "Don't you see it? He couldn't walk off. The poor devil was stuck there. He had got McNulty's lifeless hand nicely fitted onto the gun. He was ready to leave. Naturally, he looked through the door window up and down the street, normally deserted at that hour, to make sure the coast was clear. And he saw Trowbridge trudging along. He waited a minute or two for him to pass and then looked out again only to find that the young man had stopped directly across the street and gave no indication of moving on. And in a minute or two the passengers from the Albany train would be along. And after that, perhaps our friend the Colonel, early for his appointment."

"So my investigation of Trowbridge wasn't entirely fruitless, eh?" I exclaimed, rubbing my hands together gleefully. "At least, that puts me one up on the Colonel."

Nicky nodded. "A brash young man, that. What branch of the service did he say he was connected with?"

"Intelligence."

"Indeed!" Nicky pursed his lips and then relaxed them in a frosty little smile. "I was infantry, myself, in the last war."

Lawrence Block

GENTLEMEN'S AGREEMENT

THE BURGLAR, a slender and clean-cut chap just past 30, was rifling a drawer in the bedside table when Archer Trebizond slipped into the bedroom. Trebizond's approach was as catfooted as if he himself were the burglar, a situation which was manifestly not the case. The burglar never did hear Trebizond, absorbed as he was in his perusal of the drawer's contents, and at length he sensed the other man's presence as a jungle beast senses the presence of a predator.

The analogy, let it be said, is scarcely accidental.

When the burglar turned his eyes on Archer Trebizond his heart fluttered and fluttered again, first at the mere fact of discovery, then at his own discovery of the gleaming revolver in Trebizond's hand. The revolver was pointed in his direction, and this the burglar found upsetting.

"Darn it all," said the burglar, approximately, "I could have sworn there was nobody home. I phoned, I rang the bell—"

"I just got here," Trebizond said.

"Just my luck. The whole week's been like that. I dented a fender on Tuesday afternoon, overturned my fish tank the night before last. An unbelievable mess all over the carpet, and I lost a mated pair of African mouthbreeders so rare they don't have a Latin name yet. I'd hate to tell you what I paid for them."

"Hard luck," Trebizond said.

"And just yesterday I was putting away a plate of fettucine and I bit the inside of my mouth. You ever done that? It's murder, and the worst part is you feel so stupid about it. And then you keep biting it over and over again because it sticks out while it's healing. At least I

144

do." The burglar gulped a breath and ran a moist hand over a moister forehead. "And now this," he said.

"This could turn out to be worse than fenders and fish tanks," Trebizond said.

"Don't I know it. You know what I should have done? I should have spent the entire week in bed. I happen to know a safecracker who consults an astrologer before each and every job he pulls. If Jupiter's in the wrong place or Mars is squared with Uranus or something he won't go in. It sounds ridiculous, doesn't it? And yet it's eight years now since anybody put a handcuff on that man. Now who do you know who's gone eight years without getting arrested?"

"I've never been arrested," Trebizond said.

"Well, you're not a crook."

"I'm a businessman."

The burglar thought of something but let it pass. "I'm going to get the name of his astrologer," he said. "That's just what I'm going to do. Just as soon as I get out of here."

"If you get out of here," Trebizond said. "Alive," Trebizond said.

The burglar's jaw trembled just the slightest bit. Trebizond smiled, and from the burglar's point of view Trebizond's smile seemed to enlarge the black hole in the muzzle of the revolver.

"I wish you'd point that thing somewhere else," he said nervously.

"There's nothing else I want to shoot."

"You don't want to shoot me."

"Oh?"

"You don't even want to call the cops," the burglar went on. "It's really not necessary. I'm sure we can work things out between us, two civilized men coming to a civilized agreement. I've some money on me. I'm an openhanded sort and would be pleased to make a small contribution to your favorite charity, whatever it might be. We don't need policemen to intrude into the private affairs of gentlemen."

The burglar studied Trebizond carefully. This little speech had always gone over rather well in the past, especially with men of substance. It was hard to tell how it was going over now, or if it was going over at all. "In any event," he ended somewhat lamely, "you certainly don't want to shoot me."

"Why not?"

"Oh, blood on the carpet, for a starter. Messy, wouldn't you say? Your wife would be upset. Just ask her and she'll tell you shooting me would be a ghastly idea."

"She's not at home. She'll be out for the next hour or so."

"All the same, you might consider her point of view. And shooting me would be illegal, you know. Not to mention immoral."

"Not illegal," Trebizond remarked.

"I beg your pardon?"

"You're a burglar," Trebizond reminded him. "An unlawful intruder on my property. You have broken and entered. You have invaded the sanctity of my home. I can shoot you where you stand and not get so much as a parking ticket for my trouble."

"Of course, you can shoot me in self-defense—"

"Are we on *Candid Camera*?"

"No, but—"

"Is Allen Funt lurking in the shadows?"

"No, but—"

"In your back pocket. That metal thing. What is it?"

"Just a pry bar."

"Take it out," Trebizond said. "Hand it over. Indeed. A weapon if I ever saw one. I'd state that you attacked me with it and I fired in self-defense. It would be my word against yours, and yours would remain unvoiced since you would be dead. Whom do you suppose the police would believe?"

The burglar said nothing. Trebizond smiled a satisfied smile and put the pry bar in his own pocket. It was a piece of nicely shaped steel and it had a nice heft to it. Trebizond rather liked it.

"Why would you want to kill me?"

"Perhaps I've never killed anyone. Perhaps I'd like to satisfy my curiosity. Or perhaps I got to enjoy killing in the war and have been yearning for another crack at it. There are endless possibilities."

"But—"

"The point is," said Trebizond, "you might be useful to me in that manner. As it is, you're not useful to me at all. And stop hinting about my favorite charity or other euphemisms. I don't want your money. Look about you. I've ample money of my own—that should be obvious. If I were a poor man you wouldn't have breached my threshold. How much money are you talking about, anyway? A couple of hundred dollars?"

"Five hundred," the burglar said.

"A pittance."

"I suppose. There's more at home but you'd just call that a pittance too, wouldn't you?"

"Undoubtedly." Trebizond shifted the gun to his other hand. "I told you I was a businessman," he said. "Now if there were any way in which you could be more useful to me alive than dead—"

"You're a businessman and I'm a burglar," the burglar said, brightening.

"Indeed."

"So I could steal something for you. A painting? A competitor's trade secrets? I'm really very good at what I do, as a matter of fact, although you wouldn't guess it by my performance tonight. I'm not saying I could whisk the Mona Lisa out of the Louvre, but I'm pretty good at your basic hole-and-corner job of everyday burglary. Just give me an assignment and let me show my stuff."

"Hmmmm," said Archer Trebizond.

"Name it and I'll swipe it."

"Hmmmm."

"A car, a mink coat, a diamond bracelet, a Persian carpet, a first edition, bearer bonds, incriminating evidence, eighteen and a half minutes of tape—"

"What was that last?"

"Just my little joke," said the burglar. "A coin collection, a stamp collection, psychiatric records, phonograph records, police records—"

"I get the point."

"I tend to prattle when I'm nervous."

"I've noticed."

"If you could point that thing elsewhere—"

Trebizond looked down at the gun in his hand. The gun continued to point at the burglar.

"No," Trebizond said, with evident sadness. "No, I'm afraid it won't work."

"Why not?"

"In the first place, there's nothing I really need or want. Could you steal me a woman's heart? Hardly. And more to the point, how could I trust you?"

"You could trust me," the burglar said. "You have my word on that."

"My point exactly. I'd have to take your word that your word is good, and where does that lead us? Up the proverbial garden path, I'm afraid. No, once I let you out from under my roof I've lost my advantage. Even if I have a gun trained on you, once you're in the open I can't shoot you with impunity. So I'm afraid—"

"No!"

Trebizond shrugged. "Well, really," he said. "What use are you? What are you good for besides being killed? Can you do anything besides steal, sir?"

"I can make license plates."

"Hardly a valuable talent."

"I know," said the burglar sadly. "I've often wondered why the state bothered to teach me such a pointless trade. There's not even much call for counterfeit license plates, and they've got a monopoly on making the legitimate ones. What else can I do? I must be able to do something. I could shine your shoes, I could polish your car—"

"What do you do when you're not stealing?"

"Hang around," said the burglar. "Go out with ladies. Feed my fish, when they're not all over my rug. Drive my car when I'm not mangling its fenders. Play a few games of chess, drink a can or two of beer, make myself a sandwich—"

"Are you any good?"

"At making sandwiches?"

"At chess."

"I'm not bad."

"I'm serious about this."

"I believe you are," the burglar said. "I'm not your average wood-pusher, if that's what you want to know. I know the openings and I have a good sense of space. I don't have the patience for tournament play, but at the chess club downtown I win more games than I lose."

"You play at the club downtown?"

"Of course. I can't burgle seven nights a week, you know. Who could stand the pressure?"

"Then you *can* be of use to me," Trebizond said.

"You want to learn the game?"

"I know the game. I want you to play chess with me for an hour until my wife gets home. I'm bored, there's nothing in the house to read, I've never cared much for television, and it's hard for me to find an interesting opponent at the chess table."

"So you'll spare my life in order to play chess with me."

"That's right."

"Let me get this straight," the burglar said. "There's no catch to this, is there? I don't get shot if I lose the game or anything tricky like that, I hope."

"Certainly not. Chess is a game that ought to be above gimmickry."

"I couldn't agree more," said the burglar. He sighed a long sigh.

"If I didn't play chess," he said, "you wouldn't have shot me, would you?"

"It's a question that occupies the mind, isn't it?"

"It is," said the burglar.

THEY PLAYED IN THE FRONT ROOM. The burglar drew the white pieces in the first game, opened king's pawn, and played what turned out to be a reasonably imaginative version of the Ruy Lopez. At the sixteenth move Trebizond forced the exchange of knight for rook, and not too long afterward the burglar resigned.

In the second game the burglar played the black pieces and offered the Sicilian defense. He played a variation that Trebizond wasn't familiar with. The game stayed remarkably even until in the end game the burglar succeeded in developing a passed pawn. When it was clear that he would be able to queen it, Trebizond tipped over his king, resigning.

"Nice game," the burglar offered.

"You play well."

"Thank you."

"Seem's a pity that—"

His voice trailed off. The burglar shot him an inquiring look. "That I'm wasting myself as a common criminal? Is that what you were going to say?"

"Let it go," Trebizond said. "It doesn't matter."

They began setting up the pieces for the third game when a key slipped into a lock. The lock turned, the door opened, and Melissa Trebizond stepped into the foyer and through it to the living room.

Both men got to their feet. Mrs. Trebizond advanced, a vacant smile on her pretty face. "You found a new friend to play chess with. I'm happy for you."

Trebizond set his jaw. From his back pocket he drew the burglar's pry bar. It had an even nicer heft than he had thought. "Melissa," he said. "I've no need to waste time with a recital of your sins. No doubt you know precisely why you deserve this."

She stared at him, obviously not having understood a word he had said to her, whereupon Archer Trebizond brought the pry bar down on the top of her skull. The first blow sent her to her knees. Quickly he struck her three more times, wielding the metal bar with all his strength, then turned to look into the wide eyes of the burglar.

"You've killed her," the burglar said.

"Nonsense," said Trebizond, taking the bright revolver from his pocket once again.

"Isn't she dead?"

"I hope and pray she is," Trebizond said, "but I haven't killed her. *You've* killed her."

"I don't understand."

"The police will understand," Trebizond said, and shot the burglar in the shoulder. Then he fired again, more satisfactorily this time, and the burglar sank to the floor with a hole in his heart.

Trebizond scooped the chess pieces into their box, swept up the board, and set about the business of arranging things. He suppressed an urge to whistle. He was, he decided, quite pleased with himself. Nothing was ever entirely useless, not to a man of resources. If fate sent you a lemon you made lemonade.

David Kaufman

MR. HANCOCK'S
LAST GAME

IT WAS VOLTAIRE, I think, who contended that, as with all truly useless endeavors, there are men who would die for chess. Or Hugo. I have tried and cannot find such an implication in either man's work. No real matter, for it is true—men *have* died for chess. The historian can cite examples, and I myself know of one man who died for the game. For, or perhaps *because* of it.

It happened just before we moved away from Garlock's Bend. The fellow's name was Batchelder Hancock, an odd, odd, hairy little man with a pug nose, a small mustache, and a protruding belly. He was a quite close friend of my father. They often played together in the sunroom with the wicker chairs and the fish tanks when I was a child.

We lived then in the Trostle house on the high edge of the valley, and the long, marvelous sun porch of that house overlooked the lake and the whole of Garlock's Bend. In miniature so far below us, it was a pretty sight indeed. The wonderful memories I have of that house and that view and that sun porch! After all this time they are still precious to me. They help me in some measure to forget the awesome loathing I feel to this day when I think of Mr. Hancock.

At once it both thrilled and frightened me, sitting quietly to the left of my father—my designated spot—to watch the two men wait for what seemed to me hours between moves.

Each had an entirely different approach to the game. My father was a man of many interests. Chess was no more to him than one of many hobbies, and he could play or not with no bother. But Mr. Hancock was a quite different man, a man who seemed almost literally to live for chess. He constantly carried the pocket set and the texts which so quickly mark, the real addict. He recited to my father the results of Berlin, Hastings—*all* the famous tournaments, could play the great games by heart, and my father had said that he knew as much chess lore as any living man.

It is true, however, that not all chess addicts are fine players. When Mr. Hancock played with my father, at least, he won few games, for my father was a player of excellent strength, but the odd little man played with a zeal that even I as a youngster realized was quite remarkable. It was possible even for me, little though I then knew, to tell the course a particular game was taking—just by watching the color of his face: white losing, red winning. The redder his face became, the closer he was to victory. As the end approached of a game he was winning, he would shout clippingly, "Check. Check! *Check! CHECK AND MATE, SIR!*" in a louder and louder voice. A terrible, snarling demon to one my age. At the finish of one of these infrequent wins he would expel much pent-up air, his face all the while cooling to normal coloring, his features appearing much relieved. He would then giggle gleefully. My father would smile patiently and tell me to stop banging my shoes on the rung of my chair.

As I have noted, Mr. Hancock's wins were few in number, for my father was a very strong player. The vehemence of his outbursts as he approached one of these wins made the little man seem all the more frightening to me. His shouting sent shudders up and down my back, and I can even yet see his wild-eyed stare as I huddled as close to my father as he would allow. Yet, with all the distastefulness of Mr. Hancock, I could not bring myself to leave the sun room when he was there because I found him strangely fascinating.

I was very pleased that my father almost continually won against him. I knew only vaguely *what* he won, for I had only the simplest notion of the principles of the game, but I remember that each time Mr. Hancock lost it made him very angry and upset. Because I did not like him, it pleased me to see him lose.

Things went on the same way for quite a period—my father victorious in all but a few games, these few seeming to make Mr. Hancock thirst for more wins. He would give almost anything, he said, almost anything to be able to win consistently. My father said something about not attaching too much importance to a game which was, after all, only a game, but Mr. Hancock seemed inordinately serious.

Then one day, after having been beaten by my father in at least twenty straight games, Mr. Hancock disappeared. We did not see him or hear a word from him for about three months. For the whole of that last summer. My father, a very tolerant and understanding man, and generally imperturbable, grew quite excited as the days of Mr. Hancock's disappearance increased in number. He checked the mailbox constantly for a letter from him, began to sit nervously at the bay window of our front room, and soon literally lived waiting for some word from the missing chess player. I did not understand, of course, but he would not discuss the matter with anyone. He locked himself in the sunroom for hours at a time, reading one of the ugly-looking books that Mr. Hancock had lent him just before the disappearance. It was a very large book and it had a powdery black leather cover and yellowed pages. I had seen them sitting over those books, and although I was not allowed to be near and thus could not tell what they were talking about, I had heard them quarrel harshly over that one black book.

When Mrs. Berger, our housekeeper, saw fit to question my father about Mr. Hancock, of whom she seemed quite fond, he sent her from the room in a huff and a puff. He was very abrupt with her. She fretted for days, often muttering things to herself.

By inclination my father and I slept in the same room of that immense house—or rather *I* slept, for he tossed fitfully most nights after Mr. Hancock disappeared. His dreams must have been very troublesome, for he often moaned strange phrases in his sleep. I can yet remember some. "Eldritch mass . . ." he said several times, and ". . . loathsome walls . . ." and ". . . in the water. . . ."

These phrases meant nothing to me, I confess, and I remembered them only because of the upset state of my father and because several of them were new words for me, rather than for any meaning they might convey.

One day I opened the back door intending to play in the yard— and there he was, his fist raised, ready to knock. I jumped back, startled, then turned and ran for my father. "Daddy! Daddy! Daddy, he's back!" I shouted, glad to give my father the news he seemed so anxious to hear. I had expected him to be relieved at hearing of Mr. Hancock's return; he looked, however, completely shaken, looked as if he were going to faint. I had never seen him like that before, and I burst into tears. Remarkably, almost immediately he seemed to control and compose himself; he stopped my crying, took my hand, and we both went to the back door where I had left the fat and terrible Mr. Batchelder Hancock.

My father did not shake Mr. Hancock's extended hand, but said, "So you have come back." I huddled close to him. "You shou . . ."

"I did it!" Mr. Hancock shouted. "I did it! And I am ready for chess." He hurried off his heavy black overcoat, looked at my father, then down at me. "A game of chess, sir. If you please." He seemed quite excited.

"Some tea first," insisted my father, "and an explan . . ."

"First a game of chess," Mr. Hancock grunted firmly. "I will play chess." He would have it no other way.

My father shrugged as he directed me to bring out the board and pieces. Mr. Hancock almost seemed beside himself in anticipation. They sat at the board, and I took my customary place by their side. Mr. Hancock announced loudly, "I shall take the black pieces." My father protested that they should choose sides by chance, but Mr. Hancock was quite insistent on giving my father the advantage of taking the black pieces for himself.

Relenting, my father moved. He moved, but not carelessly as he had before. He moved with hesitation, with apprehension, staring at the hunched-over form opposite him.

Mr. Hancock moved.

My father moved again.

Mr. Hancock moved.

At Black's thirteenth move Mr. Hancock gave up a knight. At his seventeenth he lost a bishop. I knew enough about chess to realize that my father must be ahead. He had two of Mr. Hancock's pieces. But it was my father who now struggled at the board, who got red in the face and gesticulated. Mr. Hancock, smiling at me in a very casual way, absently moved a pawn and said, "And how is school, little sir?"

I did not answer, but stared at my father who now sat stonily, his brow wet, his breath heavy. He moved after ten minutes of intense thought.

"Knight on bishop four to knight six, check," said Mr. Hancock quickly and confidently, moving the piece as he spoke. He made the move even before my father had taken his fingers from his moved piece.

Five long and painful minutes passed before my father moved his king out of check. "Check again," Mr. Hancock grunted, moving a pawn forward immediately. My father's king had one square. He moved. "Check!" announced the fat little man.

My father again found a square for his king.

"Check!" shouted Mr. Hancock, slamming down a rook.

My father lasted three more checks before he was mated in the middle of the board. It was an ignominious experience for a player of his strength. Mr. Hancock was indecent enough to laugh loudly at my father, who insisted upon another game. He lost again, this time worse than the first. They played a third and again Mr. Hancock won. At the end of the session my father was so agitated that he could hardly speak. He had suffered Mr. Hancock's terrible laughter as well as his flawless chess, but it somehow seemed not so much the loss or ridicule he minded, not the chess, but some *other* thing. I did not understand, of course, and was extremely frightened.

Mr. Hancock would not stay for tea, a development that somehow seemed to relieve my father, for he showed the victorious man to the door, closed it, and immediately went to the sunroom and sat at the board. He sat for some time. Then he moved the pieces over the squares, touching each of them idly. "I knew it," he said at length. "I knew it."

Thinking he wanted me to respond in some way, I asked, "Knew what, Daddy?"

He said nothing, but flicked me out of the sunroom with a petulant motion of his hand. Through the French doors I watched him sit for hours, moving the pieces over the board; not playing over a game, for he never started the pieces. He just moved them, sometimes quickly and sometimes slowly, but always with what seemed to be extreme agitation.

Mr. Hancock came to our house very often after that. Each time it was the same. He never lost a game, and at the end of each game he was rude, almost contemptuous of my father. I could not understand why it was that my father did not insist he never return. But no such thing. He seemed obsessed with the little chess player, and he waited, frantically it seemed, for him to appear each day. My father was a moderately wealthy man and did not leave home very often, except perhaps on rare occasions to visit Miller's General Store, to pass the time of day and listen to Bill Miller's gossip.

We had spent much time together, my father and I. With the reappearance of Mr. Hancock, however, he had little time for me, as he spent most of his waking hours either with Mr. Hancock, taking the little man's abuses, or alone in the sunroom studying from Mr. Hancock's book, or moving the inevitable chess pieces.

It was about this time, or perhaps just a little before Mr. Hancock's return, that the Garlock's Bend Cemetery burglaries took place. There were six robberies in all, each progressively more mystifying in that state police protection was provided after the third and was increased with each subsequent robbery. At the sixth the place was literally surrounded. Yet no one was ever seen in the cemetery.

This part of my story is a bit hazy, for my interest at the time was centered about Mr. Hancock and his effect upon my father, but I do remember Mrs. Berger, who was something of a gossip, stating something to the effect that down in Garlock's Bend she heard that the cemetery guards were obsessed with the idea that there was something uncanny about the graveyard each time a grave was robbed—something they tried to and could not identify—something oppressive in the air. Just *something*.

It was difficult for me to make anything of it—she always stopped altogether or became very vague when I came into a room where they were talking. And the newspapers (I have since gone back to check) stated only that all possible was being done, that the crimes were heinous, and that investigation had shown in each case that jewelry was stolen. Mrs. Berger's informants had it that something else had been taken, and that the jewelry was but a decoy, or was all that the newspapers felt they could decently reveal. This I have since tried to justify, but cannot.

My father grew more and more agitated during the course of Mr. Hancock's visits. He slept but little, spent much time in the sunroom, had almost no time for me, and several times shouted at Mrs. Berger. When he did sleep, his dreams seemed progressively more troubled. The mysterious phrases became more and more pronounced, and in his sleep I heard him link Mr. Hancock's name with some evil-sounding words which I cannot even now pronounce but which sent shivers through me.

Something was very wrong with my father, and Mr. Hancock seemed to be the cause.

Things got progressively worse. My father became more and more curt to Mrs. Berger and me. Then one afternoon, after hours of isolation, he came quickly from the sunroom and said to us, "I will be out for some time." It was all he said. He left Mrs. Berger and me staring at each other, for it was rare that my father should leave on an afternoon, and unheard of that he should not tell us where he was going.

He came back just as it was becoming dark outside, carrying an armload of books. As he hurried past he said something to the effect that we were forbidden to touch the books for they were quite rare and valuable. He hurried into the sunroom and locked the door. Mrs. Berger, always mundane and practical, called after him. "I've seen about enough of books in this house."

One Sunday, soon after my father had brought home the books, and had spent great lengths of time studying them, it came to a head between the two men. Mr. Hancock, since his return, had won some hundred games. None of the games had even been close. My father was resetting the pieces as he said, "Chess is only a game."

"You cannot beat me," Mr. Hancock said. "No one can. I have not told you yet—I will be champion." It was obvious even to me that he was quite serious. His eyes narrowed, and glancing at me to see how closely I was listening, he leaned toward my father and said, "I have improved each time. I get stronger each time."

"You will be stopped," my father said slowly. "You will be stopped soon. Chess is not everything. It is a game."

"For you," the little man said. "But it is I, not you, who will be champion." He stood up as he said, "You cannot stop me. Not now. No one can stop me. No one."

My father rose also, and the two men faced each other. I huddled close to my father, who, fear and agitation somehow mastered, matched Mr. Hancock in determination. I confess that I was extremely frightened and cannot relate any of the details of the argument which followed. It was all a noisy whirl in my mind. It ended with much anger on both sides, and my father insisting that Mr. Hancock leave the house.

All the rest of that day and evening my father was even more excited than before Mr. Hancock's visit. He seemed not fearful or hysterical but keyed up—alert and charged for action. He was extremely restless, as if desiring time to pass quickly. He spent his time at odd and incidental tasks, largely attending to domestic troubles Mrs. Berger had long before complained about—but which had been forgotten in the light of my father's recent difficulties. Too, I remember his going once or twice to the sunroom and the musty black books. Not, I should say, for study, but rather for a quick glance, as if to solidify some point in his mind.

That night he did not dress for bed, but sat in the bedroom in the large leather Queen Anne that was just opposite our bed. He did not do much but stare at me—or, rather, past me—and once I thought I heard him mumbling. I did not sleep. He thought I did, however, and at length he rose and I felt him standing over me for some minutes. He left, and I had a deep, sickening sensation as I heard the outside door latch click and my father's footsteps scratching down the driveway gravel.

I was quite frightened all night and could not help imagining terrible things that were happening to my father, not to mention the awful things I supposed him to be doing.

It was four or five o'clock, just beginning to dawn, when he returned. He undressed and came to bed, and although he did not sleep for some little time—he just stared at the ceiling—he soon dropped into a deep repose. I assumed my father's calm and slept soundly.

When I dressed and went down to breakfast, my father was talking matter-of-factly to Mrs. Berger. She, as usual, had an excellent breakfast ready, and, relieved from sleep and cheered by my father's good mood, I satisfied an intense and sudden hunger.

My father did not eat much, but seemed, although better and although he talked to us intermittently, somewhat preoccupied. He responded to questions sometimes with an answer and sometimes with a startled glance. I suppose I bothered him too much, for Mrs. Berger's strict looks indicated clearly to me that I had best leave off.

His better mood (for he was not nearly so badly off as he had been) cheered us both. Too, as a small boy I had a small boy's fickle concentration, and my interests quickly returned to my own world. I excused myself and left the table.

In the afternoon of that day all was as it had been before. I was allowed back into the sunroom, and I sat idly playing Carrom while my father sat at the chess board setting the pieces and then making eight or ten moves for both sides. He stopped, reset the men, and played another eight or ten moves—all this over and over. I know now, but did not then, that he was doing what chess players call "studying the openings." He was calm and relaxed, almost casual. I look back now and recognize this attitude as some sort of newly acquired confidence.

I sat on the floor in the middle of that bright sunny room as I played, my legs straddling the Carrom board. Of a sudden I became aware of a presence in the doorway. It was Mr. Hancock. I could not seem to control myself, for the sight of the awful man sent the blood rushing through me, and I crayfished back across the floor until I was between my father's legs.

He looked up and said, "I have been waiting for you."

"Our game," said Mr. Hancock.

"Of course," my father said, resetting the pieces. "We will play only one game today. I shall play the white." Mr. Hancock looked startled, and it seemed as if he were about to say something, but my father insisted. Mr. Hancock tilted his head quizzically and gazed long at my father, but then seemed to recover his confidence and nodded assent.

My father moved.

Mr. Hancock rushed to the board, dropped his coat to the floor, and with pudgy fingers hastily moved his king pawn two squares, opposing my father's moved pawn. My father moved the knight to king bishop three, and again his move was imitated by Mr. Hancock.

"The Petroff," grunted my father, naming the game.

"I love to play it," said Mr. Hancock, smiling as my father captured the pawn.

My father stopped suddenly and looked at me. "I think you had better leave," he said. I could not help being hurt when he said it, for I was certain that everything was about to start over, and I did not want again to see my father so terribly upset. I left and stood behind the closed french doors for some time, watching. My father moved as he had of old, and Mr. Hancock moved quickly also, but both slowed down quite soon and then both moved slowly, my father perhaps a little the slower. I could neither see the game nor hear what they said, so I left after a time. I went down to the riverside to play for a while by the water and then to sit and watch the fishermen, a pastime that had become one of my favorites. But I could not get that terrible game out of my mind.

IT WAS MRS. BERGER, next morning, who discovered it. She was reading the Scranton *Tribune* and said suddenly, "Oh, my God! Mr. Hancock's dead."

My father looked up from his coffee.

"Oh, my sweet Jesus!" she cried, dropping the newspaper. "It happened early this morning. He was hit by an automobile."

My father said nothing, and I just stared at him, feeling, I am ashamed to say, just a little relieved that Mr. Hancock *was* dead. Mrs. Berger was quite shocked, and started to cry. She raved on and on about him—saying that he seemed so gentle, so harmless, so devoted to chess—for quite some time. She gained control of herself somewhat, and then asked the inevitable, "Why did it have to happen to him?"

"I beat him at chess yesterday," said my father quietly.

"What? What has that to do with anything?" she said.

"Nothing," my father said.

THAT IS THE SUBSTANCE of my story. I have chronicled it in as great detail as I honestly might, and I am aware of the weaknesses in its accusations. But there *are* indications, and they are not all in the mind of a romantic rehearsing his youth, either. Empirically, the evidence weighs against Mr. Hancock; taken individually each occurrence might be explained innocently. Consider, for example, the emotional changes my father suffered. These really could have been due to chess losses alone. The books he got may have been innocent of all interest in Mr. Hancock and the grave robberies, and then again they may not. Staunton College, a religious school about a dozen miles down river from Garlock's Bend, where he got the books, had a rare book collection—the Moses W. Kliendorfer Collection of the Occult and Orientalia. These are subjects which, considering everything, do not sound entirely innocent. But I have checked and the books, unfortunately, are gone—like so many important parts to this story.

My father may have left the house that last night for purely harmless reasons. Again, he may have had a significant retaliatory purpose of his own. Something to do with the books, for example.

I can say for a fact that the molesting of the graves stopped completely with the death of Mr. Hancock; *that* much is obtainable from the newspapers. It may have been a coincidence, or (can I really be saying this?) he *may have* robbed the graves. I don't know—he may have stolen some *thing* each time, these used or given in exchange for supernormal chess prowess. What it was which might have been taken is impossible to say. Nothing was ever made public, but *something else* had been removed from the graves, Mrs. Berger had said. On the face of it, this all makes me want to laugh, and yet I am almost too afraid.

Mr. Hancock's death itself may have been completely an accident, or may have been directed, caused by some evil or malignant force— a force disenchanted with him perhaps. Occult theory (I know, I *know,* I am as skeptical as the next man, but nonetheless . . .), occult theory has it that when the earthly ally or representative of evil is rendered impotent (by good or by the instruments of good), the evil thing destroys its representative, and to deflect any investigation, does it in as innocent a manner as possible. An automobile accident, for example.

Mrs. Berger is long dead, and likely could not help in any case. She made some quite pointed statements, as I look back, but I put it rather to the intuitive powers of a phlegmatic nature rather than to any knowledge she might have had.

The books are gone. Both the foul-looking ones of Mr. Hancock and those my father brought home—nowhere to be found. I have tried and can find no trace of either set. I have the uneasy feeling that they *will* one day turn up, but I pray not.

So . . . nothing positive either way. I really don't know. Perhaps Mr. Hancock was nothing more than a harmless chess fanatic. Perhaps not.

The most damning evidence was my father. He had changed somehow, after Mr. Hancock's death. He seemed a bit more aware of his surroundings than the rest of us. And he looked about all the time, this way and that, as if attempting to catch sight of something. He seemed a bit older, a bit more tired, had perhaps, I don't know, perhaps a *deeper* look. He destroyed his chess pieces and all remembrances of the game, and forbade Mrs. Berger and me to ever mention chess.

Years later I broke my promise to him and asked my father why it was that from the time of Mr. Hancock's death he played no more chess. Again the maddening ambiguity as my mind flashed to the terrible event which followed Mr. Hancock's last game.

Innocent and significant, his reply was, "I can't. I dare not lose."

H. R. F. Keating

SCRABBLE BABBLE DABBLE

MILLIE PRESCOTT LIKED TO WIN at Scrabble. Actually she hated the game. But Mike, who was very good at it, insisted on playing every evening they were at home. Even when they were round with people like the Schwartzes or Peter Remington and his sister he would often get up a foursome. So she felt that, as she was being made to play against her real wishes, she should at least be entitled to win.

And she knew a way of doing it. Something that didn't depend on cunning, things like never giving your opponent a chance to get along to a triple-word square. Or, when you were stuck with a hand chock-a-block with vowels, knowing to put a B or a W, if you were lucky enough to have either one, with an E after it alongside two letters in a word already there, so scoring three two-letter words.

Millie's secret was different. It was that you had to be careful always, when you dipped in the bag for new tiles, to put them into your rack from right to left in the exact order you took them out of your hand. If you did that, every time, no matter what, you would win. But you had to be absolutely tough with yourself. Even if, say, two tiles after you had been landed with the Q you found you had a U, you must never place them side by side until every other tile in your pick-up was in place.

If you kept to that for the whole of the game, and didn't once forget, you were bound to win. Or at least she was. It had always worked for her, every time she did it. She didn't know whether it would work for anyone else, and she was not going to try telling anybody, not even Rita Schwartz. Something like that had to be kept totally secret. And it was sensible not to use it every time.

162

So it had not much surprised her, that evening at home that began it all, when, deciding that this time she was darn well going to have a win, as she put her first pick-up into her rack in that right-to-left order they came out as E—C—R—O—V—I—D. Yes, she saw after a second, it was a Scrabble, a terrific beginning with as an extra the double points you got for starting. It just proved how you couldn't go wrong when you decided you were going to use the system.

But DIVORCE, she thought a moment later. It might be a bit tricky putting that out there on the board.

Mike might make some joke. Or no sort of a joke. Or expect her to say something herself. But what? What? She certainly couldn't think of any joke to make. Not about getting a divorce.

Her worst fears proved justified the instant she planked down the final E (just as she realized, too, that she had stupidly failed to put the V on a light blue double-letter score square; Mike never let her move tiles after they had touched the board).

"Divorce," Mike said, not even commenting on the big score she was going to make. "You're not hoping for that, baby?"

He gave a grin that could not help coming over as twisted.

"Here's one husband who isn't going to let all the world know his wife's been bed-hopping."

"I haven't—"

She stopped herself. If there was one thing worse than an evening playing Scrabble, it was an evening rowing about whether or not she and Peter Remington "had something going."

But, luckily, at the last second she was rescued. A sudden gleam flicked into Mike's eyes, and he began snatching tiles from his rack. Down they went one by one under the O she had contrived to leave directly above the red triple-word score square at the foot of the board. V—E—R—D—O—S—E. One Scrabble to set against another, and with the triple's terrific total. Maybe, after all, this was going to be the night her system failed to work.

A wash of misery flooded over her. What a life. Tied to a man she had long ago fallen out of step with. Nothing in her days really to hold her interest, just getting the house and garden the way Mike liked them. Mike and not herself. Plus occasionally going shopping with Rita Schwartz and once a month sitting on the charity committee Peter chaired. Then the evenings. Scrabble, Scrabble, Scrabble. And now, perhaps, not even getting to win tonight.

Dully she looked at the board in front of her. OVERDOSE. How different it all might be if Mike by mistake took an overdose of his damn heart medicine. Or, what about if she gave him one? She wouldn't do it, of course. But there didn't seem to be any other way she could ever get free. She hadn't needed this last blast of his about divorce to know here was one husband who would never consent to a parting of the ways. Never let her be her own woman again. Never.

In black depression she was on the point of putting the tiles she had taken from the bag into her rack from left to right. But she just managed to stop herself. Damn it, at least she would have the satisfaction of winning this game.

So, with care, she put in her seven new tiles.

Q—R—E—R—A

Thank goodness, she had been concentrating enough in the end not to have put the Q at the extreme left of her rack where, when she was not working the system, she always stashed it or the J or the X or the Z until she got a chance to put them on a dark blue square. Or, if she could ever work out how to do it, onto a simple double-letter score light blue square as part of a word that reached to a pink double-word space.

Hastily she put her last two letters in, conscious that Mike was glaring at her in the way he did if she was not playing as quickly as he liked. A U—don't stick it beside the Q—and an M.

Now, hurry, she must find something to put down. In half a minute Mike would start that finger-drumming routine, and every thought would go flying out of her head.

She peered at her rack.

And saw it. Yes. Forget about the Q, even if she had the U, and there was a good word. Using the D of her DIVORCE. And it would give her a double-word score, too.

With nervously fumbling fingers she put down the tiles.

M—U—R. And now that D. And E—R.

Only then did she realize what it was she had said. Or Scrabble had said it for her. Really, it had been the thought that had been in her mind, or half in her mind, after that little spat about DIVORCE. The only alternative, MURDER.

"No S," Mike said, liking as always to comment on her play, though he would jump down her throat if she dared say anything about his. "Pity you don't have an S. It would have got you two doubles. A solid forty points. Or, if you'd had a Q, you could have put that on a triple with QUEER, using the E in my OVERDOSE, and have scored yourself a nice thirty-six, exactly twice what you total now with MURDER."

She fought to keep the blush from rising up. Mike would see it at once and know that she did have the Q and had missed her chance. He could always catch her out like that.

How could she have failed to see it? An opportunity to get rid of her Q straight away, and one scoring all that much more. Now, if she knew anything, she would be stuck with the damn letter for the rest of the night. Or in the end be reduced to sticking it in front of the U of MURDER with just an A after and only score a total of twelve for QUA, one of Mike's favorite clever-clever words, whatever it meant.

But MURDER. The word had seemed to leap out at her in a way she had been unable to resist.

Like the idea.

She thrust the thought away.

And now, it seemed, Mike was in difficulties. He was moving his tiles about on his rack, this way and that, frowning and muttering.

She waited as patiently as she could while he made up his mind. Damn it, he must have at least one letter he could put down some-where. Even if he had got stuck with no vowels, as sometimes hap-pened to her on the nights she had decided not to risk overworking her system, there were opportunities in plenty on the board, BE or HE or WE or ME using the E of her MURDER. Or, better—how was it she never saw things like this when it was her turn?—if he had nothing more than an N he could at least score twice with that by tucking it into the corner of MURDER and DIVORCE, EN—some-thing to do with printing, Mike always said—and IN. There must be other places to go, too, even if he had the most awkward bunch of consonants. But, no, fiddle, fiddle, fiddle. He would go on endlessly, hoping something would appear.

And if she were to drum her fingers, or look at her watch, even accidentally, what a storm of abuse would spew out at her.

At last Mike gave a grunt of disgust and planked down two letters, one on either side of the second O of OVERDOSE.

"LOW," he snapped. "I've reached a low point in my play, all right. Big score of eleven, with those two double-letter squares."

Well, at least he had put something down. And she was not going to point out to him that he was already so far ahead that getting a score of only eleven now was not the end of the world. However much he had been, in fact, angling for open recognition of how well he had begun.

She stared, hardly taking anything in, at the new lot of letters she had drawn. At least she had remembered to put them one by one to the left of her remaining Q and A.

K—E—Y—L—S—Q—A. What on earth could she do with that lot?

God, how she would like to murder Mike with an overdose. But there was no way to do it. Give him enough to put an end to him, and the symptoms would be immediately evident. Dr. Parker had explained all about it, at excessive length, when he had first put Mike on to the stuff.

No, there was no way she could fake things, even though it would be easy enough to dissolve every single one of the tablets in Mike's final whisky of the day. Okay, they were tasteless, as Dr. Parker had pointed out, solemnly warning her of—so far as she could make out—an entirely imaginary danger. But, as he had immediately added, it would require a dose of at least twenty tablets to be fatal. "Two, instead of the prescribed one, will just give him a mildly rough ride." God, how that man talked.

"Are you going to play, or not?"

Mike's voice cut in on her thoughts, and she realized, too, that his fingers had been drumming away hard. And yet—she could swear—she had not kept him waiting even half as long as he had taken over his last turn.

She gave her tiles a desperate look.

And, as if by magic, saw a word she could put down. Pretty clever, and never mind if it turned out not to score all that much.

In front of Mike's LOW that S, and at the other end of it an L and a Y.

SLOWLY.

Slowly. Was that, like the word MURDER, telling her something? She felt somehow it was. Was it a message? From Scrabble to her? A hint of a possible answer to the twanging question that had been in her mind as she had looked sightlessly at the letters on her rack? Would it be possible to murder Mike SLOWLY?

"Score twelve," Mike said, with open triumph, before she had even had time to tot it up herself. "Only one point more than my lulu last go."

Okay, she thought revengefully, but at least it was one point more.

She dug in the bag for her three replacement tiles. Ah, another U. So maybe she would be able to get rid of that damn Q sooner than she had thought. She put it down neatly on the right of the Q.

And at once realized that she had broken the rules of her system.

Damn, damn, damn. No hope of winning now. Not unless Mike happened to get a really lousy hand. As he almost never did.

This stupid game. Why, why, why did she have to play it? Night after night. Oh, what a wonderful world it would be if instead of that fanatic sitting opposite her she shared her life with someone else. Not even necessarily Peter Remington. Anybody. Anybody who didn't play Scrabble.

Well, maybe there was a chance for that. Perhaps Scrabble wouldn't punish her for her mistake this time, if what it had been telling her so far tonight really meant anything. So, right, ask Scrabble what it had meant by SLOWLY. How exactly could she murder Mike with an overdose SLOWLY?

Just think the question. That must be the way. Think it hard. And wait to see what letters came out of the bag. Give him small overdoses, do it slowly . . . But then what? Small overdoses were not going to kill Mike. Just make him have a few of Dr. Parker's "rough rides." She would have to do something a whole lot more effective than that.

Mike had already put down HOMES, tacking the S on to DI-VORCE. Some pretty good score. Well, damn it, let him win. He wouldn't have many more times to. Not if what Scrabble had told her turned out to be any use, and if it would only follow it up.

She forced herself to think her question once more. Hard as she could. Till she felt tiny beads of sweat coming up behind her ears. And then looked again at the letters on her rack.

But no message pulsed out at her, look as she might. All right, she had an I and an E which could let her get that damn Q onto a triple-letter square by putting QUIRE round the R of MURDER. But, relief though that would have been if this was an ordinary game, it was absolutely no use now.

Sadly, she admitted it to herself. By forgetting to keep strictly to her system when she had put that U next to her Q, she must have forfeited any help she had been getting from Scrabble.

But would it come to her aid the next time they played? If she was totally tough in the way she put letters onto her rack?

As the game wore on she hoped so more and more fiercely. Because from that point onwards she had the most diabolical letters. The J and the Z both coming into her hand at once while she still had not got rid of the K—always a difficult letter—which she had picked up before she had put down SLOWLY. And there had never seemed anywhere to get rid of any of them, till right at the end she did at least manage to put the Z on a double-letter square.

Mike won 447 to 308.

Well, here's to the next time, she thought.

IT WAS THREE NIGHTS LATER that the next time, as Millie had thought of it, arrived. They had gone out the two evenings before, first to the Schwartzes, then to the Remingtons. Each time they had played Scrabble. Mike had really insisted, although Rita Schwartz had said quite plainly she wasn't too keen and Peter Remington had obviously, at least in Millie's view, wanted to spend the evening discussing neighborhood problems. But on both occasions, when they had eventually settled round the board, Millie had deliberately not operated her system. She wanted to make sure it would be in working order when she came to play without anyone other than Mike being there to comment on the nature of the words she hoped Scrabble would spell out for her.

So on the third night, at home, she was for once really eager to play. Not that Mike noticed, any more than he had noticed her reluctance in the days when she had still thought it was possible to get him to do something else.

Mike picked an A when they were drawing tiles to see who was to begin. Bad sign. For a few moments Millie thought with spiraling dismay that her system had somehow stopped operating forever. But when she put her first pick-up into her rack, taking, of course, every care to place each new letter to the left of the one before, her spirits began to rise. No obvious word was being spelt out, backwards or forwards, but the batch looked decently hopeful, even if rather lacking in vowels. Still, whatever Mike put down first was bound to supply at least one more of those. H—C—T—P—S (always good to get an S early, to tack on with luck to something high scoring) and then the vowel, an I, and finally a D.

She was about to begin fiddling around to see what word might emerge, something allowable under the system provided all the tiles had first been put in the rack in the correct way, when, noisily clicking, Mike jabbed down his starter. ABACK. Just the sort of damn old-fashioned word he was always so proud of knowing.

"Not bad," he said, actually rubbing his hands together. "See, I get my K on a double, and, with the double score for going first, that's twenty with just that one letter. So, total, thirty-six. Beat that."

Millie felt a sudden tumble of depression. The bastard had made a good start. A very good start. And, when he did, the game was apt to go on the way it had begun, with her trailing along the whole time getting further and further behind.

She looked at the tiles in front of her. No longer did they seem promising. So, after all, Scrabble was not going to do right by her. That one mistake the last time she had played against Mike must have put an end to the whole marvelously magic process.

All right, Mike had given her an A now, two in fact, to make up for her lack of more vowels than that I. But, damn it, she couldn't see any word that—

And then she could.

With fingers that were actually trembling she put down the seven letters she had collected in the exact reverse order she had placed them in her rack, slotting them neatly round the first A of Mike's clever-clever ABACK.

D—I—S—P—A—T—C—H

Maybe it wasn't instructions about what to do about Mike—a dispatch was some sort of a military message, wasn't it?—but, by God, she had had a Scrabble to start the game with.

Rapidly she counted her score. Four for the D, which luckily had landed on a double letter light blue square, plus one for her I, plus one for S, plus three for P, plus one for Mike's A, plus one for T, plus three for C, plus four. Pity the final H hadn't quite landed on a double-letter. One off. But never mind. Total eighteen, with fifty for the Scrabble, sixty-eight. That made his thirty-six look pretty silly.

As she could see from his face when she glanced up from the board.

And, what's more, she thought gleefully, he's having trouble finding anything to make a decent score in his new pick-up.

She toyed with doing some finger-drumming, but decided to let him off. He had worse coming to him than that. Much, much worse. Even if Scrabble had not yet begun to produce any messages.

But wait. Wait. Surely Scrabble had. Didn't *dispatch* mean something else? *I will dispatch him on the instant.* Wasn't there a line like that in some old play? Shakespeare or somebody. She must have been made to read it in school.

So Scrabble was coming to her aid after all.

Now, she must ask, thinking the question as hard as she could, just how Scrabble thought Mike could be finally disposed of. Dispatched. Slowly. That had been the beginning of the message last time. Slowly. So somehow it must be possible to get rid of Mike slowly, and because of that not be found out.

And then . . . Then never another game of Scrabble as long as she lived.

At last, face contorted with disappointment, Mike put down his next word, HONE. ONE running down from the last letter of DIS-PATCH and at least scoring a double, though even with that he had made no more than fourteen.

Still way behind. And long may he stay there.

Only now did she take a proper look at the seven letters she had picked up after her Scrabble, careful though she had been to put them down in the correct way. T—E—U—Q . . . Lucky the U had come before the Q, otherwise she might have forgotten in her excitement at picking them both up at the same time, and put them in with the U on the right of the Q. And that would have shut off all messages for this night, if not forever. Bound to.

But what were these last two letters? Two Vs. She was never going to get those down all in one go. It was hard enough to get rid of a V anyhow. The number of times she had had to put down just VIA for a score of six.

Oh God, Mike's fingers on the arm of his chair were beginning to twitch. If he started drumming now every half-seen idea would go out of her head.

Ah, but look. Reading backwards, she at least had QUET there. Could she find a spare I on the board and put down QUIET. If it came on a double she would certainly settle for it. Mike would lecture her, of course, about not making full use of the Q, but to hell with him. She was well ahead, and often—surely—it was quite a good idea to get rid of a Q rather than have it hanging about in your hand, leaving you effectively with only six tiles to play with.

Then, peering at the board to see if QUIET did hit a double-word square somewhere, she realized that—better, better, better—the Q would go on the triple-letter space, two squares up from the I of DISPATCH. She banged the tiles down. Thirty-four. Not bad. Not bad at all. Even if it didn't seem to be a message.

And Mike's face was looking glummer than ever. Good.

Until suddenly a light came into his eyes, and, without hesitation, he clipped down two letters on the end of her QUIET. A U and an S.

QUIETUS. What the hell was that? No point in challenging it. Mike's store of funny words was always too much for her.

And in any case—she could tell from the fat-cat look coming onto his face—he was going to tell her all about it.

"Quietus," he said. "An old-fashioned word, of course. But still extant, I think. You remember Hamlet. The 'To be or not to be' speech. *Shall his quietus make with a bare bodkin.* A bodkin, of course, is not the heavy sewing-needle of today, but any sort of a dagger, if I've got it right."

You damn well know you have, Millie thought. You self-satisfied prig.

And then she realized. A dagger. A dagger making somebody's *quietus.* Murder, in ordinary language. Scrabble was talking to her, even using Mike to do it. Babbling a bit, maybe. Scrabble babble. But it was making its point. *Stand by for further information.* That's what Scrabble was saying. All right, she'd stand by okay.

In the event she had to stand by longer than she had expected. It was only after four more goes that Scrabble managed to take advantage of the letters Mike had put down to produce a word she recognized as being instructions. SLOWLY. Once again the word she had been given just before communication broke down last time. Scrabble picking up where it had left off.

Then, two turns later, she found in her hand L—L—I—P, together with the two Vs she had still not managed to put down and the Z. Obviously, those last three were no help. But, she saw suddenly, using the still vacant S of QUIETUS she could put down PILLS. Now Scrabble was talking. And she had the P on a double-letter square, too, and the whole word hit a pink double-score. Total—she counted rapidly on her fingers, ignoring the fact that it always brought Mike's scorn down on her—of twenty. Not bad at all. So never mind that the P came to the edge of the board only a tempting three blank squares from the red triple-word in the corner or four away from the red above. Let Mike use one or the other of those if he could. She still had a good many points to spare.

She kept her lead, too, even though Mike produced UFF to get down from her P to the triple and score thirty-six. But soon she hardly worried whether she would win or not: Scrabble began contriving to send its messages fast as faxes. First, following on from PILLS, there had come DOSE, and then DOUBLE. Right, she thought, double his dose of the heart pills. Okay, it would do no more than give him

Dr. Parker's rough rides each night, but for sure Scrabble had something more up its sleeve.

It had.

MONTH, it spelt out for her. At first she had believed this could not be part of her instructions. But then she wondered. It had scored only eleven, as to get it down at all she had had to make use of a spare O on the board. So why had Scrabble given her such rotten letters? The answer came in her next pick-up, put into her rack, of course, in the magic order. P—I—R—T. At once she saw, reading the letters the right way, that, with a leftover L and E, she had TRI-PLE and she could get that down on the board by putting the final E next to an N going begging. Scrabble, plainly, was telling her to give Mike double doses of his tablets for one month and then increase that to triple. It would make his rough rides seem gradually to be getting worse.

And then . . . Then—the whole scheme came to her in a flash—after Mike had mysteriously become more and more sick she would have to slip him something that would give him a final fatal coronary, but not be poison itself. Dr. Parker would believe death had occurred in the course of an illness he had never quite succeeded in controling. What she would have to use for the final fatal dose she could not guess. But she could rely on Scrabble, Scrabble who had told her so much already, to give her the answer when it was needed.

But then a snag came into her mind. A terrible snag. Adding an extra tablet each night to Mike's final whisky, never mind adding two, would exhaust the supply Dr. Parker had prescribed for him in half the time he had allowed, less when she moved on to the triple dose. How could she get over that? Had Scrabble failed to work out the implications? Or . . . Or was it—this was worse, far worse, awful—was Scrabble deliberately leading her down the primrose path to . . . To arrest, trial, prison for life? \

She must have been asking these questions in her head with tremendous force, it occurred to her afterwards, because the six replacement letters she picked up in place of TRIPLE at once supplied her with the necessary answer.

She had laid them in her rack, not for a moment forgetting the magic order, to the right of an X she had been left with, R—E—H—T—O—N. What did that spell? Then in an instant she saw it. Mike, the turn before, had put down PANDA—typical of him to think of a word like that—and now, as soon as he had had his next go, she could get her letters down, in order, starting from the spare A of PANDA and at least score with a good word. Unless Mike used that A first.

She waited, screwed up with tension, for him to make up his mind where he was going to go. If he did use the A, she decided, it would mean her word was not part of Scrabble's instructions. But if she was allowed to get ANOTHER down, she had already worked out without Scrabble even having to tell her, what the whole message would be. ANOTHER DOCTOR.

Of course, it was the simple answer. Go to some other doctor and tell him or her she was suffering from exactly the symptoms Mike had had when his heart trouble began. Heaven knows, he had gone on about them enough. She could remember down to the last, tiniest detail. Then, almost certainly, she would be prescribed the very same tablets. She would have an automatic supply that would last as long as Scrabble thought the rough-rides treatment should continue. It was perfect.

Provided Mike didn't use that A. It was—she looked over the whole board once more—the only possible one she could take advantage of. If she couldn't have it she would be left with just plunking down OTHER. Meaning perhaps *Think of some OTHER way out of your misery.*

Mike was in one of his fiddling states. Probably trying for a Scrabble with a lot of letters that had just too many Es or some other vowel among them ever to make a word. The sort of thing that, when it happened with her, would set Mike's fingers drum-drum-drumming till she could have reached across the board and hit him.

Then, at last, he selected some tiles from his rack. How many? Not seven, surely. No, only three. And with extremely bad grace he was putting them down to score a very feeble, if Mike-ish, word, DELL. But, thank goodness, it was right at the other side of the board from PANDA.

She swooped down with NOTHER.

"I am taking the last three tiles," Mike said, dipping into the bag. "It's one's duty to give warning of that."

"Okay, take, take," she replied. "I should worry. I'm a good fifty points ahead."

"Fifty-two, to be accurate. And I will remind you that I still have a total of seven tiles in my hand, and a Scrabble would give me fifty points, let alone what else it might score."

So it was all the more a pleasure to her when the best that Mike could manage to do, after endless jigging on his rack, was to get down just three tiles, POD. And at the same time that gave her—ha, ha— a neat chance to put her last remaining tile, that X, on to a light blue double-letter space in a corner under the O of POD and next to an E in PENCIL. OX and EX. Well, pretty soon she would be Mike's ex. Or, better, his widow. Fair, free, and forty-something.

"Seventeen plus seventeen," she said. "Thirty-four, and out."

AFTER THAT NIGHT Millie deliberately refrained from operating her system. Scrabble had told her plenty to be getting on with, and she hardly cared now whether she won or lost at their almost nightly games (Mike seemed less and less willing to go out in the evening, even to the Remingtons or the Schwartzes).

But if she refrained from using the system, she did not refrain from following Scrabble's instructions. She went at once to a certain Dr. Kochowski and got from him, as she had somehow known she would, exactly the same prescription as Dr. Parker had given Mike, only without all Dr. Parker's long over-cautious warnings. For a month precisely, she had dropped a single extra tablet into the last-thing Scotch Mike liked her to prepare for him, a routine that dated back to their first lovey-dovey married days—before even they had played Scrabble together once.

Mike, she noted with quiet triumph, had rough rides at night from the very first dose onwards. Then, when in the next month she in- creased the dose by one more tablet, his rides became correspondingly rougher. It was now that she urged him to consult Dr. Parker again, delighting in the fact, as a sign that Mike had no idea what was happening, that getting him to make an appointment had required a lot of persuasion. She even contrived, as a precaution against any eventual suspicions, to confide in Rita Schwartz fears that Mike was ignoring worrying symptoms of some mysterious sort.

It was even more of a pleasure to her when Mike, after a third consultation at the surgery, came back saying Dr. Parker was "no damn good at all."

Then, as the end of the month of triple-dose rough rides drew near, she decided it was time to have a consultation of her own. With Dr. Scrabble.

So, next evening she reverted to arranging her tiles strictly from right to left. And, the moment she put the last of her first batch into place, she realized what they had spelt. G—N—I—L—L—I—K, KILLING. Triumph running through her like a great draught of wine, she scooped the whole bunch up—she was the one to go first—and banged them down on the board, even getting that five-point K onto the double, four squares away from the starting star, almost without having to think about it.

"Wow," Mike said, "you certainly look as if you're going to make a killing tonight."

He hooted—in that disgusting way he had—at his own joke.

"Just luck," she replied, calm as could be. "Everyone has to have a bit of luck sometimes."

"Yeah. And, you know, I think I've worked out what brings you yours. I happened to notice it weeks ago when you had a terrific run of wins, and now you've done it again. You put your tiles into your rack in reverse order, from right to left, for some damn womanish reason. But, whenever you do it, things seem to go like a breeze for you. I think I'm going to try myself."

"Oh, no. No, Mike, don't."

She felt sick.

She didn't know whether the system would work for anyone other than herself. But she had a horrible feeling that if anyone else used it—and especially Mike—the magic was bound to come to an end for her. And she couldn't afford that. Not now. Now when she needed the final piece of information Dr. Scrabble had promised her. The name of whatever it was that she could use to finish the job. She had to have that. She had to.

"Oh," Mike was saying, "so I've guessed your little secret, have I? No wonder you don't want me to try it."

"It—it isn't that," she said.

"No? So what is it? You can't stop me seeing how well it'd work for me, baby. I know the trick now. Nothing you can do about it."

She thought furiously.

"Oh, come on," she managed to say at last. "You can't believe a silly superstition like that will really make a difference."

"It did for you, sweetheart."

And down onto his rack went the tiles he had been keeping in his big fist ever since he had fished them from the bag. Down from right to left.

"Now, let's see what we have," he said. "Hm. Yeah. Hey, yeah. Watch this."

Onto the board went, click, click, click, on top of the G of her

KILLING an N. Then an I, and two Ts, then another I, and then a U. Now, above, there was only one square left, at the top of the board. And Millie realized at once, with a quick thump of defeat, what letter was bound to go there. The Q. QUITTING. A Scrabble, and God knows how much it would score.

In a moment Mike told her.

"I make that twenty-two, with the U and the second I on triple-letters," he said. "Plus fifty, seventy-two. Gives me a nice edge on your sixty-seven for KILLING."

Millie dipped her hand in the bag and gathered up seven new tiles. But how was she to put them down in her rack, she asked herself. To do it in right-to-left order would only confirm Mike in his discovery. But to stick them down anyhow would be to lose the advice of Dr. Scrabble. Certainly for this evening, perhaps even forever.

She was still hesitating when Mike spoke again.

"You know," he said, in a voice a good deal more reflective than his habitual nowadays bawl. "You know, I've got a feeling there's even more to this trick of yours than you think."

"What do you mean?"

Could he have guessed? Surely not. Even Mike, proddingly sharp as he was, could never have penetrated so far as to have discovered she was receiving murder instructions from the fall of Scrabble tiles.

"Yes," he said, still in that subdued tone. "I can't help thinking that I'm getting a message here."

"A message? You?"

Then she realized that in her astonishment she had betrayed herself. That "you" could only mean she herself had been getting messages. But too late. Too late.

Yet Mike did not appear to have seized on the point. For once he seemed too wrapped up in whatever it was he was thinking.

"Quitting," he said. "Would you believe that very word has been in my mind, buried but in my mind, for—oh, I don't know—certainly a couple of weeks now."

"What do you mean *quitting*?" she said.

Quitting was not something she had ever associated with Mike. He would never quit at anything he put his hand to. She had once admired it in him. But since he had taken so unquittingly to Scrabble she had come to find it a quality as much bad as good. More bad, really.

"Well," he answered slowly, "you know I've not been feeling too well for a long time now. Dr. Parker doesn't seem to have any explanation, but I think it's actually because I'm just tired out. Hell, I've given my all to the company ever since I started work, and I just think I've had enough."

"Enough? Enough of what?"

"Of work, stress, slog, responsibility. It's killing me. Maybe it is really killing me, and perhaps the mere chance of you having that Scrabble KILLING was what made me finally realize it. Frankly, the time has come for me to retire. A little prematurely, okay. But when your whole health's at stake, I think you've got to make the decision. However tough it is."

He gave a quick smile, a little like the smiles she remembered from the days before their marriage.

"You know," he said, "I think that my Scrabble was telling me something, too. I really do. As if it was some sort of message. From beyond. Quitting: it was telling me it's time I did just that."

Millie sat and thought.

This was a whole new ball game. Was it something she wanted? What would it be like having Mike around all the time? Would it mean that she had, there every minute from breakfast to bedtime, the Mike she saw nowadays, the loudmouth, the know-it-all, the constant aggressor? Or would it perhaps be like going back to the old days? Back to the days when he had hurried home from the office every evening as early as he could, not for any special purpose, and certainly not so as to play Scrabble, but just for the pleasure of being with her?

"Like the idea?" Mike said.

Did she? Perhaps she did. She looked at the new life that had so unexpectedly opened out in front of her. Would she and Mike do things together, as they had done in those early days? Go out together in the mornings or afternoons? To a show perhaps, or even simply shopping. Or they could take up golf, both of them. Or they could just work in the garden. Side by side. Yes. Yes, Mike in retirement could make her a life she would like. Yes.

How had it come about that she had let herself think of killing him? Killing her husband? Worse, how had it happened that she had actually begun the process. Dabbling in murder. That's what it had been. How could she have let herself be guided, controled, by Scrabble? Scrabble dabble, after Scrabble babble. What a mercy she had never learnt what it was that had been going to deliver the deathblow.

And she couldn't ever now, not when Mike had guessed the secret of how to get Scrabble to help you.

"Hey, you know what?" Mike's voice came to her.

"No? What?"

"Scrabble," Mike said. "When I'm retired we could play Scrabble in the afternoons. Maybe in the mornings too, if we felt really hot. We could have all-day sessions. Best man at the end has to—has to what? Say, give the other dinner or something. How about that? How about that? Good old Scrabble every day and each day all the rest of our lives."

Theodore Mathieson

THE CHESS PARTNER

SWEATING WITH APPREHENSION, for he was gun-shy, Martin Chronister cocked the trigger of the Colt .38 and sighted down the barrel for
the last time.

The gun, held between the jaws of a vise clamped to the top of a
bookcase in his bedroom, was aimed—through a small hole he had
cut through the plywood wall—at a chair drawn up to a chess table
in the adjacent livingroom.

After examining, without touching, the dark twine that was tied to
the trigger and which passed through a staple to the floor, Chronister
followed the line through the door and into the livingroom, making
sure it lay free along the wainscoting, to where it ended at his own
chair at the chess table, opposite the first chair.

For a moment he thought he heard Banning's car, but decided that
it was the evening wind beginning to sough among the pines. He
added a log to the fire, then turned to look at the painting of his
deceased father in the heavy, gilt frame, beneath which the lethal hole
in the wall was concealed in shadow.

"I'm using your old Army gun, too." Chronister smiled up at the
portrait which he'd lugged down from the attic that afternoon. In the
gloomy oils, the medals on the uniform of the disabled old soldier
shone dully, like golden poppies through the smoke of battle, and the
grim lips seemed to be forming a question.

Why pull a string to do it?

Sure, the Old Man knew what it was to kill an enemy, and might
even understand doing it across a chessboard instead of on a battlefield,
but he'd always had contempt for his son's fear of guns.

"It isn't just gun-shyness, Martin," he'd said once. "You shrink
from every bit of reality and involvement in life!"

No matter, Chronister knew that if he faced Banning with a live gun, he'd botch the job. Doing it his way made the act less personal and more—mechanical.

A crunch of footsteps on the path outside the cabin alerted Chronister to the fact that, having missed the sound of Banning's motor, the zero hour was almost upon him. Flinging open the front door, he greeted his enemy with a false smile of friendship. . . .

IF BANNING WERE ACTUALLY TO DIE that night, it was because he'd made three mistakes, one of which he couldn't help.

First, he'd barged into Chronister's relationship with Mary Robbins. Not that the relationship was much to speak of at the beginning. For two years Chronister had met Mary at the store in town every week when he went to buy his groceries, but the contact had become a cherished event. Always a loner—he had worked for years as a bookkeeper in small-town businesses before he'd retired, unmarried, at forty-nine—Chronister had always been afraid of women. But Mary was different.

She, too, lived in the woods, tending an invalid father, in a house at the foot of Chronister's hill, but he'd always been too shy to pay them a visit. Although she might be, as the storekeeper said, rather long in the tooth, she had a gentle voice and nice hands and eyes, and above all she seemed maternal, which perhaps was her greatest attraction for him.

Then came the Saturday when he'd met Mary in the canned goods section, and they'd struck up a conversation that seemed even livelier than usual, over the quality of different brands of tuna fish. Suddenly Banning happened along, looking remarkably distinguished in his tan raincoat, with his prematurely graying hair.

"I couldn't help overhearing," he'd said in his knowing way. "Fresh *anything* is better than canned, unless you're afraid that building up your red corpuscles will make you wayward."

Mary had looked uncomfortable, and murmuring something about finding it difficult to buy fresh fish in a mountain community, moved away. Chronister was outraged, but he waited until they were outside the store and he had put his groceries in his pickup before he spoke.

"When I'm talking with my friends, I'd appreciate your waiting until you're introduced before you volunteer your opinions."

"I hate to hear phony talk, that's all," Banning said. "She isn't really interested in tuna fish, Martin. What she really wants is a man in bed with her. You'll never make the grade with that kind of talk!"

Chronister felt a sudden rush of blood to his head. "What gives you the right to interfere in my business?" he shouted. "Just because you come out once a week and play chess with me doesn't make you my adviser. And your winning lately doesn't make you my mental superior!"

"You must feel it does, or you wouldn't mention it," Banning said.

Chronister nearly struck out at him then. Until a few months ago, Banning and he had been pretty evenly matched upon the board. Then his chess partner had started winning relentlessly, which seemed to Chronister to give his partner a psychological ascendency over him. No matter how hard Chronister worked to improve his game, he had continued to lose, and Banning seemed to grow more sure of his domination.

After what had happened in the store, Chronister was beside himself. "Well, Miss Robbins and I are not chessmen," he said, "so keep your damned fingers off us!"

"Sure," Banning said.

He walked away abruptly, crossing the highway to the hotel where he lived alone on a modest disability pension.

"I always wanted to be an intellectual bum," he'd told Chronister once, "and the Army helped me do it."

Banning had lost his left arm in Korea. . . .

For the next two weeks Chronister lived without having a single visitor at his cabin. Twice he saw Mary at the store and the last time she asked him to come to visit her and her father.

Chronister kept putting off the visit, largely out of a lifetime habit of avoiding entanglements, but Mary was often in his thoughts.

Meanwhile he worked hard at his chess books, playing games against the masters. He had a hunch that Banning would be back, and sure enough, one Friday around the end of April his chess partner appeared, full of conciliatory smiles.

"No use holding a grudge, I figure," Banning said. "Besides, I miss our games."

"So do I," Chronister agreed. "I've been boning up on the books, and I think I can take you now."

"Let's find out."

The struggle this time was more even, and up to the end game Chronister felt he had a fair chance of winning. But in the final moves, Banning brought his hopes down crashing, and then checkmated him.

Once again came Banning's smile of superiority, his almost physical levitation—which was Banning's second mistake.

"By the way," he said from his height, "I paid a couple of visits to Mary and the old man. You're quite right in giving her the eye. In a housecoat she's not bad at all. Although her pa is a dreary lump. Every time he looks at my arm, he fights the Battle of the Marne all over again!"

If Chronister had had his gun handy, he might have used it personally then. Instead, he played another game and lost, and invited Banning back the following week.

The very next day he dressed up and went down to visit Mary and her father.

"I wondered why you hadn't been down before," Mary said, standing beside the wheelchair in which sat a withered old man with sly eyes. For some reason, she seemed more amiable here than at the store, and Chronister remembered what Banning had said about the housecoat. Now she was wearing a kind of muu-muu which concealed all but her head and hands.

Aware of his scrutiny, she colored and excused herself, and the old man began talking about the First World War.

"If I hadn't got shrapnel in my spine," he whined, "I'd have taken up the Army as a profession. You been in the service yet, sonny?"

Chronister winced. "No, sir. My father was a colonel in the First World War, and he wanted me to go into the Army, too, but I guess I wasn't cut out for it."

"Good life for a red-blooded man!"

"My father thought so, too."

Mary returned shortly wearing jeans and a tight-fitting sweater, and Chronister saw what Banning had meant.

"My chess partner said he enjoyed a visit with you," Chronister said, following the line of least resistance.

"Oh, Mr. Banning, yes. He's quite delightful."

Chronister felt a stab of jealousy. "I guess he talks a little more easily than I do," he admitted. "Social situations have always been pretty hard going for me."

"It mustn't be that you're antisocial; you just don't like crowds. Well, neither do we. That's why Papa and I live in the woods. I see your light up there sometimes."

"And I see yours."

It went like that for perhaps an hour. Mary served tea and some cookies she'd made, and he departed, not sure what kind of impression he'd created. But he knew that Mary attracted him, and that he felt the need of her, because when he returned to his cabin that night he was aware for the first time of its emptiness.

Through the rest of the week he continued playing over the master games, but no matter how hard he tried to concentrate, thoughts of Mary interfered. Finally, on a Thursday, in the middle of a game, he threw the chess book aside in disgust, put on his hiking books, and went walking in the sunny woods.

As he sat resting under a yellow pine, he heard voices, a man's and a woman's, which presently he recognized as Banning's—and Mary's.

He wanted to run, but he felt paralyzed, and as he sat they came close enough for him to hear what they were saying.

". . . spring is the time for a walk," Banning was saying. "I don't get out half enough."

"Nor do I," Mary replied. "It's so lovely."

The two had stopped a few yards off, and Chronister prayed that the chaparral concealed him sufficiently.

"Look," Mary said, "you can see a roof from here. It must be Mr. Chronister's."

"Does he ever take you for a walk?"

"Mr. Chronister? Oh, never. He's been to see me only once in two years! Besides, I don't get out much."

"You should. Your father can do a little for himself, can't he?"

"Not much, and he's getting worse every day, so I like to be around when he calls."

"If you ever need help, Mary—I mean, with your father . . ."

"Thank you."

A silence followed, and Chronister, straining his ears, thought he heard them kiss. Then there was a sudden movement and quick footsteps sounded down the leafy trail.

"Mary!" Banning called, and then he, too, was gone.

Chronister continued to sit, his fear giving way to anger, then to rage. Finally he rose and pounded through the brush, not caring whether he was seen or heard, and by the time he reached his cabin his mind was made up. Mary was going to be his. He was going to kill Banning—tomorrow night. . . .

THE ZERO HOUR had come.

Banning, sure of himself tonight as ever, sat down in his usual chair, took out his tobacco pouch and loaded his pipe.

"Been doing some changing around, eh?" he asked, looking up to where Chronister had hung his father's portrait to hide the hole in the wall.

"I like a change every once in a while," Chronister said. He sat down opposite Banning, casually leaned over and picked up the twine, laying the loose end across his lap. Banning was staring at the picture.

"Would that be your father? He was an Army man, wasn't he?"

"Yes."

"You know, he looked familiar. I see he lost his left arm, too."

"In the Argonne. He led his own battalion."

"Must have been quite a man." Banning's eyes seemed to hold a taunt. "Well, it's your turn, Martin, I think with the white."

Chronister played pawn to king's fourth, and as the opening game developed in a conventional pattern, his hands upon the twine began to sweat.

If fifteen minutes, however, the game took an unexpected turn, and Chronister concentrated on the problems so avidly that he forgot the string, the gun, even his intent to murder. At the back of his mind he knew he was playing superbly well, with a freedom and dash that he had never before achieved. His moves seemed to flow, to dovetail, shaping themselves into a pattern that was a sheer work of art. Time and again he heard exasperated sighs from his chess companion that ignited his ingenuity further until finally, in the end game, he played simple cat and mouse, certain of victory.

"I concede the game," Banning said at last, leaning back in his chair. Chronister, looking up like one coming out of a dream, was surprised to see a new Banning, one divested of pride, humble and human.

In the objectivity of the moment he saw, too, that Banning had never deliberately meant to make him feel inferior. The guy had just been elated by winning a *game*.

"You played better tonight than I ever could," Banning said, smiling warmly. "But I guess it's just your lucky night." He put his hand into his coat pocket and pulled out a folded piece of paper. "I met Mary in town this morning, and she gave me this to give to you. I won't say I didn't read it, so I happen to know she prefers you to me."

Chronister took the note in a daze, letting the twine fall lightly to the floor.

Dear Mr. Chronister:

Papa had a bad spell last evening, and since we are without a tele-phone, and you are the closest person to me, I wonder if you'd mind my coming up to see you if I have need of your help?
I'd rather call on you than anyone.

Mary

When Chronister looked up, Banning was staring at the portrait again.

"Now I know who your father looks like," he said. "He looks like *me*—even if his arm weren't missing!"

Chronister's mouth felt dry as he rose. "Let's go into the kitchen and have a beer," he said through stiff lips. He took a step forward then, and felt the tug upon his hiking boot where the twine had caught in a lace hook. Before he knew what happened, the explosion filled the room, making the lamps wink in their sockets.

The echoes seemed a long time dying away, and the blood upon the floor grew into a pool beside the dead man.

There came a timid tapping at the cabin door.

Knowing at last the meaning of utter involvement, Martin Chronister went to answer it.

Bill Pronzini

SHADE WORK

JOHNNY SHADE BLEW INTO SAN FRANCISCO on the first day of summer. He went there every year, when he had the finances; it was a good place to find action on account of the heavy convention business. Usually he went a little later in the summer, around mid-July, when there were fifteen or twenty thousand conventioneers wandering around, a high percentage of them with money in their pockets and a willingness to lay some of it down on a poker table. You could take your time then, weed out the deadheads and the short-money scratchers. Pick your vic.

But this year was different. This year he couldn't afford to wait around and take his time. He had three thousand in his kick that he'd scored in Denver, and he needed to parlay that into ten grand—fast. Ten grand would buy him into a big con Elk Tracy and some other boys were setting up in Louisville. A classic big-store con, even more elaborate than the one Newman and Redford had pulled off in *The Sting,* Johnny's favorite flick. Elk needed a string of twenty and a nut of two hundred thousand to set it up right; that was the reason for the ten-grand buy-in. The guaranteed net was two million. Ten grand buys you a hundred, minimum. Johnny Shade had been a card mechanic and cheat for nearly two decades and he'd never held that much cash in his hands at one time. Not even close to that much.

He was a small-time grifter and he knew it. A single-o, traveling around the country on his own because he preferred it that way, looking for action wherever he could find it. But it was never heavy action, never the big score. Stud and draw games in hotel rooms with marks who never seemed to want to lose more than a few hundred at a sitting. He wasn't a good enough mechanic to play in even a medium-stakes game and hope to get away with crimps or hops or

186

overhand runups or Greek-deals or hand-mucks or any of the other shuffling or dealing cheats. He just didn't have the fingers for it. So mostly he relied on his specialty, shade work, which was how he'd come to be called Johnny Shade. He even signed hotel registers as Johnny Shade nowadays, instead of the name he'd been born with. A kind of private joke.

Shade work was fine in small games. Most amateurs never thought to examine or riffle-test a deck when he ran a fresh one in, because it was always in its cellophane wrapper with the manufacturer's seal unbroken. The few who did check the cards didn't spot the gaff on account of they were looking for blisters, shaved edges, blockout or cutout work—the most common methods of marking a deck. They didn't know about the more sophisticated methods like flash or shade work. In Johnny's case, they probably wouldn't have spotted the shade gaff if they had known, not the way he did it.

He had it down to a science. He diluted blue and red aniline dye with alcohol until he had the lightest possible tint, then used a camel's hair brush to wash over a small section of the back pattern of each card in a Bee or Bicycle deck. The dye wouldn't show on the red or blue portion of the card back, but it tinted the white part just lightly enough so you could see it if you knew what to look for. And he had eyesight almost as good as Clark Kent's. He could spot his shade work on a vic's cards across the table in poor light without even squinting.

But the high rollers knew about shade work, just as they knew about every other scam a professional hustler could come up with. You couldn't fool them, so you couldn't steal their money. If you were Johnny Shade, you had to content yourself with low rollers and deadheads, with pocket and traveling cash instead of the big score.

He was tired of the game, that was the thing. He'd been at it too long, lived on the far edge of riches too long, been a single-o grifter too long. He wanted a slice of the good life. Ten grand buys a hundred. With a hundred thousand he could travel first class, wine and dine and bed first-class women, take his time finding new action— maybe even set up a big con of his own. Or find a partner and work some of the fancier short cons. Lots of options, as long as a guy had real money in his kick.

First, though, he had to parlay his Denver three K into ten K. Then he could hop a plane for Louisville and look up Elk Tracy. Ten days . . . that was all the time he had before Elk closed out his string. Ten days to pick the right vics, set up two or three or however many games it took him to net the seven thousand.

He found his first set of marks his first night in Frisco. That was a good omen. His luck was going to change; he could feel it.

Most weeks in the summer there was a convention going on at the Hotel Nob Hill, off Union Square. He walked in there on this night, and the first thing he saw was a banner that said WELCOME FID-DLERS in great big letters. Hick musicians, or maybe some kind of organization for people who were into cornball music. Just his type of crowd. Just his type of mark.

He hung out in the bar, nursing a beer, circulating, keeping his ears open. There were certain words he listened for and "poker" was one of them. One of four guys in a booth used it, and when he sidled closer he saw that they were all wearing badges with FIDDLER on them and their names and the cities they were from written under-neath. They were talking the right talk: stud poker, bragging about how good they were at it, getting ready for a game. Ripe meat. All he had to do was finagle his way among them, get himself invited to join the play if the set-up and the stakes were right.

He was good at finagling. He had the gift of gab, and a face like a Baptist preacher's, and a winning smile. First he sat himself down at a table near their booth. Then he contrived to jostle a waitress and spill a fresh round of beers she was bringing to them. He offered to pay for the drinks, flashed his wallet so they could see that he was flush. Chatted them up a little, taking it slow, feeling his way.

One of the fiddlers bought him a beer, then he bought them all another round. That got him the invitation to join them. Right away he laid on the oil about being in town for a convention himself, the old birds-of-a-feather routine. They shook hands all around. Dave from Cleveland, Mitch from Los Angeles, Verne from Cedar Rapids, Harry from Bayonne. And Johnny from Denver. He didn't even have to maneuver the talk back to cards. They weren't interested in his convention or their own, or San Francisco, or any other kind of small talk; they were interested in poker. He played some himself, he said. Nothing he liked better than five-stud or draw. No wild-card games, none of that crap; he was a purist. So were they.

"We're thinking about getting up a game," Harry from Bayonne said. "You feel like sitting in, Johnny?"

"I guess I wouldn't mind," he said. "Depending on the stakes. Nothing too rich for my blood." He showed them his best smile.

"Then again, nothing too small, either. Poker's no good unless you make it interesting, right?"

If they'd insisted on penny-ante or buck-limit, he'd have backed out and gone looking elsewhere. But they were sports; table stakes, ten-buck limit per bet, no limit on raises. They looked like they could afford that kind of action. Fiddle-music jerks, maybe, but well-dressed and reasonably well-heeled. He caught a glimpse of a full wallet when Mitch from L.A. bought another round. Might be as much as four or five grand among the four of them.

Verne from Cedar Rapids said he had a deck of cards in his room; they could play there. Johnny said, "Sounds good. How about if we go buy a couple more decks in the gift shop? Nothing like the feel of a new deck after a while."

They all thought that was a good idea. Everybody drank up and they went together to the gift shop. All Johnny had to do was make sure the cards they bought were Bicycle, one of the two most common brands; he had four shaded Bicycle decks in his pocket, two blue-backs and two red-backs. Then they all rode upstairs to Verne from Cedar Rapids's room and shed their coats and jackets and got down to business.

Johnny played it straight for a while, card-counting, making conservative bets, getting a feel for the way the four marks played. Only one of them was reckless: Mitch from L.A., the one with the fattest wallet. He'd have liked two or three of that type, but one was better than none. One was all he needed.

After an hour and a half he was ahead about a hundred and Mitch from L.A. was the big winner, betting hard, bluffing at least part of the time. Better and better. Time to bring in one of his shaded decks. That was easy, too. They'd let him hold the decks they'd bought downstairs; simple for him to bring out one of his own instead.

He didn't open it himself. You always let one of the marks do that, so the mark could look it over and see that it was still sealed in cellophane with the manufacturer's stamp on top intact. The stamp was the main thing to the mark, the one thing you never touched when you were fixing a deck. What they didn't figure on was what you'd done: You carefully opened the cellophane wrapper along the bottom and slid out the card box. Then you opened the box along one side, prying the glued flaps apart with a razor blade. Once you'd shaded the cards, you resealed the box with rubber cement, slipped it back into the cellophane sleeve, refolded the sleeve ends along the original creases, and resealed them with a drop of glue. When you did the job right—and Johnny Shade was a master—nobody could tell that the package had been tampered with. Sure as hell not a fiddler named Dave from Cleveland, the one who opened the gimmicked deck.

The light was pretty good in there; Johnny could read his shade work with no more than a casual glance at the hands as they were dealt out. He took a couple of medium-sized pots, worked his winnings up to around five hundred, biding his time until both he and Mitch from L.A. drew big hands on the same deal. It finally happened about 10:30, on a hand of jacks-or-better. Harry from Bayonne was dealing; Johnny was on his left. Mitch from L.A. drew a pat full house, aces over fives. Johnny scored trip deuces. When he glanced over at the rest of the deck, he saw that the top card—his card on the draw—was the fourth deuce. Beautiful. A set-up like this was always better when you weren't the dealer, didn't have to deal seconds or anything like that to win the pot. Just read the shade and it was yours.

Mitch from L.A. bet ten and Johnny raised him and Mitch raised back. Verne from Cedar Rapids stayed while the other two dropped, which made Johnny smile inside. Verne owned four high spades in sequence and was gambling on a one-card draw to fill a royal or a straight flush. But there was no way he was going to get it because Mitch had his spade ace and Johnny had his spade nine. The best he could do was a loser flush. Johnny raised again, and Mitch raised back, and Verne hung in stubborn. There was nearly a grand in the pot when Mitch finally called.

Johnny took just the one card on the draw, to make the others think he was betting two pair. Mitch would think that even if Johnny caught a full house, his would be higher because he had aces up; so Mitch would bet hot and heavy. Which he did. Verne from Cedar Rapids had caught his spade flush and hung in there for a while, driving the pot even higher, until he finally realized his flush wasn't going to beat what Johnny and Mitch were betting; then he dropped. Mitch kept right on working his full boat, raising each time Johnny raised, until he was forced to call when his cash pile ran down to a lone tenspot. That last ten lifted the total in the pot to twenty-two hundred bucks.

Johnny grinned and said, "Read 'em and weep, gentlemen," and fanned out his four deuces face up. Mitch from L.A. didn't say a word; he just dropped his cards and looked around at the others.

None of them had anything to say, either. Johnny grinned again and said, "My lucky night," and reached for the pot.

Reaching for it was as far as he got.

Harry from Bayonne closed a big paw over his right wrist; Dave from Cleveland did the same with his left wrist. They held him like that, his hands imprisoned flat on the table.

"What the hell's the idea?" Johnny said.

Nobody answered him. Mitch from L.A. swept the cards together and then began to examine them one at a time, holding each card up close to his eyes.

Harry from Bayonne said, "What is it, shade work?"

"Right. Real professional job."

"Thought so. I'm pretty good at spotting blockout and cutout work. And I didn't feel any blisters or edge or sand work."

"At first I figured he might be one of the white-on-white boys," Verne from Cedar Rapids said. "You know, used whiteout fluid on the white borders. Then I tumbled to the shading."

"Nice resealing on that card box, Johnny," Dave from Cleveland said. "If I hadn't known it was a gimmicked deck, I wouldn't have spotted it."

Johnny gawped. "You knew?" he said. "You all *knew?*"

"Oh sure," Mitch from L.A. said. "As soon as you moved in on us down in the bar."

"But—but—why did you . . . ?"

"We wanted to see what kind of hustler you were, how you worked your scam. You might call it professional curiosity."

"Christ. Who are you guys?"

They told him. And Johnny Shade groaned and put his head in his hands. He knew then that his luck had changed, all right—all for the bad. That he was never going to make the big score, in Louisville or anywhere else. That he might not even be much good as a small-time grifter any more. Once word of this got out, he'd be a laughingstock from coast to coast. And word *would* get out. These four would see to that.

They didn't belong to some hick music group. They weren't fiddlers; they were FIDDLERs, part of a newly formed nationwide professional organization. Fraud Identification Detectives, Domestic Law Enforcement Ranks.

Vice cops. He'd tried to run a gambling scam at a convention of vice cops. . . .

R. L. Stevens

KING'S KNIGHT GAMBIT DECLINED

NEARLY EVERY EVENING during the summer months Harry Lawn could be found at the little park in the town square, along with the other gray-haired elders and an occasional farm boy down from the hills. The attraction was the line of public chessboards set in stone tables along the north side of the square. It was just like in New York, someone had remarked, though perhaps the town's chess players lacked the skill and sophistication of those in Washington Square or in Central Park.

Certainly in the limited sphere of the town square Harry Lawn was considered something of a champion, ready to play all comers. During the summer of '72, when Bobby Fischer won the world's championship from Boris Spassky in Reykjavik, Iceland, and raised interest in the game to a new peak, Harry often played several games in a single evening, invariably winning with a minimum of skillful moves.

This night, a muggy Wednesday in early September, he was seated on one of the wooden spectators' benches, enjoying a particularly spirited game between two friends, when the big green limousine pulled up and parked across the square. Harry Lawn recognized Stringer at once, because it was Harry's business to know people; but he went on watching the game as if he hadn't seen Stringer. After a few moments he heard a voice at his side say, "Hello, Harry."

He turned, feigning surprise. "Well—Stringer! What brings you to my part of the state? Thinking of buying a farm?"

Stringer was a big man, twenty years younger than Harry Lawn. More than that, he was a city man out of place in small-town life. Harry enjoyed kidding him during his infrequent visits.

"You know what I'm here for, Harry," the big man said.

"Checkmate!" one gray-haired man shouted in triumph from the board. "I licked him, Harry! I'm ready now to take on the champ!"

Harry Lawn smiled at the compliment. "Not right now, Syd. I've got a visitor." Then, as an afterthought, he turned to Stringer. "How about it? Want to play me a game?"

Stringer stared at the chessboard in open distaste. "I haven't played in years."

"It'll come back to you."

Stringer glanced at the sky. "Getting dark."

"The park lights will go on soon. We'll be able to see the pieces. Chess has always been a big sport in our town."

"I don't know. I came on business."

"From George Danzig?"

"Of course from Danzig—you know I don't work for myself." He had dropped his voice, so it would not carry to the men at the chess tables.

"You have the envelope?"

Stringer reached into his coat pocket and extracted a fat white envelope. "It's all in there—the money and the name."

Harry Lawn nodded. He opened the envelope enough to see the thick wad of one-hundred-dollar bills and the slip of white notepaper with a single named printed on it in thick black ink. The name was that of Ralph Andow, a downstate judge rumored to be under investigation for underworld ties.

"Big name these days," Harry said with a grunt.

"That's why Danzig is paying so much. We don't want any mistakes."

"I never make mistakes," Harry said. He slipped the envelope into his pants pocket. "Now how about that game?"

Seeing there was no chance of playing the champ, Syd and the others were drifting away. Harry and Stringer were almost alone in the little park, and perhaps this gave Stringer the courage to try it. "Sure, I'll play you, Harry. I might even beat you!"

The park lights went on, bathing the chess table in a soft glow that vied with the last traces of daylight. "Which color do you want?" Harry asked.

"I don't care. Black."

"Then I'll be white. I go first."

Stringer frowned. "Why's that?"

"You really haven't played in a long time. White always moves first." Harry moved his king pawn forward two squares.

"How long you been playing chess, Harry?"

"Nearly all my life. My father and grandfather played, too." He watched Stringer move his king pawn forward two squares, and Harry followed immediately with knight to king bishop three.

"Who's going to do the job on Andow?" Stringer asked suddenly, already beginning to lose interest in the game.

"You know I don't talk about things like that, Stringer."

"Danzig would like to know. After all, he's paying the freight."

Harry watched the big man move a knight. "I thought Danzig understood the way I worked. I'm a middleman and nothing more. I take my cut and pass the money along. Danzig never knows who did the job, and my man never knows who hired him to do the job. That way nobody gets hurt if there's a slip."

"You just said there wouldn't be a slip."

Harry Lawn sighed and ran a hand through his white hair. "I said I never make mistakes, and I don't. But there still could be a slip somewhere."

"Danzig figures he should know who the guy is, in case anything happens to you."

"I'm not that old yet, Stringer. I've got a few good years left."

"Danzig wants to know."

"So he can cut me out of the deal and save himself a grand every time?" Harry reached toward his pocket. "Hell, you can take back your money if that's the way he wants to play!"

"Calm down, Harry. The judge has got to go. He knows your man will do a nice neat job." Stringer touched one of his knights. "You and I are just knights, Harry, working for the king, doing his killing for him, just like in the Middle Ages."

"Yeah," Harry agreed, studying the board.

They played a few moves in silence, then Stringer asked, "How long will it take with Judge Andow?"

Harry Lawn shrugged. "I have to mail the money and the name to my man. That'll be a couple of days. Then he has to find Andow and set the thing up. It's got to take a week, maybe longer."

"Danzig wants it done fast. The judge is getting ready to talk to a grand jury in two weeks."

"No sweat. It'll be done by then."

"And we know you won't be talking about it."

"Have I ever?"

"This one's especially important. That's why Danzig wanted the name of your man."

Harry captured a knight. "You tell him I can handle my affairs without any help from him. Tell him I've been down here running my little business for a hell of a lot longer than he's been bribing judges."

Stringer glanced around nervously. "Take it easy. What if someone hears you?"

"They're all in bed. The whole town's in bed by now, Stringer."

"The mosquitoes aren't—they're eating me alive! Let's quit this foolish game."

"I think I can beat you in three more moves, Stringer,"

"The hell with it! Play with yourself!"

"I guess chess isn't your game."

"Damn right! One trip to see you in this one-horse town every three or four months is plenty for me."

"You could mail me the money. Then there'd be no chance of people seeing you."

"These hicks? They probably think I'm a traveling salesman." He stood up and stretched. "Besides, Danzig wanted me to talk to you this time. Make sure we all understood each other."

"We understand each other. You're not getting the name of my man."

"Well, there's something else that's bothering him."

"What's that?"

"On the last job, a couple of months ago, your man stopped long enough to take some money off the body."

"You mean the Foster hit?"

Stringer nodded. "Foster was collecting some money for Danzig when he got it, which was just bad luck. But the money was missing from the body—maybe twenty grand. Your man heisted it."

"Hell he did! My man shoots and runs."

"Not that time. There were no witnesses. He stayed long enough to take the money. Maybe he even split it with you."

"Come on, Stringer. You're making an old man lose his temper."

He took a step forward, but Stringer was faster. His beefy hand grabbed Harry by the shirt, shoving him backward onto the chessboard. Harry rolled off the stone table and fell on the grass, scattering chessmen around him.

Stringer stood above him, breathing hard. "Harry, you know I'm just doing my job. One of the king's knights."

"Is that your message?" Harry asked, getting to his feet.

Stringer stared hard at him. "I guess so, Harry. Do your job so Danzig stays happy. He's a bad guy when he's unhappy."

"Yeah."

Stringer ground one of the chessmen into the soft earth beneath his heel. "Keep your nose clean, Harry. See you next trip." He turned and walked across the square to his car.

Harry watched him for a long time, until the big green limousine rolled away and vanished into the night. Then he walked slowly around the chess table, bending to pick up the fallen chessmen. He placed the pieces gently in their wooden box and went home.

THE HOUSE WHERE HE'D LIVED alone since the death of his wife was just down the street from the town square. He turned on the lights and went to sit at the kitchen table. He noticed that his hands were still shaking from his encounter with Stringer.

Damn! He was getting too old for this sort of thing. Too old, when the young hoods thought he was soft enough to be bullied and threatened!

But he knew it wasn't Stringer's fault. The big man did what he was told. Obviously Danzig had decided Harry Lawn could be leaned on. Harry Lawn was just an old guy who played chess in the town square and happened to have some good guns for hire. Harry Lawn couldn't hurt anybody.

He sighed and opened the envelope, counting out the one-hundred-dollar bills. He placed ten of them to one side and slipped the rest into a fresh envelope. On its face he printed the name and address of a young man who lived in a city fifty miles away. He'd had many occasions to send the young man money, and he'd never been disappointed.

Lastly he picked up the piece of notepaper on which Ralph Andow's name was printed. He stared at it for some moments. Then, remembering the expression on Stringer's face when he'd ground the chessman into the earth, Harry crumpled the piece of paper and dropped it into the waste basket.

He drew a note pad toward him and carefully printed the name of George Danzig on the top sheet. Then he sealed it in the envelope with the money and went out to the mailbox.

As he dropped the letter into the slot he said, very softly, "Knight to king bishop six, checkmate."

Nedra Tyre

THE MURDER GAME

IT WAS TIME for the murder game.

To play it, my brothers and sisters and I, all six of us, were gathered as usual on the first Tuesday night of the month in our Aunt Felicity's huge and impressive bedroom which was big enough for a royal levee. From its high stuccoed ceiling hung two Venetian chandeliers. A vast canopied bed dominated one end of the room. We were sitting in the other end at small candlelit tables set in the bay window that overlooked the rolling expanse of lawn that swept down to the river.

We had finished eating a simple but superbly cooked dinner. Our three tables were grouped in a semicircle around the Récamier sofa on which Aunt Felicity, beautiful and elegant but badly crippled from arthritis, had half reclined as she ate from a tray.

I didn't like the foolish game, nor as far as I could see did my brothers and sisters; but five months previously Aunt Felicity had proposed it out of the blue, and she had been so kind to us, so loving and generous, that none of us dared protest at first, and by now it had become a monthly ritual.

Five of us were not the least bit good at parlor games. As children we hadn't played them. My three brothers were competitive and excellent sportsmen, and competitive in business and spectacular successes for such young men—Carl and Matthew were lawyers, but not partners, and Andrew was an investment banker. Alicia, our oldest sister, was competitive socially and the most prominent young hostess in the city; her parties were famous—people literally clawed each other for invitations to her balls.

However competitive my brothers and Alicia were in the professional and social worlds they were inept at Aunt Felicity's murder game.

Jeanine—next to me the youngest girl—always won the game. Always.

She was the scholar among us, the bright one. I don't think she had a competitive bone in her body, and she discounted the prodigious store of knowledge that she possessed. She was genuinely modest about it. Her attitude seemed to be that she could not take pride in having mastered some information when there was so much more to be acquired. All the same, I think it irked my brothers that the murder game was so easy for her.

I will describe the game as we played it. Perhaps it's a variation of a well-known game. As I say, we hadn't played parlor games either as children or adults. Previously we had only talked when we had dinner together on the first Tuesday of each month. We never ran out of things to say to each other. It was our one night together when there were no outsiders; not even our brother's wives or Alicia's husband joined us.

When we had finished eating, Jeanine and I would clear away the dishes and pile them in the dumbwaiter and send them down to the kitchen where Mr. and Mrs. Finch were waiting for them. Our brothers would draw up chairs around Aunt Felicity. Alicia and I sat together on a loveseat, and Jeanine, as if to hide herself and her brightness and her inevitable triumph, sat in a small Louis XV chair behind our brothers.

The game began when Aunt Felicity reached into the drawer of a table near her and took out six sheets of rather ratty-looking scratch paper on which she had inscribed with a red nylon-tipped pen the first names of the persons suspected of murder; then she would tell us that the murdered person, before expiring, had been able to write something which indicated the name of the murderer, but that the murderer himself, or herself, intent on getting away from the scene of the crime, was not aware of having been incriminated, since the clever victim had been able to point to the murderer in an oblique way.

Aunt Felicity handed the sheets to Carl and he distributed them.

We read the names of the suspects: Horace, Llewellyn, Mary Ann, Joan, Louise, Margaret, Lawrence.

Before the victim died he had been able to scrawl one word: George.

Again Carl rose. Again he took six sheets from Aunt Felicity and handed them around to us. We now held a sheet with the names of the suspects in red and a sheet with the one word George in black.

We all—except for Jeanine, of course—began to frown in disgruntled perplexity.

Aunt Felicity asked if anyone had the solution. No one answered. She quizzed us in turn beginning with Carl who was nearest to her. When my time came I said I had no idea who was guilty. Occasionally Alicia would make a stab, but it was always a futile, incorrect one. And our brothers invariably became jocular, charming, bluffing, willing to take a chance, and on rare occasions one of them made a lucky guess, but he could never prove it by evidence or any sort of clue.

Aunt Felicity didn't let the game drag on or permit our brothers to become too rollicking with their random guesses. She would suddenly say, "Jeanine, who is the murderer?"

Tonight, as usual, Jeanine was neither coy nor hesitant in answering. Her voice was clear but modest. "The murderer is Mary Ann."

"That's right," Aunt Felicity said. "Now tell us why Mary Ann is the guilty one."

"Well, the victim wrote down George. George Eliot is the name under which Mary Ann Evans published her novels. Therefore George equals Mary Ann."

"Good Lord," Matthew said. "I haven't thought about George Eliot since I was a freshman in high school and had to read *Silas Marner* and *The Mill on the Floss.*"

With Jeanine's naming the murderer our evening together was over. I gathered up the twelve pieces of paper we had used in the game and threw them into the wastebasket. My brothers and sisters lined up around the sofa and kissed Aunt Felicity good night and then they left me alone with her. We were an affectionate family, in touch with each other two or three times a day by telephone, and my brothers and their wives and Alicia and her husband and Jeanine, who wasn't married but lived on campus at a nearby university where she was an assistant curator in the Museum of Fine Arts, made numerous brief visits nearly every week.

My brothers relied on Aunt Felicity's advice and counsel and she relied on theirs. She had been our guardian ever since our parents had been killed in a plane crash, the same crash that had killed Aunt Felicity's husband. At the time of that tragedy Carl, the oldest child, had been twelve and I, Sue, the youngest, five. Aunt Felicity had taken us into her large house copied from an English manor and had given us a wonderful life, and by shrewd investments had made a substantial fortune for us out of our parents' estate, so that we were all well off financially when we came of age.

I had neither my brothers' drive for professional success nor Jeanine's brains nor Alicia's flair for society, and so I stayed with Aunt Felicity. She needed me, especially after she was stricken with arthritis. I found it satisfying to give back a little of the care and devotion she had given us. I did her errands and her telephoning. She found it difficult to dial or to hold the telephone, but liked to be in immediate and constant touch with people. I made dozens, sometimes scores, of calls for her every day. I invited her continuous flow of guests. She was a witty and informed conversationalist who liked to have witty people around her. I bought books for her to read, sent presents and flowers for her, got up at dawn to go to the farmers' market when Aunt Felicity wanted special food to prepare for a gourmet friend. I searched the shops for kaftans and long elegant dressing gowns that would hide Aunt Felicity's crippled body.

That night when my brothers and sisters had left after Jeanine had said that Mary Ann was the name of the murderer, I wanted to say as I helped Aunt Felicity make the painful, labored journey from the sofa to her bed, "Why do you have us play that silly game? Don't you see that none of us really likes it? And it embarrasses Jeanine to win all the time. I've never known you to make other guests ill at ease. Why don't you stop insisting that we play it?"

But I didn't complain.

And the game did end soon.

Or at least we were to be given a respite when Jeanine left town at the end of the semester. She took a brief leave from the university to spend the spring in Italy studying art in churches and museums.

I had thought that perhaps at our last gathering before Jeanine left, Aunt Felicity wouldn't make us play the game, but I was wrong.

As always, when our meal was finished and the dishes were cleared away, Aunt Felicity told us to take our places for the game, and once we were settled she reached into the drawer and handed Carl the slips with the names of the suspects. Carl handed a slip to each of us and we read the names: Cleo, Annette, Josephine, Melissa, Maude, Frank, James, Warren.

Then came the sheet with the clue: a serpentine line, an irregular, lopsided S.

Andrew was brash and even before Aunt Felicity asked for volunteer answers he said, "The guilty person is Cleo. The clue that looks like an S is a serpent, the asp that caused Cleopatra's death. Cleopatra equals Cleo. Sorry, Jeanine, to end your unbroken streak of victories, especially on your last night."

"A very good guess," Aunt Felicity said. "But the name on the list of suspects is Cleo, not Cleopatra. Your answer is wrong."

After Andrew's gaffe no one else guessed or offered any kind of comment. It was, I think, the shortest game on record.

As always, Aunt Felicity turned to Jeanine and asked for the answer.

"The murderer is Josephine," Jeanine said. "The clue—the S—is the outline of a swan. The swan was Empress Josephine's motif or emblem or whatever you want to call it. She had swans embossed everywhere. So the swan equals Josephine and Josephine is the guilty one."

Aunt Felicity gave Jeanine a congratulatory smile.

Then we all kissed one another good night and wished Jeanine a wonderful trip.

And that, as it happened, was the last time that we ever played the game of murder.

The next week was frantic for me. Even more than usual the telephone was like an appendage, an extra limb I'd grown in order to function. Aunt Felicity gave a large reception for the curator taking Jeanine's place and introduced him to the young painters and writers in town. Then a famous conductor, an old friend of Aunt Felicity, arrived for a concert and Aunt Felicity invited him and his entire orchestra to a late supper party.

I had never made so many telephone calls or done so many errands, and the night after the supper party when I handed Aunt Felicity her dinner on a tray she insisted that I go to bed immediately.

"You look dead tired," Aunt Felicity said. "I've imposed on you too much. I don't need you tonight. I'll have Finch come up for the tray and he can send any caller upstairs. If any of the children"—she still referred to my brothers and sisters and me as children—"come they have their own keys."

I glanced at the bedside table to be sure everything she needed was at hand. Two books of her two favorite poets—Keats and Gerard Manley Hopkins—were there; the sherry decanter beside them was full—Aunt Felicity liked to sip sherry as she read, the last thing she did before going to sleep.

"Sue, darling, everything I can possibly want is within reach," she said. "Now go and get some rest." She lifted her forehead toward me and I kissed it and we said good night.

Twelve hours of sleep was all I needed to give me back my energy.

I woke up the next morning feeling equal to a hundred telephone calls and errands. I bathed and dressed quickly, then went as usual into Aunt Felicity's room. I tidied up a bit and picked up the Hopkins book that had fallen to the floor and set it in its accustomed place beside the volume of Keats. I often found a book on the floor where it had fallen out of Aunt Felicity's hand when she had dozed off to sleep. I adjusted the shutters so that the sunlight streamed in.

Then I went to the bathroom and moistened a washcloth so that Aunt Felicity could sponge her face and hands. I leaned under the canopy and pushed back the heavy curtains of the bed and called to Aunt Felicity.

Her alert eyes did not look up at me.

She did not give me her usual radiant smile.

She was turned so that she seemed to be submerged, drowned in the deep mound of pillows.

I realized then that she was dead, but that did not keep me from repeating her name again and again, as if I might somehow arouse her; and then I compelled myself to do what must be done.

I made one telephone call after another that morning. The first one was to Dr. Cowan who came to the house immediately.

"Don't grieve for Felicity," he said as we stood beside her dead body, and even as he ordered me not to grieve I saw that he was weeping for his dear friend. "Every moment of her life was pain." He wiped his eyes and recovered his professionalism. "Her death seems a perfectly natural one. I'll examine her, of course. When you call your family and friends, just say that Felicity died in her sleep."

As I left the room to make the sad announcement, I saw Dr. Cowan stoop over her body.

Whatever he had said to me about not grieving for Aunt Felicity, I mourned for her. I knew that life was precious to her and that however acute her pain and the inconvenience of being an invalid, she considered them a small price to pay for the pleasure and exhilaration of living.

Carl and Andrew and Matthew and their wives and Alicia and her husband arrived within minutes after I telephoned them, a prelude to an invasion of friends and acquaintances. Soon the house was crowded with people. After some delay I had reached Jeanine in Florence and managed to convince her that there was no reason for her to come home for the funeral—Aunt Felicity wouldn't have wanted her to interrupt her studies.

Late that morning I went to the kitchen to brew more tea for the guests and Matthew was coming up from the cellar with four bottles of sherry to replenish the supply. He motioned me into the pantry out of hearing of Mrs. Finch and the maids preparing refreshments.

"Sue," he whispered, "she didn't leave one of those pieces of paper with a clue on it, did she?"

"What do you mean?"

"That game of murder meant so much to Aunt Felicity. Maybe she had a premonition that she was going to be killed. Maybe that's why she made us play it so that we could discover her murderer."

I couldn't answer Matthew. I stared at him. He might have said an obscenity over Aunt Felicity's body.

My lack of answer was evidently answer enough for Matthew. "I know it's far-fetched," he said. "I—well, my God, I suppose I'm crazy but I thought maybe she had been murdered. Whatever you do, don't mention my suspicions to the others."

And then Carl and Andrew in turn stalked me, each cornering me privately in that house teeming with callers and prodding me to learn whether Aunt Felicity had left a clue that might point to her murderer. My shock and disbelief made them back away with apologies. The suspicions appalled me; and each swore me to secrecy, none of them wanting his dark mistrust to be told to the others.

But when Alicia grabbed my arm and pulled me into the downstairs powder room and locked the door behind us and asked if Aunt Felicity had left a clue I was less shocked. I now had questions of my own.

"Who would be the suspects, Alicia?"

"Any of us. All of us."

"But why? Why on earth would any of us want to murder Aunt Felicity?"

"Money," Alicia said. "Aunt Felicity was very, very rich and she left her fortune to us."

"Money? We all have money of our own. We don't need Aunt Felicity's money."

"Don't be naive, Sue. No one ever has enough money. I happen to know that Andrew is desperate for ready cash, and Carl has a new love affair but his wife won't give him a divorce without stripping him of everything he owns. And Matthew—"

I held up my hand for her to stop talking.

"Little baby sister," she said, "you're much too unworldly. You've spent your adult life being an errand girl and making telephone calls. I didn't mean to upset you or to make monsters out of our brothers.

Someone could have murdered Aunt Felicity out of pity. It was unbearable sometimes to watch her hopeless fight against pain. I've longed for her to die so that her suffering would be over."

"But, Alicia, how could she have been murdered?"

"I don't know. Maybe an overdose of sleeping pills or something else put into her sherry. We all knew she drank it before going to sleep."

I slumped into the chair at the dressing table.

"Stop looking so horror-struck," Alicia ordered. "And get up out of that chair. We've guests to attend to. Come on."

AT LAST AUNT FELICITY'S HOUSE was empty of all the callers; my brothers and sister, about to leave, insisted I not spend the night alone; each invited me to be an overnight guest.

"Alone?" I said. "I'm not alone. Mr. and Mrs. Finch are here. I want to stay where I belong—in Aunt Felicity's house."

I had no intention of leaving, and I was relieved finally to close the front door on my brothers and Alicia and go to my room.

It had been a long difficult day and the night was almost over. I needed rest for the approaching funeral and all the details that would precede and follow it.

But I could not sleep.

Seemingly the only thing alive in that dark and silent house was my small bedside clock and its regular tick and its illuminated hands that kept circling around and around as the slow and sleepless hours marched past.

Then a breeze swirled up from the front door and ascended the stairway and turned the corridor and swept into my room, and the most cautious footsteps I ever heard mounted the stairs and eased into Aunt Felicity's room.

And I knew that either Carl or Matthew or Andrew or Alicia was searching there for a sheet of paper bearing a clue that would point to Aunt Felicity's murderer. They had been right to be suspicious. I was, as Alicia had said, the naive one.

Aunt Felicity's game of murder had been played all along for a real purpose.

But I tried to persuade myself that the darkness and my tiredness had exaggerated everything, that I had only imagined the breeze that had entered with the opening of the front door. I could not have heard any footsteps—the chatter of the clock would have muffled them.

But perhaps I ought to make sure.

Perhaps I ought to get up and look into Aunt Felicity's room.

Then above the ticking of the clock I heard descending footsteps and then the front door opened and closed.

There was still time for me to find out who had come in. I could rush to the entrance and see whose car was driving away.

Then I told myself that surely our loving family had not bred a murderer. Whoever had entered had only wanted to check to be sure that Aunt Felicity had not left a clue; it was not a murderer intent on destroying a clue. Aunt Felicity's game of murder had only been an innocent pastime with the slight moral purpose of proving Jeanine's superiority over Matthew's and Carl's and Andrew's and Alicia's worldliness and my aimlessness.

That idea reassured me and I managed to fall asleep.

But I was not reassured when I awoke. My one resolution was to play out the murder game.

I had never liked the game, but that didn't matter now. For once I must be adept at it. Jeanine, the only one good at the game, was thousands of miles away, and if Aunt Felicity had left a clue she would have meant it for me. She knew I wasn't subtle like Jeanine, so she would have left a clue easy for me to decipher.

I went resolutely into Aunt Felicity's room.

The last time I had been in there I had found her dead body.

But before I had discovered she was dead I had gone about the ordinary morning routine. I had picked up a book of poetry from the floor and had set it on the bedside table where it was now. I had opened the shutters and had gone to the bathroom to dampen a washcloth.

I looked around me.

Nothing about the room resembled itself. The bed with its hangings seemed almost pretentious, the tambour organdy curtains looked too stiff, the French sofas and armchairs belonged to a stage set, the chandeliers should light a palace ballroom, the paintings ought to hang in a museum.

Without Aunt Felicity's presence the room had lost its elegance, all its personality.

I walked over to the small table near the Récamier sofa from which Aunt Felicity had taken, as she began the murder game, the sheets listing the names of the suspects. The drawer contained pads of scratch paper. I fluttered through them, but I could find nothing written on any sheet.

Then I realized that if Aunt Felicity were in the last moments of her life and aware of her predicament she must certainly have been in bed, and would have had no way to make the arduous journey from her bed to the table and back again without help, which she could surely not have requested of her murderer.

So she would have left the clue near or in the bed.

But the bedside table had nothing to offer. The books of poetry and the sherry decanter and wine glasses were on it. Inside the top drawer were my aunt's cosmetics and medicines. The bottom drawer held stationery and various pens and pencils, but everything was innocent of the clue in Aunt Felicity's handwriting for which I was searching.

I pulled back the bedcovers. No doubt Mrs. Finch had changed the sheets after Aunt Felicity's death and had dislodged the clue if Aunt Felicity had left it in the bed. Mrs. Finch would have thrown it in the trash if it had fluttered out at her. I found nothing in the bedsheets or stuffed under the mattress or in any of the pillowcases.

There was no clue.

Or if there had been one the early morning visitor had found it and removed it.

But I will not give up.

I looked again at the collections of poetry. I picked up the Keats book and riffled its pages. There was nothing it in. I put it back and took up the Hopkins book; the only extraneous thing in it was a small piece of paper that marked Aunt Felicity's reading place.

I snatched the paper. It was not identical in size to the pads of scratch paper which Aunt Felicity used for the murder game, but it did not need to be. A single word was written out on it with the black nylon-tipped pen that Aunt Felicity always used when she wrote down the clues.

The word was TERENCE.

I said the name aloud. It was vaguely familiar. Terence was a writer of antiquity, wasn't he? I didn't know. I didn't have Jeanine's fund of information. Holding the sheet of paper, I ran downstairs to the library and pulled a biographical dictionary from a shelf. " 'Terrence,' I read. 'Publius Terentius Afer C. 190–159 B.C.' " My eyes raced down the rest of the entry but I paid no attention to what I was reading. It was of no use to me. Aunt Felicity would have known I couldn't make deductions from a literary reference. She would have made it easier for me.

But however simple or easy she might have thought she was making it she had not made it simple enough or clear enough for me.

Terence.

Terence.

Terence.

It meant absolutely nothing.

The telephone rang, summoning me to all the duties and details attendant on Aunt Felicity's funeral.

It was Mr. Frame, Aunt Felicity's attorney, telling me that the undertaker had tentatively arranged for the service to be held at two the next afternoon if it would be satisfactory with us. He asked me to telephone Alicia and my brothers and then to let the undertaker know.

I would telephone them and then I would call Dr. Cowan and ask if Aunt Felicity could possibly have been murdered. I would tell him I thought that as Aunt Felicity had grown drowsier and drowsier after her last caller had left she realized that the caller had put something lethal in her sherry when it was poured out for her, and that just before she died she had managed to write something that incriminated the caller and had put the slip of paper in a book just before it fell out of her hand.

First, though, I must telephone about the time of the funeral.

As always I began with Carl, since he was the oldest.

His telephone was busy, so I called Matthew. Two o'clock was satisfactory with him. I called Carl again, but his line was still busy. So I dialed Alicia and then Andrew; each said the hour was agreeable.

Carl was the only one left to question and his line was still busy; I kept dialing.

And then I realized that Aunt Felicity *had* made it simple for me. Terence.

My finger, plucking at numbers, had also been dialing letters of the alphabet, and Carl's number was 837-3623.

I wanted the line to stay busy forever, but on my next try Carl answered. I told him the proposed hour of Aunt Felicity's funeral and, as with the others, it was all right with him.

Then I said, "Carl, Aunt Felicity did leave a clue. I found it a little while ago. The clue she wrote was Terence. It was directed at me because I use the telephone so much. When I dialed your number—

837-3623—I also dialed T-E-R-E-N-C-E. As Jeanine would say, Terence equals Carl. You killed Aunt Felicity."

There was a long pause and then a sound I had never heard on a telephone. I thought at first that a door might have slammed, but then I heard my sister-in-law scream and I knew that Carl had shot himself.

James Holding

CARD SENSE

ALTHOUGH I READILY ADMIT that I earn my livelihood by means not usually considered honest, I like to think I am not an entirely unredeemed human being.

For one thing, I never cheat at poker.

Not because I have scruples against it, of course. Not at all. But rather, because I consider it contemptibly picayune as well as physically dangerous if one happens to be caught at it. Besides—and I confess this with all due modesty—I am an exceptionally observant poker player and do not normally find it in the least necessary to stoop to cheating in order to win handsomely at the game.

In my experience, careful observation of one's opponents contributes infinitely more to winning at poker than does the fickle jade affectionately known to many gamblers as Lady Luck. Give me an hour or two of play in which to observe my fellow gamblers as they draw, bet, raise, call, hold, or fold, and I can usually detect, from their individual mannerisms in correlation to the hands they ultimately expose, a pretty good evaluation of the cards they hold. Such individual mannerisms are valuable clues which the keen observer can interpret to his profit.

For example, a sudden attentiveness of posture after a draw, an increase in a player's volubility, a more than usual eagerness to get on with the betting—all these may signal a good hand. A slight increase in the loudness of a certain player's voice, a tiny thread of strain in another's tone may be a clear signal that he is bluffing. Some players, when they plan to raise or call, will unconsciously fiddle with their stacks of chips, or hold their hands with unnatural rigidity. You see what I mean?

Anyway, my name is Henry Carmichael.

At home my colleagues and friends call me "Professor" as a satirical comment on my scholarly speech and my one year of higher education at Dartmouth College.

The five men gathered with me around the poker table in Naples, Florida, that night were neither colleagues nor friends—merely five congenial companions with whom I had played golf occasionally during the two weeks of my annual vacation, and who had invited me to help them improve the evening with a little poker while their wives attended a fashion show in one of the public rooms of the Colony Sands Hotel.

Actually, they were a bit above me, socially and financially, these friendly fellows. Stainton, vice president of a steel company; Corrigan, ex-chairman of an insurance company; Hoblitzel, a Detroit pediatrician; Lasher, a retired broker; and Bellamy, our host, who, I gathered, had been something rather important in the trucking industry.

We had been playing for two hours and I was, as usual, comfortably ahead. It was a comparatively modest game for such tycoons as my opponents—ten-dollar limit with only three raises permitted. In spite of that, I estimated the chips in front of me might add up to winnings of perhaps ten or eleven hundred dollars.

We took a short break around ten o'clock to freshen our drinks and sample the sandwiches that Bellamy had hospitably provided. Lasher looked at my stacks of chips and said, "Henry, how do you do it?"

"Do what?"

"Win so consistently?"

I shrugged modestly. "Just lucky, I suppose."

Lasher shook his head. "I guess luck accounts for some of it, of course, but I have this odd feeling, watching you play tonight, that you can actually sense beforehand whether you'll draw the cards you want."

I smiled. "That sounds like a definition of cheating."

"I don't mean that," Lasher hastened to apologize. "I'm certain you're not cheating, Henry. What I mean is—"

Hoblitzel spoke up. "What you mean is, Henry has exceptionally acute perceptions where cards are concerned, right? An extra helping of card sense, in other words."

"That's it," Lasher said. "What about it, Henry?"

I waved a deprecatory hand. "An extra helping of card sense? Well, yes, I suppose you could say that. Or even a little touch of ESP, perhaps. Because with me, it sometimes seems to go beyond mere card sense in the accepted meaning of the term."

"Like how?" Bellamy asked.

"In that last hand we played, for example, I felt a definite, though inexplicable, premonition that I would draw the king that gave me a full house. Hence my aggressive raising before the draw when I had nothing but two pair. I felt certain I would fill. And I did."

"Who can win against a guy with second sight?" Stainton said in mock disgust. "Deal me out of this game, friends. If Henry can read the future—"

I sipped my drink. "I can't, really," I said. "Only occasionally. Very, very occasionally. And then only in draw poker."

"How does your card sense work with stud?" Corrigan asked. "Maybe we'd better switch to dealer's choice."

There was general laughter in which I joined. Then I said ruefully, "My card sense, as you call it, is more an embarrassment to me than anything else. I don't understand it. And I really don't want it. But I am afraid there is nothing I can do about it. It runs in my family, like hemophilia or twins."

Lasher said, "Everybody in your family has ESP?"

"No, not everybody, thank God. But somebody in each generation seems to come up with it. My own card sense is minuscule when compared with that of a niece of mine in Indianapolis." I spread my hands in a wide gesture. "She's truly incredible."

"With cards?" Hoblitzel asked. "Like you?"

I nodded. "With one important added improvement, as the ads say. Her ESP, or card sense, or whatever, works over long distances."

Silence. At length Bellamy said, "All right, Henry, I can go along with a gag. What do you mean, 'long distances'?"

"Hundreds of miles," I replied. "Don't ask me to explain it, because I can't."

"Wow!" exclaimed Stainton. He slapped his knee. "That does it, for me. Card sense I'll accept. But *long-distance* card sense? No way!"

Hoblitzel, who must have studied some aspects of the subject while in medical school, murmured, "There *have* been instances of it, Jerry."

"Name one," Stainton said.

"Well, if I remember correctly," Hoblitzel said, "some researcher at Duke University or somewhere claims he has known primitive Australian bushmen, the aborigines of the outback, to communicate mentally with each other while physically separated by two thousand miles of desert."

"Nuts!" said Lasher. "Where'd you hear that fairy story?" Then to me, "You're kidding, aren't you, Henry?"

I shook my head. "No," I said earnestly and a little apologetically, "I'm not. I've known my niece to identify correctly a card drawn from a deck of cards by a stranger five hundred miles away."

At this there was a moment of dead silence, as though I had uttered an obscenity at a church picnic. Finally Lasher cleared his throat and said, "No reflection on you and your niece, Henry, but that's pure unadulterated hogwash, if you'll pardon a contradiction in terms." He reached out a hand and cut the deck of cards on the table before him, turning up the four of diamonds. "You are trying to tell me that your niece in Indianapolis could identify this four of diamonds by ESP, even though she's hundreds of miles away?"

"I am not trying to tell you anything," I said wearily. I hitched my chair closer to the table. "Why don't we get on with our game? Whose deal is it?"

"Wait a minute," Corrigan said slowly. "Let's not overlook the fact that Henry here has demonstrated his own superior card sense tonight by winning a lot of money from us as easily as though we were children who had never played poker before." He flashed the other players a conspiratorial look which I pretended not to see. "So maybe he's being honest with us about his niece." He eyed me curiously, half intrigued, half suspicious. "How does she do this remote control ESP trick, Henry? Do you help her? By broadcasting thought waves to her in the form of the four of diamonds, perhaps?" He laughed.

"I have nothing to do with it," I said with ill-concealed impatience. "I told you, I don't understand how she does it and I don't want to. All I know is that she *can* do it."

Bellamy said baldly, "I don't believe it, Henry. I'm sorry, but I just don't believe it." He winked at Corrigan. Again, I pretended not to notice. "I'm willing to bet you anything it's utterly impossible." There was a faint undertone of challenge beneath the raillery.

I sighed. "I'm sorry I mentioned my niece," I said. "I had no intention of starting an argument, believe me."

"You haven't started an argument," Corrigan said. "What you've done is to arouse our betting blood, Henry. I agree with Joe that it's impossible for anyone to identify correctly a card cut from a deck that's hundreds of miles away. I'm willing to bet on it, too."

Stainton raised a hand. "I'd like to have a small piece of that action."

I sighed again, more deeply than before. "I don't want to take your money," I protested. "You're betting against something I know is a sure thing."

"Wait a minute," Lasher said. "You can't leave me out of this. But before I make any bets, I want to know just how we put your niece to the test?"

"We call her on the telephone," I said, "and ask her what card you just cut."

"Oho!" Lasher crowed. "I'm beginning to get it now." He gave me a mock-knowing look. "When you telephone your niece, you give her some sort of signal that tips her off to the four of diamonds. A prearranged signal. Right?"

"Wrong," I said. "*You* put in the call. Or have the hotel switchboard place it for you. Do it anyway you like. Then you talk to my niece yourself. I'll stay out of it. You don't even mention my name, although the chances are she'll guess who's put you up to calling her. She's been called a few times before"—I smiled around at them—"by other skeptical card players like you."

"You won't go near the phone? You won't say a word?" Corrigan said.

"Not a word."

"That's good enough for me," Hoblitzel said. "I never did believe that ESP jazz about the Australian bushmen. I'll take a piece of the bet, too. How much, Henry?"

I counted the chips stacked in front of me, an action commonly considered an augury of ill fortune to follow. "This is foolishness," I said. "However—" I finished my counting. "I seem to have won just over a thousand dollars from you tonight. So shall we say two hundred dollars apiece? If you insist on betting, that is. Personally I'd rather play poker. That's what we're here for."

"I think I detect a slight attack of cold feet, Henry," Bellamy said.

"You can't back out now," Lasher said, rubbing his hands. "Two hundred is great with me, Henry. Okay with the rest of you guys?"

His four friends chorused their agreement.

"The phone's there beside you," Bellamy said to Lasher.

Lasher reached for it. "Here we go," he said. "What's your niece's name, Henry? And her address? Or do you have her telephone number?"

"Her name's Pamela Rogers. And her telephone number is—" I got out my wallet and rummaged in it until I found the folded scrap of paper bearing Pamela's telephone number. I read it off to Lasher.

"What if she's not home?" he asked as he lifted the receiver.

I shrugged. "You'll save two hundred bucks apiece," I said.

Lasher asked the switchboard operator for an outside line and dialed

Pamela's number himself. Faintly, as he held the receiver away from his ear so that the rest of us could hear, came the distant ringing of Pamela's phone in Indianapolis. On the fifth ring we could all hear a click as the receiver was lifted. A female voice said, "Hello?"

Lasher said, "Is this Pamela Rogers?"

"Yes," came the crisp reply.

"My name is Lasher. And I'm calling—"

Pamela broke in, "What? Who did you say? Dasher? I don't know you, do I? Are you calling long distance? You sound so far away. Or else this is a rotten connection."

"Lasher," Lasher said, "with an 'L.' I'm calling you from Naples, Florida, Miss Rogers, to ask if you'll be good enough to settle a bet that I've made with a friend of mine—"

"Hold it!" Pamela said. "This friend of yours wouldn't happen to be my Uncle Henry, would it?"

"Could be," Lasher said cautiously.

"I thought so! And I suppose he's in trouble again?"

Lasher flashed a glance at me. "What do you mean in trouble again, Miss Rogers?"

"You're playing poker with him, right? And he's a big winner, isn't he? So somebody in the game suspects him of cheating, and Uncle Henry gives you his song and dance about having superior card sense. And you don't quite believe him. So he uses me to prove that unusually keen card sense *does* run in his family, right?"

"Well . . ." Lasher hesitated. "Something like that, yes. Only we don't believe your uncle is cheating. He's not in any trouble at all. This is just a friendly bet, Miss Rogers, and we'd appreciate it if you could help us settle it."

We could hear an exaggerated sigh of irritation at the other end of the line.

"Okay," Pamela said, "I'll try. But this is absolutely the last time. Tell Uncle Henry that, will you? I'm sick and tired of having him make me out as some kind of a freak!"

Lasher laughed and said, "I'll tell him, all right. And thank you for being so accommodating. Now then: I've just drawn a card from our deck here, and the bet is that you can identify it, even though you're in Indianapolis and we're in Florida. So can you tell me which card I've drawn?"

A hush descended on us. We held our collective breath until Pamela said tentatively, "Uh . . . yes, I probably can. But give me a minute, you're awfully far away for me to get any vibes. So far, it isn't clear at all." She said nothing more for a long moment, then plaintively, "It isn't coming through, Mr. Rasher. I'm terribly sorry."

I counted five triumphant expressions flitting simultaneously across the faces of Lasher, Corrigan, Stainton, Hoblitzel, and Bellamy.

Lasher almost chortled. "We're sorry, too, Miss Rogers. At least, your Uncle Henry is sorry, I'm sure." A thread of quite ungentlemanly malice crept into his voice. "It was very good of you to try, anyway."

"Wait a minute," Pamela said, "don't hang up yet. Will you hold on a minute while I get a cigarette? Smoking helps me to concentrate for some funny reason."

"Sure, go ahead," said Lasher blandly. "I'll hold on." He put his hand over the telephone mouthpiece and said to us with a snicker, "She's gone to get a cigarette to help her concentrate. Did you hear that?"

We nodded. "Give her a chance," I said. "She may surprise you yet."

Corrigan said jovially, "Two hundred more says she doesn't."

I shook my head.

"Chicken," Stainton said.

Lasher, holding the phone, said, "It's taking her a hell of a long time to find a cigarette, it seems to me."

"Maybe she had to run down to the corner store for a new pack," Hoblitzel suggested, smiling.

"Probably can't find her lighter," I hazarded. "She's a great one for mislaying things."

"Including her ESP," Lasher said smugly. "You suppose she just left me on 'hold' and went back to bed, maybe?"

"She wouldn't do that," I said. "Not Pamela. Give her another minute or two."

"This is a long-distance call, for God's sake!" Corrigan said. "If she doesn't get back to us pretty soon, the charges will eat up our profit!"

At this bit of infantile humor everybody laughed loudly, including me.

The seconds ticked by, each one seeming of inordinate length. Corrigan built himself another drink. Hoblitzel sat quietly, tapping his fingers on the table. Bellamy urged Stainton to have another sandwich. Lasher yawned.

Then, suddenly, he snapped to attention. "Here she is!" he said out of the corner of his mouth. He uncovered the mouthpiece of the phone. "We were beginning to think you'd left us for good, Miss Rogers. Couldn't you find your cigarettes?" Slight rallying tone.

"Yes, but not my lighter," Pamela said. "I'm sorry to be so long. I'm all set now." The sound of a woman exhaling cigarette smoke from deep in her lungs came to us quite clearly over the line. Pamela said, "There, that's better. Isn't it peculiar how a cigarette seems to help? It's coming through to me much clearer, now, Mr. Lasher. Oh, yes . . . now I can see it. I think the card you drew from the deck is . . ." She paused and blew smoke noisily.

"Is what?" Lasher demanded. "What card did I draw?"

"It's the four of diamonds, isn't it?" Pamela asked.

To say that my companions were thunderstruck is to minimize the shock effect of thunder. They were stunned, frozen into immobility by surprise and incredulity. For a moment we all sat like statues, staring at Lasher and the phone in his hand. At length he said very quietly indeed, "Thank you, Miss Rogers," and hung up as gingerly as though he were placing a heavy boulder on a fragile piece of window glass. "Did you hear that?" he whispered. "She said the four of diamonds."

Another long moment went by in silence. Then Hoblitzel gave me a crooked grin and said, "Henry, you're the first Australian bushman I ever played poker with. Here's your two hundred."

WHEN I RETURNED HOME a week later, I met Dixie at the Elite Cocktail Lounge to present her with her share of the loot. As she entered the café and swivel-hipped her graceful way toward the booth in which I awaited her with a martini in front of me, she seemed the very embodiment of wholesome, unsophisticated young innocence— the last person in the world one would suspect of harboring larceny in her heart. I realized once more how fortunate I was to have won her friendship—and on many occasions, her expert cooperation.

I stood up to greet her. "Miss Pamela Rogers, I presume," I said, bowing from the waist.

She dimpled at me. "The same, Professor," she answered, bowing in her turn. She sat down, waited until the waitress had brought her a frozen daiquiri, then asked brightly, "You have something for me, Professor?"

I passed her an envelope containing $500 in cash. She thrust the envelope into her shoulder bag without even counting the money. Dixie is the only person I know who completely trusts me.

We raised our glasses in a congratulatory toast to each other. Then I said, "So you took up smoking the minute I left town?"

She twinkled at me. "You meant the 'cigarette-to-help-me-concentrate' bit that I laid on your friend Mr. Dasher or Smasher or whatever his name was?"

"THAT WAS JUST A STALL FOR TIME," Dixie said. "We had an ice storm up here that night you wouldn't believe, Professor. It downed a lot of power lines and blacked us out for over an hour, just when your friend called. So I had to stall while I tried to remember where I'd left my flashlight." She took a sip of her daiquiri. "And you know how I am about mislaying things. Did the wait make you nervous?"

I patted her hand. In our prearranged code of four surnames to designate the four suits in a deck of cards, and thirteen first names to denote the different cards in each suit, the name "Pamela Rogers" instantly identified the four of diamonds—except, alas, to Dixie, whose memory is as unreliable as mine is photographic. Wherefore I had prepared a written list of our code names for Dixie to keep conveniently beside her telephone for ready reference when a call like Mr. Lasher's came in. "Did the wait make me nervous?" I said. "I haven't stopped shaking yet. I thought you'd mislaid our name sheet!"

George C. Chesbro

FOUR KNIGHTS GAME

GIVING A SIMULTANEOUS CHESS EXHIBITION against 50 players was
nothing new for Douglas Franklin. A prodigy as a child, an international grand master at 18, Douglas had spent the last 10 of his 29 years
wringing out a living doing what he loved best: playing chess. He
had been around the world a half dozen times. He had little money,
a small walk-up flat in New York City, an unbroken string of invitations to all the major international tournaments, and he called that
freedom.

Like most grand masters, Douglas was accustomed to playing simultaneous exhibitions in a kind of trance. Not that he didn't know what
was happening on the boards; but he relied on his prodigious skills,
natural instincts and vast experience to sustain him through the long
hours as he moved around the inner circle formed by the players'
tables, working to obtain an advantage in the openings, then allowing
each game to take its course, to play *him*.

This exhibition was different. The girl was a distraction.

She was good, Douglas now realized; too good to be a casual week-
end player like the majority of participants on the "Chess Cruise" he
had been hired to host. He had underestimated her and chosen a line
of attack that was quick and powerful, but ultimately inferior. She had
withstood the attack, and Douglas now found himself in *zugzwang*,
where all the moves available to him were bad ones.

Sensing a game of unusual interest, a number of spectators had
crowded around the girl's board. Armand Zoltan, the ship's owner,
had positioned his huge bulk directly behind the girl's chair and was
staring over her shoulder at the score sheet she had been keeping.
Zoltan's eyes were large and black, like two pieces of coal shoved
into the puffy dough of his face. His gaze momentarily flicked upward

218

as Douglas approached. Then he turned his attention back to the score sheet.

There was one other man who appeared more interested in the record of moves than in the actual position on the board. He had slipped between two of the tables and was standing inside the circle, studying the piece of paper by the girl's hand. He was tall and thin, with pale, almost yellow eyes that seemed to blink in spasms. A bald pate was sparsely covered with a few strands of hair combed from one side to the other and plastered down with hair lotion. His suit was obviously well-tailored but failed to disguise the fact that he needed a bath. He smelled of spicy after-shave and sweat.

Douglas touched the man on the shoulder. "Excuse me, I need some room." The man stared hard at Douglas for a few moments, then moved quickly back.

Douglas lighted a cigarette and pretended to study the position on the board in front of him. He knew the position was hopeless; what he was really interested in was the girl. If she were nervous, she didn't show it. She was cool and poised, despite the crush of onlookers and Zoltan breathing down her neck. She had a high forehead framed by silky, raven black hair; cold, penetrating green eyes that seemed to reveal little were contradicted by a full, sensual mouth.

The score sheet had no name on it.

Douglas tipped over his king in the traditional gesture of defeat. "I resign," he said easily.

There was scattered applause, quickly stilled by the angry shushing of the other players.

"Thank you," the girl said quietly. She rose and began to fold her score sheet.

Douglas gently touched her arm. "May I ask who just beat me?"

The girl smiled and extended her hand. "My name is Anne Pickford." Her grip was firm, like her game. She spoke with a pronounced British accent.

"You play a fine game, Anne. Do you mind if I borrow your score sheet? I'd like to look it over."

Anne laughed as she handed him the paper. "If you like. But my guess is that you know every move that was made. The line you used was refuted three years ago in Copenhagen. You were the one who refuted it, against Barslov."

Douglas grinned and slipped the sheet into his pocket. Many of the spectators had moved on to the other boards, but Douglas was aware that the man with the yellow eyes was standing close by, watching them. Douglas leaned closer. "Actually, I was looking for an excuse to ask you to have a drink with me."

"Why must you have an excuse, Mr. Franklin? Where's your natural grand-master egomania?"

"It's badly bruised at the moment. Eight o'clock in the upper lounge?"

"Fine."

The girl nodded curtly, then turned and walked away. Douglas waited until she had disappeared from sight out on the deck, then moved on to the next board. He studied it for a moment, then reached down and moved a bishop. "Checkmate," he said cheerfully.

"PICKFORD," DOUGLAS SAID. "There was an English grand master, Samuel Pickford."

Anne smiled and sipped her drink. "My father. He taught me how to play."

Douglas tapped the score sheet in his pocket. "Of course. It really was a beautifully played Sicilian."

Anne shrugged. "We both know you'd beat me easily in a match."

Douglas' glass was empty. He looked inquiringly at the girl, who shook her head. He ordered another Scotch for himself, then leaned back and studied her.

"Why haven't I heard of you? Judging from the way you play, I'd say you were at least an expert. Considering the state of women's chess, I'd think you'd be in international competition."

Something moved deep in the girl's eyes, a dark, silent laughter that Douglas found disconcerting.

"I find my own game more interesting," Anne said quietly.

"Really? What game would that be?"

"I'm a journalist." Her eyes were veiled again. "Actually, this is a working trip for me."

"You're not here as a player?"

"No. I'm afraid I sneaked into the exhibition."

"I'm glad you did."

"I was in Barcelona when I heard about this junket to Glasgow for the Interzonal elimination. Obviously, chess is very chic now and I thought there might be a good story in the cruise. I was right. Here I am in the middle of the ocean, having drinks with the infamous Douglas Franklin. . . ."

Douglas laughed. "Infamous?"

"Well, perhaps that's overstating the case. But it's true that most serious players resent you, and non-chess players admire or envy you. For the same reasons."

"What reasons?"

"Take the Glasgow Interzonal. You won't be playing in it because you never bothered to try to qualify. Instead, you're hosting a boatload of *patzers* on their way to sit in the audience. Who else but Douglas Franklin would win his share of major tournaments every year, then turn his back on the chance to play for the world championship? The chess Establishment thinks you're irresponsible."

"What do you think?"

"I think you're having a lot of fun. You're waiting for your wanderlust to burn itself out. When you want the world championship enough, you'll go after it."

Douglas shrugged. He felt it was time to change the subject.

A steward arrived with his drink. As Douglas pushed back his chair to give the man room he noticed two men watching them from a table in a far corner of the lounge. One was Zoltan, and the other was the man with the yellow eyes.

Douglas waited for the steward to leave, then pulled his chair back close to the table. "Let's see how good a journalist you are," he said quietly. "The two men at the corner table—the fat one's Armand Zoltan, right?"

Again, something moved in Anne's eyes. She glanced quickly over his shoulder, then back into his face. She seemed puzzled. "Yes. He owns this ship. But didn't he hire you?"

Douglas shook his head. "I was hired by the travel agency booking the cruise. Who's the guy with him?"

"I don't know." Her voice cracked almost imperceptibly and she quickly swallowed some water. "Why do you ask?"

"Just curious. They seemed to take a special interest in our game this afternoon. Maybe they think it's still going on."

Anne paled and her eyes shifted slightly out of focus, as if she were looking at something ugly and menacing far in the distance, beyond the confines of the ship.

Douglas tried to bring her back. "Does Zoltan play chess?"

"A Four Knights Game," Anne said absently.

"I must have missed a move. How's that again?"

Anne's eyes came back into focus and she smiled disarmingly. Whatever she had been looking at was gone, sunk in the depths of the ocean, or her mind. "Nothing," she said easily. "I was just talking to myself." She stifled a yawn that could have been feigned. "I'm sorry," she said. "I'm very tired."

Douglas summoned the steward and signed the check, then escorted Anne out of the lounge. Zoltan and the yellow-eyed man had already left.

Anne chatted pleasantly on the way back to her cabin, but Douglas could sense that something in her had changed. She was distracted, and he had become nothing more than a shadow at her side that talked. This bothered him, and he tried unsuccessfully to break down the barrier that the mention of a man's name had erected.

Douglas' mind rapidly shifted to other things when he reached his own cabin. He was positive he had locked it before leaving, but the louvered door swung open at his touch.

He stepped inside and switched on the light, then froze. His berth had been torn apart, thoroughly and professionally. His suitcases had been opened and their linings torn out; his clothes and personal possessions were strewn over the floor.

In the air was the faint but unmistakable odor of the man with the yellow eyes.

Douglas sensed rather than heard a movement behind him. He had just started to turn when something hard and heavy smashed into the base of his skull. What started out as a terrible, rending pain ended as a warm wave sloshing back and forth inside his brain. He didn't even remember falling.

"HELLO, DOUGLAS," THE GIRL SAID. "You look terrible."

"I had a rough night." Douglas gently touched the back of a head that felt like it was filled with broken glass. "I got mugged."

"Really?"

"Really. And the man who did it was the same man who was with Zoltan in the lounge last night."

Anne's eyes narrowed. "How do you know that?" She tried to adopt a casual tone, but her voice was tight and had a sharp edge to it.

"I smelled him," Douglas said evenly.

"Did you report it to the captain? I suppose you've done that."

"Sure. He was properly upset. Said he'd look into it."

"Was anything taken?"

"That's why I called you. You see, I don't have that much to begin

with, and it was all there when I woke up. I double-checked. It
wasn't until I took off my jacket that I realized what was missing. It
was the score sheet you gave me. That's what the man was after."

Anne paled and quickly looked away. "You could have lost it."
Her voice was strangely muffled, as though damped by some intense
emotion held tightly under rein.

"I didn't lose it."

Anne quickly regained control of herself. The face that she now
presented to Douglas was totally expressionless, the green eyes cold
and distant. Suddenly, without warning, she laughed. "Is *that* what
you wanted to talk to me about?"

Douglas felt his face grow hot. He'd realized before he called Anne
that he would risk sounding foolish, and she was not making things
easier for him. Still, he felt sure that whoever had sapped him had
known exactly what he wanted to find. If the score sheet had been
taken, there was a reason.

"I know it sounds strange," Douglas said tightly. "That's the point.
I thought you might have some idea why somebody would want to
steal that particular score sheet."

"Please leave me alone," Anne said coldly. "I've heard some stupid
lines before, but this tops all." Her eyes flashed. "Really, Douglas,
you're such a child. Is this another game? Must you make everything
into a game?"

"What is it, Anne? What's wrong?"

"Stick to your chess; that's obviously what you do best. You've
already begun to bore me." She punctuated the last sentence by slamming the cabin door in his face.

Douglas stared at the closed door for a few moments, then turned
and walked slowly back the way he had come. When he reached his
cabin he found Armand Zoltan and the ship's doctor waiting for him.
The room had been straightened; his clothes had been neatly folded
and packed in two new, expensive-looking suitcases. There was a large
basket of fruit and a bottle of Scotch on the table beside his bed.

The doctor, a thin, reedy man with a chronic case of dandruff, sat
stiffly on a chair at the opposite end of the room, a huge, leather medical
bag propped on his knees. He smiled nervously as Douglas entered.

Zoltan rose from his chair and gestured expansively around the
room. "Mr. Franklin!" Zoltan's smile did not touch his eyes. "I hope
you will now find everything in order. I wished to take the liberty
of coming personally to apologize for this terrible incident. The man

you described to Captain Barker is under close surveillance." Zoltan took a check from his pocket, signed it with a flourish, then held it out to Douglas. "I trust this will be sufficient compensation for the suffering and inconvenience you've been caused."

"Nothing was stolen," Douglas said evenly, but it suddenly struck him as odd that Zoltan should be on this particular ship. From various newspaper accounts Douglas knew that Zoltan was a multi-millionaire, with a large fleet of ships trafficking on the oceans of the world. What was he doing on a five-day cruise from Spain to Scotland? It was unlikely that he had even had anything to do with the decision to book a boatload of chess players. That type of mundane business affair was usually taken care of by mundane business managers. Zoltan should be on his island hideway, counting his money. What was he doing here?

"Please take the check anyway," Zoltan insisted. "You've proven yourself to be a most valuable part of this cruise, without a doubt underpaid. Accept this as a token of my appreciation."

Douglas took the check and shoved it into his pocket without looking at it.

"I've brought Dr. Macklin with me to examine you," Zoltan continued. "We want to make absolutely certain that you're all right."

"All I've got is a headache," Douglas said. "It'll pass." He suddenly wanted to escape from Zoltan, the cabin, the questions. He glanced at his watch. "I have a class on chess openings in twenty minutes," he continued. "I want to make sure I earn my keep."

"As you wish, Mr. Franklin. The captain, the crew and myself are at your disposal. Please let me know if there's anything you require."

Douglas started for the door, then stopped and turned. "By the way," he said, watching Zoltan's face, "I'm going to be discussing the Four Knights Game. What do you think of that opening, Mr. Zoltan?"

Zoltan looked puzzled. Finally he shrugged. "I'm aware that it's a very old opening, and not particularly aggressive. But I'm certainly no expert by any means."

If the question meant anything else to Zoltan, he had managed to disguise it well. Once again Douglas felt foolish, a participant in a shadow game that might exist only in his mind. He excused himself and walked out of the cabin.

DOUGLAS' CLASS WAS WELL ATTENDED, his lecture and demonstration enthusiastically received. Still, he found his mind constantly returning to Anne Pickford, for reasons that he could not fully explain to himself. Probably it was pride; he was not used to having doors slammed in his face.

Douglas finished with the class at one, then went to the dining lounge. He had hoped to catch sight of Anne, perhaps try to speak to her again. She wasn't there.

After lunch he went to the girl's cabin, knocked repeatedly on the door, but got no answer. He tried the door and found it locked.

Douglas had no responsibilities for the afternoon so he set out to look for Anne. He started on the upper deck. It was a calm, clear day at sea and the European coastline could be seen far in the distance, off the starboard bow. A number of passengers were sunning themselves or playing chess. Douglas strolled casually among the players, greeting familiar faces, occasionally stopping to answer questions or give advice. All the while he kept looking for the girl. There was no sign of her.

Next, Douglas traversed the lower deck, swimming pool, cocktail lounges, and any other place he could think of where the girl might be. By five o'clock his head was splitting and he went back to his cabin to take a nap. He arose in an hour, showered and dressed for dinner. He ate and stayed in the dining lounge until it closed, nursing coffee, watching the doors. Anne did not appear. He went to her cabin; there was still no answer to his knock.

Douglas felt a cold chill pass through his body. Once again he searched through all the areas of the ship that were open to passengers. Then he headed for the ship's bridge.

"I think you're missing a passenger," he reported.

The deck officer stared at him. "I beg your pardon, sir?"

"I said I think one of your passengers may be in trouble. Her name is Anne Pickford. If she's on the ship, I can't find her."

The officer, a Greek of moderate build and deep-set, soulful eyes, shook his head. "It is possible that you simply missed this person, sir. The *Argo* is a large ship."

"It's also possible that she fell overboard. I think you'd better call the captain."

The officer hesitated a moment, then said, "As you wish, sir."

Captain Barker arrived a few minutes later, with Zoltan. There was no question as to who was in charge, and who would do the talking. Barker's face was flushed with interrupted sleep, and his coat was only half-buttoned. His eyes darted nervously about the room and refused to meet Douglas' gaze.

Zoltan stepped forward and took Douglas' elbow solicitously. "Mr. Franklin, how are you feeling?"

Douglas eased himself out of the other man's grip. The expression on Zoltan's face was imponderable. "It's one of your passengers I'm worried about," Douglas said tightly. "Miss Pickford is not in her cabin. I've been—"

Zoltan made an impatient gesture with his hand. The folds of flesh on his face rearranged themselves into something that might have been a leer. "You have a taste for the finer things in life, Mr. Franklin— Douglas, if I may call you that—but you needn't concern yourself about Miss Pickford. She's in good hands."

"Is that right? Whose hands?"

"Miss Pickford took ill quite unexpectedly this morning. Dr. Macklin examined her in her cabin and diagnosed her illness as acute appendicitis. As you may know, appendicitis can often strike without warning. Dr. Macklin thought it best that she be hospitalized immediately. As luck would have it, there was a British patrol boat in the area. Our request for assistance was immediately granted. By now Miss Pickford is undoubtedly in an English hospital."

"I didn't see any patrol boat."

"Of course not. I believe you were giving a demonstration-lecture at the time. In fact, I hope none of the other passengers saw it. We try to keep these unpleasant matters as unobtrusive as possible. The sight of a woman being carried off on a stretcher would be, at best, unpleasant. Before you know it there would be rumors of food poisoning, or something like that. The cruise would be ruined for many passengers. Miss Pickford was transferred from the loading platform at the bow of the ship. Are there any other questions, Douglas?"

There were many other questions, but Douglas decided he would keep them to himself. If Zoltan were telling the truth, everything was fine; if he were lying, nothing could be gained by arousing his suspicions.

"No," Douglas said, fixing his gaze on Zoltan's chest, "I'm glad you acted quickly."

"You are a good person to have on board, Douglas," Zoltan said with a wide grin that could have meant anything. "Most people would not notice the absence of a casual acquaintance. Such concern is to your credit. Now I suggest we all go back to bed and leave the deck officer to his duties. Good night, Mr. Franklin . . . Douglas."

There was a note of finality to Zoltan's voice, and Douglas knew he was being dismissed. He nodded curtly and left the bridge. As he stood near the rail in the moonlight, smoking a cigarette, he stared at the red lettering on the door leading to the lower levels of the ship: NO ADMITTANCE. AUTHORIZED PERSONNEL ONLY. If Zoltan had lied and Anne was still on the ship, that was where she must be. It was the only place he had not looked.

The thought that he was actually considering going through the door bothered Douglas—perhaps the blow on the head had transformed him into an idiot. At best, if he were caught below, he would have compromised himself and his job. At worst, assuming Zoltan was involved in some criminal activity, he might never reach Glasgow. The sea was the ultimate garbage dump, and a ship at sea was a world unto itself, with no place to run and no place to hide; and it was obvious that Zoltan was the final arbiter of the law on the *Argo*. An outside observer might be fascinated by Zoltan's story of how he disappeared, but Douglas had no interest in allowing such a situation to develop. Money was power and power was often more potent than truth. There was no doubt in Douglas' mind that Zoltan had a number of high-voltage connections. One person had already disappeared, and Zoltan was evidently not distressed by that.

Had Anne actually disappeared? *Why* would Zoltan lie?

Douglas mentally reviewed the reasons for his uneasiness: a bump on the head during the course of a robbery that wasn't a robbery; Zoltan's acquaintance with the yellow-eyed man who had hit him; a vague reference to a chess opening that Zoltan hardly knew. Finally, there was the girl's strange behavior. Beneath Anne's cold exterior there had been fear—he was sure of it.

Douglas flipped the cigarette into the wet darkness beyond the railing. He glanced around to make sure he was unobserved, then slipped through the hatchway, closing the steel door quietly behind him.

He found himself at the top of a steep, narrow stairway that was only faintly illuminated by a string of naked, low-wattage electric bulbs. The steps led down to a narrow corridor lined on both sides with cabins. The corridor was empty. Douglas removed his shoes and moved past the cabins, which he assumed held sleeping crew members. He reached the opposite end of the corridor and tried the door there. It was open. He passed through the door, closed it behind him, then put on his shoes.

The corridor beyond the crew's quarters was wider, lined on the right with recessed steel doors on which the word *Cargo* had been stenciled. At the opposite end of the corridor, fifty yards away, was another door.

Douglas tried the first cargo hold. It was locked, as were all the others. Frustrated, he tried the door at the end of the corridor. It, too, was locked. He cursed softly to himself as he realized that he had maneuvered himself into a *cul de sac*.

He turned and started back the way he had come. He froze when he heard the footsteps. They were echoing off the metal floor beyond the closed door leading to the crew's quarters, and they were coming toward him.

Douglas was abreast of the second, recessed steel door. The recess wasn't very deep, but it was the only conceivable hiding place. He flattened himself against the steel plate, and heard the door at the end of the corridor open and close, and the footsteps resume. He peered around the edge of the recess.

The footsteps belonged to the man with the yellow eyes. He was in his shirt sleeves, and the shoulder holster he wore was stuffed with a large, ugly, blue-steel automatic.

Douglas braced, ready to kick out at the man's groin as he came abreast. Then the footsteps stopped. Douglas again looked around the corner of the recess in time to see the yellow-eyed man turn a key in the lock of the first door, open it and pass through. He left the door open behind him. Douglas waited thirty seconds, then slipped down the corridor and looked in the open door.

The cargo hold was large and brightly lit, with two doors at the opposite side. One of the doors was open, revealing a corridor, and Douglas assumed that was where the yellow-eyed man had gone. The right side of the hold was filled with large wooden crates stacked neatly in piles of four.

Douglas entered the hold, darting across the concrete floor and ducking behind one of the piles of crates. A few moments later he heard the sound of footsteps again. The yellow-eyed man emerged from one of the corridors, walked quickly across the cargo hold and exited through the steel door. The door closed behind him with an ominous click.

Douglas stepped out from his hiding place and examined the crates. There were no markings on them, and each was circled by a tight, metal band. There was a large pair of wire clippers hanging on the wall. He took down the clippers and cut through one of the bands. The band snapped with a loud, singing crack that reverberated throughout the closed confines of the hold. Douglas ducked behind the crates again, his heart hammering in his chest, but the silence returned. He waited a few more minutes to make sure no one was coming, then used the handle of the clippers to pry back four of the plywood slats.

The crate was filled with machine pistols; a protective coating of light oil glistened on the black metal. Douglas picked up one of the guns, wiped off the oil with his handkerchief and examined it. The serial number on the frame had been carefully filed off.

The pistol felt heavy and alien in his hand. He searched through the crate for ammunition but couldn't find any. It was just as well— he wouldn't know what to do with a loaded gun.

He replaced the pistol in the crate, found a tarpaulin and threw it over the broken band and slats. Then he crossed the hold and moved down the passageway from where the yellow-eyed man had come. The corridor was about fifty feet long. At the end it branched off at right angles to form another corridor. There were small, glassed-in office cubicles on either side.

He found the girl in the last cubicle on the left. She was lying on a cracked leather couch, tightly bound. There was a wide strip of adhesive tape over her mouth. Her eyes widened when she saw him.

Douglas suddenly realized that he was trembling; his clothes were pasted to his body, and he could smell his own fear in his nostrils. He took a deep breath, then went to the top of the T formed by the intersecting corridors and glanced around the corner. There was no one there.

To the left and right were steel ladders leading up to hatch covers. Douglas quickly climbed one of the ladders and tested the wheel gear on the bottom of the cover. It turned easily. Douglas breathed a sigh of relief at the discovery that there was another way out from below decks without going back through the cargo hold and crew's quarters. If they could manage to get back to the passengers' section, Zoltan just might be forced into a sort of Mexican standoff. He climbed back down the ladder and slipped into the office.

Anne's breath exploded in an urgent whisper as Douglas stripped the tape from her mouth. "Douglas! Zoltan will kill you if he finds you here! Get out!"

Douglas laughed shortly. "That's a strange request. What's he going to do to you if I leave you here?"

The girl said nothing.

Douglas knelt beside her and examined the ropes. They were thin, and the knots had been tied by an expert. There was blood on the girl's wrists and ankles where the rope had cut into the flesh. He searched through the cubicle but could find nothing sharp to cut the ropes so he went to work on the knots with his fingers.

"Who are you?" Douglas asked quietly.

"I'm a British agent," Anne said after a pause.

Douglas smiled wryly. "That's your game?"

"That's my game."

"Well, it certainly isn't very ladylike."

Anne smiled. "Don't talk like a male chauvinist pig, Douglas."

"Chauvinist, hell. None of my opponents has ever tried to tie me up."

"It adds a different dimension," Anne said dryly.

"You like to play word games, too," Douglas said seriously. "The Four Knights Game you referred to: that's the Four Horsemen of the Apocalypse, right?"

Anne winced but did not cry out as Douglas pulled the ropes free from her wrists. Her hands and feet were swollen and inflamed. "Death, war, pestilence and famine," she said through clenched teeth. "Zoltan deals in death: drugs, guns, adulterated medicine. If the price is right, he'll smuggle anything in or out of any country in the world."

"I've seen the guns. Where are they going?"

"Northern Ireland. Special delivery to the terrorists. My job was to notify my superiors when and where the drop was to be made. I had a portable transmitter, but they found it."

"I don't suppose you can explain to me how I got involved in all this."

"Somehow, Zoltan found out about my cover and mission, but he didn't dare move against me until he could be sure I was working alone. My playing in the exhibition aroused his suspicions. He became even more suspicious when he saw I was beating you, and that you wanted my score sheet. He thought you might be a contact, and the score sheet might contain some sort of code. That's why Hawkins—"

"Hawkins. He's the one who's allergic to soap?"

Anne nodded. "You might say Hawkins is the executive director of the seamier side of Zoltan's business enterprises. In any case, they realized they'd made a mistake when they examined the score sheet. They tried to cover up, but by then you'd already talked to me. They knew I'd make the connection, and that's when they moved in."

Douglas finished removing the ropes. Anne eased her legs over the side of the couch and tried to stand. The blood drained from her face.

"Can you walk?"

"Just give me a minute to get the circulation back." She bent over and started to massage the muscles in her legs. "I acted toward you the way I did because I didn't want you involved," Anne said quietly, without looking at Douglas. "I must say, I'm glad you're so persistent. It must be that grand-master egomania."

The odor hit Douglas' nostrils a split second before he heard the words.

"You should have minded your own business, sonny."

The voice and smell belonged to the man with the yellow eyes, the one Anne had called Hawkins. Douglas spun and crouched. Hawkins was standing in the doorway, his legs braced. His lips were drawn taut as a bowstring in a strange, cruel smile. The pistol in his hand was aimed at Douglas' head.

"Checkmate, sonny," Hawkins said, and pulled the trigger.

However, Douglas was already moving, warned by his sensitivity to other people's moods. He knew that Hawkins intended summarily to execute him and that he had little to lose by trying to fight back. He ducked low and drove for the man's legs.

Douglas' speed saved him. The sudden movement caught Hawkins by surprise, throwing off his aim. The bullet smashed into Douglas' wrist, shattering the bone. Numbed by the effects of a massive surge of adrenaline, Douglas barely felt the pain as he hurled himself through the air and hit Hawkins at the knees. Douglas hit the floor hard. Hawkins crumpled over the top of him.

"Run, Anne!" Douglas heard himself shouting. "Get out of here! There's a hatch cover around the corner!"

"Douglas—"

"*Run!*"

He was vaguely aware of a lithe body hurtling through the air over his head, then the sound of footsteps turning the corner. A few seconds later there was the sound of a steel hatch cover clanging shut.

He was not dead yet. Douglas interpreted that as meaning that Hawkins had lost control of his gun. The yellow-eyed man's breath was coming in short gasps, and he was moaning with pain.

Douglas started to wiggle out from beneath the other man's body. It was then that the pain hit him, exploding in his wrist and coursing through his body like bolts of electricity. He cried out and clutched at his wrist. The fingers of his right hand were immediately enveloped in a warm, sticky fluid.

Hawkins rolled off of him. Douglas lifted his head and almost vomited with terror as he saw the gun lying on the floor a few feet away. There was no way he could get to it before Hawkins.

Hawkins took a step toward the gun, then screamed in pain, clutching his right knee as he slumped to the floor. He then began crawling across the floor toward the gun.

Douglas pushed himself to his feet with his good right arm. His head swam with pain, and for a moment he was afraid he would pass out. Then it cleared enough for him to see that Hawkins had the gun. Douglas wheeled and ran out through the door at the same time as a loud explosion thundered in his ears and a bullet smashed into the wood paneling beside his head.

Douglas sprinted around the corner, let go of his wrist and pulled himself up the ladder to the right. He managed to turn the wheel gear, then, bracing his legs on the rungs of the ladder, pushed against the hatch cover with his shoulder. The steel cover was jammed.

He started to climb down, intending to try the other cover. He froze when he saw Hawkins suddenly emerge from around the corner. The man was staggering, clutching his ruined knee with one hand. His eyes were clouded with pain and hate.

For the second time Douglas pulled himself up the ladder and pushed against the hatch cover with his shoulder. His head was filled with a sound like crashing surf—the sound of terror.

Hawkins leaned against the wall, lifted his gun and fired, but the pressure on his shattered knee ruined his aim. The bullet bit into the metal inches from Douglas' left side, then whined off down the corridor.

The hatch cover suddenly burst open. Douglas scrambled up through the opening as a second bullet whined through the air beneath him. He slammed the hatch cover shut, then lay on his back, gasping for air, drinking in the cold, wet sea breeze.

He would have given anything to be able to lie there, not moving, and wait for them to come and get him. There seemed no sense in resisting; Anne and he had not really gotten away, but had merely escaped into a larger pen. They were still trapped on a ship at sea.

The thought of the girl brought him to his feet. He was not ready to die yet, and he would not be a grand master if he had not learned to play out some end games that were apparently lost.

He looked around him and immediately saw that he had made a

tactical error—he had come out the wrong hatch. He was on a narrow walkway, blocked off from the passenger section by a steel bulwark.

Hawkins' voice, fogged by pain and rage, came out of the darkness above him. "You should have taken the trouble to learn the layout of the ship, sonny. You came up the hard way—*I* took the freight elevator." There was a pause filled with hoarse, heavy breathing, then, "You're going to have a lot of company in a few minutes, sonny. But I'm going to take care of you personally."

Douglas pressed flat against the bulkhead. To his left, separated from him by twenty yards of moonlit walkway, were dark, undefined shapes in the open storage area at the stern of the ship. *Twenty yards.*

"Where's the girl?" Douglas asked.

"We'll find her," Hawkins said. The voice seemed closer, almost directly above Douglas.

Douglas tensed, clutching his injured wrist to his side. "You can't afford to do a lot of shooting, Hawkins. It'll wake the passengers."

The answer was a soft, spitting sound, like the cough of a cat. The wood on the walkway to Douglas' left splintered.

"End of the line, sonny."

Douglas pushed off the bulkhead and dashed toward the black shapes at the stern. Bullets whined in the air like angry steel bees. Finally he dove through the air, landed heavily on an oil drum and rolled off on the other side. His wrist felt as if it were bathed in molten metal, and he bit off the scream that formed at the back of his throat.

Finally, after what seemed an eternity, the pain subsided. Douglas lifted his head slightly and looked around him. He was on the edge of a forest of oil drums that had been loaded on pallets and lashed onto the deck. He lowered his head and crawled backward, deeper into the tangle of steel drums.

Somewhere in the darkness in front of him a door opened and closed. Then he heard the curious, shuffling footsteps of a man dragging one foot behind him. The drums could explode from the impact of a bullet, Douglas realized. Hawkins knew that too. The yellow-eyed man would be very careful, wait for a sure shot at close range.

Douglas turned as far as he could without making noise and desperately searched for something with which to defend himself. His knee brushed painfully against something—a chain. Douglas' mouth went dry. He reached down and caressed the thick, rusted links with his fingers.

The chain was heavy, perhaps too heavy for him to use in his weakened condition. Still, it was the only weapon he had. One end was anchored firmly beneath a wooden pallet, probably having become lodged, then abandoned, during the course of loading. He estimated the loose end to be about eight feet long.

Douglas peered over the top of a barrel. Hawkins was about fifteen feet away, moving carefully, the gunmetal extension of his hand glinting in the moonlight. Douglas sank back down to the deck. It was only a matter of time before Hawkins or one of the other men moving out in the dark found him, and the longer he waited the weaker he would be. He would be executed, shot like a helpless, wounded animal. His left arm had begun to smolder with a white heat. He could wait no longer if he hoped to take Hawkins with him.

Douglas kicked at the nearest barrel. The drum produced a dull, thudding sound. The shuffling footsteps stopped, then started again, coming directly toward him: twelve paces, ten paces . . .

"Where the hell are you, you stinking—"

Douglas gripped the chain in the center with his right hand and sprang to his feet, shifting his weight and pulling on the chain with all his strength. The steel links clanged against the drums, skipped free and described a wide, whistling arc. The end of the chain caught Hawkins in the center of the forehead. There was a sound like the popping of a knuckle and the yellow-eyed man fell to his knees, then crumpled onto the deck.

Douglas leaped from behind his barricade, intending to search for Hawkins' gun. Out of the corner of his eye he saw two crewmen, guns drawn, converging on his position. He ducked down, frantically groping in the dark for the gun.

Douglas!"

Douglas glanced up at the sound of Anne's voice. He could see the girl standing at the railing on the upper deck, silhouetted by the moonlight. She was frantically waving her arms and could not see the man coming up behind her.

"Anne!" Douglas yelled. "Behind you!"

He didn't see what happened next. He ducked down behind a barrel as a bullet ricocheted off steel. He heard Anne call out his name again; he looked up in time to see her body hurtling down. The sound of her body hitting the water floated up to him through the darkness.

Douglas reacted instinctively, although he probably would have done the same thing if he'd had time to think about it—he would be no worse off in the water than he was on the ship. Bending low, using the barrels as a shield, Douglas raced for the side of the ship, then leaped over the rail, aiming for the area where he had seen Anne fall.

His own fall seemed interminable, and when it finally ended he wished it hadn't. The water came up to meet him like a slab of concrete and once more pain shot through his wrist, blinding him, tearing the breath from his lungs. The icy cold of the water kept him conscious, but his strength was gone; the water was closing over his head and his lungs burned. In a moment, he knew, he would end it all, open his mouth and suck in the water.

Someone was yanking at his hair, pulling him up. Douglas kicked the last few inches to the surface, drinking in great drafts of air. Anne was supporting him in the water.

"Hey," Douglas sputtered at last, "I was supposed to rescue *you*."

Anne smiled. "I didn't want you to rescue me, I just wanted you to follow me."

Douglas shook his head. "I can't swim. My wrist is broken."

"Can you float?"

Douglas slowly lay on his back in the water, resting his left wrist on his chest. "Uh, I don't mean to sound pessimistic, but I'm not sure this is a solution. It's cold out here."

Anne glanced toward the east. The sun was just breaking over the horizon. "If you can hold out for an hour or so, we'll be eating breakfast on a British destroyer."

"How'd you manage that?"

"By being unladylike toward a very surprised radio operator. That's why I had to leave you down there with Hawkins. Duty, and all that. Besides, I thought you'd be able to handle him."

"Thanks a lot. What about Zoltan?"

"Well, I suspect he's going to have to take a big loss on this particular shipment. That ship will be a lot lighter by the time it pulls into Glasgow. By the way, did I thank you for saving my life?"

"I don't think you had time. Did I thank you for saving mine?"

"We can properly thank each other later."

Douglas smiled. "Are you any good at blindfold chess?"

"Pawn to king four."

Douglas thought for a moment, then said: "Pawn to queen bishop four."

Stanley Ellin

FOOL'S MATE

WHEN GEORGE HUNEKER came home from the office that evening he was obviously fired by a strange excitement. His ordinarily sallow cheeks were flushed, his eyes shone behind his rimless spectacles, and instead of carefully removing his rubbers and neatly placing them on the strip of mat laid for that purpose in a corner of the hallway, he pulled them off with reckless haste and tossed them aside. Then, still wearing his hat and overcoat, he undid the wrappings of the package he had brought with him and displayed a small, flat, leather case. When he opened the case Louise saw a bed of shabby green velvet in which rested the austere black and white forms of a set of chessmen.

"Aren't they beautiful?" George said. He ran a finger lovingly over one of the pieces. "Look at the work on this: nothing fancy to stick away in a glass case, you understand, but everything neat and clean and ready for action the way it ought to be. All genuine ivory and ebony, and all hand-made, every one of them."

Louise's eyes narrowed. "And just how much did you pay out for this stuff?"

"I didn't," George said. "That is, I didn't buy it. Mr. Oclrichs gave it to me."

"Oclrichs?" said Louise. "You mean that old crank you brought home to dinner that time? The one who just sat and watched us like the cat that ate the canary, and wouldn't say a word unless you poked it out of him?"

"Oh, Louise!"

"Don't you 'Oh, Louise' me! I thought I made my feelings about him mighty clear to you long before this. And, may I ask, why should our fine Mr. Oclrichs suddenly decide to give you this thing?"

"Well," George said uneasily, "you know he's been pretty sick,

236

and what with him needing only a few months more for retirement I was carrying most of his work for him. Today was his last day, and he gave me this as a kind of thank-you present. Said it was his favorite set, too, but he wanted to give me the best thing he could, and this was it."

"How generous of Mr. Oclrichs," Louise remarked frigidly. "Did it ever occur to him that if he wanted to pay you back for your time and trouble, something practical would be a lot more to the point?"

"Why, I was just doing him a favor, Louise. Even if he did offer me money or anything like that, I wouldn't take it."

"The more fool you," Louise sniffed. "All right, take off your things, put them away right, and get ready for supper. It's just about ready."

She moved toward the kitchen, and George trailed after her placatingly. "You know, Louise, Mr. Oclrichs said something that was very interesting."

"I'm sure he did."

"Well, he said there were some people in the world who *needed* chess—that when they learned to play it real well they'd see for themselves how much they needed it. And what I thought was that there's no reason why you and I . . ."

She stopped short and faced him with her hands on her hips. "You mean that after I'm done taking care of the house, and shopping, and cooking your hot meals, and mending and darning, then I'm supposed to sit down and learn how to play games with you! For a man going on fifty, George Huneker, you get some peculiar ideas."

Pulling off his overcoat in the hallway, he reflected that there was small chance of his losing track of his age, at least not as long as Louise doted so much on reminding him. He had first heard about it a few months after his marriage when he was going on thirty and had been offered a chance to go into business for himself. He had heard about it every year since, on some occasion or other, although as he learned more and more about Louise he had fallen into fewer traps.

The only trouble was that Louise always managed to stay one jump ahead of him, and while in time he came to understand that she would naturally put her foot down at such things as his leaving a good steady job, or at their having a baby when times were hard (and in Louise's opinion they always were), or at buying the house outright when they could rent it so cheap, it still came as a surprise that she so bitterly opposed the idea of having company to the house, or of reading some book he had just enjoyed, or of tuning in the radio to a symphony, or, as in this case, of taking up chess.

Company, she made it clear, was a bother and expense, small print hurt her eyes, symphonies gave her a splitting headache, and chess, it seemed, was something for which she could not possibly find time. Before they had been married, George thought unhappily, it had all been different somehow. They were always in the midst of a crowd of his friends, and when books or music or anything like that were the topics of discussion, she followed the talk with bright and vivacious interest. Now she just wanted to sit with her knitting every night while she listened to comedians bellowing over the radio.

Not being well, of course, could be one reason for all this. She suffered from a host of aches and pains which she dwelt on in such vivid detail at times that George himself could feel sympathetic twinges go through him. Their medicine chest bulged with remedies, their diet had dwindled to a bland and tasteless series of concoctions, and it was a rare month which did not find Louise running up a sizeable doctor's bill for the treatment of what George vaguely came to think of as "women's troubles."

Still, George would have been the first to point out that despite the handicaps she worked under, Louise had been as good a wife as a man could ask for. His salary over the years had hardly been luxurious, but penny by penny she had managed to put aside fifteen thousand dollars in their bank account. This was a fact known only to the two of them since Louise made it a point to dwell on their relative poverty in her conversations with anyone, and while George always felt some embarrassment when she did this, Louise pointed out that one of the best ways to save your money was not to let the world at large know you had any, and since a penny saved was a penny earned she was contributing as much to their income in her way as George was in his. This, while not reducing George's embarrassment, did succeed in glossing it with increased respect for Louise's wisdom and capability.

And when added to this was the knowledge that his home was always neat as a pin, his clothing carefully mended, and his health fanatically ministered to, it was easy to see why George chose to count his blessings rather than make an issue of anything so trivial as his wife's becoming his partner at chess. Which, as George himself might have admitted had you pinned him down to it, was a bit of a sacrifice, for in no time at all after receiving the set of chessmen he found himself a passionate devotee of the game. And chess, as he sometimes reflected while poring over his board of an evening with the radio booming in his ears and his wife's knitting needles flickering away contentedly, would seem to be a game greatly enhanced by the presence of an opponent. He did not reflect this ironically; there was no irony in George's nature.

Mr. Oclrich's, in giving him the set, had said he would be available for instruction at any time. But since Louise had already indicated that that gentleman would hardly be a welcome guest in her home, and since she had often expressed decided opinions on any man who would leave his hearth and home to go traipsing about for no reason, George did not even think the matter worth broaching. Instead, he turned to a little text aptly entitled *An Invitation to Chess,* was led by the invitation to essay other and more difficult texts, and was thence led to a whole world of literature on chess, staggering in its magnitude and complexity.

He ate chess, drank chess, and slept chess. He studied the masters and past masters until he could quote chapter and verse from even their minor triumphs. He learned the openings, the middle game, and the end game. He learned to eschew the reckless foray which led nowhere in favor of the positional game where cunning strategy turned a side into a relentless force that inevitably broke and crushed the enemy before it. Strange names danced across his horizon: Alekhine, Capablanca, Lasker, Nimzovich, and he pursued them, drunk with the joy of discovery, through the ebony and ivory mazes of their universe.

But in all this there was still that one thing lacking: an opponent, a flesh-and-blood opponent against whom he could test himself. It was one thing, he sometimes thought disconsolately, to have a book at one's elbow while pondering a move; it would be quite another to ponder even the identical move with a man waiting across the board to turn it to his own advantage and destroy you with it. It became a growing hunger, that desire to make a move and see a hand reach across the table to answer it; it became a curious obsession so that at times, when Louise's shadow moved abruptly against the wall or a log settled in the fireplace, George would look up suddenly, half expecting to see the man seated in the empty chair opposite him.

He came to visualize the man quite clearly after a while. A quiet contemplative man much like himself, in fact, with graying hair and rimless spectacles that tended to slide a bit when he bent over the board. A man who played just a shade better than himself; not so well that he could not be beaten, but well enough to force George to his utmost to gain an occasional victory.

And there was one thing more he expected of this man; something a trifle unorthodox, perhaps, if one was a stickler for chess ritual. The man must prefer to play the white side all the time. It was the white side that moved first, that took the offensive until, perhaps, the tide could be turned against it. George himself infinitely preferred the black side, preferred to parry the thrusts and advances of white while he slowly built up a solid wall of defense against its climactic moves. *That* was the way to learn the game, George told himself; after a player learned how to make himself invulnerable on the defense, there was nothing he couldn't do on attack.

However, to practice one's defense still required a hand to set the offense into motion, and eventually George struck on a solution which, he felt with mild pride, was rather ingenious. He would set up the board, seat himself behind the black side, and then make the opening move for white. This he would counter with a black piece, after which he would move again for white, and so on until some decision was reached.

It was not long before the flaws in this system became distressingly obvious. Since he naturally favored the black side, and since he knew both plans of battle from their inception, black won game after game with ridiculous ease. And after the twentieth fiasco of this sort George sank back into his chair despairingly. If he could only put one side out of his mind completely while he was moving for the other, why, there would be no problem at all! Which, he realized cheerlessly, was a prospect about as logical as an ancient notion he had come across in his reading somewhere, the notion that if you cut a serpent in half, the separated halves would then turn on each other and fight themselves savagely to death.

He set up the board again after this glum reflection, and then walked around the table and seated himself in white's chair. Now, if he were playing the white side what would he do? A game depends not only on one's skill, he told himself, but also on one's knowledge of his opponent. And not only on the opponent's style of play, but also on his character, his personality, his whole nature. George solemnly looked across the table at black's now empty chair and brooded on this. Then slowly, deliberately, he made his opening move.

After that, he quickly walked around the table and sat down on black's side. The going, he found, was much easier here, and almost mechanically he answered white's move. With a thrill of excitement chasing inside him, he left his seat and moved around to the other side of the board again, already straining hard to put black and its affairs far out of his mind.

"For pity's sake, George, what *are* you doing!"

George started, and looked around dazedly. Louise was watching him, her lips compressed, her knitting dropped on her lap, and her manner charged with such disapproval that the whole room seemed to frown at him. He opened his mouth to explain, and hastily thought better of it.

"Why, nothing," he said, "nothing at all."

"Nothing at all!" Louise declared tartly. "The way you're tramping around, somebody would think you can't find a comfortable chair in the house. You know I . . ."

Then her voice trailed off, her eyes became glassy, her body straightened and became rigid with devouring attention. The comedian on the radio had answered an insult with another evidently so devastating that the audience in the studio could do no more than roar in helpless laughter. Even Louise's lips turned up ever so slightly at the corners as she reached for her knitting again, and George gratefully seized this opportunity to drop into the chair behind black's side.

He had been on the verge of a great discovery, he knew that; but what exactly had it been? Was it that changing places physically had allowed him to project himself into the forms of two players, each separate and distinct from the other? If so, he was at the end of the line, George knew, because he would never be able to explain all that getting up and moving around to Louise.

But suppose the board itself were turned around after each move? Or, and George found himself charged with a growing excitement, since chess was completely a business of the mind anyhow—since, when one had mastered the game sufficiently it wasn't even necessary to use a board at all—wasn't the secret simply a matter of *turning oneself into the other player* when his move came?

It was white's move now, and George bent to his task. He was playing white's side, he must do what white would do—more than that, he must feel white's very emotions—but the harder he struggled and strained in his concentration, and more elusive became his goal. Again and again, at the instant he was about to reach his hand out, the thought of what black intended to do, of what black was surely *going* to do, slipped through his mind like a dot of quicksilver and made him writhe inwardly with a maddening sense of defeat.

This now became the obsession, and evening after evening he exercises himself at it. He lost weight, his face drew into haggard lines so that Louise was always at his heels during mealtimes trying to make him take an interest in her wholly uninteresting recipes. His interest in his job dwindled until it was barely perfunctory, and his superior, who at first had evinced no more than a mild surprise and irritation, started to shake his head ominously.

But with every game, every move, every effort he made, George felt with exultation he was coming nearer that goal. There would come a moment, he told himself with furious certainty, when he could view the side across the board with objectivity, with disinterest, with no more knowledge of its intentions and plans than he would have of any flesh-and-blood player who sat there; and when that day came, he would have achieved a triumph no other player before him could ever claim!

He was so sure of himself, so confident that the triumph lay beyond the next move each time he made a move, that when it came at last his immediate feeling was no more than a comfortable gratification, and an expansive easing of all his nerves. Something like the feeling, he thought pleasurably, that a man gets after a hard day's work when he sinks into bed at night. Exactly that sort of feeling, in fact.

He had left the black position on the board perilously exposed through a bit of carelessness, and then in an effort to recover himself had moved the king's bishop in a neat defensive gesture that could cost white dear. When he looked up to study white's possible answer he saw White sitting there in the chair across the table, his fingertips gently touching each other, an ironic smile on his lips.

"Good," said White pleasantly. "Surprisingly good for you, George."

At this, George's sense of gratification vanished like a soap bubble flicked by a casual finger. It was not only the amiable insult conveyed by the words which nettled him; equally disturbing was the fact that White was utterly unlike the man that George had been prepared for. He had not expected White to resemble him as one twin resembles another, yet feature for feature the resemblance was so marked that White could have been the image that stared back at him from his shaving mirror each morning. An image, however, which, unlike George's, seemed invested with a power and arrogance that were quite overwhelming. Here, George felt with a touch of resentment, was no man to hunch over a desk computing dreary rows of figures, but one who with dash and brilliance made great decisions at the head of a long committee table. A man who thought a little of tomorrow, but much more of today and the good things it offered. And one who would always find the price for those good things.

That much was evident in the matchless cut of White's clothing, in the grace and strength of the lean, well-manicured hands, in the merciless yet merry glint in the eyes that looked back into George's. It was when he looked into those eyes that George found himself fumbling for some thought that seemed to lie just beyond him. The image of himself was reflected so clearly in those eyes; perhaps it was not an image. Perhaps . . .

He was jarred from his train of thought by White's moving a piece. "Your move," said White carelessly, "that is, if you want to continue the game."

George looked at the board and found his position still secure. "Why shouldn't I want to continue the game? Our positions . . ."

"For the moment are equal," White interposed promptly. "What you fail to consider is the long view: I am playing to win; you are playing only to keep from losing."

"It seems very much the same thing," argued George.

"But it is not," said White, "and the proof of that lies in the fact that I shall win this game, and every other game we ever play."

The effrontery of this staggered George. "Maroczy was a master who relied a good deal on defensive strategy," he protested, "and if you are familiar with his games . . ."

"I am exactly as well acquainted with Maroczy's games as you are," White observed, "and I do not hesitate to say that had we ever played, I should have beaten him every game as well."

George reddened. "You think very well of yourself, don't you?" he said, and was surprised to see that instead of taking offense White was regarding him with a look of infinite pity.

"No," White said at last, "it is you who thinks well of me," and then as if he had just managed to see and avoid a neatly baited trap, he shook his head and drew his lips into a faintly sardonic grimace. "Your move," he said.

With an effort George put aside the vaguely troubling thoughts that clustered in his mind, and made the move. He made only a few after that when he saw clearly that he was hopelessly and ignominiously beaten. He was beaten a second game, and then another after that, and then in the fourth game made a despairing effort to change his tactics. On his eleventh move he saw a devastating opportunity to go on the offensive, hesitated, refused it, and was lost again. At that George grimly set about placing the pieces back in their case.

"You'll be back tomorrow?" he said, thoroughly put out at White's obvious amusement.

"If nothing prevents me."

George suddenly felt cold with fear. "What could prevent you?" he managed to say.

White picked up the white queen and revolved it slowly between his fingers. "Louise, perhaps. What if she decided not to let you indulge yourself in this fashion?"

"But why? Why should she? She's never minded up to now!"

"Louise, my good man, is an extremely stupid and petulant woman . . ."

"Now, that's uncalled for!" George said, stung to the quick.

"And," White continued as if he had not been interrupted at all, "she is the master here. Such people now and then like to affirm their mastery seemingly for no reason at all. Actually, such gestures are a sop to their vanity—as necessary to them as the air they breathe."

George mustered up all the courage and indignation at his command. "If those are your honest opinions," he said bravely, "I don't think you have the right to come to this house ever again."

On the heels of his words Louise stirred in her armchair and turned toward him. "George," she said briskly, "that's quite enough of that game for the evening. Don't you have anything better to do with your time?"

"I'm putting everything away now," George answered hastily, but when he reached for the chessman still gripped between his opponent's fingers, he saw White studying Louise with a look that made him quail. White turned to him then, and his eyes were like pieces of dark glass through which one can see the almost unbearable light of a searing flame.

"Yes," White said slowly. "For what she is and what she has done to you I hate her with a consuming hate. Knowing that, do you wish me to return?"

The eyes were not unkind when they looked at him now, George saw, and the feel of the chessman which White thrust into his hand was warm and reassuring. He hesitated, cleared his throat, then, "I'll see you tomorrow," he said at last.

White's lips drew into that familiar sardonic grimace. "Tomorrow, the next day, any time you want me," he said. "But it will always be the same. You will never beat me."

★   ★   ★

TIME PROVED THAT White had not underestimated himself. And time itself, as George learned, was something far better measured by an infinite series of chess games, by the moves within a chess game, than by any such device as a calendar or clock. The discovery was a delightful one; even more delightful was the realization that the world around him, when viewed clearly, had come to resemble nothing so much as an object seen through the wrong end of a binocular. All those people who pushed and prodded and poked and demanded countless explanations and apologies could be seen as sharp and clear as ever but nicely reduced in perspective, so that it was obvious that no matter how close they came, they could never really touch one.

There was a single exception to this: Louise. Every evening the world would close in around the chessboard and the figure of White lounging in the chair on the other side of it. But in a corner of the room sat Louise over her knitting, and the air around her was charged with a mounting resentment which would now and then eddy around George in the form of querulous complaints and demands from which there was no escape.

"How *can* you spend every minute at that idiotic game!" she demanded. "Don't you have anything to talk to me about?" And, in fact, he did not, any more than he had since the very first years of his marriage when he had been taught that he had neither voice nor vote in running his home, that she did not care to hear about the people he worked with in his office, and that he could best keep to himself any reflections he had on some subject which was, by her own word, Highbrow.

"And how right she is," White had once taken pains to explain derisively. "If *you* had furnished your home it would be uncluttered and graceful, and Louise would feel awkward and out of place in it. If she comes to know the people you work with too well, she might have to befriend them, entertain them, set her blatant ignorance before them for judgment. No, far better under the circumstances that she dwells in her vacuum, away from unhappy judgments."

As it always could, White's manner drove George to furious resentment. "For a set of opinions pulled out of a cocked hat that sounds very plausible," he burst out. "Tell me, how do you happen to know so much about Louise?"

White looked at him through veiled eyes. "I know only what you know," he said. "No more and no less."

Such passages left George sore and wounded, but for the sake of the game he endured them. When Louise was silent all the world retreated into unreality. Then the reality was the chessboard with White's hand hovering over it, mounting the attack, sweeping everything before it with a reckless brilliance that could only leave George admiring and dismayed.

In fact, if White had any weakness, George reflected mournfully, it was certainly not his game, but rather in his deft and unpleasant way of turning each game into the occasion for a little discourse on the science of chess, a discourse which always wound up with some remarkably perverse and impudent reflections on George's personal affairs.

"You know that the way a man plays chess demonstrates that man's whole nature," White once remarked. "Knowing this, does it not strike you as significant that you always choose to play the defensive— and always lose?"

That sort of thing was bad enough, but White was at his most savage those times when Louise would intrude in a game: make some demand on George, or openly insist that he put away the board. Then White's jaw would set, and his eyes would flare with that terrible hate that always seemed to be smouldering in them when he regarded the woman.

Once when Louise had gone so far as to actually pick up a piece from the board and bang it back into the case, White came to his feet so swiftly and menacingly that George leaped up to forestall some rash action. Louise glared at him for that.

"You don't have to jump like that," she snapped; "I didn't break anything. But I can tell you, George Huneker: if you don't stop this nonsense I'll do it for you. I'll break every one of these things to bits if that's what it takes to make you act like a human being again!"

"Answer her!" said White. "Go ahead, why don't you answer her!" And caught between these two fires George could do no more than stand there and shake his head helplessly.

It was this episode, however, which marked a new turn in White's manner: the entrance of a sinister purposefulness thinly concealed in each word and phrase.

"If she knew how to play the game," he said, "she might respect it, and you would have nothing to fear."

"It so happens," George replied defensively, "that Louise is too busy for chess."

White turned in his chair to look at her, and then turned back with a grim smile. "She is knitting. And, it seems to me, she is always knitting. Would you call that being busy?"

"Wouldn't you?"

"No," said White, "I wouldn't. Penelope spent her years at the loom to keep off importunate suitors until her husband returned. Louise spends her years at knitting to keep off life until death comes. She takes no joy in what she does; one can see that with half an eye. But each stitch dropping off the end of those needles brings her one instant nearer death, and, although she does not know it, she rejoices in it."

"And you make all that out of the mere fact that she won't play at chess?" cried George incredulously.

"Not alone chess," said White. "Life."

"And what do you mean by that word *life,* the way you use it?"

"Many things," said White. "The hunger to learn, the desire to create, the ability to feel vast emotions. Oh, many things."

"Many things, indeed," George scoffed. "Big words, that's all they are." But White only drew his lips into that sardonic grimace and said, "Very big. Far too big for Louise, I'm afraid," and then by moving a piece forced George to redirect his attention to the board.

IT WAS AS IF WHITE HAD DISCOVERED George's weak spot, and took a sadistic pleasure in returning to probe it again and again. And he played his conversational gambits as he made his moves at chess: cruelly, unerringly, always moving forward to the inescapable conclusion with a sort of flashing audacity. There were times when George, writhing helplessly, thought of asking him to drop the subject of Louise once and for all, but he could never bring himself to do so. Something in the recesses of George's mind warned him that these conversational fancies were as much a part of White as his capacity for chess, and that if George wanted him at all it would have to be on his own terms.

And George did want him, wanted him desperately, the more so on such an evening as that dreadful one when he came home to tell Louise that he would not be returning to his office for a while. He had not been discharged, of course, but there had been something about his taking a rest until he felt in shape again. Although, he hastily added in alarm as he saw Louise's face go slack and pale, he never felt better in his life.

In the scene that followed, with Louise standing before him and passionately telling him things about himself that left him sick and shaken, he found White's words pouring through his mind in a bitter torrent. It was only when Louise was sitting exhausted in her armchair, her eyes fixed blankly on the wall before her, her knitting in her lap to console her, and he was at his table setting up the pieces, that he could feel the brackish tide of his pain receding.

"And yet there is a solution for all this," White said softly, and turned his eyes toward Louise. "A remarkably simply solution when one comes to think of it."

George felt a chill run through him. "I don't care to hear about it," he said hoarsely.

"Have you ever noticed, George," White persisted, "that that piddling, hackneyed picture on the wall, set in that baroque monstrosity of a frame that Louise admires so much, is exactly like a pathetic little fife trying to make itself heard over an orchestra that is playing its loudest?"

George indicated the chessboard. "You have the first move," he said.

"Oh, the game," White said. "The game can wait, George. For the moment I'd much prefer to think what this room—this whole fine house, in fact—could be if it were all yours, George. Yours alone."

"I'd rather get on with the game," George pleaded.

"There's another thing, George," White said slowly, and when he leaned forward George saw his own image again staring at him strangely from those eyes, "another fine thing to think of. If you were all alone in this room, in this house, why, there wouldn't be anyone to tell you when to stop playing chess. You could play morning, noon, and night, and all around to the next morning if you cared to!

"And that's not all, George. You can throw that picture out of the window and hang something respectable on the wall: a few good prints, perhaps—nothing extravagant, mind you—but a few good ones that stir you a bit the first time you come into the room each day and see them.

"And recordings! I understand they're doing marvelous things with recordings today, George. Think of a whole room filled with them: opera, symphony, concerto, quartet—just take your pick and play them to your heart's content!"

The sight of his image in those eyes always coming nearer, the jubilant flow of words, the terrible meaning of those words set George's head reeling. He clapped his hands over his ears and shook his head frantically.

"You're mad!" he cried. "Stop it!" And then he discovered to his horror that even with his hands covering his ears he could hear White's voice as clearly and distinctly as ever.

"Is it the loneliness you're afraid of, George? But that's foolish. There are so many people who would be glad to be your friends, to talk to you, and, what's better, to listen to you. There are some who would even love you, if you chose."

"Loneliness?" George said unbelievingly. "Do you think it's loneliness I'm afraid of?"

"Then what is it?"

"You know as well as I," George said in a shaking voice, "what you're trying to lead me to. How could you expect me, expect any decent man, to be that cruel!"

White bared his teeth disdainfully. "Can you tell me anything more cruel than a weak and stupid woman whose only ambition in life was to marry a man infinitely superior to her and then cut him down to her level so that her weakness and stupidity could always be concealed?"

"You've got no right to talk about Louise like that!"

"I have every right," said White grimly, and somehow George knew in his heart that this was the dreadful truth. With a rising panic he clutched the edge of the table.

"I won't do it!" he said distractedly. "I'll never do it, do you understand!"

"But it will be done!" White said, and his voice was so naked with terrible decision that George looked up to see Louise coming toward the table with her sharp little footsteps. She stood over it, her mouth working angrily, and then through the confusion of his thoughts he heard her voice echoing the same words again and again. "You fool!" she was saying wildly. "It's this chess! I've had enough of it!" And suddenly she swept her hand over the board and dashed the pieces from it.

"No!" cried George, not at Louise's gesture, but at the sight of White standing before her, the heavy poker raised in his hand. "No!" George shouted again, and started up to block the fall of the poker, but knew even as he did so that it was too late.

LOUISE MIGHT HAVE BEEN DISMAYED at the untidy way her remains were deposited in the official basket; she would certainly have cried aloud (had she been in a condition to do so) at the unsightly scar on the polished woodwork made by the basket as it was dragged along the floor and borne out of the front door. Inspector Lund, however, merely closed the door casually behind the little cortege and turned back to the living room.

Obviously the Lieutenant had completed his interrogation of the quiet little man seated in the chair next to the chess table, and obviously the Lieutenant was not happy. He paced the center of the floor, studying his notes with a furrowed brow, while the little man watched him, silent and motionless.

"Well?" said Inspector Lund.

"Well," said the Lieutenant, "there's just one thing that doesn't tie in. From what I put together, here's a guy who's living his life all right, getting along fine, and all of a sudden he finds he's got another self, another personality. He's like a man split into two parts, you might say."

"Schizoid," remarked Inspector Lund. "That's not unusual."

"Maybe not," said the Lieutenant. "Anyhow, this other self is no good at all, and sure enough it winds up doing this killing."

"That all seems to tie in," said Inspector Lund. "What's the hitch?"

"Just one thing," the Lieutenant stated: "a matter of identity." He frowned at his notebook, and then turned to the little man in the chair next to the chess table. "What did you say your name was?" he demanded.

The little man drew his lips into a faintly sardonic grimace of rebuke. "Why, I've told you that so many times before, Lieutenant, surely you couldn't have forgotten it again." The little man smiled pleasantly. "My name is White."

Ellery Queen

THE GAMBLERS' CLUB

ELLERY WAS ADMITTED INTO THE sacred mysteries of The Gamblers' Club one winter morning, when a stainless town car which the slush of 87th Street seemed unable to sully deposited three men on his doorstep. Inspector Queen, who was home that morning working on a confidential report, raised his birdy brows at the size of the car and retired with his papers to the study—not, however, without leaving the door ajar the irreducible minimum for eavesdropping.

The three men introduced themselves as Charles Van Wyne, Cornelius Lewis, and Gorman Fitch. Van Wyne was slender and bluish, Lewis was huge and brown, and Fitch was roly-poly and pink.

The Gamblers' Club, they explained to Ellery, was an association of seventeen retired businessmen with a passion for gambling and the means to indulge in it. In addition to the conventional group games of chance played in the clubrooms, members were pledged to suggest unusual gambling adventures to one another on an individual basis, being expected in this oath-bound obligation to display imagination and ingenuity. Suggestions were made by mail, anonymously, on special letterheads of The Gamblers' Club available to members only.

"Why anonymously?" asked Ellery, fascinated.

"Well, when someone's been hurt," squeaked pink little Mr. Fitch, "we don't want him holding a grudge."

"Of course, we're all reliable characters," murmured Van Wyne, nibbling the head of his stick. "Quite the whole point of the Club."

"But apparently someone's developed an unreliable streak. Is that it?" Ellery asked.

"You tell it, Van Wyne," boomed the large Mr. Lewis.

"Lewis dropped in on me this morning," said Van Wyne abruptly,

251

"to ask if I happened to be a party to a certain individual Club gamble he'd been enjoying, and when we compared notes we found we were both in the same thing. The two of us wondered if anyone else was in it and, since Mr. Fitch lives in my neighborhood, we dropped in on him and, sure enough, he was involved, too.

"Exactly three weeks ago each of us received a long envelope in the morning mail, with a typewritten message on Club stationery—quite in order—giving us a tip on the market. The stock suggested is unstable as the deuce—way up one day and way down the next—making it a real gamble, so each of us bought. It took a big jump, and we cleaned up. Two weeks ago this morning we each received a second letter proposing the purchase of another stock, equally jittery. Again we made a lot of money.

"And just one week ago today—"

"The same thing," rumbled Cornelius Lewis impatiently.

"You want to know," asked Ellery, "how he does it?"

"Oh, we know how he does it," said pudgy Mr. Fitch testily. "He's got inside information, of course. It's not that—"

"Then it's the letter you all received this morning."

The big ex-banker glowered. "How the devil did you know we got letters today?"

"Let's call him Mr. X," said Ellery, getting into the spirit of the thing. "Mr. X's first letter came three weeks ago today, his second two weeks ago today, his third one week ago today—so it was a pretty good bet, Mr. Lewis, that a fourth came today. What's disturbing you about it, gentlemen?"

Charles Van Wyne produced a long envelope. "Read it, Mr. Queen."

The envelope was of fine quality. It had no imprint or return address. Van Wyne's name and address were typewritten, and from the postmark it had been mailed the previous night.

Ellery removed from it a sheet of weighty stationery with a tony

THE GAMBLERS' CLUB at the top in gold engraving:

"Dear Fellow-Member:

How did you like my three market tips? Now something new has come up and it looks like the best yet. Secrecy is important, though, and I have to handle it personally or it's all off. If you'll gamble $25,000 on a hot chance to double it in seven days, no questions asked, leave the cash at the foot of Dominicus Pike's grave in Trinity churchyard tomorrow at 3:30 A.M. on the button. No prying, or you'll spoil the deal."

THERE WAS NO SIGNATURE.

"Now I've told Lewis," said Van Wyne, "that this is a sporting gamble. The man's proved himself. I'm for it."

"I don't say I'm not," growled Cornelius Lewis. "The only thing is—"

"Isn't that why we're here?" demanded Gorman Fitch with a sniff. "What do you think, Queen? This sound on the level to you?"

"Fitch, you're impugning the integrity of a fellow-member," said Van Wyne coldly.

"I'm just asking a question!"

"It's possible, Van Wyne, isn't it?" grumbled Lewis. "And if somebody's turned crooked, that's the end of the Club, and you know it. What's your opinion, Queen?"

"Sounds good to me," murmured Ellery. "But I'd want to dig a bit before committing myself. Did either of you other gentlemen bring your letters of this morning with you?"

"Left mine home," stated Lewis.

"They're practically identical with Van Wyne's," objected Fitch.

"I'd like to see them, nevertheless, envelope and all. Suppose you send them right over to me by messenger. I'll phone the three of you before noon."

The moment the front door had closed, the study door opened; and there was Inspector Queen, incredulous.

"Did I hear right?" snapped Ellery's father. "Did you say to those three this sounds 'good' to you? Good for what, laughs?"

"The trouble with you," said Ellery in a pained way, "is that you've got no gambling blood. Why not wait for developments?"

EMERGING FROM THE STUDY again just before noon, Inspector Queen found his celebrated son examining two envelopes and their contents. Cornelius Lewis's envelope, postmarked the night before, was exactly like the one Charles Van Wyne had received, and the wording on the Club letterhead was the same except that where Van Wyne's time for depositing the $25,000 at the Trinity Church grave had been 3:30 A.M. The small plain envelope Gorman Fitch had received, also postmarked the previous night, contained the same message on Club stationery except that Fitch was to deposit his package of cash at 4:00 A .M.

"I suppose," said the Inspector, "you're going to recommend that your three clients follow these instructions to the letter?"

"Sure thing," said Ellery cheerfully; and he telephoned his approval to Van Wyne, Lewis, and Fitch in turn.

"Are you out of your mind, Ellery?" howled Inspector Queen as Ellery hung up for the third time. "The only sure thing in this racket is that three suckers are going to be taken for twenty-five thousand lollypops!"

"Racket?" murmured the son.

The old gentleman controlled himself. "Look. This smoothie operates on a group of—"

"Mr. X? And what do you mean by 'group'? Specify."

"Seventeen! One of the seventeen Club members has gone sour. Maybe he's broke. He picks a stock that's always acting like a pogo stick and he writes half the members to play this stock to go up, the other half to play it to go down. Whichever way the stock moves, half the members lose, *but the other half win,* and he's a genius.

"Step two: He ignores the losers in the first operation and sends his second tip only to the winners—"

"Figures," pleaded Ellery. "Exactly how many would receive the second tip?"

"Half the original sixteen! Eight, the eight first winners. Now he tips half these eight to play the stock up, the other half to play it down. Again, half have to win—"

"Number, please," said Ellery.

"Can't you do kindergarten arithmetic? Half of eight is four! Now he's got four two-time winners. He picks another kangaroo stock, sends the third letter, this time telling half the four to play the stock up, the other half to play it down. So now he's got his three-times-winning chumps primed and he's ready to spring the big one. He sends his fourth letter—"

"To how many?" inquired Ellery.

"To the two remaining winners!"

"That's what it should boil down to, all right," mourned Ellery. "The only thing is, it doesn't. *We've got three.*"

Slowly, the Inspector sat down.

"An extra man," said Ellery. "Question: Who is he, and how could he possibly defy the laws of mathematics? Answer: He can't, so he's the con man himself, our friend Mr. X, not one of the suckers at all."

"Van Wyne, Lewis, or Fitch. One of them's the bunco . . ."

"I'm afraid so. Whichever one of the three he is, this morning, to his annoyance, he found himself in a consultation with his two victims. The letters setting up the graveyard payoff had been mailed last night and were already delivered, so he couldn't do anything about *them*. He could only pretend he'd been a three-times winner, too! If I warned his innocents to lay off, Mr. X would simply fail to show up tonight at Trinity. But if I didn't seem suspicious or a threat, he'd go through with his scheme. Does if figure?"

"Like Einstein," chortled the Inspector; and he hurried downtown to Police Headquarters to make certain arrangements about a church-yard and the grave of one Dominicus Pike.

GHOSTS WALKED ABOUT Broadway and Wall Street that night, but by 1:00 A.M. they had subsided behind various illustrious headstones in the churchyard, and the area grew quiet.

Ellery insisted that his father share George Washington's old pew in the chapel with him, murmuring something about the long wintry wait and the Father of Truth.

But at 3:15 the Queens were skulking behind one of Mother Trinity's skirts. At 3:30 A.M. on the nose the slender shadow of Charles Van Wyne fell eagerly across the grave of Dominicus Pike.

It deposited something on the frozen ground and slithered away.

At 3:45 the black hulk of Cornelius Lewis appeared, something dropped behind the headstone, and the black hulk melted away.

At the last stroke of 4:00 A.M. the dumpy blur that was Gorman Fitch repeated the process, and then he, too, disappeared into the darkness.

"Whichever he is, he's taking no chances," chattered Inspector Queen. "If anything went wrong, he'd be one of the suckers depositing his twenty-five grand. Now he'll wait a while. Then he'll sneak back to pick up the cash. I wonder which one it'll turn out to be."

"Why, Dad," said Ellery in an amazed undertone as he turned to his parent, "do you mean to say you don't *know?*"

"No, I don't," whispered the Inspector malevolently. "And don't tell me you do!" he added.

Ellery sighed. "Of course I do . . . X certainly didn't send any letters to himself—he didn't expect to have to enter the problem as a 'victim' at all. When accident forced him into it yesterday morning, he was in a jam. Yes, he could lie to the other two and *say* he had also received the fourth letter, but I asked him to produce it—along with the envelope. To look genuine, the envelope he gave me had to have the same postmark as the other two—the postmark of the night before! But that was impossible—it was now the morning after, and our conspirator found himself faced with a bit of a problem.

"So X did the best he could. He looked through his legitimate morning mail and found a plain envelope addressed to him, with no return address, which bore the correct postmark of the previous night; and he sent that envelope along to me with the note he had hastily typed as an enclosure. The only trouble was, the envelope was *of a different size* from the ones he'd been sending his victims. He hoped, I suppose, that I wouldn't notice the discrepancy in the sizes."

"Van Wyne's envelope was *long* . . ." the Inspector said.

"And Lewis's was identical with Van Wyne's. But the third envelope," said Ellery, "was a *small* envelope, and since that was the one sent over to me by—"

A shout profaned the churchyard, lights popped, and in their beams a figure was caught kneeling over three bundles on the grave like a boy in a melon patch. It was the pudgy little figure of Gorman Fitch.